Mr. Murray has also written
two other novels

TRUMPETER, SOUND!

REGENCY

THESE ARE BORZOI BOOKS, PUBLISHED BY
ALFRED A. KNOPF

COMMANDER OF
THE MISTS

COMMANDER

OF THE

MISTS

by

D. L. MURRAY

NEW YORK · ALFRED · A · KNOPF

1938

IN HOMAGE TO

THE SCOTTISH NATION

FROM

A DISTANT KINSMAN

FOREWORD

THE historical novelist, who is compelled to mingle fiction with the facts, may as well lay his cards upon the table. Besides the inevitable minor manipulations required for the entries and exits of my imaginary characters, I confess to having released a celebrated State prisoner from the Tower of London some ten months before his actual liberation (page 405); I have let him behave during this new lease of liberty as he is known to have behaved after gaining his real freedom. Further, I have caused an illustrious personage to visit Scotland (page 494) in a year during which there is no satisfying evidence that he was in this island. Beyond this I have sought to represent historical characters and episodes as, in spirit and in substance if not always in strict detail, I believe them to have really been; but I would emphasise that the Maceachans of Glenmarisdale are a purely fictitious family and clan, living in an imagined locality.

Treading over ground so rich in history and historical interpretation, it would be impossible for me to enumerate every book, ancient and modern, to which I owe a debt. But among those which I should feel most ungrateful to pass over are W. Drummond Norie's superb, illustrated "Life and Adventures of Prince Charles Edward Stuart" and Compton

Foreword

Mackenzie's small gem of biography, "Prince Charlie"; F. Adam's "Clans, Septs and Regiments of the Scottish Highlands"; W. B. Blaikie's "Itinerary of Prince Charles Edward Stuart"; E. M. Barron's authentic account of the Battle of Culloden in the *Inverness Courier* Official Guide to the town and moor; John Geddie's "Romantic Edinburgh" and Robert Chambers' "Traditions of Edinburgh"; Sir Bruce Seton Gordon and Jean Gordon Arnot's "Prisoners of the '45," and Beresford Chancellor's "The Eighteenth Century in London." On page 94 I have quoted from J. L. Campbell's translation of Alexander Macdonald's Gaelic "Song to the Prince" with the kind consent of Messrs. John Grant, publishers of "Highland Songs of the 'Forty-Five." To the three grand educators, Scott, Stevenson and Neil Munro, let a humble concluding tribute be paid.

I cannot thank all the living friends in Scotland and England who have given me the benefit of their knowledge and advice, and must beg them to accept a collective expression of gratitude that is most sincerely felt.

D. L. M.

Commander of the Mists

CONTENTS

Contents

BOOK THREE
THE RECKONING: 1746–1747

EPILOGUE

BOOK ONE

THE GATHERING

1 7 4 5

Chapter I

AULD SLEEPY

1

THE July sun beat down upon Edinburgh from a sky without a cloud. The Law Courts had risen ten days ago, leaving their benches as dumb as the great Parliament Hall itself, stilled now for thirty-eight years since the Union with England. From Holyrood Palace, dreaming with shuttered eyelids on its fading bloodstains and decaying splendours, to the drowsy routine of the Castle garrison, the pulse of the widowed capital beat low and languid.

But the lawyers, with arrears of papers still to sort, had not yet all left for their country seats or vacation haunts; and while they lingered with their families some shadow of fashion continued to decorate Edinburgh. Under the starveling trees of Hope Park a flight of silken butterflies hovered about a red-coated escort from the Castle; here a physician, there a minister in sedate bands promenaded his lady. In the more romantical wilderness of the King's Park adjoining a few sedans swung wearily under the pitted face of Salisbury Crags, one or two English officers galloped their horses. Down the centre of curving King's Drive, blind to fair

3

faces and fine horseflesh, blind equally to the majesty of Arthur's Seat cresting lion-like above the vanes of the palace and to the airy panorama of the Old City mounting as though to storm heaven with the lance-points of its spires, walked two lawyers in professional black. On the roadway, as they came, they cast shadows grotesquely disparate, one long and lean, the other short and paunchy. One was a young man and the other old, the former wearing a neat bag-wig, the latter an out-of-date periwig, broad-bottomed and ill-brushed. Pallor contrasted with convivial ruddiness, and the Lowland humour that creased the cheeks of the elder as he picked over the bones of a venerable legal anecdote found no reflection in the gaunt, raw-boned face of the junior, with its pale eyes sunk in deep hollows.

"Then," continued Counsellor Penicuik, "then quoth his lordship to the panel,* 'I misdoot me ye are a pair of abandoned rogues that have come from overseas in conjury to levy war upon oor Sovereign Lord King George.'"

"A pair?" interjected the younger lawyer, with a worried pucker in his forehead. "Did you not say, Counsellor, that there was but one person accused?"

The Counsellor chuckled, his small, diamond-bright eyes almost disappearing on either side of his beaky nose. "Ah! Mr. Duncanson, have ye so sune forgot what I tauld ye, that his lordship had been brought the very morn straight from Johnny Dowie's cellar into court, and an unco deefficult task he had found it to mount the bench at a'?"

Mr. Duncanson made a disgusted sound.

"'A pair of abandoned rogues!' quoth his lordship. Upon which I rose and humbly submitted, 'My lord, the panel is *singularis*, and canna have been in conjury wi' his ain self. Forbye, he hath made solemn abjuration of the Pretender and his party.' His lordship sets his wig straight, drinks nigh

* Prisoner.

on a pint of gude port from the decanter that aye stood beside him on his desk, and glowering at the panel wi' eyes as yellow as a scrauch-owl's, 'Ah!' says he. 'To whom then will ye be leal? Ye may be but ane man, as ye pretend, but I ken from the double face of ye that ye are a traitor to twa kings!' . . . Ah! Mr. Murray, a gude day to ye!"

Counsellor Penicuik broke off to raise his hat to a sharp-looking little gentleman in elegant lavender clothes with a lace *jabot*. "And what brings you from Broughton, Mr. Murray? How does your hairvest ripen?"

"We shall reap a fair harvest this year, I think," replied the gentleman from the country. "I have come to town concerning a lease. And what is your Edinburgh news, Mr. Penicuik?"

The Counsellor shrugged his shoulders. "What news can ye expect in Edimbro' in July? My Lord Justice Clerk departed last night to his country residence; of the other judges, my Lord Brounhill—"

"Remains in town a day or two with his young wards, the Laird of Glenmarisdale and his sister," interposed Mr. Duncanson.

"Aye, and is that a fac'?" remarked the Counsellor. "Weel, Mr. Murray, ye hae oor Edimbro' budget."

Mr. Murray's eyes shifted from side to side, then came to rest on a folded newspaper under the Counsellor's arm.

"You have the *Courant* there, I observe. There is no news from France?"

"Fra' France?" exclaimed the Counsellor. "What news suld there be fra' France? If ye will hae my rede of it, Mr. Murray, neither side has ony mair fight in them for the present. The French hae brawly chappit the English at Fontenoy this May, but they hae their ain sores to lick by my way o't. There will be naething attempted against us thence for this year at the least."

"You may be right," agreed Murray of Broughton, a faint relief in his voice, and passed on his way with short, self-important steps.

Mr. Duncanson reverted to the Counsellor's anecdote. "And did you gain the acquittal of your client, Mr. Penicuik?" he asked.

"What, are you still on my auld tale? Do you never tire, then, of hearing law cases, Mr. Duncanson?"

"Would I have chosen the profession of the law if I were like to tire of it?"

"Troth! Ye may say there are mair onlikely things for a callant! I could name six that have read in my ain chambers that would mair gladly have carried the sword. And ye have the build of an officer yoursel', Mr. Duncanson, gin ye were not inclined to stoop."

The young man squared his shoulders rather uneasily. "You cannot read without stooping," he murmured. "But you are right, Counsellor. Even a volunteer officer should pay heed to his physical vigour."

"And have you never desired, Mr. Duncanson, to be mair than an officer—God save us!—of volunteers?"

"I would gladly draw a sword, Mr. Penicuik, in defence of my country, her laws and her King. But I conceive that there is no more vain glory than swashbuckling."

"Cannily spoken! What for suld I break ma heid in their quarrels? It is eneuch to defend ma ain hearthstane. But for a' that do ye never feel that hot blood in ye rebel, as it were, against musty statutes and precedents?"

"I know no way but constant study to advance in my profession."

"And you may claim to have studied to some purpose!" Mr. Penicuik shot a respectful side-glance at his young companion. "Did you not qualify for practice at the English Bar as well as in our Faculty of Advocates? And while in

London did you not attract the favourable notice of Maccallum More himsel'?"

"The Duke of Argyll was graciously pleased to retain me in a cause of his."

"And then, as I am tauld, he brought you back to Edimbro' to undertake a' his land business! Your foot is in the stirrup, Mr. Duncanson! Land tenures and heritages—that is the wark o' to-day! The study of them will advantage ye mair than a' these auld tales of treason and rebellion."

"You may rest assured I do study them, diligently."

"Too diligently, if I may tak' in some sort the liberty of a father to you! Your cheeks are hollow; your eyes are bleared wi' poring over auld vellums. I hae been regarding you whiles we promenaded here. You have no glances for the gran' thoroughbreds these young Southron officers bestride. Not once hae you jowked to steal a peep in at a sedan-window. . . . What kind of a young man am I to mak' o' ye, Mr. Duncanson? . . . D'ye hear me, sir? . . . Gude sakes, am I wrang a' the time? Will he be loupin' on those lang legs of his after a sedan in spite of a'?"

2

MR. DUNCANSON had, in fact, stopped short in their walk with a muttered apology, and with long strides was pursuing a sedan chair that had passed them on the way towards Holyrood, and that was now slowing down in obedience to imperious taps upon the window from within.

Mr. Penicuik hobbled after as quickly as his legs would allow, his face crumpled with malicious wonder, his eyes sharp points of curiosity.

He came up with the sedan in time to see his young friend uncover with a well-bred bow, and to hear a female voice exclaim, "You are a traitor, Mr. Duncanson!"

"Gude sakes! Mair treason trials!" he grunted as he raised his hat in turn with a stiff, old-fashioned gallantry.

Framed in the curved window of the sedan was a girl's face, angrily flushed beneath its rouge. A contemptuous spark lurked in the large pupils with their shifting tints from cloudy brown to grey, set in wide, white ovals. A contemptuous quiver ran through the small, heart-shaped red mouth, which seemed to conform to the elongated heart-shape of the face as a whole, with its high cheeks and delicate aquiline nose. Flashing from the gloom of the sedan padding, it was a vision that caused Mr. Penicuik to mutter, "The canny lad! When he does chuse to notice a face, it is the flower of the whole promenade!" Aloud he said, "What is this indictment I hear against my friend, Mistress Maceachan? Ye maun allow me the privilege of appearing as his counsellor."

"Of course you shall, Mr. Penicuik, if you fancy you can benefit the panel. I am charging him," she levelled her green sun-fan in her long, nervous fingers for emphasis, "I am charging him with treasonable desertion. He has abandoned my laigh-shop party to-night for Lady Stair's rout— base betrayer!"

"Wi' submission, my Lady Justice," pleaded the Counsellor, "I move that ye canna eat oysters in July."

"And what of that, Counsellor? There is a plenty of good things to eat and drink in Lucky Middlemast's cellar in July, more appetising than Lady Stair's stale cakes and orangeade. And the company will be less like to make one expire of tedium."

"A verra mixed company, believe you me, Mistress Maceachan! Caddies and chairmen, the barber's lad and the water-carrier, foot-pads and pick-pockets—"

"Advocates, Counsellor, and Judges!"

"Is that a fac'?"

"Wits and men of letters!"

"Aye, and is that a fac' too? Yet I see one bonnie reason why I had liefer escort you to Stair House, mistress, than to Lucky Middlemast's."

"You see a bonnie reason?"

"Aye! I see it this minute!" The old man glanced at her face, and then gazed heavenwards, his hat held over his heart, his eyes screwed up to invisibility. "I see it this minute," he gurgled in a voice coated with ancient sugar. "Now at the oyster-shop I wad only be permitted to see your mask!"

He stepped back, hugely pleased with his little effect, which the lady acknowledged without a trace of embarrassment. Then, slowly fanning herself, she turned to the younger man. "And what will Mr. Duncanson be saying in his own defence?" she asked. "No, Mr. Penicuik, he is *not* to be heard only by the mouth of his advocate!"

Mr. Duncanson suddenly smiled, and the smile was disarming. "My plea must be 'Not guilty,' Mistress Maceachan. I was pre-engaged to Lady Stair."

"And what of that?" she demanded with a charming impudence. "Could you not be breaking your engagement to that old despot? It is time there was a rebellion against her!"

"What!" The Counsellor held up horror-struck hands. "Will ye be advising a lawyer, ma'am, to engage in breach of covenant and rebellion? Forbye that Mr. Duncanson would be desairting his ain clanswoman."

"I forgot, truly!" Miss Maceachan's eyes and voice turned frigid. "You will be a Campbell, of course."

Again Mr. Duncanson yielded to his shy and wavering smile. "It is not a name by which I know myself."

"But Maccallum More is your chief!"

"The Duke of Argyll is my client."

"Come, sir, come!" remonstrated the Counsellor. "You

canna deny that the Duncansons of Inveralsk form pairt and paircel of great Clan Campbell; only mair than the leddy here can deny that the Maceachans of Glenmarisdale are a sept of mighty Clan Ranald."

"Under your leave, Mr. Penicuik!" Miss Maceachan turned upon him with more than her usual vivacity. "The Maceachans will be no sept; we are an independent clan, and have been since the days of our founder, Hector, King of the Great Glen. When my brother comes of age he will be acclaimed as chief by our people on the Isle of Graves in Loch Maris, and to their acceptance of him Macdonald of Clan Ranald will have naught to add."

"Hum!" The Counsellor snuffed his beak dubiously. "Clan Ranald, I trow, holds feudal superiority over you by charter, howe'er ye may be pleased to phrase it."

"He may be our superior, and for five hundred years our flag has flown beside his on every field. There is a saw in both clans, 'Black dawn when Maceachan from Clan Ranald's side shall fall!' But he will not be my Chief for all that."

"Such notions," struck in Duncanson gravely, "are as Gothick and barbarous to-day, by my way of thinking, as the ruined Abbey that clings to the flank of Holyroodhouse yonder. Though, if it be true," he added with a touch of caution, "that Mr. Macdonald has a parchment establishing superiority, the law will on occasion take account of it."

"I am thinking, sir," said Miss Maceachan, "that you have no objection to Gothick antiquity—in your hostesses."

"But Lady Stair's invitation, ma'am, was to meet the Lord President."

"Aye! he canna afford to miss that," asserted the Counsellor. "What young advocate could?"

"There will be very little gallantry, I see, among gentlemen of the long robe." Miss Maceachan with a peevish shrug prepared to sink back upon her cushions. "You think only of your prospects, of your advancement."

"And what for no?" demanded Mr. Penicuik. "A lawyer has a mouth, Mistress Maceachan, like ilka man."

"I am thinking all men are the same!" cried the disgusted beauty. "Not one of my invited guests but has spurned me. All, all pre-engaged to that wrinkled Sultana! And so, it seems, my last night in Edinburgh is to be spent yawning by the chimney corner or seeking my fortune from the cartes."

"But surely," objected Mr. Duncanson, furrowing his anxious brows, "surely your Tutor, Lord Brounhill, is bidden to meet the Lord President?"

"And what is that to me, Mr. Duncanson?" Miss Maceachan thrust flaming cheeks through the window again. "There was an invitation doubtless to 'Lord Brounhill and family.' I am not his family, at least not when bidden upon that tone; nor is Hector. My brother and I have both vowed to give Lady Stair the go-by—and now I bethink me, since there seems to be no other gentleman in Edinburgh who has sufficient regard for me"—she was slyly watching Duncanson's troubled expression from under her curling lashes—"to forego for my sake an evening's pleasure—hem! —with the prospect of advancement, of course, why, Hector shall e'en be my cavalier to-night."

"What is this? What is this?" rapped a voice like a pistol-crack behind her. "My name in vain? What devilry will you be plotting against me now, Darthula?"

A short, slim youth of eighteen in tartan trews had pounced on the party from the back of the sedan, and stood grinning at the success of his trick. His swart brows and sallow complexion were in crude contrast to his powdered wig; an assumption of half-fatuous humour lit his blue-grey eyes. Across the turf a few yards behind him shambled a thick-legged and red-headed caddie, wearing the three-cornered hat of an Edinburgh chairman, and carrying a bag of golf clubs in his hand.

"Well met, Mr. Maceachan," said Duncanson with a friendly nod.

"A gude day to you, Glenmarisdale," said the Counsellor with a more ceremonious salute. "You come in the nick o' time to compose our quarrels here."

"Quarrels? Oh! Darthula is ever quarrelling . . . it is, as it were, the vital breath she draws. She cares for nobody with whom she does not quarrel at least once in the day; and him whose cheeks she has clawed thrice before bed-time," his gaze flickered facetiously over Duncanson's rigid face, "him, Mr. Duncanson, she loves."

"I will never have quarrelled with you, then, Hector!" There was a flash of menace in the cloudy-brown eyes.

"Never?" Hector Maceachan spun into a pose of reflection, finger on forehead. "You would not be calling it a quarrel, maybe, that day I left you crying on the peak of Fraoch Bheinn, to find your own way home, for your tantrums?"

"Hector! What will it import for these gentlemen to know that when you were a lad you were too great a coward to climb Fraoch Bheinn?"

"Coward? Oh! defamation! Duncanson, take note! I retain you in my cause. Mark well! I had a stone in my brogue that day."

"My grief! A bone in your leg, rather, Hector! But anyhow you shall not be too lazy to take me to sup at Lucky Middlemast's to-night."

"Alack! Too late! Too late! Your loathed rival hath forestalled you in my graces. Lady Stair—"

Darthula exploded. "Hector! You *shall* not be going to that woman's! My loss! Why am not I haggard and wrinkled and deaf?"

"Patience, sister of mine! It is you that will be!"

"You see, Mistress Maceachan," chuckled Mr. Penicuik, "you are desairted on all sides! . . . I canna thole it though, to think o' your lonely evening wi' the cartes."

"Lonely? Is it I will be moping in my corner if they are all going? No, forsooth! I shall be present. I will be out-facing my lady in her own fortalice. Do you hear me, Mr. Duncanson?"

"I shall warn Lady Stair that to-night she needs no candles."

("That was nae sae dooms slow," mused the Counsellor, tapping his snuff-box. "This young man is verra delusive.")

"Well, Duncanson," said the young Chief, "I grieve to be leaving Edinburgh to-morrow without giving you that swingeing defeat I promised at the golf."

"Ned Burke tells me you are mending," said the lawyer kindly.

"Glenmarisdale," broke in the chairman-caddie, "will neffer pe keeping his eye upon the ball."

"My grief! Would you have me strike and not measure how far I may be carried? Pure unreason!"

"Hector," grumbled his sister, "has always an excellent reason for doing what he is told not to do . . . and for taking the side that is not his own. That is why he will be doing nothing—even at the golf."

"So you will be awa' to the Hielan's the morn, the pair o' ye?" Mr. Penicuik raised his hat in leave-taking. "I wish ye a peacefu' journey."

"The Highlands are always peaceful," replied Hector solemnly. "It is we have no Captain Porteous, and no contentious chairmen."

"Awa' wi' ye, Glenmarisdale!" laughed the Counsellor. "As if oor chairmen were not a' Hielanders, like yon ruffian Ned Burke! They are the cause a' our tuilzies. Aweel, I hope we four may meet again in the King's Park when the leaves turn. And so we humbly tak' our leave."

3

"AND now, Hector," asked his sister severely, as he strolled beside her chair on the way back to the city, "who is it that will have been persuading you to go to Lady Stair's this evening?"

"My Tutor."

"My sorrow! Since when has Brounie dictated your social diversions?"

He mimicked a passionless, grating voice. " 'Hector, I require your presence and your sister's in attendance on Lady Brounhill and mysel' the nicht. Sae let's hae nae havers aboot it, mon, at a', at a'."

Darthula shuddered at his mimicry of the Lowland Doric. "And is that a way to be speaking the English? And he a Maceachan!"

"Our Uncle is a man of fashion, Darthula. And I am thinking he does his best to forget that he is a Maceachan. It will mean a great deal more to him to be Laird of rich Brounhill in the Lowlands than Tutor to beggarly Glenmarisdale. I am not blaming him."

"My shame on you, then! And you should not subserve his whimsies."

"But I am needing money, little sister, needing it sorely. And my Tutor holds the pouch-strings."

"Will it be the cartes again?" Her eyes were reproachful.

"And the dice. And diverse other fascinating toys."

Darthula sighed. "It's glad I'd be of the day you were honourably discharged from your Hellfire Club, Hector. How can a gentleman be passing all his evenings in a filthy cellar?"

"What! Not if it were Lucky Middlemast's, Darthula?"

Darthula shifted irritably on her cushion. "Everyone of note pays at least one visit to Lucky's, and 'tis I will not be left behind! But you would seem to take unending delight in squalor and . . . and . . . what else does the Hellfire Club provide?"

"Tedium. To speak the truth, I am for turning saint if Hell hath no more variety than it shows at the Club."

"In good time, Hector! I was ever wondering you should stomach such associates."

"Stop you! You yourself, Darthula, I have observed, are on excellent terms with the Devil."

"Hector! How dare you? I on terms with the Devil? Explain yourself!"

"Our President. I do but render him his official style. I thought you and he were grown monstrous confidential."

"Of whom are you speaking?"

"Of Alastair Ruadh."

"Young Glengarry! He will never be one of your rake-helly companions!"

Hector chuckled. "Will he not then? A properer ring-leader for our orgies you would not be finding in all Edinburgh, or in all Paris either."

"I could never be dreaming it."

"He did not mean that you should dream it, my love. No man more adroit at changing his skin to suit his company. I admire chameleons, but . . . but," his dancing grey eyes of a sudden shone tremulous with anxiety, "I am not thinking they are the proper sort of creature to be crawling on my Darthula's skirts."

Darthula laughed. "Poor, mad Alastair! Will you be speaking so of your friend?"

"My associate . . . or better still, my creditor."

"It will be to Alastair, then, you owe this money?"

Hector drew a folded paper from his pocket. "I was drawing out this promise to pay in six months before I went to the links. I will be meeting Elcho at the White House presently, who will back it. The Devil will accept of it . . . and some day I will have to be honouring it."

"You can be making no instrument, being an infant at law, Hector!"

"It will hold good in honour," he answered with a shrug.

Darthula examined the document in dismay. "There hundred guineas . . . it is mad you must be, Hector! And what way," she added fretfully, "will you be signing like that?" She pointed her little finger at the school-boyish scrawl:—

Hacktor Mackeichen

"You aye subscribe yourself 'Maceachan of Glenmaris-dale' like a Chief," she reminded him, "and can you not yet be spelling our name?"

He whistled with mock consternation. "Perhaps I was feeling that it was not a meet document for a Chief to be setting his name to, although most of us, I fear, must execute such deeds in these days. Aye, and we will be signing more and more of them, unless the wheel political takes another spin in time to save us from bankruptcy. . . . But I marvel, Darthula, that you will still be flirting with Glengarry. I had thought you were favouring the lawyer-chap Duncanson. There is a man wrapped in him somewhere, if you could break the vellum bands."

Darthula greeted this suggestion in a manner very different from the coolness with which she had accepted the charge of fondness for Glengarry.

"I am admiring at you!" she cried with eyes darting

sparks and a deep-rose spot on each high cheekbone. "And I am admiring at my own patience in hearing you! A boy to be parading my suitors for me! We will soon have you, Hector, playing your part in high affairs of State!"

"But 'tis I am always the one that is right, Darthula," he pleaded. "It has been my settled aim since childhood."

"And you to be hitting it as oft as you do the golf-balls! Away with you lest I scratch your face for your pains!"

Miss Maceachan had fanned herself into coolness again by the time that her bearers, after passing through the gates of the Netherbow, tightened their muscles to breast the long ascent of the High Street. It was recovering a little by now from its mid-day stupor, and the return of the tide was shown by the rivulets and pools of folk that were forming across the causeway and round the shops and booths in the first relenting of the sun. The human honeycomb of the ancient city was discharging its tightly-packed denizens from the black skyscrapers with their twelve to sixteen storeys, and the relentless swarm was beginning again to buzz and hover round the sculptured doors.

Just where the island of the Luckenbooths narrowed the street to a passage-way, she checked the chair again outside a silk-mercer's, to examine some ribands that the owner came trotting deferentially out to show her.

"There will not be *one* of the shade I expressly ordered," she complained.

"The broun matches brawly with your een," replied the merchant, thrusting it up against her cheek with a perfectly respectful familiarity.

"Guiser's tatters!" she scoffed, letting the stuff fall among the cabbage-stalks upon the causeway.

"My ribands are no that bad. Gude e'en to you," said the man, placidly picking it up and retiring.

Miss Maceachan threw herself back with an irritated movement into her chair, and then became conscious that the outside window of the sedan was shadowed. Turning with a little start, she observed a man's face, slightly distorted, regarding her through the glass, which she had raised for protection against the dust. In a moment she recognised him, and lowered the window with an arch smile. "What will you be doing here, Alastair Ruadh?" she demanded.

"*Pardon, Mademoiselle!* I was overhearing you say last night at the Assembly that you would be choosing ribands at Nicholson's booth to-day. So I have been watching from the wineshop opposite."

"My grief! Spying, Mr. Macdonnell of Glengarry?"

"I take the means to gain my ends, whateffer," he answered smiling.

She could not resist an admiring glance at his well-knit military figure and proudly-set head, with the red hairs peeping under the powder.

"Is it true, Miss Maceachan," he asked, "that you will be leaving us to-morrow?"

"Without fail. It is fixed."

"Then I must see you to-night."

"You will not, unless you too are bidden to Lady Stair's."

He scowled, and she saw that he had received no card. "I would not be demeaning myself by visiting a Whig and a Campbell."

"Since Glenmarisdale and I will both be present—we are thanking you for the compliment!"

He shrugged his square shoulders. "It will be but too plain that you are both of you ignorant of your Uncle's plot."

"Glenmarisdale's Tutor does not plot against him, Mr. Macdonnell."

"See you if he does not unmask his engines to-night!

What way do you think Duncan Forbes, the Lord President, will be coming to sit among the animated corpses of milady's *salon*, except to give his blessing to the great plan?"

"I confess I am not comprehending so much as one word of what you are saying, Alastair Ruadh."

"Is it desired by the hunters that the deer should know how they have set the ambush?"

"More riddles! Will I be the deer?"

"You are to be the pledge of a reconciliation between Light and Darkness. *A la bonne heure!* It will be a braw day for the Whigs when they get Glenmarisdale within maw. A Maceachan and a Campbell unholily mated—!"

Darthula brought her fan down with a rap on the ledge of the window. "Now it is impertinent you are pleased to be, Mr. Macdonnell!"

"Since I would be giving my life for you, Darthula Maceachan, shall I not be braving a trifle of your displeasure—to warn you?"

She relented a shade. "Listen, Alastair! I am not loving my Uncle's politics. But, my faith, his position is none of the easiest! It was by his zeal and suppleness in the law alone that Glenmarisdale was saved from forfeiture and our Father from attainder after the misfortunes of 'Fifteen."

"Your father was in no peril—believe one who has studied the evidences! And your Uncle's solicitude for the lands of Glenmarisdale will be a resolve to add them one day to the estate of Brounhill. If he could now be bringing Inveralsk, too, into the family, *mon Dieu!* what a *coup!*"

She looked at the young soldier curiously. "You will have been scrutinising our affairs like a lawyer, Alastair Ruadh."

He bowed with a simple dignity. "*Madame*, I am the soldier of a Cause, our exiled King James's,—and it trampled upon, discouraged, betrayed too often in the house of its friends! You must not be blaming me if I count jealously over again and again every asset upon which we may still rely, if I am trembling at the thought of even one more defection."

Darthula raised her head proudly. "Defection is not a word that may be spoken of Glenmarisdale!" She would have added more, but at that moment the back-chairman's face appeared at the other window of the sedan. "They will pe asking you to move forward, ma'am," he said. "There waas three chairs and the Lord Advocate's coach wanting to pass."

"It is they may wait!" rapped back Miss Maceachan; for though she had been on the point of signalling the chair to go forward, she would not be moved on even by the King. Thus Glengarry found himself forgiven, for she turned to him smiling and asked, "Will you be for Invergarry Castle next month?"

"If no business recalls me to France." He turned a haughty head at the objurgations coming from the blocked traffic behind him, and then brought his florid, handsome face with its full chin almost inside the sedan-window. "Will I be seeing you, if I stay?" he whispered. "Will you be pleased to see me?"

The reply was a smile of a dozen possible meanings, and the chair swung forward, releasing the angry throng behind.

As Glengarry moved back again to the wine-shop where he had been waiting, a figure met him in the arch of the doorway and handed him a package. It was a small Highlander, in Glengarry tartan, with a pale, pointed face, and lizard-like eyes, so watchful that you might fancy he never slept. Glengarry passed into the shop and broke the seals of the missive. It contained a second sealed packet, with a covering letter. This he read attentively, sitting on the edge of one of the wooden tables. The sun shot through the narrow window of the stone-vaulted room, with its rows of bottles and shadowy, iron-hooped casks, and fell full on the handsome face, upon its forehead drawn into puckers and its wavy lips gnawed by a single projecting tooth. At last he looked up and said to the walls or his gillie, equally impassive listeners, "Murray of Broughton will be writing this at least a month too late, by all I hear. But I must strive to carry this packet to whom it concerns. . . . Go down to Leith, Mungo, and find if any ship sail for France the morn."

Chapter II

THE POLITICIANS

1

Darthula Maceachan at last dismissed her chair by the entry to Advocate's Close. Through its archway opened a long vista of stairs, plunging down to a garden between the leaves of which the Nor' Loch glanced. The door into which she turned bore carved above its lintel the text Introibit Rex Gloriae; but she spared no look for the familiar words before pressing her skirts to her sides to guard them from the grease of the narrow stair that wound up to Lord Brounhill's lodging on the first floor.

A single large apartment, fronting on the High Street, served the wealthy Lord of Session's family for dining-room, drawing-room and sitting-room—while at present it did duty also at night as the Laird of Glenmarisdale's bed-chamber.

Hector had to sleep there or nowhere; for in the back-part, beside Lord and Lady Brounhill's bedroom, there was only a tall, coffin-shaped closet, book-lined to its roof, which served the judge for library and official chambers. From this closet, a private door, opening direct upon the outside

22

stair, was found useful by the less obtrusive agents of the law. Lord Brounhill's daughter Jean, and his niece Darthula, when she stayed with him, squeezed themselves into a cupboard rather than a room, reached from the tiny kitchen up three more stairs. Space was dear in Edinburgh, and my Lord Brounhill no believer in expense for display.

He would, nevertheless, not have spared himself on any account the cost of yet one more chamber, a minute closet fitted into a turret overhanging the stairs at the back, which he used for his oratory, in literal compliance with the text, "But thou, when thou prayest, enter into thy closet." To this dark alcove, furnished with a Bible on a ledge, a wooden arm-chair and a collection of cobwebs, Lord Brounhill was used to climb three times a day, his after-dinner visit being the most prolonged. Groaning sounds from the oratory at this hour were by the tip-toeing servants taken for signs of spiritual struggle; though his daughter Jean, who had wits like a knife under her shining, neatly-banded hair, knew them for snores—and kept silent about her knowledge.

Jean was sitting now in the window over the High Street, with the casement of green bottle-glass shut against the stench from the gutters—closeness and lack of outlook being lesser evils in the summer. The noises of the street came faintly into the room, the warning cries of the chairmen, the drawl of peddlers hawking broadsides, the rumble of an infrequent coach upon the stones, the fairy call of bugles from the Castle. As Darthula entered, her cousin looked up from the embroidery of red apples that she was working with plump fingers that never could rest idle, and, "My father will be wishful to see you, Darthula," said she.

Darthula dropped into an arm-chair, and, unbuckling one of her shoes, kicked it off upon the parquet, for it pinched her. Jean frowned at the patch of untidiness the unfastened shoe made upon the polish of the boards, and, "It is *now* that my father will be wishful to see you, Darthula," she emphasised.

"And when, pray, am I to be dressing for Lady Stair's?"

"You will be coming, then, to her ladyship's with us, after all?"

"Did I ever say I would not?" Darthula irritably forced her slender, roe-like foot into the shoe again.

"We thought when you threw Lady Stair's invite upon the floor and stamped your heel on it, that, maybe, you would not be giving us the pleasure of your company. But, do you hear, Darthula, my father *waits*."

"It is he may wait," said Darthula, rising from her chair, "until I have set myself in a little order."

"Why, Darthula, I am sure you look as if you had got yourself up to meet a King's eye, not just to parade among chairmen and riband-merchants."

Darthula flounced off to her bedroom, from which she did not emerge for a good quarter of an hour, though she had done no more to her appearance than touch her face with a powder-puff.

"Come in!" cried a harsh voice as she tapped upon the door of her uncle's study. The judge was sitting at his table in legal black with bands, for he had been across to Parliament Close on official business earlier in the afternoon. Lord Brounhill had the high cheek-bones and reddish colouring of the Highlander, displayed just now by the removal of his wig; but his mask of dour impassivity was less characteristic of his race. The low forehead, the small green eyes set close to either side of the high-ridged nose, the morose and sensual mouth running down in gashes at the corners did not betoken high intelligence. "A stupid man!" onlookers in Lord Brounhill's court often told themselves as they marked his glassy look while listening to the pleadings, his mumbled questions and slow way of taking down the answers. They were the more surprised when, at the end, his lordship, folding his hands upon his desk, and seeming to sink his head between his slightly hunched shoulders, let flow, with half-closed eyes, a summing-up, passionless, lucid and comprehensive, which left no hole for criticism to niggle at. No jury could find grounds for flouting his direction; and often as his judgments were appealed against by disgruntled suitors, not one, in that age of political passion, favour and corruption, had yet been upset by the scrutiny of his brethren. A single false step in his delicate position as the relative and legal tutor of a young Highland Chief whose clan's disloyalty to the House of Hanover was known, might have proved enough to ruin him; but he had not made it, and he was daily more trusted by the Government.

By the populace "Brounie" was reckoned a terrifying judge for the implacability of his logic. He showed, indeed, none of the sadistic cruelty that has blotted the memories of one or two of his judicial contemporaries: but neither did he know compunction or mercy. "Mitigating circumstances" was a phrase without meaning for "Brounie." If it is probable that he had never in his life procured the condemnation of an innocent panel, he automatically gave the guilty their full sentence. The springs of his soul seemed as dry as his wooden countenance; his actions were those of a reasoning-machine without bowels.

"Sit doon!" he said to his niece, in his carefully cultivated Lowland Scots, as she entered.

"Where?" enquired Darthula, pouting at the encumbered room, which was more crowded even than Allan Ramsay's nest, though with far less seductive folios.

"Where ye chuse!"

She tilted a valuable law-book upon the floor with crumpled leaves, and took its place upon the only stool the study contained.

"Ye will pay me, Darthula, for re-binding those *Pandects*," observed Lord Brounhill, making a note. "And now," he continued, folding his hands in his customary gesture when delivering judgment, "what is this that I am tauld by Leddy Brounhill, that ye mak' difficulties aboot accompanying me to Lady Stair's the nicht?"

"I am not caring to go to Lady Stair's."

"That is, nae doot, a calamity. But I am enforced to bid baith you and Hector to attend me. The Lord President hath done the twa o' ye the honour to desire your acquaintance."

"The honour of meeting a Whig grandee leaves me cold, sir."

"Is it e'en sae? But your feelings, Darthula, maun give place the nicht to fam'ly interests. I design, and the Lord President deigns to grant his approval, that Hector, acting as my deputy, shall raise an Independent Company for the Watch of Glenmarisdale and the Great Glen."

"Hector raise soldiers for the usurper!"

"For the presairvation o' law and order in the Hielan's. There is nae question o' politics here, girl, King James or King George! We hae lost, by ma reckoning, upwards o' sixty heid o' cattle at Glenmarisdale in the last four years."

"My grief! We know who lifts our cattle!"

"Ye hae no need to inform me."

"But," Darthula hesitated, "Macdonell of Barisdale is supposed to hold the Watch."

"I am no just minded to go on paying the *black mealh* to a villain—ye'll mind that this is *in foro domestico*—wha shares in our plunder wi' Lord Lovat."

"Barisdale is the ruffian, no doubt, and he a bad neighbour too. I am not desiring for all that to see Hector in the Elector's uniform."

"You are no desiring! But what if it be ma will?"

"You know very well, Uncle, whom Hector will be obeying!"

Lord Brounhill glinted stonily at her. "I ken he has aye been in an unnatural subjection to you, Darthula. 'Twas the fault o' Glenmarisdale himsel'."

"I will not hear our father censured! My sorrow! It would be unnatural, and against religion!"

"Hector was left too much to your care as a bairn."

"It was I had to stand for father and mother too to the poor laddie."

"Ye sair o'erstretched your office, in ma opeenion. But I presume ye have wit enough to see that we maun protect our herds at Glenmarisdale?"

"What way, then, are we needing so many cattle? Since you have been our manager the byres have increased and the cottages decreased. It was my father's boast that Glenmarisdale could bring fifty claymores to the following of Clan Ranald. Now, I have reckoned, we could be mustering a bare thirty, if the call came."

Lord Brounhill began with deliberation to sharpen a pen. "You have been pleased to raise there, Darthula, twa', three points upon whilk I will mak' it my duty to instruct you mair pairfectly. I have increased the cattle on our lands, for the reason that cattle are wealth and men are poverty. There is nae benefit to us in forty, fifty caterans lying idle around the shielings . . ."

"If they can wield a broad-sword—"

"I will thank ye to allow me to speak. Broad-swords are the curse o' the Hielan's. There will never be peace nor prosperity amang us whiles ilka Chief reckons his strength in claymores, and is able to disturb the country wi' tramplings of an armèd host at the first rumour of ceevil disorder or rebellion. The Scripture saith, 'They shall beat their swords into pleugh-shares.' I could weel dispense wi' your clamjamfrey o' clansmen that hae nae occupation but to wait for the day of trouble, and mak' it waur when it comes. For why should the estate be burdened wi' their maintenance?"

"Our poor lads must live!"

"Let them betak' theirsel's to Barbados or Ameriky! There is nae mair scope for them in Scotland. I can see far aheid. The slogan o' to-morrow will be 'Cattle!' not 'Claymores!' Lastly. I merked ye saying that it was the duty of Glenmarisdale to follow Clan Ranald. Ye hae likely forgot, or maybe, ye hae never heard, that Glenmarisdale holds fra' the Crown direct, not fra' Clan Ranald?"

"Clan Ranald has always been our superior!" declared Darthula, flying into a very different tone from that she had used earlier in the afternoon.

"An auld sang!" sneered her Uncle. "But I can tell you an older!" His voice lifted, his accent changed. "The sons of Hector held Glenmarisdale before effer the sons of Donald came upon the continent of Scotland. The ancient tower above our house was built before one shtone of Tirrim shtood upon another! I am flinging Clan Ranald's claim in his teeth, and I will be fighting to my last breath before I will pay him fealty whateffer!" The pen snapped in the clenched fists of James Maceachan, and Lord Brounhill came back on a laboured breath. "That is," he added, "if there were ony sense in fechting these days. It is a question of law, and I ken Clan Ranald has nae parchments."

"Well, sir, you will doubtless be having your way about the Watch. Is that all you wish with me?"

"Resume your seat! I will tell ye when I am done with

ye! I will now ask you to direct your attention to your ain future. Hae ye given that matter ony serious consideration?"

"I had supposed, sir, that so long as my brother was needing my presence at Glenmarisdale—"

"In my opeenion, as you know, you are *functa officio* a lang while syne, so far as dry-nursing the lad goes. He needs to be freed fra' female leading-strings. Ye are of marriageable age, Darthula; it is time to consider how best to dispose of your hand for the advantage of the fam'ly."

"Possibly my own inclination might be permitted to play a part?"

"Your inclination, as ye ca' it, must bend to the requirements of your situation. Unless I am deceived, but I think I hae my wits aboot me, the opportunity now offers to ally our fam'ly wi' the wealthy lands of Inveralsk."

Flame leapt into Darthula's face. She had dismissed Young Glengarry's talk of a design to wed her with Mr. Duncanson of Inveralsk as part of his insatiable craving for gossip. Now, here was the plot springing full-armed from the Tutor's head! And she had been too careless to mark its development! Swift fury seized her. "I am not knowing, sir," she cried, "what can have led you to suppose that I would be willing to bestow my hand upon Duncanson of Inveralsk . . . and he a Campbell!"

"I have occupied mysel' rather in ascertaining, Darthula, whether there were grounds for hoping that Mr. Duncanson might be willing to accept of you in marriage."

"You asked him such a question! You were having no more regard for my modesty?"

"I see naeth'n a marriageable spinster o' your age need to blush at in the thocht of a treaty of marriage between yoursel' and young Duncanson, who is under the especial protection o' the Duke of Argyll, and weel looked upon by the Lord President, Duncan Forbes—twa great aids to advancement."

"But Mr. Duncanson himself . . . is it he has ever hinted . . . is it he has shown signs of willingness . . . ?" Darthula broke off, her face crimson, her heart beating painfully.

"I hae not asked young Mr. Duncanson," replied Lord Brounhill. "I hae been in correspondence wi' his father, Inveralsk himsel'."

"Indeed! And so the pair of us are to be disposed of by two old men to forward their family views, as if we had no will nor inclination of our own! My sorrow! I would not be having Allan Duncanson now, if he asked me."

"Young Duncanson, I'll uphaud ye, will do as his father bids in the matter. He is a young man o' prudence and good dispositions . . . aye, and one who will maybe mak' a great name as an advocate some day. He will not be for breaking his parritch-platter aboot his ain heid. And you, Darthula," he sat looking glumly at her, with a face that seemed carved out of wood, "you had best pay heed to ma direction . . . or ye may see cause to regret your contumacy. D'ye hear? Gin young Duncanson should mak' approaches to ye at Lady Stair's this e'en, ye maun, wi'out cheapening yoursel', show him some civeelity."

2

DARTHULA found that her hands were still shaking as in the cramped sleeping-closet she unhooked the dress she meant to put on for Lady Stair's. It was a plain gown, with a pointed stomacher and elbow-sleeves trimmed with tartan ribbons, rather worn, but good enough, she held, for the Sultana. Over this she would drape her silk *arisaid* of the crimson, green and black barred, Clan Ranald dress tartan,

worn by the Maceachans of Glenmarisdale with a slight difference of sett peculiar to themselves. One dark-red flower
would adorn the brown curls that fell with coppery gleams
like a cascade upon her neck.

But as she stood with these articles in her hands, gazing
through the slit of the window, swift melancholy came upon
her. The falling of the sun had brought but little relief from
the heat. Through the open window the air came stale and
oppressive. It would be a welcome thing, she sighed, if the
thunder broke.

She would be glad to breathe mountain air again. On a
sudden she felt weary of all the agreeable titillations of
Edinburgh society, and infuriated—she felt the tide of
anger rising afresh—at the way in which her Uncle and
Allan Duncanson had presumed to dispose of her, as if she
were their chattel. She did not analyse—her bird-like
thoughts skimmed away from these depths—what it was
right down in her soul that had wounded her so sorely. If
she had heard that there was a design afoot to marry her to
anyone else—to Glengarry, for example!—she would have
quizzed them all and led them a wild dance of annoyances.
But Allan Duncanson to slight her so, and he with his shy
airs and respectful mien! Well, if he looked for "civilities"
to-night he might guard himself!

Wax-candles lit the *salon* of Lady Stair's house, with its
black-oak gallery formerly used by the minstrels. They
flung their radiance up to the beam-divided ceiling with its
rich medallions of plaster, and flashed on the finely-wrought
iron grates and firedogs, now glistening with summer cleanliness.

All that the advancing year had left of society in the
metropolis was gathered into this last reception of the season, and the room, large as it was for an Edinburgh resi-

dence, was crowded with silk dresses and velvet coats. Every chair had been seized, and the remaining guests had lodged themselves in the deep embrasures of the windows, where they sat precariously balancing tiny cut-glass goblets filled with the orangeade at the thought of which Darthula had shuddered.

Her eye, as she entered behind her Uncle and Aunt, took in familiar figures. The Lord Advocate's family were there, and the Commander of the Castle garrison was just taking his leave. In a corner behind the skirts of three young women, Counsellor Penicuik's snuff-box rattled, and Darthula, as she passed, caught the words, "Then quoth his lordship to the panel, 'I misdoot me ye are a pair of abandoned rogues—.'" Then she caught sight of the lean back of Mr. Duncanson, who was lending attention to the pudding-faced Lord Provost, Archibald Stewart, condescendingly delighted at finding such a patient listener to his municipal woes. For a moment she almost wished she had a dirk.

Then she was forced to join in Lord Brounhill's wooden reverence to their hostess, and in Lady Brounhill's vacantly brilliant smile under her rouge, as she billowed in a curtsey that spread her hooped skirts for yards on the glimmering floor-boards. When Darthula made her own bob and smile she saw a tiny glint in the black pin-points that pierced the Sultana's wrinkled mask, and knew that she was the prisoner at the triumph.

With a flick of her shoulders she turned aside, and then started in genuine surprise. By the further fireplace she had gained a glimpse of a figure that had been concealed from her on her entrance by a group paying it an even more accentuated court than was enjoyed by Lady Stair.

It was that of an enormously fat old man, lolling in an armchair. His great belly, in a waistcoat worked with tiny nosegays, rippled down almost to his knees, which were clad in greengage plush; while the swollen legs, dangling below, half-impotent through gout, ended in huge soft-leather shoes adorned by gold buckles. A scarlet plaid, barred with green, was brooched over his shoulder. Despite the inertness of his bulk there was a continuous liveliness in his hands, with their slim, sensitive fingers and splayed thumbs working and pressing one against the other as he talked. Life gleamed, too, from the ancient, deeply-furrowed face, with its glittering eyes and arched brows habitually twitching. There was seduction in the long mouth when it smiled, and in the broad nose flairing to left and right like a hunting-dog's.

He was chattering to two or three handsome women whom he had coaxed from the side of their husbands, to receive his flatteries. From time to time their laughter, shrill with excitement, floated over the room, seeming almost to alarm the demure hum of the general conversation, which died away for an instant whenever this happened. At those moments the old man rolled about in his chair with childish enjoyment.

Behind this magnate Young Glengarry lounged against the black panelling, a smile on his full, wavy lips. "So my friend has slipped in, after all," thought Darthula. "What a magnificent screen!" A half-reluctant smile softened her heart-shaped mouth. "Hector," she said over her shoulder to her brother, who had followed her into the room, "did you know Lord Lovat was in Edinburgh?"

"Will the old spider's own henchmen be knowing where he will be spinning the next moment?" laughed Hector. "Go to him, Darthula, he is signalling to you."

Lord Lovat in fact had paused in his rotatory enjoyment, and was now bending forward so that his belly almost hid his knees, looking towards Darthula. His eyes shone with candid delight, his eloquent fingers opened with such a fatherly invitation, that Darthula, smiling and blushing, floated over the floor towards him as though drawn on a silken string. "Ask him how many of our kine he has in those great pockets of his," hissed her brother in a lamentably loud whisper as she went.

"Welcome, welcome indeed, Flower of Glenmarisdale," cooed the old man. "You bring a breath of true Hieland air into the oppression of Edinburgh!"

Darthula was conscious of Glengarry's smile overhead as she curtsied.

"We did not know," she said, "that you had come to town, Macshimi."

"It was not for my pleasure, indeed," sighed Lovat, "that I left Beauly. But pleasure hath rewarded me!" He kissed his fingertips. "I came to plead recovery of a right, and Heaven rewards me, undeservedly, with a favour! Tell me, Darthula," he went on, "is Hector wedded to this scheme of a new Watch? Is he so ambitious to become Captain of a Company? I would he would allow old Simon Fraser, his friend, to give him a wee word of warning. There will be a load of affliction in that service! My sorrow, should I not know it? I who held the Watch for all Inverness-shire with my own Independent Company until seven years ago, when I gladly laid down the burden! One is out of pocket, out of heart, hated by the country for executing justice, neglected by the Government for whose sake you have toiled! Truly, I would not be seeing a son of mine earn white hairs before his time in such a task!"

Darthula's brain worked nimbly as she listened. Lovat had not gladly surrendered his Company, she knew. He had been removed from the command for his political untrustworthiness. Did this fulsome address mean that the old spider resented a young Chief being given a place that might well signify his own permanent exclusion? The plan, she knew, was the Tutor's. Now with Lovat, as with all the great Chiefs of the neighbourhood, Lord Brounhill had always been at cat-and-dog. Here were deep waters.

"Then," wheedled Lovat sibilantly, "then, there iss Barissdale! Poor Barissdale! This will be a sair blow to him. He hath held his own Watch these seven years, and done it well. There will be scarce a heid of cattle that goes astray now from Inverness to Fort William!"

This lie was too egregious. Darthula looked her incredulity, but was met by a gaze of humid innocence. "Let me speak to Hector!" coaxed Lovat.

"I will try to find my brother, Macshimi," she answered coldly, and withdrew into the throng without the least intention of exposing Hector for any cause whatever to the Chief of the Frasers' blandishments. In a moment the Tutor was at her side. "Upon what was Lord Lovat conversing so airnestly wi' you?" he demanded.

"You had best beware, Uncle!" she replied with a point of malice. "He is here to countermine your grand scheme for Hector's Watch Company."

"The auld rogue!" growled Lord Brounhill. "His words wad cause the angels fa' from grace! Ach! But I canna' believe," he knit his brow gloomily, "I canna' believe the Lord President wad be misled by sic a traitor! In gude time, here is Duncan Forbes!"

There was a stir round the door in humble greeting to a tall man, formally but richly dressed in judicial black, with a full-bottomed, elaborately-powdered wig upon his head. Duncan Forbes of Culloden, Lord President of the Council and Lord Justice General, entered the room with the condescending briskness of one who knew himself to be the Government of Scotland, and thoroughly enjoyed the position. On his long, thin face, with the ruddy glaze of the deep drinker of years gone by, sat a quaint admixture of complacency and benignness; the eyes had a kindly twinkle, yet withdrew slyly all the time towards their corners under the drooping lids. His bow to his hostess exquisitely wafted homage from a superior to a venerated inferior; and as he turned round after his salutation to study the company, he had the air of a man only waiting to be asked to distribute favours, and also a little—to Darthula's mocking fancy—of the preacher about to pour forth the balm of the Word.

Then his look, as it glanced from side to side, fell upon Simon Lord Lovat, now sitting still in his corner, his finger-tips delicately touching, his mouth wreathed in a honey-dropping smile, his lids fluttering over eyes that had turned to gleaming slits.

For a second Darthula saw the smile wiped from Duncan Forbes's face, and a haggard look steal over it. Mr. Peni-cuik's epithet, "sour," would in that moment have suited the lank and melancholy visage that stared at the old spider. Then in a flash the smile returned, and with a hearty "Simon! What gude wind blaws you all unexpected into Edinburgh?" the Lord President walked with stately tread to greet the Fraser Chief.

Then was seen a wondrous sight, as the old nobleman, with an apparently heroic courage, struggled to upheave his vast bulk to salute the Lord President standing. He tottered as he stood with his spine bent into a hump and one hand clutching the chair-arm for support. His face was bowed down as if in the presence of an archangel.

"Sit ye doon, my lord! Sit ye doon!" begged Duncan Forbes, palpably pleased by this expensive homage, and he patted Lovat's shoulder as he helped him back into his seat. A footman hastened to place a second chair for the Lord President, and so for a while the twin-gods of the High-lands and the Lowlands sat chatting together, while the rest of the company conversed with eyes that kept straying to the mighty ones by the fire-place. Darthula suddenly missed Glengarry. As the Lord President entered he had glided away into the most distant of the window-embrasures out of sight.

Lord Brounhill glowered behind Lady Stair's sofa, and Lady Brounhill showed a scornful dint in her Roman nostrils. Hector Maceachan sighed, and began to put absurd acrostics to his cousin Jean. His high voice rose, tittering, above the subdued talk of the other guests and mingled with the grave murmur of the magnates. Once Forbes looked up with a puzzled frown, and Darthula quenched her laughter in her handkerchief.

"You draw amusement from this spectacle?" asked a familiar voice behind her. "Now what is it, I wonder, that excites your risible faculty?"

Darthula swished her skirts round upon Allan Duncanson . . . and in an instant, as she looked into those pale, anxious eyes, her carefully-banked fury seemed to run out at her fingers and toes.

"My grief, Mr. Duncanson," she said with but a feeble pettishness, "may one not laugh without reason?"

"That would appear to me a highly superfluous procedure. I can laugh, when I am satisfied that there is a jocosity before me. But I never felt less like laughter than to-night."

"Will you be so anxious over your presentation to the Lord President?"

"So anxious lest you should never come back to Edinburgh."

"Why should you be thinking that? My uncle insists that we spend part of every year in the city."

"I do not trust the Highlands, Miss Maceachan. I aye fear they will spirit you away, and imprison you, like the nymphs we were taught to read of, in some stone of a waterfall, or cleft of a pine. I speak by way of metaphor, you will understand."

"I understand. And what way will it trouble Mr. Duncanson if I am falling a victim of one of my native divinities?" Her smile suddenly dazzled him.

"It would then be a barren glory to me, were I made a Lord of Session!"

"Fie on you, Mr. Duncanson! Are not you the tragic one!"

"I am no saying there is immediate likelihood of such promotion."

"Promotion! Do you know whither I would like to see you promoted, Mr. Duncanson?"

"I cannot guess."

"To Inveralsk. To your own land, and to be leading your own people!"

"I have chosen otherwise than to be a petty Chieftain."

"We will not, then, I fear, be seeing so much of one another in the years to come."

He creased his brow as though faced by an anguishing problem. "You could never bring yourself to live in Edinburgh, then?"

"All the year? It is stifled I would be!"

"If you were endowed with an estate in the vicinity? A Lowland estate brings much consideration, Miss Maceachan."

"It would be a barren glory to me, Mr. Duncanson, did Lady Stair's own royalty go with it."

"That is gey ill news to me, Miss Maceachan."

"How might that be?" She arched her eyebrows.

"I have a wish for further converse with you, Miss Maceachan, on a very weighty matter."

"I would not be suspecting you of frivolity, Mr. Duncanson." He felt that her voice had gone hard as granite. "Unfortunately," she added, "I will be away with the dawn."

"Lord Brounhill," he said, hesitatingly, "has had the condescension to bid me visit you and Glenmarisdale with him in August."

"And be sure we shall be giving you a welcome!" The Highland instinct of hospitality prevailed over everything and her smile came back in a flash.

"That," he replied, "is the best word I have heard spoken these many weeks!"

Gazing curiously at him, she saw his eyes in their deep hollows brighten like bits of sun-lit sky. An unaccountable thrill ran through her, and she forced herself to look away.

Just at that moment the mighty pair concluded their conference. Duncan Forbes rose, and two gillies in the brown and green hunting-tartan of the Frasers entered to assist their Chief to his feet. From one of them he took a crooked stick of black wood to support his steps; then, looking round, beckoned to Hector Maceachan.

The young laird advanced with a sheepish look in spite of Forbes's welcoming smile. Darthula edged forward to hear what Lord Lovat would be saying.

"My dear lord," he swung about on his stick towards Forbes, "I have pleasure in presenting my young friend to you. Hector, dear lad, I have persuaded his lordship to make you my successor in the Captaincy of the Watch. I know you will be diligent, and loyal . . . and loyal." He patted the boy's arm; and with a last adoring look at the Lord President turned to go. As he painfully revolved he almost bumped into Darthula, but without noticing her. His face was crumpled with hatred.

Darthula followed him with her eyes, as, leaning with his other arm upon one of the gillies, he limped through the doorway. His second attendant followed, with a swing of his plaid that pleased the watcher to see. It marked, she felt, the independence of the humblest Highlander in this simpering and drawling Lowland society.

Then she faced back where Duncan Forbes stood chatting to her brother, who was making the impulsive and *mal apropos* interjections to which he was given when in the state of shyness. She was indignant at Lovat's diplomacy. With characteristic craft the old spider had shifted his ground and flung out new threads to win Forbes's favour and represent Hector as his own *protegé*. Little as she loved Lord Brounhill, she felt that the family had been slighted by this theft of their natural privilege. And it gave her a pang to realise that Hector, her baby-brother, whom she had come to regard pretty well as her private possession, was already old enough to be the centre of a whole mesh of intrigues—the great ones of the hills and the Government alike competing for his support. Well, it proved at least that Glenmarisdale, with its starveling revenues and diminished following, still counted for something in the world! And, whatever befell, she knew who would rule Hector from the background.

Like all Darthula's thoughts, these reflections darted through her mind in a second or two; then she was aware of the Tutor stepping swiftly across the floor on his bandy, black-silk legs towards Forbes, his head high, his face rigid, his little eyes smouldering. The Lord President, glancing sideways, read the menace in his mien, and hurried to disarm it. Only once or twice had any of Lord Brounhill's Edinburgh colleagues ever known him break out, and they bore the memory of it.

"So, here you are, my lord!" he cried, "I have been in sair need of you since I entered. Here is Simon Fraser has been taking the liberty—I am sure a weel-intentioned one—of commending your young relative to me as a gude friend to the King and the Law in the Hielan's. And you will weel understand that sic a recommendation weighs with me—aye, a muckle weight. But now I am asking you to present Glenmarisdale to me afresh, that I may press him to me as a pairsonal friend, vouched for by ane o' ma auldest and maist faithful brethren of the Court."

As he spoke his face radiated such a glow of sympathy, his hand, with its fall of fine lace at the wrist, dropped with such an affectionate gesture upon Lord Brounhill's arm that the angry man was checked. Darthula, however, watching closely, observed behind the Lord President's geniality that same sly, watchful look peer forth, as if he were gauging the success of his taming. She wondered which of the two glances gave the real man.

"I had desiderated the honour of this presentation mysel'," said Brounie in a grating tone, pointing to Hector, "and I had not supposed I wad be forestalled."

"Only very partially forestalled, Jamie!" remonstrated Forbes, "forbye that ye hae anither member o' your family that I wad be gey gled to be brought acquainted wi'. Glenmarisdale hath a sister."

"She wad be honoured by your lordship's condescension at some seasonable time. But since we are now to speak of business—"

"It is sometimes verra unwise to leave the petticoats out of business," Duncan Forbes warned him. "Miss Maceachan, by all I hear, is a verra positive young leddy; and I am thinking we shall do weel to make a friend of her in this scheme. May I not see her?"

Lord Brounhill looked about him and imperiously beckoned Darthula. She came up, resenting his uncompromising display of authority; but within the space of a few sentences she was charmed by Duncan Forbes, who set the four of them in committee by the fire-place, and took very little time to settle the important business in hand. He had a skill of his own in presenting a proposition in an attractive light, and in meeting, or even forestalling, objections so as to make them opportunities for gratifying the objector. A ticklish point that was bound to arise was the oath Hector would have to take to King George before receiving his commission for the Watch. "It is the same," remarked Forbes lightly, "as Cluny Macpherson hath taken." Now Cluny's loyalty to King James was unquestioned among the Highland Chiefs; and gracefully setting the small on the level of the great, the Lord President went straight on to say, "Wi' your power on the North balancing Cluny's to the South . . . weel, I look forward to sleeping in peace henceforth at Culloden."

So it was soon concluded that the Lord President was to write immediately to the Secretary of State for Scotland, Lord Tweeddale, in London, and that meanwhile Hector should hold a provisional muster of his clansmen. "We will as soon as may be," said Forbes further, "issue the licences for you to procure arms for your Company. Dinna tell me," he added archly, "that you hae already a hidden store o' weapons at Glenmarisdale, for I wadna' believe it if ye did!"

Upon this they parted on terms of mutual gratification, Lord Brounhill dourly satisfied, Hector whimsically resigned, but flattered, Darthula forgetful of the abstract point of loyalty involved, in her consciousness that the standing of Glenmarisdale would be enhanced and Lovat's pilfering of their property arrested.

3

So TRIUMPHANT was she, that a few minutes later, encountering Glengarry, who had slipped out of his refuge again as soon as Forbes departed, she forthwith spilled the tale to him.

To her surprise, a scowl crossed his face. "What way

would they be making a Captain of Glenmarisdale, a mere boy? *Dieu me damne!* For why would they not be entrusting the Watch to my father, and he the principal Chief of the region?"

"Consider his age and his infirmities!" pleaded Darthula, anxious to appease the angry youth.

"Why, then, should not I be depute in my father's stead? I am an officer of several years' standing whateffer."

"Indeed and you are an officer!" said Darthula, as though a curious thought had just occurred to her. "You will still be holding King Louis' commission, will you not, in his *Royal Ecossais*? And since the Elector is at war with his most Christian Majesty, how is it they are not clapping you into the Castle when you show your face in Edinburgh?" She glanced round a trifle apprehensively. "Are you prudent, Alastair, to be appearing at such a public assembly as this?"

"They would not be daring to pluck me from under Simon Fraser's plaid," he replied bitterly. "So you see I humiliate myself, as well as taking risks, to see you, Darthula Maceachan."

There was a heroic simplicity in Alastair Ruadh's words at certain moments which never failed to touch Darthula. Now she allowed him to beckon her under the shadow of the minstrels' gallery.

"You are not believing," he said, "that I am moved by jealousy of your brother's promotion? My soul! Be such baseness far from Alastair Ruadh! It was but of the honour of Glengarry that I was thinking. But these things must be as they may. May I hope that the other, the more *effroyable* scheme, of which I spoke this afternoon, has after all not been mooted this evening?"

"Listen, Alastair Ruadh!" said Darthula. "You may rest assured that when the time comes to dispose of Mistress

Darthula Maceachan's hand the deciding voice will be," she made a little curtsey, "that of the humble person who is now thanking you for your solicitude, and begging you henceforth lay it aside."

"That is good news for me!" he said in a heartier voice. "I will be taking ship for France to-morrow with one load less upon my mind."

At that moment a flash of lightning paled the candles in their sconces, provoking screams from the startled assembly. It was followed by a crack of thunder that seemed to burst the roof, as the slowly advancing storm of the afternoon at last broke over Edinburgh. Some ran to the windows to peer out at the lashing rain which descended at the same instant; others remonstrated and cried for the mirrors to be covered.

Alastair and Darthula stood apart, unnoticed in the excitement, under the gallery.

"Will you be for France to-morrow?" she asked him. "I was thinking you would be lingering the summer out at home."

He sighed. "A dispatch received since I left you hath shattered that hope. I am not my own master, as you doubtless know."

The thunder crackled again, and there were renewed exclamations from the body of the *salon*. Alastair leaned forward towards her in the gloom. "Darthula, I am bound on a perilous venture. It was ever I was the madman chosen for the forlorn hope. God and His Mother alone are knowing when, if ever, I shall set eyes on you again. Will you not give me some keepsake to treasure as a holy memory?"

"What do you mean, Alastair?"

"See that knot of ribbon at your sleeve, and it hanging by a thread! I could not live if I was thinking it might fall and be trampled by careless feet. Make me its guardian instead!"

She was touched, but fenced with him. "I am not knowing

what you have done, Alastair Ruadh, that you should deserve my gage."

"Darthula!" Her brother thrust his head round one of the pillars of the gallery. "I have been looking for you everywhere. Brounie and Allan Duncanson wish to have word with you. Do not be keeping them waiting longer!"

"I will come when I am free!" she threw over her shoulder.

Hector, after a long look at Glengarry, who returned his survey haughtily, withdrew, shrugging his shoulders.

Darthula, with a defiant little gesture, broke the knot of tartan from its thread. "There! Alastair!" she said, handing it to him; "it will be a token of friendship only . . . you are not to be building upon it, you know!"

He kissed it like a relic. "I will be striving to lay a foundation upon which I may be allowed to build some day," he said. "Farewell, my dear! Let the holy angels be guarding your peace!"

She watched him with lightly misted eyes as he marched through the doorway with his proud head high, while the lightning flickered in the staircase. Then she smiled at the craziness of him.

Hector meanwhile was yawning as he talked to his cousin Jean. "And is not this the fine bruilzie," he grumbled, "over the command of two or three score caterans to be going after two or three hundred cattle-lifters—upon the excellent maxim, 'Set a . . . Highland watch . . . to catch a thief'?"

"I am thinking, Hector," she answered gravely, "that you should feel honoured by the appointment."

"I was coaxed into it. Just for a moment I was dreaming it might be an entertaining change from pursuing the deer. Hunting one's fellow-men! My soul! There should be a savour in that!"

"Fie, Hector! Will you be so bloodthirsty?"

"No, Jean dear!" He grinned. "*Ennui* will be my only trophy. I will be the weariest Watch Captain that ever carried broad-sword."

"Hector!" she interrupted, looking across the room to her father, who was speaking to Darthula with a grim expression. "My father will be extremely angered soon against Darthula. And for her own sake she should not permit young Glengarry to show her such marked attentions. She will never learn our Edinburgh ways."

"And they full of peril!" he assented languidly. "Will you be expecting us simple mountaineers to be discerning all these snares and enduring these repeated alarms? One crisis of momentous events upon another's heels! Oh! for my lonely glen, where life doth not move at so heart-shaking a pace nor with such a succession of shocks. There, listen to that!"

The thunder growled again, more distantly.

"You are mocking us," said Jean placidly. " 'Tis true we distort trifles and swell gossip into accusations . . . because . . . I suppose because . . ."

"Because, sweet coz, this is the age of triviality and there will be nothing better to be done in it. And, indeed, who can tell what in the eyes of the Eternal Fates are the trifles and what the grave matters? Not I! There is your philosophy! With a beard might not I be standing by Aristippus and Diogenes? Hark! There sounds the ten-hours' drum below, bidding us all 'gang hame'! I will be defying it, and, Diogenes-like, hie to my tub—to wit, Sandy Macgliskin's cellar. Good night, and, alas! farewell, cousin—for we shall be away at dawn before you rise, to escape the heat of the day."

"And do you take me for such a lie-a-bed, Hector, that I would not be stirring to bid you farewell?" She looked at him reproachfully.

"I am not knowing," he said in a moved tone, "what we have done . . . what I have done . . . to earn your devotion, my dear. But I will be telling you this. Saving my respects to your esteemed parents, I believe you are the only person I will be leaving behind in Edinburgh with regret."

She looked up at him, and for a moment her pretty face looked like crying. Then sinking her eyes again, "I will take care this time," she said composedly, "that you take a better breakfast than a sup of brandy."

Chapter III

THE BAIRN

1

OUTSIDE in the close the rain was still pelting down, and violet flashes from the receding storm lit the northern peaks and the dark sheet of the Firth. The calling of sedans and the quarrelling of the chairmen made a wild confusion as the guests streamed downstairs.

In the narrow porch Hector was jammed against his sister, who was stooping to fit her feet into the heelless green and gold pattens that would lift her above the wet as she crossed to her chair.

"For what were you colloguing so long with Glengarry in that corner?" he grumbled. "Let me tell you the man is a danger, a stormy petrel."

"Already on the watch, Captain?" she asked ironically as she stood up overtopping him on her pattens. "Let me tell *you*! Alastair is the gallant fellow, but it will take a better man than he is, with his French oaths and his tavern-meetings, to set the heather afire or wake Auld Sleepy from her snores. Whither are you bound?"

"For hell—for Sandy Macgliskin's, at any rate. Where is

48

that ruffian Ned Burke? Will you be going home with Brounie, Darthula?"

"He left before anyone, after lecturing me, and bidding my lady take heed that no one disturbed him among his books until morning. He has an 'opeenion' to frame, it seems. I do not suppose my aunt will sob herself to sleep, but I will wait for her and Jean. Do *you* not sit too late! We make early start, remember!"

"I have not forgotten. Perdition catch that rogue Ned!" Lifting his voice to a mountaineer's shrill call, he shouted in Gaelic for the chairman, who answered him at once from across the close.

Several of Lady Stair's guests who were crammed with him into the porch turned shocked faces at hearing a gentleman employ such a tongue in the entrance to a noble house, and even Darthula sought to hush him.

"Well," he grumbled, "it has at any rate brought the scoundrel to the door!" Ned Burke and his assistant, another Highlander, glum and black, had in fact forced their way through the press by unscrupulous use of their elbows and heavy square-toed shoes, and the Laird of Glenmarisdale found his chair waiting for him in a space cleared as if for a royal personage. "Sandy Macgliskin's!" he called through the window as he seated himself, and with a grin the red-headed caddie swung to the left out of the close and began to descend the slope of the High Street.

They pursued their way through the hiss and drive of the rain, the gurgle of the over-filled gutters, which sent up a malodorous whiff from their sewage, and the splashing from the eaves of the houses. The street was deserted save for one or two cloaked and scurrying figures, and a couple shamelessly embracing under an arched entry. Outside the Town Guard House the sentry, with the rain dripping from the tip of his nose, looked like some antique, battered statue.

Passing out by the Netherbow Port with brief formalities, they began the sharp descent of the Canongate suburb outside the walls, which wore a cut-throat appearance in the dark with its few tallow-dips in the windows of the dramshops, and its few noble residences of former days now still and shuttered in their owners' absence. Straight on the chair proceeded until it entered the sordid cluster of buildings that constituted the sanctuary of the ancient Abbey of Holyrood. Here lights glimmered from almost every window, and songs, quarrels and curses floated unabashedly out upon the night. Through the alleys of this privileged Alsatia, which derided alike the Puritanism of the dark city frowning from its hill above and the melancholy of the abandoned home of kings beyond, ragged male and female figures flitted under the rain; while a group of professional beggars, with real or alleged cripplings, reeled arm in arm down the broad causeway leading to the Palace, their badges and tin bowls chinking as they moved.

The bearers stopped at a fair-sized house with a sagging roof just off the main street, and the young Laird descended.

"I suppose you will be wanting to know at what time to fetch me?" he called from the shelter of the penthouse over the door. "I wish, Ned, I knew my own desires well enough to foretell when I shall be as wearied of this den as at the present moment I find myself of Lady Stair's."

"Haaf no fears, Glenmarisdale! Hamish and I will pe taking a bit supper in the White Horse kitchen yonder, and in twa', three hours we will attend you here again. If you pe still not ready, why, we must e'en take turns to sleep inside the chair!"

"Admirable servitor! Ned, I think I must take you back to wait on me in the Highlands!"

"An' it please you, Glenmarisdale," answered Ned stiffly, "I will pe a Macleod."

"And you could not bear to leave Edinburgh either, I know."

"One grows into Auld Reekie as into a shoe, and that iss a fact, Glenmarisdale. Will I effer pe seeing ma Hieland hills again? Who can tell? Well, I will pe bidding you good cheer and good company!"

"Neither of which I am like to find here!" grumbled Hector as he rapped a code signal upon the door, and, after being surveyed through an iron grating, was allowed to enter and descend to a stone cellar where he hung hat, cloak and sword upon a peg in a line already occupied by a fair number of others. Then, approaching a door studded with nails that closed a Gothic arch, he tapped upon it three times. Again a shutter was opened, and a hoarse voiced said:

"*Maledicat te Beelzebub!*"

To which Hector responded with a yawn:

"*Et omnes angeli sui, Amen!*"

Upon this the door swung back, and Hector passed into a large vaulted room, supported by heavy pillars, which had evidently once formed part of the Abbey crypt. It had, indeed, as its plan showed, been a subterranean chapel, but was now travestied from its original purpose. In place of sanctuary lamps wooden hoops hung from the roof, bearing tallow candles that guttered and dripped and diffused a smoky light over the scene. Where the altar used to stand a fireplace and grill had been built into the apse, now tended by a one-legged man and two boys, busy cooking. Down the nave ran a wooden table at which thirty to forty persons were at the moment feasting rudely on herrings, rizzared haddocks, chops and steaks, and broiled fowls. A dozen long clay pipes added their quota to the fog made by the candles and by the smoke from the fire, which escaped with difficulty through a circular hole in the vaulting.

In this flickering chiaroscuro the company looked more

like an assemblage of spectres than a collection of live men. A smile seemed a grimace, a frown a scowl; eyes glittered diabolically, a rumpled coat-collar made a hump, a figure leaning back into shadow became a headless apparition. Yet this gathering of goblins, the Hellfire Club numbered, together with the riff-raff of the city, members of the best families and chief professions of Edinburgh. So much could not be said of their female companions, who betrayed their status by dispensing with masks.

It always tickled the humour of Hector Maceachan to see these raddled strumpets of the Canongate and Cowgate perched on the knees of rising advocates, rich merchants' sons, university professors, and heirs to noble names. They would thrust their views into the discussion of theology, law, classical scholarship or the principles of poetry; and scholars and dandies would absent-mindedly, as they resumed their discussion, sip porter or whisky from glasses streaked by illiterate harlots' mouths.

As the Laird of Glenmarisdale approached the long table, a figure rose and nodded to him. It was a young man, dressed in fastidious elegance, with a handsome profile and thin, sardonic lips.

"Good evening, Elcho," said Hector, "and did you convey our bond to the Devil?"

"This afternoon. I trust you will not default, Glenmarisdale, when some day it is presented?"

"Faith is a grace," declared Hector with a fatuous smile, at which Lord Elcho looked bleak. "Is Glengarry in the club?"

Elcho pointed to the empty Presidential Chair at the head of the table. It was draped in flame-like hangings, and had horns instead of knobs decorating its back. On the table just before it were set a skull and an hour-glass containing not sand but writhing worms. The Presidential hammer, in the form of a skeleton hand clutching a crown, lay neglected in a litter of pipes and mugs.

Hector walked off to the side of the room, where the continuous clink of coin showed that the only pursuit which really fascinated him in this place of childish and vulgar debauchery was in ardent progress. Every form of gambling could be enjoyed in the two aisles of the old chapel—cards, dice or the spinning roulette ball. After some waiting he found a place at a card-table, where for a little while he played in the style peculiar to himself. He would as a rule begin by placing huge stakes on the table, the magnitude of which forced him to play with all his natural wit and *finesse*, until his opponents were stripped. Then, bored at the sight of so much money so safely his, he would risk mad hazards, and perhaps lose both his winnings and his original stake. This again put him on his mettle, and for the next half hour he would be more dangerous than ever—until the sight of a fresh pile of winnings set him casting about for fresh means of throwing it away.

But to-night he very quickly wearied of the slow process of the cards, and crossed to the opposite aisle to find a dicing party. On his way over the paved floor, defiled with spittle and the droppings of mugs, he paused to listen to a debate on Davy Hume's new theory of causation between a student from the University and a plump Counsellor, who kept grunting, as he pulled at the unclean curls of his doxy, "Na, na; I canna thole that! 'Tis against a' religion; you will ne'er persuade me o' sic impiety!"

"In the domain of the Devil, my learned friend," whispered Hector as he passed, "piety is blasphemy and punishable by a draught of salt and snuff in hot water. You will have been warned!" The next minute a well-known prostitute with flaming hair cast her arms about him, but he sent her spinning away with such heartless force that she bruised herself on a table and started blubbering.

In a few moments he was established at a dicing-table; and now, no longer needing to keep his wits so sharp, he began to drink dram after dram of brandy from a chipped and heelless glass. As he threw he kept up a ceaseless monologue of his own forced humour, to which his neighbours at the board, two aged Writers to the Signet and a shrewd young Lowland laird, paid not the least attention, intent upon counting their gains correctly.

From time to time a player would rise and surrender his seat to another, and Hector welcomed each new-comer with fantastic panegyric. All around by now was a genuine pandemonium. Most of the other games had been abandoned, or had ended in the oversetting of the table and a brawl quickly quelled by the officers of the club. It was a rule of the Imps of Satan that they must not quarrel within the precincts of their kingdom—a necessary regulation if two or three members were not to be lost each night, and the reason why swords were compelled to be left in the ante-room. Thus in the ever-thickening smoke there had gradually collected round the table where the Laird of Glenmarisdale still held his reckless own a surging throng trying to follow the game. One clutched a woman naked to the waist to his bosom; another, who had clambered to the shoulders of a friend, was trying with tipsy fingers to pour the contents of a whisky bottle over the wigs of the dicers.

Suddenly Hector paused, as a new opponent took his place opposite to him. "The Devil!" he shouted. "Welcome, most potent, grave and reverend signor! I will be passing the throw to you."

Glengarry, his florid face empurpled with drink, seized the dice-box and rattled it in an unsteady hand. But before he could throw Hector caught his arm.

"What the d-d-devil is this," he stuttered, "that you wear at your buttonhole?"

Glengarry fumbled with a guilty hand at his lapel. He was too late. Despite his intoxication, Hector had recognised first by the Clan Ranald tartan, then by the little golden fringe, the ribbon his sister had been wearing that evening. Leaning across the table, he made a vain effort to snatch it away; then struck Glengarry with all his strength in the face. One of the pointed crystal buttons he wore at his cuff cut Alastair over the eye, and the blood poured out.

In a moment the table was over, and the Laird of Glenmarisdale had been dropped upon by half a dozen of the clubmen, who pinned him by the weight of their bodies to the floor. Glengarry, at the same time, blinded with his own blood, was borne away into the ante-chamber, loudly protesting his Presidential authority, and his honour as a "shentlemens, py Gott!" and "an officer of his most Chrishian Machesty!"

Hector meanwhile, though prostrate, raged like a mountain cat; and there seemed no way of holding him until at last Lord Elcho promised, in defiance of Hellfire law, to carry his challenge to Glengarry the next morning, if he persisted in it when he woke. "That is a pledge," said the young peer, "and now a drink upon it for confirmation!" He signalled with his sarcastic brow to the one-legged landlord, who handed him a glass.

Hector drained it feverishly, and fell flat as if he had been clubbed on the head.

2

And the club seemed still to be pounding his skull when he woke on a rope pallet in a room unknown to him, but still underground. With his hands to his aching head he tried to think. He remembered the Hellfire Club, a game of cartes, the argument on Davy Hume's theory of causation . . . after which his mind went black. Lord! how sick he felt! He gave way and felt a great deal better. He had been foully hocussed, it was evident; but how, by whom? He clapped his hands to his pockets; they were stuffed with guineas and bank-notes. No one had tried to rob him. For what purpose, then, this outrage?

Peering round in the gloom, he made out two or three pallets occupied by sleeping couples in extreme disarray. Then he discerned a figure moving over by the door, and hailed it. Sandy Macgliskin, the landlord of the Hellfire Club premises, stumped towards him on his wooden leg.

"Where am I, you rascal?" roared the Laird.

"You hae been gey ill, Glenmarisdale," he answered, "so I e'en had you carried fra' the club, and brought hither to yin o' ma ain private bedrooms."

Hector could not help laughing. "You call this a private bedroom, do you?"

"Aye," replied the landlord. "I whiles let it to a few o' the gentry for their pleesures. It is retired and apart fra' the club. And peacefu' and pleasant, as you may see for yoursel'."

"Peaceful and pleasant!" Hector twitched his nostrils. "Will these be your guests of the gentry?" he asked, turning to the snoring and mumbling couples. "I would like fine to see the faces of them, Sandy!"

"Forbear, Glenmarisdale!" exclaimed the landlord, starting forward in a sudden alarm, "I hae tauld ye these are ma ain guests, enjoying ma private hospitality!"

"There can be no harm in a glimpse!" protested Hector, his impish humour aroused. "Who, for example, is it that

snores so loud in the black corner yonder? I am thinking
that snore is familiar to me. Come! Who is this lord?" he
cried, shaking off Sandy's arm; and crossing the room he
turned the sleeper over with his foot to see his face. . . .

"A noble lord!" said Sandy Macgliskin grimly. "I tauld
ye! Ye hae nane but yoursel' to thank for what ye now see!"
Hector turned round with his hand over his eyes; then said
in a curiously shaken voice, "Bring me that coverlet from
the empty cot there! Do it, man! Or it's your head I'll be
breaking open!"

"I maun charge twopence, ye ken, for extra bedding. . . .
What whim is this, Glenmarisdale?"

"Do you never read your Bible, you that belong to the
sanctimonious Kirk, and are an elder on the Sabbath, I'll be
sworn?"

"I dinna just see what the Bible can have to say to a' this.
I wad have hoped, Glenmarisdale, that your natural reverence—"

"It forbids me at least to behave like the sons of Noah!
Come, Sandy, give me that rag of yours. . . . Poor Brounie!
. . . Is this the purpose served by your private door o' nights?
. . . Is it that I should be sitting in judgment on you? Nay,
I misdoubt I have to-night for the first time a spark of fellow-
feeling with you! You will be a man, after all, my Tutor,
and not a mere bundle of parchment and a rattle of keys!"

He spread the rag-quilt over the stupefied sleepers with an
almost hieratic gesture.

" 'Earth to earth,' " he murmured, " 'ashes to ashes, dust to
dust. Unto this shall all flesh come!' "

"Forbear, Glenmarisdale!" remonstrated the landlord,
deeply shocked. "Will ye misquote the Scriptures for your
sport? Canna the Bishop teach ye better?"

"*Parcus et infrequens cultor*, Elder, I fear. . . . Pheugh!

how my head throbs. Give me, Elder, I beseech, a hair of
the dog that hath bitten—nay, swallowed me. And what,
pray, can the time be?"

"Past twa o' the clock. I heard it strike from Holyroodhouse as I came down."

"We have all made a precious use of our time, I am thinking. Is there a way out of this den?"

Sandy hopped nimbly on his single leg up a wooden ladder
before Hector. At the house door he laid a hand on the
young Laird's sleeve as he drank a last ill-advised dram of
cheap brandy, and said meaningly, "You will not forget, will
you, Glenmarisdale, that you hae surprised my secret . . .
and anither's . . . and forbear to wag your tongue? Gin I
had known his lordship would be visiting Tron Corner Meg
this nicht of nichts, I wad have placed ye in ither quarters to
recover. But the lad maun have admitted him wi'out my
knowledge."

"Do you read Davy Hume, Mr. Macgliskin?" asked Hector gravely.

"Whiles. But I canna just bring mysel' to agree wi' his
opeenions."

"'Tis pity! Davy might have taught you, Mr. Macgliskin, how to disholve—curse my tongues! dissolve—dish-
agreeable impressions."

He dropped some coins into the landlord's hand, and
stepped out into the street while bolts and chains rattled behind him.

"A-ah!" He drew a deep breath. "I had never dreamed
a mere draught of fresh air could be such nectar!"

"*Gardy loo!*" said a gruff voice overhead, and the contents
of a domestic utensil narrowly missed his hat and splashed
on his coat-skirts.

3

THE storm had by now completely passed away, and in the rain-scoured street the freshness of the summer night over-bore the odours of the vicinity. A cool breeze was stirring with the exhilaration of a wind from the hills, while overhead a torrent of stars glimmered in a clear blue vault.

At these, while his colleague slept inside the chair, Ned Burke stood staring up with an odd rigidity. In answer to his employer's hail, he lifted his hat, as one gentleman saluting another, then resumed his astronomical posture.

"Ned!" said Hector with chattering teeth. "I perceive you are exceedingly drunken. But do not think I am re-proaching you for your beastly condition. For, *imprimis*, I will have kept you waiting long enough to drive a more seri-ous character to the dram-bottle. And *secundo*, I myself . . . am not precisely drunk . . . but something far, far worse. But what I would pray you earnestly to consider is . . . have you the wits and legs to carry me home to Advo-cates' Close?"

Ned Burke turned and approached him with a bold, almost menacing, stride. "It is I haaf had stranche visions to-night whiles you lingered in there, Glenmarisdale!"

"Why for that matter, Ned Burke, I too have had visions . . . one exceeding strange . . . and one I have forgotten." Again he racked his thudding head to recall what had gone before his lapse into unconsciousness. . . . A quarrel, surely . . . and a face. . . . Whose face?

Ned meanwhile regarded him with folded arms.

"Do you know, Glenmarisdale, that I haaf the Seeing?"

"I never yet knew a Highlander," replied Hector with wan affability, "that was not claiming it. And in Edinburgh it is mostly made the ground for demanding a silver shilling of the fortune-teller. But if, O Ap-p-pollo, you will be descending from your tripod and be pedestrian enough to carry me home, I will reward you with two silver shillings . . . of the best English coining, since the rogues no longer give us leave to mint our own!"

"Say what you will, Glenmarisdale," muttered the chairman sulkily, as he stooped with his companion to take up the poles. "It is I haaf seen stranche sights in the sky to-night!"

"Or at the bottom of your glass?" mumbled Hector, as he fell into the chair.

It was a curious course they steered back up the tasking hill. The chair pitched like a ship in the waves, and was driven from side to side as if by a gale; though the breeze was light, and the star-sown night, already paling fast, was tranquil in its vast solemnity.

They had a rough passage of the Netherbow this voyage; for the Waiter at the Gate was angry at being disturbed from slumber, and opined sourly that these were pretty hours for a gentleman to keep.

"Do not insult the shentlemans!" began Ned Burke truculently; and Hector had to cry to him out of the window not to start a brawl. "I am nigh the end of my tether, I assure you," he warned him; "and if you do not make smoother way . . . it is I will be sick again!"

"You haaf neither the heart nor the stomach of a Chief, Glenmarisdale!" retorted Ned with a stately air of offence, and they resumed their journey up the hill.

The wavering progress ended at last at the black mouth of Advocates' Close. Hector descended, and found his head spinning in the keen air of the height. Ned Burke offered his arm. "Come, Glenmarisdale, I will be leading you to your door."

It was the very knife-edge between night and dawn. A

ghostly greyness was overspreading the sky, turning the tall mansions with their crow-stepped gables into hooded apparitions. Far away beyond the Nor' Loch the call of a cock came like a wail through the silence. The silhouette of the other chairman was like that of a man enchanted into a statue.

Hector shuddered. "This is a horrid hour, Ned. An hour that makes my blood run c-c-cold! They say, Ned, it is the hour when the tide turns, and the p-pulse beats low, and the sick are caught by the cold fingers of Death at their throttle." He put his own hand to his throat, gulping. "G-give me, Ned, the gay mid-night, not this sad gloaming of the dawn!"

"Let me be your guide!" said Ned Burke. "Faith, you will be taking a fever, by my way of thinking, if you do not get speedily to your bed. Come, man, come awa'!"

They were an unsteady pair as, leaning the one upon the other, they sought to make entry into the dark passage of the Close. Ned Burke's partner, watching them, thought of two wounded men trying to support one another from a field of battle. He had been in the fighting in Glen Shiel in 1719.

On the doorstep below the carved text INTROIBIT REX GLORIAE Hector collapsed and begged piteously for something to drink.

"And how would herself pe finding you drink in this place, at this hour?" expostulated Ned Burke, nearly distracted. "Do you but make an effort! Climb your stair, and I'll uphaud you, you will can find good claret enough within!"

"I could no more be c-c-climbing all those stairs," wailed Hector, "than ascend to Heaven! Woe is me, for I am a man of unclean life, Ned Burke!"

"De'il take the Laird!" moaned Ned. "He iss extraordinar' intoxicate! I canna make it out! Come, Glenmarisdale! Come!" He shook Hector's shoulder. "Rouse yourself! Pe a man!"

"Bury me here!" sobbed Hector. "B-bury me here! Let

the g-green branches be waving over my tomb, and hang the harp of Ossian above my grave!"

"The man iss clean daft!" thought Ned, scratching his poll, and wondering if his own legs were steady enough to carry the young Laird upstairs in his arms.

"Hush!" said Hector, abruptly lifting his haggard face from his hands, "what is that?"

Ned spun round and listened. Up from the dip of the shadowy steps that sank away to the brim of the loch a footstep was approaching.

"Some other bird of the night!" Burke told himself, but he had a peculiar feeling. His hair was tickling under his wig, a trickle of cold water seemed to run down his spine, and his heart, he thought, would have jumped out of his throat had he not shut his mouth tightly.

Nearer and nearer sounded the step; but though Ned glared at the stairs till his eyes swam, no head rose out of the dip, no form appeared to accompany the impetuous patter of the footfalls.

"Christ preserve us!" groaned the Highlander, tottering against the wall, and spreading out his hands to support himself. His teeth chattered together as the steps went past him, while Hector sat staring foolishly with fallen jaw, and shivered in his turn as though struck by an icy wind, when the Invisible Walker passed by.

Breaking the spell with an uncouth cry, Ned ran through the arch into the street, and hailed his companion.

"Who went by, Hamish?"

"No man," answered the other Highlander.

"You haaf seen none?"

"Yourself alone."

"Were you not hearing the steps?"

"Yours only, Ned! What others mean you? Haaf you bestowed Glenmarisdale?"

"Not yet. The lad iss sick. Bide a wee!"

He ran back and hauled Hector to his feet. He was sweating to be gone from the place. "Come your ways, Glenmarisdale, lean on me!" he panted, and propelled him inside the doorway.

It was pitchy black in the staircase as they stumbled together to climb it. They turned the first winding, and a slant of grey light shot like a sword-thrust in mid-air from a lancet.

Suddenly Ned gave a yell. "A bairn!" he cried. " 'Tis a bairn!" He tottered backwards down the stairs.

Hector, deprived of support, fell violently forward on his hands upon the stones. The shock seemed to sober him.

"What was that?" he asked in a painful voice. "What made you cry out, Ned?"

"A bairn! A bairn!" gasped the caddie. "A bairn streaked wi' blood, and it floating in the air above your head, Glenmarisdale!"

Hector from where he lay looked sharply up at the shaft of grey light, every moment widening and deepening as the day grew clearer. Ned craned forward and stared too.

There was nothing to be seen but floating motes of grime and dust from the filthy old corkscrew that immured them.

"You have had a fantasy, Ned," said Hector gravely. "You have been drinking, you know."

"My sorrow!" sobbed the chairman. "It waas no fantasy. Neither waas there any whisky dishtilled that could cause me first to pe hearing feet with no body, and then to see yon Babe wi' the blood pearling from its hair and nose. I haaf the Seeing, I told you, Glenmarisdale."

"I hope you have not," said Hector in a calm voice, "and I hope you are drunk. Else you have seen something very disagreeable to me, Ned Burke."

"And what iss it you would pe saying I haaf seen, Glenmarisdale?" asked Ned in a wheedling tone, as he crouched down on the step beside Hector, and thrust his ill-shaven face, glimmering in the dawn, close to the young Laird's shadowed countenance.

"The Bairn of Glenmarisdale . . . our family spectre."

"The *bocan*?* May the Silent Ones take pity on us!" whined Ned. "And what may that betoken?"

"The early death of the Laird. . . . A death by violence, Ned Burke!"

* Ghost.

Chapter IV

A VIOLIN IN THE WOOD

1

On Loch Maris the soft rain was falling, dulling its waters to a steely blue, veiling the cragheads that stood trooped along its narrow length in scarves of cloud, making dim spectres of the peaks at its foot, which stood like challengers to guard the savage passes leading to the head of Loch Arkaig beyond.

The islet with its three feathery pines and ruined chapel near the head of the loch, where the graves of the Maceachans lifted their stones among the tussocks, seemed this morning to float indistinct upon the shadowy water. Bare as some fragment hewn from the rock of the hillside above was Glenmarisdale House upon the tongue of land that projected where the river swirled into the lake. In silence it offered to the beating of the rain its two grey storeys and its high-pitched roof, still only thatched in part, with chimney-stacks of stone. Outlined upon the half-moon of black firs that stretched behind it, it looked more like a comfortable farmhouse than the mansion of a Chief; save for the two plain pillars upholding the porch and the family shield with the motto *Non Obliviscor* carved above them, it made no show of ornament.

Above the House the ground rose sharply to the left of the fir plantation, till it reached the rocky cleft whence the river Maris tumbled from a twenty-foot scarp. On the brink of the fall, commanding the pass to the loch-head, stood the tower of the ancient keep, dating from the days of Malcolm Canmore, now furnished as a summer-house by Darthula. From a gate in the wall enclosing this ruin could be reached the path that ran by the gash of the river all the way to where Glen Beasdale with its fairy woods overhung the caves of Loch-nan-Uamh on the Western coast—a ten-mile walk or pony-ride.

A huddle of outbuildings, stables, byres for cattle and huts for the farm-workers and servants, filled the space at the back of the House between the old tower and the fir-wood. On the further bank of the river, where the hills receded some-what from the shore, small crofts of oats had been economi-cally carved out in a strip of fertile soil, the tiny cottages that dotted them making white patches in the faint light. Similar gleams of walls came from a cluster of houses near a creek in the strath, and more could be observed at intervals along the shores of the loch, and even here and there high up among the birches which draped the lower slopes of the encompassing mountains. These minute farms and heather-thatched cots sheltered the families whence came the swordsmen on whose arms the Lairds of Glenmarisdale still relied for their power and prestige; but on this still morning with its fresh, dank air, few seemed to be abroad. Smoke-threads rising straight from the massive chimneys of the House, and curling here and there through holes in the thatch of the huts, gave sign of human life; but the dark specks of cattle, feeding on a soggy strip of bright-green pasture just where the river joined the loch, were the only moving figures in the landscape.

Such was the habitation of the small Clan Maceachan, buttressed to West and East by the two great confederacies of the Western Highlands—the Macdonalds of Clan Ranald, whose standard they followed in broil or war, and the Camerons of Lochiel, from whose family Darthula's mother had come. Centuries ago they had surrendered land to these powerful neighbours as the price of protection; but the crumbling tower at the loch-head still testified to their antique grandeur. It might be a fable that Maceachans had ever ruled as Kings of the Great Glen, as fabulous as their bardic ancestry from Hector, son of Astyanax, son of Hector of Troy; the stern relic on the height, by its dungeon and arrow-slits, still spoke regretfully to the dwellers in the House by the sheltered lakeside of a power which had dwindled almost to a shadow.

Perhaps that regret was in the music rising at the moment from a stone wall bordering the lawn in front of the house. There sat a kilted form, fingering a set of pipes. It was Mackissock, hereditary piper of Glenmarisdale, softly trying an improvisation. He was the only human creature in sight; and in the pauses of his indecisive music the hiss and patter of the rain alone was audible.

Suddenly he stood up, saluting, as the house-door opened, and two figures came out upon the lawn. One was Darthula Maceachan, her plaid of the green hunting Clan Ranald tartan with its slight red bars drawn over her head; the other a slight old man, neatly dressed in black, with a cloak thrown over his shoulders against the rain.

Apart from these precautions, neither seemed troubled by the weather as they paced round the edge of the rough circular lawn.

"Be assured, Doctor," Darthula was saying, "that Hector has no head for politics. If we can induce him to perform his new duties as Captain of the Watch with a decent regularity, we will have taxed his public spirit as far as it will go. He has no ambitions."

The old man at her side lifted refined hands. "I had no mind to censure Glenmarisdale," he protested. "Even were there ground, it would be no business of mine to do so."

Darthula laughed. "As chaplain here you might claim the privileges of a spiritual adviser, surely, Dr. Hay!"

He shook his cleanly-powdered head. "I will wait with my counsel till it be asked. I fear," he smiled slyly, "that Glenmarisdale at present takes his religious instruction rather from the sceptic Hume."

"You must know, Doctor, that he is a fellow of infinite moods, my Hector. In the heart of him he would no more forsake his God than be disloyal to his King!"

She might for a moment have stood for a picture of St. Monica exalted; then, as she caught a tiny twinkle in the chaplain's eye, the red spot flew to her cheeks. "You are thinking now," she declared, "that I too am the creature of impulse and whim! Confess it!"

"I am thinking, dear Mistress Darthula," he answered gently, "that you at least never inflict upon us the suffering of monotony. It is no grave fault to be susceptible in youth. You had no need to be ashamed if it were true that you had a little of the variety of our Highland weather. . . . Look now, how the sun smiles a moment upon the golden field across the water! . . . Ah! it is gone, and here comes the rain closer than before!" He drew his cloak a trifle more tightly around him. "Such is the divine caprice of our native land, so much more attractive—to me, at any rate—than the set smile of Italy or the sullenness of England. Let our ladies take after our nature!" He raised his black shovel-hat. "It becomes them surely."

"I have always vowed it was you were the expert in gallantry, Dr. Hay!"

"Oh! fie, fie, Mademoiselle, will you be saying so of a Churchman?"

"And what for no? You are not bound, like our Catholic neighbour, Bishop Hugh Macdonald of Morar, to be celibate. You might have taken wife!"

"I preferred to take peace!" His sunny face, with its clear-cut, almost feminine features, shone all over with humour. "You have made me stray from my text—a heinous fault in a preacher, Miss Darthula! I did but seek to express a hope that Glenmarisdale would never make a politician. A soldier . . . yes! That is his tradition and predestination!"

"Would you have him exile himself to France? Where else, pray, is there a flag under which he could serve?"

"You have silenced me there," said the old man mournfully.

"For the moment," Darthula proceeded, "such ambition as he hath would seem rather to fit himself to become a hunting-gillie. This is the fifth day he will have been away to the hills after the deer with the Forester. Heaven knows where he is now among the crags!"

"You are not alarmed for his safety?"

"And he with Donald Dhu the Forester at his side, and old Macvarish to watch over him like a nurse? That would indeed be inventing fears to plague myself! I wish, though, he would not take Macvarish with him on these occasions. It means we have no Seneschal to house till he returns. . . . You have come to a poor family, Dr. Hay."

The chaplain uttered his pleasant laugh, while Darthula looked round at the weather. "The rain will not be ceasing the day," she said. "See, Doctor, how the mists come down!

The Dreamer is hidden, too. That is aye a bad weather-sign."

Dr. Hay tried to peer through the distant curtains now covering the foot of the loch, in an endeavour to make out the outline of the strange peak with the human profile called by that name.

"You have a legend about that mountain, have you not?" he asked as he desisted.

"About every stone and every tree at Glenmarisdale . . . as you will know to your cost before you have been with us very long, Doctor. As to the rhyme of the Dreamer . . . I ought to summon Ewen the Bard to chant it to you. But the old man is in his grave these five years, and hath left no inheritor of his gift. The son of his old age, Neil, is as crazy as a poet, but the boy makes no songs. So we lack our *Sennachie*, too."

"But by all I hear, dear Miss Darthula," protested the clergyman, "you are well able to supply his place."

Darthula looked pleased. "I long ago Englished the rhyme of the Dreamer, which, you must understand, flies about in the Erse among our people. It was no great task, and there will be small merit in my version. It runs thus." Without dramatic affectation she pointed a finger towards the hidden peak, while she recited:

> "Should the Dreamer wake,
> On his mountain-tower,
> 'Tis Maceachan's power
> Must pass from the Lake."

For a moment she was silent, a questioning look in the clouded brown depths of her eyes; then she dropped her hand to her side with a light laugh. "Whatever the rune may mean, the Dreamer is not likely to wake on such a morning. Well, I am thinking I will have my pony for a ride in the woods; there is so much singing there when the burns are full."

"And I," said Dr. Hay, "will betake me to my room to write letters. I have one must go to Edinburgh, and two at least to Paris. Mr. Sanderson tells me he will be sending a bag to-morrow to Fort Augustus for the post."

2

As soon as he had said this the chaplain became aware that he had made a *faux pas*. Darthula stood looking at him with frigid eyes. "So, Mr. Sanderson was not thinking it necessary to acquaint me!" she exclaimed. "It would seem that whether I am in residence at the House or away in Edinburgh makes no differ at all to him!"

"I fear," said Dr. Hay pacifically, "that 'tis I who am the offender. Little doubt but that Sanderson looked to me to acquaint you of his intent; he did but pause a moment on the path from Glen Liath yester morn to tell me, as he rode his pony towards the upper shielings. Had he visited the House he could not so far have forgot his duty . . . to say nothing of his courtesy . . . as to neglect to inform you, too."

The chaplain was extremely anxious to do nothing to embitter further the fierce dissension which already in the few months he had been at Glenmarisdale he had perceived to rage between Miss Maceachan and the Lowland factor appointed by Lord Brounhill to manage the Glenmarisdale estate in his absence. The Tutor was convinced that no Highlander would work or get work out of those under him; so he had sent from his own property of Brounhill the stocky little man with the eye like a hard, blue pebble, whose task it was to drive the labour on the clan lands and to check Highland wastefulness.

Under the grindstone of Rob Sanderson's personality, waste had to a good extent been checked; but longer working hours could not be extracted from the lounging, muscular clansmen; and when he had disputed the right of the crofters dwelling by the entry to the loch to spear salmon for their own use, he had one night, while lurking to pounce on them, been tripped and flung into the water. After that he had taken to riding round the estate with two enormous horse-pistols loading down his long-suffering pony, at the sight of which Darthula had politely enquired whether she should not request the officer commanding at Fort Augustus to send a six-pounder with its team to escort him on his rounds.

Yet within a month or two of this bitter sarcasm, Rob Sanderson could claim good grounds for his apprehension. It befell this way.

Without any special length of warning the factor evicted old Duncan Maceachan and his still older wife from Maol Farm, on the plea that he was too infirm to work it, and that his son Angus was a drunkard and a ne'er-do-weel, who did nothing to help his father. Now old Duncan not only claimed cousinship with the Laird; he had actually, in accordance with Highland usage, been foster-father to Hector in his infancy—until indeed his sister had snatched him away to have him for herself. But she did not recall that long-ago quarrel when she was told of the factor's unheard-of outrage on her relatives. She had remonstrated, threatened, finally implored Sanderson with tears to relent. His only answer had been, "Ye are aye fond o' daffin', Mistress; but ye canna persuade me that yon ragged cateran is sib to ye. Cousin, Gudesakes! He is only fitten to be a Wanderin' Willie on the roads, and a gaberlunzie he shall be afore the new moon! D'ye ken he owes three quarters rent and kind?"

Hector, when begged to intercede, had whistled, shrugged his shoulders, and offered to pay to place Duncan and his wife in comfort in Dunbar's Hospital in Inverness. Duncan had retorted that he would sooner die in a cave above the waters of Maris—and that so should his rheumatically-stricken wife. A joint letter to Lord Brounhill, signed by Hector and Darthula, begging for an arrest of the factor's sentence, only elicited a curt request that they would "use their influence to assist in place of impeding Mr. Sanderson's performance of his duty to me."

And abruptly Duncan Maceachan, his aged wife, and his drunken son Angus, had solved the problem by a total disappearance. In a night they had vanished into the windings of a land made for fugitives, a giant's maze of hills and caves and boulders that makes pursuit the hunting of a mirage, and not even Hector could learn from his own people one word of their whereabouts. "It will be better as it is, Glenmarisdale!" was the only answer, dutifully given, but with a glance of mute reproach at the Chief who had failed to save his kinsmen from the necessity of taking to the heather. "Nothing," Hector complained to his sister afterwards, "can make them see that I have no power to go against my Tutor's will in such a matter."

Darthula had answered with a glance that showed she was of much the same opinion as the clan; and six weeks later, when the whole business seemed to be buried, Rob Sanderson, cantering his pony through the woods at the deserted foot of the loch, had been shot at from the undergrowth. The bullet had sent a hole through his coat-skirts, and a pretty state of shaking he had been in when he fled back to the House, crying out upon "Barbarians!" and "Outlaws!" He had insisted upon a pursuit being organised after old Duncan's ne'er-do-weel son, but no glimpse was gained of the lank form of Angus Maceachan, of his bald, domed head fringed with red hair, his wild eyes, or his hollow cheeks. Hector, however, knew something that he never uttered to a soul. First, on the night of the attack upon the factor and the escape of his assailant, Darthula had casually remarked to him that her fastest pony had strayed from its feeding-ground. Secondly, he had missed the next morning one of his deer-shooting guns, with a horn of powder.

For several days afterwards the young laird would sit with his fork half-lifted at dinner, staring at his sister's smooth countenance as she exchanged anecdote or badinage with him, wondering . . . wondering . . . and reaching no conclusion.

3

THIS end of the story was not known to the chaplain, who now, after dubiously successful attempts to smooth away Darthula's fresh cause of resentment against the factor, went to his own room in the north wing. Here was also the chapel, reached by a winding stone stair in a turret at the north-east angle of the House. The prohibited service of the Scottish Episcopal Prayer Book was read every Sunday by Dr. Hay, wearing black gown and bands, to a crowd in kilts and tartan kirtles that filled the long room with its tilted roof almost to suffocation. Beneath the great brass chandelier, suspended by a chain from the central rafter, Hector and Darthula sat on crimson-covered arm-chairs in the midst of their people, old Macvarish, the henchman and seneschal, and Mackissock, the piper, occupying posts of honour, one behind each chair, which they would have fought while they had life to retain.

When not away upon his sacred duties, visiting the sick at the shielings or carrying the Sacrament on pony-back across the hills for the comfort of the dying, Dr. Hay was normally sunk in books. These, however, were seldom the folios of the Fathers, which were allowed by him to slumber on the shelves of the library below the chapel, or even the controversial tracts in favour of episcopacy, liturgy and the Usages with which he was favoured by his brethren in Edinburgh and the Non-Juring divines in England. He preferred to any professional reading an Elzevir Horace, an Ovid—the *Fasti*, not the *Ars Amatoria*—or a Theocritus of such a crabbed type that Darthula at the mere sight of it forsook her momentary desire to learn Greek. And just as he could not sit a shaggy mountain-pony without something of the air of the cavalry cadet he had been in a noble French regiment in his youth, so he could not choose a book from a row without revealing the fastidious scholar.

When he was not thus reading, or composing minute translations of Greek or Latin epigrams, or writing long letters to friends abroad on "the affairs of Scotland," Dr. Hay had yet another hobby. This was an old, browned violin; and so soon as he learned that his playing would fret no one at Glenmarisdale, he would sit for hours letting the delicate melodies of Corelli or Scarlatti drift through his window into the woods behind the house, and mount in the still, pure air towards the savage peaks above.

Darthula, whose ear for music was quick and sound, though her playing on the tremulously-corded spinet in her parlour was variable and untrustworthy, loved to accompany the chaplain so soon as she could read his tattered books of music or pick out an accompaniment by hearing—the method she preferred. This very morning, although he had said he would attend to his duties of letter-writing, she heard the violin sounding as she passed out of the back of the house to get her pony; and, turning, she called up through his open window, "I will find you a sprig of white heather, Doctor!"

She was still smiling at his lovable foibles when a few minutes later, wrapped in her plaid, she rode her sturdy pony out of the paddock, through a gate of lopped branches from which the woods could be reached. A child, almost naked, rose from the wet grass to open it for her, and saluted with a twig he was shouldering in place of a sword. The lances of the rain struck on her head as she bent supply to the movements of the pony, while it scrambled up the bank to the sheltering trees.

For a couple of miles the path ran through woods alive with the varied voices of the rain, dripping on the roof above or trickling from the leaves within, and with the song of a small burn hurrying over reddish stones—an obstacle that the pony negotiated with the daintiness of a kitten. Presently a louder voice began to sound as the path wound nearer to the gulf through which the Water of Maris flung itself in a brown and creamy torrent; boiling over rocks that shone like the skins of aquatic monsters half-sunken in the flood; rushing under bridges formed by fallen trees across the stream, their battered boughs lashing the water, the leaves on their upper side dying a bronze death, their shallow roots upstanding like dishevelled tresses.

Darthula had been singing in a low tone while she rode. But now her voice was drowned in the thunder of the Upper Falls, which tore their way down in three huge leaps from a cleft in the heights opposite, where ridge lifted itself behind barren ridge, till, dimly defined to-day, a cone-shaped pinnacle sprang over all, to menace heaven in unscalable aloofness.

A continuous cloud-spray danced over the pool into which the falls discharged themselves, and, all around, the stones, the tree-trunks glowed like green metal in their coat of dampness. The fringe of the wood had caught the fertility of this moisture, and flourished in wilder luxuriance of verdure and bright mosses. Right across the sunken river-bed the spray was tossed upon the woodland path, to fall upon Darthula's cheeks.

She pressed forward, drinking in through mouth and nos-

trils, and, as it seemed to her, through all her pores the refreshment of her native air and rain. At last she was being washed
clean of the grime and grit of Edinburgh. With an exulting
cry, she let the hood of her plaid fall on her shoulders, and
pulled away the ribbon that bound her hair. The pony, taking the sound for a call to more speed, broke gamely from his
amble to a full canter, careering along the soft edge of the
path below the branches, and forcing her to lie forward on
his shaggy mane, to keep her locks free from entanglement.
The hoofs squelched, the leaves whispered, a discontented
bird higher up in the trees let loose a chatter of notes and
abruptly ceased.

Suddenly the wood lightened, and bands of sky like grey
cotton-wool showed between the boughs. In a few minutes
they had scrambled down and up a ditch marking the bound-
ary of the wood, and were out in the loneliness of the jade-
coloured hill-side. Below, the slope sank towards the now
completely hidden river; above, it rose to meet waves of
magenta heather pallid in the rainy light. Higher still loomed
the black phantasms of mountain-peaks, with vapours steam-
ing, like smoke from an Ogre's cauldron, round their heads.
Tiny waterfalls seamed their flanks with trembles of silver,
and cloud-curtains veiled the mysterious mouths of their
passes.

Between the heather and the crags outcrops of purplish
rock split the ground, some like the fingers of a buried Giant
clutching the soil, others displaying slits like leering mouths.
Here and there, also, boulders shaped like crouching men
lurked in the bracken of the nearer slopes, and might have
alarmed a stranger to the region. But they brought no fear
to Darthula and her pony. With her streaming hair darkened to black by the rain, and sparkling with the drops as
though caught in a diamond net, she found in this wilderness
only the freedom of home.

Tirelessly the pony trotted on, for she was not much taller than her brother, and made little burden in the saddle. The song of the Maris died away to the left as they rounded a shoulder on which the mauve surges of the heather swept closer to meet them, while, with very little hope, she kept her mountain-trained eye for the fleck of white that might enable her to fulfil her rash promise to Dr. Hay. They were threading a narrow pass now, and though the rain was still falling in a thin veil, there was a lifting of the sky overhead which signalised that she was drawing alone through the wet solitude towards the Atlantic, whose vast sheet of light the cloudy weather could not stay from throwing its pearly radiance far inland. Another mile and the mountain walls broke away on either hand, to show, beneath, the woods of Beasdale in their dark-green summer livery, shot with the silvery shimmer of the birches.

The shelter of these trees once gained, Darthula leaped from the pony to rest him. With his reins looped over her arm she led him along by tracks she knew, stooping from time to time to pluck the wild flowers on the path, blue-bells, ragged robin, the tiny yellow pyramids of the bog-asphodel. By degrees she gathered a little nosegay of soft flowers, which she fastened into the circular brooch with Celtic patternings that held her plaid together at the breast.

She moved always with ears alert for sounds, for in truth she was always a trifle frightened of the silence of Beasdale Woods. They seemed so likely a place for apparitions— Hector had never indoctrinated Darthula with the maxims of Davy Hume. It might be the shades of warriors or outlaws from the coast and neighbouring isles, who must so often have found refuge in their recesses; it might be sprites of trees peeping down with green, slanting eyes from the leaves overhead; it might be some flat-headed kelpie writhing from under a stone in a rill. She did not to-day more than any other day take these fancies too seriously; yet, just as she was bending to pluck a purple orchis, she sprang erect with a jerk that made the pony snort, and stood listening with white cheeks and thudding heart.

A violin was being played through the forest, away down where the wood overhung the rocky bay of Loch-nan-Uamh. A violin! But it was impossible! For a second the wild idea jumped into her mind that Dr. Hay had followed to wreak a practical joke upon her. She dismissed it at once; such a mad prank was not for his age or character. But who else would be playing a violin in this locality? Not Angus of Borrodale, in whose demesne the woods lay, nor any of his family! Not young Clan Ranald—she believed he was on the mainland, but he practised only upon the pipes. There had been a pedlar last year who had wandered up from Glasgow, and amused the glens with songs and reels scraped on a little kit—these fine, melancholy notes were no pedlar's.

They were growing fainter as she stood straining her ears to listen, and now they had completely died away; she could hear only the beating of her heart. The pony startled her with an impatient whinny. Should she follow after, and seek to hunt down the mysterious musician? . . . She was not at all sure that she wanted to find him. She did not relish the notion of coming suddenly, under a gloom of entangled branches or between two tall, lichenous rocks, upon a creature with tiny horns peeping through its curls, or cloven hoofs showing above its shoe-buckles. . . . What ludicrous phantasies! What was becoming of her sanity?

But anyhow it was not she that would go questing in search of sorrow. In search of sorrow! she repeated to herself, as if the words had been put into her head. She turned the pony's head aside, and made towards Beasdale Burn. There was a break in the wood there, and the burn was an old friend, even if sometimes it seemed to sing ironically to her as she passed it by.

She felt relieved when at last she heard its voice, raised as if in welcome. The strip of open sky above it was still obscured by mist though the rain had ceased, and the daylight came as though filtered through milk; but she was glad to be clear of the trees, from behind which she had been feeling that she might be pounced upon at any moment.

And suddenly she succumbed to the heaviness of her eyelids. The long and strenuous ride through the rain, after Edinburgh laziness, the scented closeness of the woods through which she had been picking her way, the lullaby of the tiny torrent pouring over its stones, all coaxed her to sleep. Her fears of the unknown with the violin seemed silly now she was out of the darkness of the wood. Why should any wandering musician seek to harm her? On the bracken near the burn, she could safely trust the pony to browse with the reins tucked into his throat-lash; and a grey rock in front of her had a hollowed side as alluring as an arm-chair.

Darthula loosened her plaid, and spread it amid the bracken before this rock, refastening the brooch, with its nosegay of wild flowers, at her breast. Then, with a sigh of content, she coiled her lithe little form in its lavender-coloured dress down upon the green tartan, which matched the fern except for its blood-coloured threads. Her head lay back against the smooth stone, and the fringe of her lashes, as her eyelids drooped, seemed almost to brush the ridges of her cheeks.

She heard the burn calling as she floated off into confused dreams. . . . She heard it calling as she came slowly back to consciousness and the heady forest odours swept round her again. For a moment she lay in the puzzlement of awakening; then abruptly started to a sitting posture, propping herself on her palms, while one foot in its heavy buckled shoe shot out from the billowing folds of her long skirt.

Just across the stream under the overhanging bank a man was sitting on a flat rock with his back to her, his head bent as he tightened the keys of a violin. He was dressed in black with square cuffs and silver buttons, and for a second she thought that it was Dr. Hay who had followed her after all. Then she realised that this was a taller, slimmer figure, and that the wig upon his hatless head was brown, not powdered. Who could he be? A clergyman evidently; but whence? Visitors were rare enough upon this lonely coast for each to rouse a lively speculation.

While she wondered he turned his head, and she saw large eyes, with pale-brown rims surrounding a dark and meditative centre, fixed curiously upon her.

"So, you are awake at last," he said in a clear, rather high-toned voice. "I trust it was not my thrumming that disturbed you." He plucked softly at a violin-string as he spoke, and it uttered a sob that fled down stream with the burn.

"Who are you?" demanded Darthula point-blank, forgetting all her behaviour.

She saw the young man's mouth, red-lipped and shaped like a tiny Cupid's bow, melt in a sudden smile, and the smile agreeably dimpled his plump cheeks. She realised her *gaucherie* and blushed.

"I ask your pardon, sir," she said, "I am Mistress Maceachan of Glenmarisdale . . . and you, I believe will be a stranger to these parts?"

"Maceachan . . . Maceachan," he murmured, as if trying to recollect something about the name. "Oh, of course! I was told that your family was one—" He broke off and bent a reflective head over his instrument.

"You know us, then?" asked Darthula. He said nothing, still fingering the keys of his violin. "You have the advantage of us, sir!" she persisted.

He glanced up and she saw a flash of suspicion in his look. "Every prudent traveller," he said coldly, "will acquaint himself with the notabilities of the lands through which he passes."

"And you will be travelling in these parts, Mr.—Mr. —?" The arching of her eyebrows, the parting of her lips to draw an answer were irresistible by male flesh.

"Mr. Jameson, an it please you." He lifted his hand to his head, and remembered that he was hatless. "It fell as I peered down a cliff at a torrent in the mist," he explained.

"And is not that the misfortune!" she cried.

" 'Tis no matter; I am inured to exposure. And I shall pick up a better hat where I am going."

"And where will that be?"

"To London, ma'am, in time . . . if it concerns you to know."

"You must pardon curiosity, Mr. Jameson, in a country lass! I am thinking your coming will make a stir along this quiet coast."

"Truly, Miss Maceachan, I believe it may!"

"I see you are a Churchman, sir."

"My coat says so."

"Of what denomination, pray?"

"I am a Catholic; but I am not, to be frank with you, in Holy Orders."

"I understand. A student."

"Yes, I may admit to being a student . . . and I think I have surely lighted on a Catechist!"

Darthula got to her feet with dignity, and snatched up her plaid. "I had no thought in my mind, Mr. Jameson," she said, fumbling with the pin and the flowers, "but to offer you such civilities as might be in my power. I am *not* inquisitive; such has never been my nature. I ask your pardon once more, and now I will be going—"

"You are going, I hope, to cross to my side of this stream!" He was smiling again, this time temptingly, roguishly. "Come, Miss Maceachan," he pleaded, "I throw myself on your charity. You had it in mind—you confessed it but now —to do me kindness. Never did traveller stand more in need of faithful counsel! And I have been told that a stranger in doubt or difficulty will never turn in vain to Highland man or woman. And so," he rose, and stretched out a hand with a courtly gesture, "let me assist you to cross by these stones."

She was amused at the idea that she needed to be helped across such a little burn, but she felt pleasure none the less in taking his hand. Then she noticed that he had waded ankle-deep into the water, and cried out to warn him.

"Such warm wettings do *me* no harm," he laughed. "Come now, sit on this boulder here, and give me counsel." He flung himself on the grass at her feet, and plucked up a stalk to chew.

"This is my case," he said after a moment. "I have travelled from overseas to pursue a family dispute in England."

"It will be a matter of land?" she asked, drawing on her own experiences.

"You have hit it! A matter of land. Land that is my father's, and which he ought to be enjoying."

"Then where is there room for doubt?" Her small curved nostrils dilated pugnaciously. "Will you not defend your right?"

"That is the plague of it," he said, and a line came into his smooth forehead. "For this business will mean much conflict, sore trouble, I know, for many people."

"Nevertheless, if your right is good you should stand by it, Mr. Jameson."

He shot a quick, grateful glance at her. "You speak my own thought! I have always told them that our good cause being manifest God would declare himself of our party!"

"Why then there is nought that I can see to let you. Your *slogan*, Mr. Jameson, will be 'Forward for your right!'"

"Yes, forward! At last I hear someone who speaks like a trumpet!" The sombre pupils of his eyes blazed suddenly with light-blue fire, the brown edges darkening by contrast. "Only let me get forward!" he went on, from time to time plucking a challenging chord from the violin with his fingers. "That is my nature. Once I am in the saddle! Once I have seized the oars! Something greater than I am drives me on. . . . I care not what may withstand me in my course. But," he dropped suddenly into gloom, "I *am* being withstood; I *am* being impeded. My Scottish friends, on whose aid I was counting in this business, they meet me all discouraged. They go about shaking heads as heavy as that sky above us . . . yours is a sad country, Miss Maceachan!"

"We will be having our days of sunshine, too, Mr. Jameson," she answered resentfully, "when every glen is a green smile, and every burn showers jewels."

"It may be so," he answered dubiously. "To me it seems all barren hills and clouds, with never a prospect! . . . And I read what is in my friends' minds, that I had better never have come, and had better, far better, go back again at once . . . back with nothing accomplished," he gave a sigh that seemed to rend him, "back with no news to bring a smile to my father's worn face. That is what takes the heart out of me, Mademoiselle. That is why I have played truant, and wandered away up here alone with an old friend," he patted the violin, "who never irks me or opposes me. I wanted for a few hours to forget myself, forget my hopes and longings. Then, when, to my very great surprise," he smiled, "I came upon you sleeping by that rock, I thought, so fair was the vision, 'Why, here is the very spirit of Scotia! And she shall give me my answer!' "

He stopped out of breath at the end of his long tirade, and she felt there was something school-boyish in his excitement and his admiration. She could not help meeting his smile; but there was perplexity in her eyes, and an odd maternal feeling stirred inside her.

"Was I giving you the answer you wanted?" she asked dubiously.

He turned his head aside a little, staring at the ground, and she studied his profile—the high and beautiful forehead, the dominating nose, the plump, almost pendulous, young cheeks, ruddy with exercise and sea-voyaging. "This will be no Churchman," she thought, "no, nor no student for the Priesthood. Who, then, can he be?" She tried another cast.

"You spoke of friends of yours in these parts, Mr. Jameson. May I not know their names? Is it Macdonald of Borrodale, perhaps, or Clan Ranald himself . . or maybe it will be Cameron of Lochiel that has been advising you?"

He turned his gaze back to her. "You are the only person I have spoken with on the continent of Scotland," he said gravely, "and I thank God with all my heart for sending you to comfort me. For your words were the tonic I needed, Miss Maceachan!"

Suddenly he swung his violin to his shoulder and broke into a gay *gigue*—not a Scottish air, she knew, but more like a French *contre-Danse;* and from that passed into a military march, tapping his toe on the ground and whistling. Gradually this, too, relented, melting into a sad and wavering strain which bore the signs of improvisation. Watching his glances as he played, Darthula realised that he was seeking to interpret his surroundings—the solitude of the forest in which they sat, the solemnity of the great peaks looming through the mists above, the austerity of the rocky coast be-

yond the reaches of the wood at his back. Dimly she felt
history passing, armies on the march to oblivion, and monarchs dropping wearied into their tombs. Her eyes filled
with tears, as a fuller, purer harmony than his own inventions
swelled out, and into her mind came lines from the worm-
eaten Folio of Shakespeare's plays that mouldered in the library at Glenmarisdale:—

> "For God's sake, let us sit upon the ground—
> And tell sad stories of the death of kings."

He stopped as abruptly as he had started, but "Play that
again," she commanded him, "play that again!"

"You like it so much?" he asked, surprised at her earnest-
ness. "It is from Corelli's *Notte di Natale*. I am more used
to the violin-cello part in the quartet. But you shall have it
again," and he repeated it while she strove hard to memorise
the theme. "Oh! finish it! finish it!" she protested, as he
stopped short before the end.

"Why should I?" He laughed lazily. "Do you not weary
of it now, Miss Maceachan? I abhor repetitions. When you
have done a thing, pass on to the next!"

He felt in his fob, and drew out a gold watch so superbly
set in diamonds that Darthula blinked at it. "I must return to
those who await me," he muttered. "Do you know it is past
four of the clock?"

"So late!" She started. "Then I must bustle too!" She
whistled to her pony, which splashed obediently across
where the bank was lower, and came to her. Mr. Jameson
stooped to help her into the saddle, and seemed astonished at
her feather-weight. Then he looked about him, with the line
in his forehead again. "I am all astray," he complained. "My
boat is at a creek I think they call Nama. . . . Is it that
way?"

She laughed. "I am thinking you are no mountaineer, Mr. Jameson."

He flushed. "There you are in the wrong," he retorted sharply. "I have climbed amid mountains that can well rival these hills of yours. It is true that in that land the sky is always blue and one can see one's way."

"The Highland mists are traitors," she confessed.

"Traitors?" He stood intently gazing over the tree-tops at the shapes of the peaks, which turn by turn looked out and withdrew in the caprices of the vapours. "I think rather," he said in a low tone, "that they are sent to serve me. How they might cloak surprises! How they might aid concealment!"

"But what," asked Darthula, "will Mr. Jameson be wanting with surprises . . . or concealments?"

He looked at her with a haughtiness that she had never yet experienced from any man. Without moving from his place by her pony's head he seemed to have placed a gulf between them.

"Will you be pleased to show me the way to Nama?" he commanded.

Quite abashed, she stirred the pony forward with her heel, while he strode at her stirrup, his face almost on a level with hers, his long, muscular paces supporting his account of himself as a mountaineer. They came to a break in the woods, and had to cross a stone-strewn cup, with a rock-wall mounting from it, cut by mist. In the centre of this hollow a purple pool of heather glimmered.

"Look!" exclaimed Mr. Jameson, with a total change of mien. "Is that not a piece of your fortunate white heather?"

She was surprised at the keenness of his sight, for she herself had not detected the small white tuft.

"We must not lose that! we must not lose that!" he shouted, running on his long legs down into the dell.

"See!" he said, returning bright-eyed to her side. "Was I

not right? If I gave this to you, Miss Maceachan," he added with an almost elfish look, "would you wear it?"

"It is I will be wearing it willingly!" she replied, stretching out her fingers. She plucked it in half, and handed a sprig back to him. "That is for you," she told him. "It is true that it carries luck!"

He watched her, as she fastened her piece into the heart of her nosegay of wild flowers. "Brings luck?" he sighed. "Ah! we shall know that better in six months' time. In a year! . . . But I will not be parted from this token you have given me." He set it in his button-hole.

Again she shot puzzled glances at him as they moved forward; but he seemed so absorbed in his thoughts that she dared not interrupt him. So in silence they traversed fresh reaches of woodland, splashed with crimson foxgloves, till Darthula reined in where the trees ended in a floating sea of mist.

"We have come to the edge of the cliff," she said. "There is a way down the rocks here to the beach. It is not a difficult descent. Will you be needing any further guidance?"

"No. You are to come no farther with me!" was the peremptory reply as he peered, listening, through the trees. "Nevertheless," he turned back to her transfigured to a graciousness that overawed her, "it is my hope . . . and my firm belief, Mistress Maceachan, that we are destined to meet again."

"If you propose to linger in the neighbourhood, Mr. Jameson, my brother Glenmarisdale and I will be happy of the opportunity."

"I shall hope *not* to have to linger in the neighbourhood," he declared, "after what you have said to encourage me, Mademoiselle! But still I think that you and I . . . I must not say more now. My heartfelt thanks . . . and *adieu*!"

In a moment he had turned and vanished through the trees,

descending the low cliff face, she realised, without waiting to find the path. Well, he had not the limbs of a blunderer!

She sat still with her ears pricked for sounds of his descent, and presently was surprised to hear through the mist a voice, gruff but respectful, speak in French. Then after a minute or two came the creak of rowlocks and dip of oars. So he had rowers waiting for him at this point of the bay! The riddle of his identity piqued her furiously. What was his real business? What ship had brought him hither, and where was he staying? On one of the islands? Well, she would make it her sole business in the next few days to find out. Nothing could happen in this country-side and be long a secret from her keen curiosity and nimble wits. If only, she thought, the mists would lift and show where the boat was steering for across the bay! Vain wish! Their curtains held fast and guarded his secret.

Chapter V

THE DREAMER WAKES

1

A HALF-MOON was floating amid cloud-floss over Loch Maris by the time Darthula returned, dimly revealing the indented course of the promontories that marked its length and the gathering of mighty peaks at its foot. The chapel on the burial isle shone palely, and the tufts of the three pine trees made ink-blots in the moonlight. Wavering silver paths ran hither and thither over the waters as they peacefully lapped the shore below the house.

She was consumed by famine; and, knowing that Dr. Hay would have dined long since, called for a tray of food to be brought to her own parlour upstairs. "The candles, quick! quick!" she cried, pushing the little black-haired maid who was hurrying before her with a taper into the room. In a minute there flickered into visibility the old brown spinet by the farther window, the beribboned mandolin over the stone fireplace—a gift from a cousin in the Spanish Army—the book-case half filled with leather-bound volumes; the cabinet crammed with the china shepherdesses Darthula had collected in her school-days at Edinburgh and Paris; her riding-whips and silver-mounted hunting-gun piled in a corner; the settee with slim gilt legs standing on a deer-skin rug, the only covering for the oaken floor-boards.

While the little maid pulled out a small table to prepare her meal Darthula went straight to the spinet and unbrooched her plaid. The bunch of wild flowers she was about to throw upon the window-seat, when the sprig of white heather caught her eye, and (false to her promise to the chaplain) she pinned it back again at her breast. Then she began the task that had occupied her mind during the last part of the ride home, that of reproducing from memory the theme of the Corelli piece that Mr. Jameson had played for her.

She did not break off when the tiny, sighing voice of the girl told her in Gaelic that her dinner was served; but carried her plate to the instrument and fed herself with a fork in one hand, while she strummed with the other. At length it began to take shape, and, pouring herself a glass of claret from the table, she went back, sipping it while she tried to correct the weak places. Satisfied at last, she settled herself on the stool, and played the completed theme with the full force of her wrists, till it rang through the silent house steeped in moonshine.

"I do not think you have the bass quite right," said a voice behind her; and turning with a start she saw Dr. Hay smiling in the beams of the spinet candles.

"Forgive my eaves-dropping," he said, "but surely this is the way of it." He reached over her shoulder, and with his delicate white fingers played the erring phrase over two or three times.

"At least, Doctor," she said with some pride, "you recognised the piece."

"The *Notte di Natale*? I ought to remember it. I heard it last in circumstances that should stamp it on a man's memory . . . yes, and bring it back to him in his dreams!"

"Why, where did you hear it, Doctor?"

"Well . . . it was in Rome."

"Go on! Do not be secretive, I implore! There can be no treason involved, surely?"

"Why, I am not so sure about that either, Miss Darthula."

She spun round on her stool. "This is too entrancing! Now I *must* have your tale. Sit, Doctor, sit . . . yes, in the arm-chair there . . . kindle your pipe in peace . . . you know I pardon it . . . and now the story, the whole story, or I shall die of curiosity!"

"I will try to preserve you for the delightful torment of the Highlands!" he chuckled as he lit his long clay pipe from one of the candle flames. "Well, the last time I heard that piece was, as I told you, in Rome . . . in the Palazzo Santi Apostoli."

Darthula started a little.

"Yes, I warned you there might be treason in it. His Majesty himself deigned to attend a grand concert of music in his palace, to his faithful adherents and to the aristocracy of the city. You may well ask how I was to be found in such exalted company. I was granted a card of admission by favour of Macgregor of Bohaldy, who, indeed, sponsored me to the reception. You may judge if it were a grand occasion, Miss Darthula, for both his Majesty's sons were to play parts among the string performers: the little Duke of York the violin, Prince Charlie—the Prince of Wales, that is—the violincello."

"The violincello part in a Corelli quartet?" she whispered, the ovals of her eyes widening.

"This same *Notte di Natale*." He had turned to the fireplace to knock the ashes out of his pipe, and did not observe her agitation.

"A more splendid scene," he continued with his back to her, "I do not look to behold in this life. The great *salon* with its columns and gilding and frescoes ablaze upon the ceiling. The goodly company, the Roman nobles so richly attired, our own poor Scots and faithful English so threadbare despite the attempt to maintain appearances. But the Blue Ribbon here dignified a worn coat, and there the diamonds of the Bath shone beside pewter buttons. Good King James in his chair had a sad face that seemed to show a mind hundreds of miles away—in London, perhaps, or Windsor . . . or heaven, it may be, where no hopes are frustrated. . . . And I shall always remember, too, Mistress Darthula, the courtesy of the Prince of Wales. For there was a French gentleman bidden to this concert, a man of weight in his own land, the President of the Court of Dijon. This worthy gentleman, through some mischance, involving, I believe, no intended discourtesy to his Majesty, arrived late for the opening; and as we were all applauding the Royal musicians he was heard to say in his own tongue how much he grieved to have missed their performance. Upon which Prince Charlie, overhearing the words, cries out in his pleasing way, 'We will render that last composition again, gentlemen, for the express benefit of M. le Président.' So they fell to with a will, and repeated it— until near the very end, when the Prince laughs, pushes back his chair and signs to the others to stop, saying—"

"Saying, Doctor," Darthula's voice rang tremulous through the dimly-lit room with the candle-light struggling against the moonbeams from the uncurtained windows, "saying, 'I abhor repetitions! When you have done a thing, pass on to the next!'"

The clergyman swung round in his chair to face her. "His very own words . . . or as near as gospel! But how can you know? You were not there? . . . Miss Darthula, what has come over you? You tremble. . . . You look as if you had seen a ghost!"

He rose in concern as she came towards him, almost tottering, but her eyes shining as he had never before seen them do.

"No ghost, Doctor! No ghost!" she babbled. "Himself! The Prince! 'Tis I have seen him this day. He has come!"

Dr. Hay recoiled a step and his pipe fell upon the hearthstone, breaking in two. "Prince Charlie here!" he stammered; "it is impossible!"

"It is true, I am telling you, *true*!" She flung her arms wide in exultation. "I have spoken to him. Alone in the woods above Loch-nan-Uamh! Look! he gave me this!" She touched the heather at her bosom. "The White Cockade!

> " 'Joyful I am, he is coming,
> 　　Son of our rightful exiled King,
> 　　A mighty form which becomes armour . . .' "

she chanted, and then clapped her fingers over her mouth. "I am mad," she whispered, "to make such outcry! Even here it will not be safe to sing our joy."

The old man stood staring at her, his hands shaking. "It is impossible!" he repeated hoarsely. "How has he come?"

"How? I know not! I care not! On the wings of the morning! But he played that piece to me upon his violin in the woods. He used your very words!"

Dr. Hay stooped down without a word, and picking up the broken pieces of his pipe from the hearthstone, tried aimlessly to fit them together. Then he turned almost savagely upon her, one fragment clenched in each fist. "I *will* not believe you!" he cried. "You do not know Prince Charlie? Have you ever as much as seen his portrait? Ah! wait! wait! I will convict your error!"

He hurried out of the room, and in the silence of the house, where all the servants were long since abed, she heard his footsteps crossing to his own apartment. She waited by the window, looking out upon the loch, bathing herself ecstatically in the magical radiance.

In a few minutes the Doctor returned, bearing under his arm a wooden box, painted with a varied design of wreaths and rosettes and curving gold lines, which she had often admired upon his table.

"Is it the portrait of the Prince, then, that you keep ever locked in that box, Doctor?" she asked curiously.

"Scarcely!" he answered, smiling, his self-possession to some extent regained. "That would be too dangerous a treasure to keep under a lock that a pen-knife could turn! No. I have a device to show you."

He set the painted box down upon the table, and asked leave to set two candles from the mantel-shelf beside it. Then he produced from his skirt pocket an odd little flashing cylinder. Darthula watched him, bewildered.

"A mirror!" he explained, still smiling, though his face, she could now see by the close candle-light, looked ten years older.

"Now will you give me your attention?" He set the cylinder upright upon the table behind the box. "I beg you to look into the glass," he said.

She obeyed with the eerie feeling of one summoned to participate in an act of the Black Art.

"What do you see?" he inquired.

"Just your box with its patternings, the garlands and so forth."

"Clearly?"

"Brilliantly. But what has this to do—"

"Wait! Keep looking!" He laid his hands upon the box and slowly revolved it to a new angle.

Darthula started back from the mirror with a stifled cry. Glimmering in its depths, and endowed with a stereoscopic solidity, as though it had been some actual homunculus shut within the tiny prison of the cylinder, there smiled at her the musician of Beasdale Woods. Her eyes flashed white with fear as she turned to the doctor. "What is it?" she whispered. "Some wizardry?"

"No, no!" He gave a little laugh. "A mere play of mirrors! The lines on the box-lid here combine to make the face when the cylinder is correctly turned. An artist craftsman made the device for me in the Via del Babuino at Rome. I have placed it on my dinner-table many times to drink the loyal toast with my friends. . . . But now!" the anxiety crept back into his voice. "Tell me, that is *not* the face of the man you met by the shore of Loch-nan-Uamh this day? Say it is not, I implore you! Do not practise with me, Miss Darthula. It is matter of life and death—for all of us perhaps!"

"As God hears me!" pronounced Darthula solemnly, "this is the very face I saw to-day in Beasdale Woods!"

"Then," said the old man, falling into the nearest chair and burying his face in his hands, "may God have pity upon poor Scotland!"

Darthula turned on him, bristling. "What do you mean by that?" she cried. "Is this your welcome to your Prince, and you the loyal man, we believed! Oh! shame!"

"You understand nothing," he replied, shaking his head. "You are a wild girl, craving excitements and adventures . . . do I not know you? But cannot even you recognise the fatal rashness of such a landing . . . if it be a fact . . . unannounced . . . unprepared for? What can be done without French troops . . . without artillery? What the end of this may be, Miss Darthula, no man can tell: I may say in the words of the ancient, 'This day is the beginning of great evils'—for Scotland! Aye, and before that, it is the beginning of great evils for the young man himself. Not a chief will come out to follow him on these terms."

"Oh! slander!"

"Macleod of Macleod will hang back. See if I do not prophesy truth! . . . Macdonald of the Isles will not embark his men . . . Cameron of Lochiel will keep his borders."

"Oh! never! never! That is false! Is it gentle Lochiel will betray his Prince?"

"You speak ever like the green girl you are," retorted the chaplain severely. "Has Lochiel, then, no duties to his own people, to withhold the men from flinging their lives vainly away, to preserve the women from widowhood and outrage, the children from perishing by hunger, the flocks from spoiling, the farms from devastations? . . . As for Clan Ranald—"

"It is I will be answering at least for Clan Ranald! There will not be a claymore that will not leap from its sheath! . . . And Hector, oh! why is he not to be found? I will rouse every man here at the loch-head, and send him into the mountains to search!"

"Beware!" said the chaplain in a changed voice. "How will it profit his Royal Highness for you to fill the glens with clamour before he has formed his plans? All must be done in darkest secrecy. Your people, I am sure, have arms hidden somewhere. Do you know if the hilts are fitted to the sword-blades, or are they still packed in their cases as they came, I suppose, from Italy? In any case they must be distributed as stealthily as though the red-coats from Fort Augustus were in garrison here."

Darthula stopped in her restless pacing. "Then, you are with us, after all, Doctor?" she asked in surprise.

He threw out his arms. "What choice have I or any loyal man if his Highness chooses to raise the standard? We can at least die with him—the swordsman on the field, the Churchman on the scaffold. . . . But if only the Chiefs can

persuade him to go back. . . . Hush! what is that I hear?"
He turned his head towards the window opening on the
back of the House. "Someone rides through the woods!" he
said.

2

BOTH ran to the window and looked out. The ancient tower
stood stark in the moonlight; in the cottages and farms on
the strath by the riverside not a light was to be seen. Their
inmates were all at rest, preparing for the easy work and
simple enjoyments of the morrow. The Doctor's heart was
wrung as he thought of his flock. Then he looked towards
the black curtain of the woods in which the frantic tattoo of
the horse's hoofs, muffled for a few moments by a turn of the
path, had broken out again.

"It is Rob Sanderson!" exclaimed Darthula, as a figure on
horse-back came plunging down the slope towards the paddock. "Now what foul fiend will be bringing him riding by
night in such a frenzy, and he ever so tender of his precious
limbs!"

A step crunched on the path at the back of the House. The
factor had tied his horse to the gate and was peering up at
the lighted window.

"Wha stirs so late?" he called up.

"It is I, Mr. Sanderson," said Darthula sweetly. "What
brings *you* from your bed at this hour? No ill news, I trust?"

"Who is that with you?" asked the factor. "Is it Glenmarisdale?"

"No, Mr. Sanderson, it is I, Dr. Hay," rejoined the chaplain.

"Whaur is your brither, Miss Maceachan?"

"The Lord knows, Mr. Sanderson. He was away to the
hills after the deer, three days gone, and has not returned."

"And can you no find him?" The factor's tone was urgent.

"Only by combing the braes from here to Loch Arkaig and Loch Beoraid!"

"That is gey ill news." Sanderson hesitated. "May I tak' the liberty o' coming up to confer wi' you, Mistress?"

"But, of course, Mr. Sanderson, ever welcome! You must take a glass of wine, too, after such a night-ride!"

The Doctor turned back into the room, and slipped the cylindrical mirror into his pocket, leaving only the painted box with its innocuous patternings on the table, while the factor unlatched the ever-open door below and clumped up the stairs.

"I thank you. I will tak' nothing," he said sourly in answer to their invitations. "Nor will I sit, I feel no fatigue. Miss Maceachan, in your brither's absence, I maun appeal to you as standing in place of the head of the family. . . . It is true I am for maist purposes the lawfu' authority, holding Lord Brounhill's agency; but I misdoot your people wad no tak' an order to stand to arms at my lips."

"I am doubting it too," said Darthula dryly.

"But what do you mean, stand to arms, Mr. Sanderson?" inquired Dr. Hay. "The Clan has no arms. They were all surrendered to Government, long before I came here, surely?"

"How far that may sort wi' the truth, you maun know better than I, Doctor," replied the factor with a glint of his cold blue eye. "But I have had the maist disturbing news, judge ye! There came a man at nightfall to ma house in Glen Liath to tell me of a foreign ship o' war, a Frenchman, anchored in Loch-nan-Uamh. For what purpose are they here? Wha hae they aboard? I could mak' a gude guess . . . you, too, maybe . . . only this will I say. At any moment they may land foraging parties to drive in our cattle!"

"Is that all you fear?" asked Darthula, betraying relief.

"Gudesakes! And is that no eneuch? Messengers should be sent instanter to the garrisons at Fort Augustus and Fort William, baith."

"I am fearing you will induce none of our people to quit their haymaking to carry messages for you to the red-coats, Mr. Sanderson."

The factor scowled. He knew well enough that he could not compel or coax any clansman to go near the English Forts.

"In that case," suggested Dr. Hay smoothly, "perhaps you could find messengers, Miss Darthula? Let Mr. Sanderson write his letters now—and entrust them to us to send."

Darthula seized his point—Dr. Hay's alertness in conspiracy was beginning to surprise her. "Will you do that, Mr. Sanderson?" she asked.

"I hae no better choice," he assented grudgingly. "But shouldna the new Watch Company be embodied at sic a perilous moment?"

"There is no Watch Company yet," said Darthula. "My brother has but made a scrawl of names. His men are designate, but not enrolled, nor drilled nor taught the use of arms."

"I tak' the liberty of holding," retorted the factor, "that there is nae need to teach any Hielander the use of arms, neither the broad-sword, nor," he glanced obliquely at Darthula, "the gun."

"The cattle, though, should be collected, and put in a secure place," said Dr. Hay. "Mr. Sanderson is right there; there is nothing the invaders would more desire than to lay hands on our herds."

"Aye, they should be gathered to the loch-foot," said Sanderson, "as far away as possible."

"Why not here, to the House?" asked Dr. Hay. "They will be under our eye, and we have at least stout fellows enough to be able to deal with a raiding party as they merit."

"We will be able," agreed Darthula, admiring the swiftness with which the frail little old man's mind was seeing and planning ahead. *She* ought to have realised that the Prince would need supplies from all his adherents, and that it was not too soon to be gathering them. "Collect as many head as you can, Mr. Sanderson," she ordered, "in the byres and pastures round the House. I will be responsible for them till my brother returns."

"Aweel," Mr. Sanderson gave another wrung-out assent; "it properly appertaineth to ma office as factor to determine where the stock shall be placed on occasion of emairgency; but, to speak sooth, I am no' that desirous to move them as near to Cameron country as the loch-foot. I hae ma doots o' Young Lochiel's loyalty."

"He is not needing your good word!" cried Darthula sharply.

"Let us not keep Mr. Sanderson longer than we must from his bed," put in Dr. Hay. "Will you come to my room, my dear sir, to indite your missive to the Forts? I have good quills there."

He led the factor upstairs, and in a few minutes returned, closing the door carefully, and drawing Darthula away into the embrasure of the farthest window.

"You understand, Miss Darthula, do you not, that someone must carry a message immediately to his Royal Highness, if he can be found, to warn him that at least one enemy already entertains suspicions of his presence . . . and may at any moment hold them confirmed?"

"It is I will do that, so soon as this man has gone. . . . Indeed, it is best it should be me, for I am aye known to ride hither and thither without reason, to please my fancy. . . . But what will you be doing in my absence? Should not the men here be armed against Hector's return . . . the fiery cross despatched for the others . . . Mackissock bidden to hold himself in readiness to march at our head, playing 'Sons of Hector,' our ancient battle-song?"

"Not so fast! Not so fast." Dr. Hay hushed her with a deprecating hand. "You must take less pleasure, let me say it, and more thought over this business; it is perchance the weightiest you will ever have on your hands in your lifetime, be it short or long. It is not your part . . . far less mine . . . to bring out the Clan. None but the Chief may unfurl the war-flag of the Sons of Hector, just as none but the Priest may consecrate the Holy Symbols in the Liturgy."

"But Himself is not to be found!" She pressed her hands together in anguish. "Is not that Hector?"

"He cannot delay much longer. The very eagles will be bearing this news to the remotest corners of the hills! Meanwhile, send Mackissock with the scroll of names of all those chosen for the Watch to bid them not depart from the neighbourhood of their houses or bothies. The Chief may have need of them, let him say: and even Rob Sanderson must approve that order."

It was some time before the factor descended, yawning, and looked with suspicion at their conclave by the window. The moon had paled, and the greyness of dawn was making stark and terrible outlines of the peaks around the House. Some seemed to uplift jagged saws to the dim sky; others like lances vertiginously stabbed at its impalpable vesture. Towards the foot of the loch the Dreamer was beginning to show his familiar profile, the immense bearded face with beetling brows. Darthula, watching it, fancied almost that she could hear his respiration, slow and solemn, driving the mists that yet clung to the lower slopes in puffs before it.

Rob Sanderson coughed to demand her attention. "Here," he said, holding out two fat packets, sealed with splodges of red wax, "here are the briefs. I hae thought proper to explain at some length ma apprehensions and ma deeficult position here," his pebbly eye glanced sullenly at Darthula and her adviser, "baith to the Commander at Fort Augustus and to him at Fort William. Ma repoort to Lord Brounhill I will prepare at more leisure at hame. I bid ye baith tak' note that ye are put upon your allegiance to see these missives conveyed by safe hands to their destinatories!"

"My dear Mr. Sanderson!" Dr. Hay laughed pleasantly. "You grow somewhat portentous, surely. Has his Majesty appointed you to a military or civil jurisdiction over Mistress Maceachan and myself? As the Chief is from home, you may safely leave all that touches honour or allegiance in the hands of his sister. Let me advise you now, go home and—"

"I need nane o' your counsel, Priest o' Baal!" roared Sanderson, letting loose upon the clergyman the smouldering fury with which Darthula's disdain always filled him. "I ken weel your aims and your treasons. Your mere presence in Scotland is an offence against the law. Your idolatrous mummings are an offence against God's ain Majesty—"

"Mr. Sanderson!" Darthula turned coldly from the window. "Will you be holding your peace, or is it I must have you thrown into the loch!"

"Nay, nay!" protested the chaplain good-humouredly. "There is no need for such words! Mr. Sanderson mistakes me entirely!"

"And is that a fac', Papist?" sneered Rob. "I wad be gey and gled to see you hangit in your ain massing-house. . . . My services to *you*, Mistress, as in duty, if not in pleasure bound. . . . I hae nae mair to say."

He banged down the stairs, and the chaplain watched from the window while his squat figure, staggering a little with fatigue, crossed to the paddock-gate, and unhitched his horse.

Then, as the hoofs beat away through the wood, Dr. Hay broke the seals of the letters, read them smiling, and thrust them into the flames of the guttering candles. Coils of feathery ash fell upon the floor.

"So much for that," he said coolly, dusting his blackened fingers together. "Miss Darthula, you should slumber for an hour before riding to Loch-nan-Uamh. . . . Why, what troubles you? Is there anything amiss out yonder?"

Darthula was leaning right out of the window, and he could see her fingers quivering on the sill. He stepped swiftly to her side and looked out.

The day was coming strongly on; and though the mists still trailed like strips of muslin over the waters of the lake, the sky was a shell of pale blue, precursor of scorching heat. Behind the tormented peaks in the East pink flames still ribboned the firmament; but it was towards the opposite shore, to the Dreamer, that Darthula now pointed with a trembling arm.

The giant face was clear of all vapour now, and plain upon the deepening blue. Just underneath it a single woolly cloud curled like a scarf with the ends loose. Suddenly Dr. Hay gave a light exclamation and laughed.

"That is certainly a curious phenomenon!" he declared. "I never observed it before."

The rays of the mounting sun, pouring from a cleft in the East, struck full upon the Dreamer, and were refracted also from the bank of cloud at his throat. They caught the lodes of mica just below the overhanging ledges that formed the eyebrows of the imaginary face, and lit them up. For a few minutes, and a few minutes only, the eyes of the Dreamer sparkled with fire and life.

"They are open! They are open!" gasped Darthula, with eyes wide in terror. "The Dreamer wakes!"

Dr. Hay glanced at her with some concern. "That is a way of putting it!" he told her soothingly. "But you will agree, Miss Darthula, that the sight must often be visible at sunrise, when you are not stirring, perhaps, or not strung up with expectations."

She paid no heed to his suggestion. "What will it mean," she kept whispering, "what will it mean?

" ' 'Tis Maceachan's power
Must pass from the lake!'

Pass away to destruction and oblivion? Or pass out with banners to conquest and to glory?"

Chapter VI

SEVEN MEN OFF MOIDART

1

THE dawn had fulfilled its promise by the time Darthula reached the edge of Loch-nan-Uamh; a few grey-purple wisps alone streaked the tender radiance of the sky. No mists now obscured the arm of the sea that made the Loch of Caves. Its waters extended, dancing with diamonds, to the darker blue line at the horizon, and the tufts of heather in the grey rocks, the woods rising above the beaches waved gaily in the breeze that blew inshore. Down the middle of the Loch stretched a chain of islets graceful as sculpture, their surfaces, like those of the boulders on the strand, draped in beige-coloured weed that mixed its health-giving odour with the sea-wind.

A good way out, with the headlands of Moidart shadowy behind it, the French brig-of-war was anchored, its sails furled, its brass cannon glinting through the port-holes, the red caps of its crew dotting the decks and rigging. Darthula, sitting her pony, marvelled at the tranquillity of the scene. There lay the ship that was, at the moment, the storm centre of Britain; and round it the woods stood silent, the fierce heights capping them to the South lifted their heads, ignoring

all on earth, towards Heaven. The little white farm of Borrodale, up its gorge, showed no concern; the strand itself was
deserted; and cattle nosed among the weed.

Then Darthula perceived that she had been over-hasty.
Through a cleft in the low rock-wall to the North of the
beach there came into view a group of men who marched to
the water's edge and stood looking out towards the ship.
Three figures wearing tall bonnet-feathers stood together in
front, one of them gesticulating excitedly; while behind were
massed ten or a dozen swordsmen, the sun-rays making points
of their target-bosses and claymore-hilts. Darthula at once
recognised the foremost of the three leaders. "Mac'-ic-
Ailein himself!" she ejaculated, giving his patronymic to the
son of the Chief of Clan Ranald, and put her pony to a canter
across the strand toward him.

The new-comers did not notice her approach at first, for
the weed and the sand had dulled her pony's hooves. They
were all intent upon a boat that had put off from the *Du Teillay* and was being rowed towards the beach. The swordsmen in the background, however, saluted her, and Young
Clan Ranald turned his handsome face and sleepy eyes towards her wonderingly.

"You here, too, Darthula?" he asked as she dismounted.
"I doubt this is to prove no woman's business whatever!"
He smiled with a shade of grimness at his two companions,
both of whom Darthula now recognised. They were brothers of Donald Macdonald of Kinlochmoidart, the Chieftain
whose house and territory lay in the bay just round the sun-
hazed headland that pointed out into the Atlantic behind the
Du Teillay. Alan, the elder, was of discreet age; Ranald, the
younger, whom Darthula had known as a boy, had just blos-
somed into a warrior wearing his sword and dirk, his plaid
and Clan Ranald badge of golden heath, with a pretty swagger.

While she greeted them, the Chief watched the boat drawing nearer, manned by red-capped rowers, and bearing in its
stern a bent figure wearing a gold-laced hat and wrapped in
a cloak. Then he glanced again at her. "Will you be for the
ship, too?" he asked dubiously. "Where is Glenmarisdale?"

"He is away to the hills hunting, Son of Alan," she answered. "I come in his place with a warning for the Prince,
and I may advise you," she dropped her voice, "our men are
all held ready, our arms—"

"Who talks of arms?" interrupted Young Clan Ranald,
closing his sleepy eyes for a moment in irritation. "You are
another of those who will be running before their own pony,
Darthula! Since you appear to know so much about this
business, I may tell you now I am from the Isles with bad
news for His Highness . . . bad news for his hopes, that is.
Nor Macleod, nor Sir Alexander Macdonald will bring out
their powers. But you may e'en as well come with us to the
Prince, and learn what is to be decided.

The boat had grated on the pebbly shore, and Clan Ranald
and his kinsmen from Moidart moved down to meet the old
gentleman it had been carrying, who now disembarked with
some stiffness, aided by one of the sailors.

Darthula following, with her long riding-skirt looped over
her arm, saw him sweep off his gold-laced hat in a bow that
seemed oddly incongruous, with its air of St. Germains, upon
this wild beach. The yellow frogs with black-spotted backs
that were leaping in and out among the rocks stood still at
the sight, as though amazed. The three Highlanders lifted
their bonnets together with a silent solemnity, and stood
waiting. Clan Ranald's broad-sword clinked against his
slung targe, and the little waves uttered a sudden sigh against
the stones.

"Gentlemen," began the old man, wrinkling his ancient
face into a smile, "allow me to inthrojuice myself! Sir

Thomas Sheridan, entoirely at your service, for many years tutor to His Royal Highness. And which of you may I have the honour of addressing as the Chief of the Clan Ranald?"

"I," said the tall young Chief, "act as Captain of Clan Ranald by delegation from my father, who is ill upon the island of Uist."

"Deloighted!" Sir Thomas twirled his hat in another of his exquisite bows. "I understand, sir, you are returned from a mission to the Chiefs of the Isles, and have doubtless brought us news of glad adhesions to His Highness's cause?"

Clan Ranald's brow gloomed. "As to that, Sir Thomas, I am fearing my news will not prove to His Royal Highness's liking."

"Sure, then, there can be no need to give it him, can there? It is encouragement His Royal Highness needs. . . . I will say on your behalf that the Chiefs of the Islands do but wait upon those of the continent for leadership."

Clan Ranald opened his eyes wide with astonishment. "It is I myself," he replied curtly, "who will be relating to the Prince the issue of my visits. Surely His Highness should be acquainted with the truth, however unpalatable?"

"H'm!" The aged Irish courtier shrugged his shoulders. "His Highness likes to hear *good* news, Mr. Macdonald. . . . Will you gentlemen do me the honour?" He lifted his hat again, as he proffered a tiny, jewelled snuff-box, into which the Highlanders, used to their great mulls, dipped nervous fingers. As he hobbled from one to the other on legs like little thin sticks, he caught sight for the first time of Darthula standing behind them. He started, and made yet another bow, this time bringing his hat to his heart with a flavour of gallantry.

"I present to you, Sir Thomas," said Clan Ranald, "Mistress Maceachan of Glenmarisdale. She is here in the place of her brother, the Laird of Glenmarisdale, who is from home.

He is one of the principal Chieftains of my Clan—"

"The Chief of Clan Maceachan," corrected Darthula.

"—who brings thirty or forty claymores to my standard," continued Clan Ranald, ignoring her interjection.

"To the standard of His Royal Highness," corrected Sir Thomas in his turn. "Sure, Miss Maceachan is welcome in her own right, and needs not appear as any man's proxy. We will not keep her waiting here longer than we can help, but our audience upon shipboard, sir, is already overdue."

"Wait!" exclaimed Clan Ranald. "Mistress Maceachan accompanies us to pay her duty to His Royal Highness."

Sir Thomas's face expressed utter desolation. "I am sorry . . . so sorry; but it is impossible. Faith, it breaks my heart to say so to a lady, but it is *quoite* impossible!" He fumbled in his flowered vest, and drew out a set of ivory tablets. "His Royal Highness is graciously pleased to receive in audience," he brought the tablets close to his eyes and read:

" 'Mr. Ranald Macdonald, the Younger, Captain of Clan of Ranald,

" 'Mr. Alan Macdonald, brother to Mr. Donald Macdonald of Kinlochmoidart.'

"And that is the list . . . no one else is mentioned at all, at all."

Clan Ranald flushed a slow red; his sleepy eyes began to glow. "Not only I and Mr. Alan Macdonald will be waiting upon His Royal Highness, but also Mr. Macdonald's brother here, and likewise Mistress Maceachan. Otherwise . . . our ponies wait for us at the cliff yonder, and I return from whence I came . . . with my men."

He imparted such a fearful significance to the last three words that the courtier began to stammer. "But what am I to do? It's desthroyed I am! Have compassion on my situation, my dear sir, I implore you! You are summoned to the presence of a great Prince, Mr. Macdonald! There is an etiquette that must be observed!"

Clan Ranald threw his arm up in a menacing sweep towards the mountains. "Seek, if you can, Sir Thomas, to impose your etiquette upon yonder crags!" He pointed down to the wavelets slapping against the rocks with little insistent noises that had a curious strength in them, as if they carried the whisper of the immeasurable Atlantic itself from whence they came. "Marshal these waves in order of Court precedence! But do not you hope to be binding with your rules the sons of Allan, and they the children of Kings!"

With these words he clapped his bonnet, which in deference to Sir Thomas's repeated uncoverings, he had been holding in his hand, upon his head again. His two companions followed him, and the three feathers nodded proudly in the air.

Sir Thomas Sheridan recoiled as if expecting to be hewn down next by their broad-swords. But as they stood still as statues, he pressed his hand on his startled heart and began to temporise.

"I had no such intention, sir, I assure you! And indeed it is more than I can bear even to seem to disobloige you, Mr. Macdonald! I will have the honour of conveying you with all your party aboard . . . on my own responsibilitee! But you, sir, must in your turn give me your word that none of you will attempt to . . . ah! . . . force an entry upon His Royal Highness, should he feel indisposed to accord further audiences."

"And is it we," said Clan Ranald, relapsing into his slumbrous good-humour, "that would be intruding upon the privacy of any gentleman, let alone our Prince? But it is our right to wait upon him, and we will not be kept sitting like gillies in the doorway."

Sir Thomas took another pinch of snuff to calm his nerves, and looked curiously at them. Darthula suddenly realised

that they must puzzle him. The Chief, indeed, with hi
splendid sporran of white fur and his silver-studded targe dis
played a certain rude magnificence; but the dress and ac
coutrements of the other two gentlemen were plain even to
rusticity. The cluster of swordsmen following them showed
bare legs and patched plaids. She herself, she was conscious
betrayed by her disordered hair and the streaks upon her skirt
her headlong ride over torrents and through woods. But did
this ancient marionette, she wondered, as they took their
places in the boat, really see no difference between the
orangeries of Versailles and the rocks of the Highlands? The
first of the Prince's advisers she had met seemed to her to
bode ill for his relations with the Scottish Chiefs.

2

As soon as they had reached the deck of the brig Darthula
perceived another old man in some kind of blue foreign uni
form coughing and spitting up upon the poop. And yet a
third came, limping heavily with gout, out of the cabin to
greet them. For what motive, she wondered, had the Prince
chosen to set out upon a wild adventure with so many infirm
greybeards?

However, the new-comer both gave and received a very
different welcome from Sir Thomas Sheridan's. "Clan Ran
ald!" he cried, with moist eyes shining, and embraced the
young Chief.

Clan Ranald seemed deeply moved. "Atholl!" he replied
"Welcome, welcome home at last, Atholl!"

"Well," laughed the old nobleman at the repetition of the
title. "I go as Tullibardine, for the present! But soon, no
doubt, I must dispute with my Whig brother to surrender my
Dukedom to me!"

Clan Ranald presented his companions. The Marquis of

Tullibardine received each with quiet courtliness. Darthula liked the bright way the eyes twinkled in his worn, lined face. Here was one, she thought, who had not lost his fire with age.

He led the way now to a rough tent or awning of sail-cloth, set up with poles, under the poop. A table underneath it bore a goodly array of bottles, long-necked ones for liqueurs and square ones for whisky. Behind it sat a gentleman with the watchful eyes of the practised courtier and the purplish flush of the habitual drinker. He was introduced as he rose as Colonel Strickland; and, though his manner was dry, he set about offering refreshment with alacrity. The old military gentleman climbed laboriously down from the poop to join them, and was presented as Colonel Sir John Macdonald, of the French King's Irish Brigade.

Darthula, after taking a glass of claret to join in the general pledging that went on, withdrew towards the bulwarks, not wishing to intrude upon the apparently confidential discussion that was beginning between the Chiefs and the elders. Young Ranald from Kinlochmoidart also strolled away to the side of the ship. Darthula, however, kept her sharp eyes on the council; noticed how Strickland seemed to take little part except to refill glasses; how Clan Ranald kept giving his slow head-shake, and Tullibardine looked gloomily at the deck.

She sighed, and gazed away across the sunlit waters of the loch, to where the woods rippled in gold-flecked splendour, the heather spread a King's carpet on the slopes above, and the peaks glistered like beacons in the sky. The sea wind blew with a salt tang through her curls. The whole scene was bathed for her in the exhilaration of hope—and there were those aged men quavering and head-shaking. Ah! why would not the Musician of Beasdale issue from the cabin with his enchanted violin, and banish all these doubts and despondencies?

The doors swung open and her heart leapt. But it was no'
the Prince who emerged. It was, however, a friend, who
started at sight of her and then waved cheery greetings. Clad
with medical gravity, and dignified by a finely-powdered
wig, Dr. Archibald Cameron, with his powerful, aquiline
nose and keen brown-berry eyes, was a figure known and
loved by all the country-side, from Arisaig and Moidart to
the Great Glen and farther Lochaber. To all he was physician, counsellor and friend . . . and the importance of his
presence here was not lost upon Darthula. Without a doubt
he had come as the ambassador of his brother, Cameron of
Lochiel, the greatest Chief, when all was said, of the Western
Highlands. Lochiel, their mighty neighbour at Achnacarry,
could put a force of eight hundred or a thousand claymores
into the field at the disposition of the Prince . . . if he
wished. But Darthula quickly seized upon this further point.
If he had not come himself, but sent his brother as his agent,
it meant either that he had refused—she went cold at the
thought—or had at least not yet made up his mind.

Meanwhile Dr. Cameron was approaching her through
the obstacles of coiled rope and gun-carriages on the deck,
followed by a majestic-looking stranger, who wore his own
red hair curled instead of a wig, and had a great coat flung
carelessly open upon some kind of undress uniform. As he
swaggered along in the wake of the Doctor she noticed with
amusement that on shipboard he was wearing huge spurs.

Archie Cameron took her hand affectionately. "I will not
ask how you come here, Darthula," he said. "As well question a *sithiche* of the woods upon its flights! But how comes
Glenmarisdale not to be with you?"

"How comes Lochiel not to be with *you*, Archie?" she
retorted, looking him challengingly in the eye.

"My brother is not finding himself in the best of health,"
answered Dr. Cameron, with a smile that showed he had no

intent to deceive her by the phrase.

"Glenmarisdale, thank God, is in the best of health! He will be back from the hills in a day or two."

"Aye?" nodded the Doctor, "and then will be the time for him to be very careful . . . of his health." He cast a keen glance at the group under the awning. "I am finding no cheering medicine in those faces," he remarked.

"Archie!" she caught at his arm. "You would not betray the Prince?"

"Whisht, woman!" he hushed her with a mock severity. "What is all this emotion? Come, let me present you to Captain O'Sullivan. This, sir, is Mistress Maceachan of Glenmarisdale, and I would rather be having her on my side . . . or at least not against me . . . than all the broad-swords her brother can bring into the field."

"Deloighted by the privilege!" The officer made a stately bow, and Darthula took a vague distaste for his statuesque face and contemptuously curling nostrils. . . . She was also beginning to tire of Irish brogues.

"Sure, I can well understand, Dr. Cameron," he went on with a languid self-assurance, "that Miss Maceachan would be worth a score of swords. Is there a blade that would not leap from its sheath at the bidding of those oyes?"

"Come, Captain!" interrupted Archie Cameron sharply. "Did you put in, pray, at your own country on the voyage hither to kiss the blarney-stone? We are too canny in the Highlands to accept your small change of compliment as good coin. You must deal with us without flattery, sir; we are simple folk."

Tullibardine beckoned to him, and he joined the conference under the awning. O'Sullivan watched him go, propping his massive form against the bulwark. "And isn't he the grand fellow, entoirely, Miss Maceachan?" he murmured in a tone that made an insult of the compliment. "Faith, it's in love I am with you Highlanders, every man . . . and woman . . . of ye all. They look stout gossoons, the men, too. Tell me, d'ye think they'll foight?"

"It is we will very soon be showing you, Captain O'Sullivan!" replied Darthula, firing up.

The Captain flicked his gauntlet towards the men of Clan Ranald's retinue, who were lying or strolling about on the edge of the shore, their red legs shining in the sun.

"Are those specimens of the infantry yonder? Some of them look to have stolen the clothes off the scarecrows as they came along!" he sniggered.

"They keep their swords bright!" Darthula cut back at him.

"And they show foine muscle, too," agreed O'Sullivan warmly, realising his *faux pas*. "We'll drill them into something we can use, never fear, never fear! Still, I wish with all my heart, His Royal Highness had come with some five or six thousand good trained soldiers of his cousin's, the King of France. I do, upon my honour, Miss Maceachan."

"His Highness," Darthula threw her head back, "can safely trust himself to his own people."

"Sure, he seems to be meeting with white faces so far!" The Captain flicked his glove again, this time towards the council under the tent. "Ah! here is himself!" he added in a changed tone, and drew himself up in a flourishing salute, as the Prince stepped out of the cabin, still dressed in his clerical clothes, but (as Darthula noted with amusement) wearing a hat fastened by a cord to his buttonhole against the wind.

For an instant Darthula saw him hesitate, and scan the cluster of counsellors under the little sail-cloth pavilion with that sharp, suspicious glance he had thrown upon her yesterday in the woods when she questioned him indiscreetly.

Then he called up a smile, and walked over with his lithe, springy step to join them.

Everyone rose and bowed low, and the Prince was lost to sight in the midst of the group. "Pray, excuse me, Miss Maceachan," said O'Sullivan importantly. "If there is to be a council of war it will not be long before I shall be required." He strode off, making his cavalry boots thud heavily upon the planking, and took up a posture at an angle where he judged it likely that he would soon catch the Prince's eye.

"May I inthrojuice myself?" said yet another brogue in her ear, and she turned to see a small man, also in clergyman's dress, smiling at her out of a pale, irregular face, with a genial if slightly wild eye. "I go by the name of O'Brien, a Churchman, I avow myself; and you, they tell me, are sister to one of the Chiefs of the localitee. I always believe in making friends of the ladies. They are our foinest recruithing-sergeants entoirely!"

"I am thinking, Mr. O'Brien," answered Darthula, "that His Royal Highness appears to be his own best recruiting-sergeant!"

The group under the awning had parted for a moment, to allow the Prince to make a gesture towards the mountains of the South-West. He held his other hand down upon a map that had been spread among the bottles on the table, and his face was alight with enthusiasm.

The clergyman looked at her blankly. Then he burst into shrill laughter. "Sure, you don't believe *that*, do you, Miss Maceachan? That is not the Prince Regent. Don't you know that dress? It is the uniform of the Students of the Scots College in Paris. That young gentleman has studied the lie of the land in these parts, and is no doubt giving valuable advice."

Darthula gave her shoulder to the clergyman in disgust.

The conference seemed in danger of breaking up. The grey-beards drew together in one group. The Prince, after accepting a large glass of wine from the obsequious hands of Strickland and draining it with a violent gesture, strode away alone, and began to pace the deck between the two masts. Clan Ranald, almost furtively beckoning Dr. Cameron and Alan Macdonald to his side, made a third little knot.

At that moment a thick-set man with eyes rather close together, wearing a brown bag-wig, came up with a heavy step to O'Brien.

"May I have a word with you, Mr. Kelly?" he asked; and then, noticing Darthula, who had been half-hidden from him by a gun-carriage and the shrouds running up near it, he apologised. "Not at all," said the clergyman affably. "This is Mistress Maceachan of Glenmarisdale. Mr. Æneas Macdonald, ma'am."

Darthula raised her eyebrows with a look that made the little man crackle into his shrill laugh again. "That is without any *double entendre*, Miss Maceachan," he declared. "It is really the famous banker, Mr. Æneas Macdonald of Paris."

"Of Kinlochmoidart," said the banker with a sigh. "I should be a neighbour of Miss Maceachan's if I had been wise enough to stay at home like my brothers yonder." He sighed again. "Well, 'tis no matter, Mr. Kelly. What I had to say can wait . . . like so much else in this business. His Highness seems to be at loggerheads with his followers already, as to who shall do the leading!" He rolled ponderously away again.

Darthula turned upon the little clergyman with a scornful lip; but he disarmed her with upraised hands and a quirkish smile. "No, no, Miss Maceachan!" he protested, "I know everything you would say. I have told you no falsehoods. I would shame my cloth if I did."

"You were saying you were O'Brien—!"

"I said I went by the name of O'Brien. I do—for my safety's sake!"

"—and that that was not the Prince!"

"Not the Prince *Regent*—he has not yet reached the throne!"

"You were saying, Mr. Kelly, he was a student of the Scots College in Paris!"

"I said he wore the dress of one. It is a fact. I borrowed it for him."

"Do you ever speak the simple truth, Mr. Kelly?"

"Is truth ever simple, Miss Maceachan?" A wistful look pointed his haggard, irregular face. "As for me, I have so often been in places where the simple truth would have been the last word I spoke . . . yes, and not only that, which would have been but a trifling matter, I agree with you . . . but the death-sentence likewise of the engaging young gentleman yonder, in the dress, I repeat, of a student of the Scots College . . . that I am left wondering. I have tried to find a *via media* between the truth that destroys and the falsehood that damns, but no doubt it is hard to find. Well: I see that I am like to find a hard confessor and get no shrift at all from you, Miss Maceachan. So I will e'en take my leave and go and console honest Æneas. Sure, his money-bags are a hump that sits heavy on his shoulders!"

He ambled off with his nose stuck defiantly in the air, and Darthula, with the ruthlessness of youth, began to analyse the confidants whom the Prince had chosen for his arduous, delicate and exalted enterprise. Three aged men—"Allagrugous old fellows!" she said to herself in the vernacular, recalling the grim lines on their faces—of whom only the Marquis seemed to retain any sparkle of life; the popinjay O'Sullivan, and the banker already foreboding losses; the supple, intrusive little cleric to teach him conspiracy, and the purple-faced Englishman Strickland over there to train him in toping!

She left quite angry for the moment with her musician; then, hearing a step on the deck near her, she turned her head and saw him standing with eyes that did not see her just on the other side of the gun-carriage. He was clutching the knob at the end of the brass cannon with agonised fingers, and pearls of sweat hung on his forehead as he gazed out seawards with a look on his young face that filled her heart again with that strange uprush of maternal tenderness. She hardly restrained herself from rushing round to embrace him and offer words of consolation.

The sun glittered, the blue loch-water sparkled now with an air of mockery. The mountains still upheaved themselves all around in disdain of mortal coils.

Then as the Prince swung away from the bulwarks, young Ranald came padding towards her, his weapons clapping as he moved. "Darthula!" he breathed in her ear. "This is cruel! It is I am shamed by my own kin. I must speak for myself!"

"Wait, Ranald, wait!" she answered, catching him by his plaid. "Your moment will come, but not yet, not yet!"

3

CLAN RANALD with the other Highlanders at his heels was marching across the deck to meet the Prince. The deputation wore an air of finality. A few yards from where the girl and the boy waited behind the shrouds, Charles stood still to meet them, his feet pressed together, every line of his body taut.

"Well, your decision, gentlemen?" he asked in a high voice.

"We are agreed upon the advice it is our duty to tender your Royal Highness," answered the Chief.

"Speak . . . speak freely, Clan Ranald!"

"Dr. Cameron here, sir, agrees with me. Sir Thomas Sheridan," he beckoned the old tutor forward to support him, "has been convinced. Sir, there are two great Chiefs in these parts without whose adhesion it would be madness to attempt any enterprise. They are Macleod of Macleod and Sir Alexander Macdonald of the Isles. At your command I have visited them; I have pleaded with them. They will not under present conditions raise their standards."

"But I have their promises," cried Charles in a voice breaking with pain and indignation. "I have Macleod's own written engagement in my *portmanteaux*!"

Clan Ranald and Dr. Cameron looked embarrassed at this revelation, and turned their eyes away.

"Then there is Lord Lovat!" pursued Charles. "He writes my father and myself continual assurances of his fidelity. Surely he will not betray too?"

There was another awkward silence, in which Archie Cameron could not by biting his lip refrain from a smile.

"What in God's name am I to do, gentlemen?" demanded Charles.

"Go home, sir," replied Clan Ranald bluntly.

"Home!" cried the Prince. "Why, I am come home! Do you take me for a foreigner, Clan Ranald?"

The Chief went red. "I hope your Royal Highness will not dwell upon a *façon de parler*."

"No, Clan Ranald, no, my friend," declared Charles with impulsive affection. "But can you not see that in another five years your fashion of speaking will have become a fashion of thinking? Yes, gentlemen, I assure you it will!" for there had been a movement of remonstrance among the Highlanders. "From saying that our home is in Rome or in Paris you will be coming to look upon us as foreigners. I have been feeling that . . . oh! longer than I care to remember . . . and that is why I am resolved at all hazards to make entry into my own house. Yes, I will at least be buried at home, if I may not live there!"

"And we are ready to be buried with you!" growled Clan Ranald, and at the murmur of assent that followed Darthula felt her first little thrill of returning hope. Their spirits were not quite dashed, then! She had again to hold back young Ranald, feeling still, to her quivering finger-tips, that the moment was not yet come.

Then she strained her hearing to catch the rest of the debate, which tended to be carried away from her ears by the increase of the wind, which was ruffling the surface of the loch and humming through the rigging, as though excited. She moved a little closer to the disputants in time to hear Clan Ranald say, "—it was agreed, not less than six thousand French troops."

Again Prince Charles's high tones rang out. "And did you think I would come shedding Scots and English blood by the hand of foreigners?"

"We cannot be doing everything by ourselves, sir," persisted the Chief. "It was supposed, too, that you would bring artillery with you."

"Oh! cannon!" The Prince smiled confidently. "If it be cannon that are troubling you, I have them, be assured!" The Highlanders looked surprised. "Yes," he went on, "I have twenty swivel-guns on this very ship that can be unscrewed and brought ashore."

There was a disappointed rustle among his listeners. "You might as well use catapults, sir, against the Elector's artillery-train," said Clan Ranald cruelly.

The Prince stared at him with fallen jaw, like a schoolboy whose tin sword has been snapped.

"But my guns—" he began, and then broke off. "Well, if they do not content you, have we no hearts, no hearts in the Highlands?"

"Yes, sir," interjected Dr. Cameron, "we *have* hearts—hearts that needs must bleed at the thought of the people entrusted to our care. We dare not, in the sight of God, lead them to mere massacre!"

Charles turned away from them all with a despairing gesture, throwing clenched fists skywards.

Darthula gave a push to Ranald Macdonald's shoulder. "Now," she hissed, "now speak, Ranald! All hinges upon you!"

The boy shot forward like a stag of the mountains, his hand on his claymore-hilt.

"Stop that man!" roared Captain O'Sullivan, mistaking the gesture.

"Do not stop him!" cried Charles, as Ranald fell on his knees before him. "You will assist me, Ranald, will you not?" he demanded, seizing the lad by his shoulders.

"I will, I will. *Phrionnsa Tearlach!*" * cried the boy. "Though no other man in the Highlands should draw sword, it is I will be fighting for you and dying with you!"

The Prince raised him from his knees and flung his arm round him. "The first!" he exclaimed exultantly.

Immediately Darthula glided from the shelter of the gun-carriage, and swept in a curtsey to the deck. "I crave to be the second, sir!" she cried in a clear voice. "I offer you, in my brother's name, the claymores of Glenmarisdale!"

"Thank you! Thank you!" Charles seized her hand and kissed it fervently. "I knew I had friends in Glenmarisdale; they told me it would be so!" He faced about, holding Ranald by one hand and Darthula by the other.

"See here, gentlemen!" he challenged. "A boy and a woman are ready to die for their Prince and their King. Is there no one else will stand by me?"

Ranald's brother made a stifled sound, and thrusting aside

* Prince Charles.

his Chief's detaining hand, rushed across to Charles's side. "I cannot be outdone by my baby brother!" he declared. "Moidart shall come out for you, sir, I promise!"

"Clan Ranald!" said the Prince, in a voice, Darthula afterwards related, that would have seduced an archangel. "I am waiting for *you*!"

There was a moment's pause; then with a smile half-moved, half-cynical, the young Chief, with his slumbrous eyes inscrutably veiled, stalked over to Charles, and knelt to kiss his hand. "I must not be letting my vassals filch the leadership," was all he said.

Darthula clapped her hands for joy. Clan Ranald, with its septs and allies, she reckoned, would not put many short of five hundred swords into the field: it was already the nucleus of an army!

Alone now Dr. Cameron held out, pulling and pinching his lower lip.

"Doctor," said Charles kindly, "will you be alone in standing out against my hopes?"

"Whether I resist, sir, as reason and humanity dictate, or whether I yield to my heart, and range myself with those who, it seems, no longer dread a desperate venture . . . dicing with the lives of men and the future of Scotland . . . that weighs little in the event. It rests with my brother Lochiel, not with me, to bring out the Camerons."

"But it is to you he will give ear! Why else did he choose you for his ambassador?"

Dr. Cameron shook his head, and made a half-turn away, as though seeking to break the spell.

"Very well, sir," said the Prince haughtily. "Go! These gentlemen have engaged themselves to win with me, to die with me, or skulk in the heather with me. Lochiel, who, my father told me, was his closest friend, may rest at home and learn his Prince's fate from the news-sheets."

"No! no!" Dr. Cameron turned back again, profoundly distressed. "That shall never be said, never! I will take your appeal to my brother, sir, and I can prophesy his answer."

"He will come?"

"He will say, 'I will be sharing the fate of my Prince, and so shall every man over whom nature or fortune has given me any power.'"

"Then," said the Prince, "what more have I to fear?"

He looked round, radiant, upon the little band that had crept closer to him during the last few decisive moments. There they stood, the seven men who had come with him to the point of Moidart to conquer three Kingdoms; and there opposite them were their first reinforcements: one Chief, two gentlemen in arms, a doctor of medicine in civil sobriety— and a girl with flushed cheeks and starry eyes.

Suddenly the old Marquis of Tullibardine hobbled forward on a stick, and lifted his hat. "Huzza for King James!" he cried in a bloodless, cracked voice, and a cheer broke from the tiny assembly, dominated by Ranald's shrill mountain call and Darthula's bird-like note.

The sound rang through the brig, startling the sailors at their work; it floated thinly across the water ever weaving and unweaving its aimless ripples, and startled a flock of seagulls on the nearer rocks, who rose and scattered with mocking squawks.

The handful of clansmen on the beach ran together in wonder and perplexity, looking towards the ship.

Not a leaf stirred responsive in the ancient woods; the great peaks, drawing their veils close round their heads, continued to dream their dream of all the ages, their faces unchangeably raised towards the Eternal.

Chapter VII

FAMILY MATTERS

1

BEFORE Darthula made her way home that evening she had
seen the Prince established in the first of his Scottish palaces,
under the care of Angus of Borrodale in his white-washed
farmhouse high up the romantic glen that led from the shore.
Sea-gulls perched upon the chimneys like guards; and in
front of the plain door a bearded warrior from Clan Ranald's
suite did sentry-go, his accoutrements glinting in the wester-
ing sun.

Here in his little room upstairs, piled with *portmanteaux*
and bags of papers, while his violin rested in the deep embrasure of the window, Charles listened while she warned
him that one enemy, a small reptile, but a dangerous one, was
already busy for his undoing. Neither the Prince nor Clan
Ranald, who was with him, saw much immediate danger in
Rob Sanderson's activities, however; especially as his des-
patches to the red-coats of the Forts had been intercepted—
how the Prince's eyes had laughed when she told him of the
trick. "I have agreed," Charles added, "to the advice of these
gentlemen that I should, so soon as things may be made a
little ready, withdraw into Moidart, there to gather my sup-

porters in greater secrecy, and fix the day and place for raising my standard." And, after Clan Ranald had withdrawn to visit his sentries, Charles had thanked her for her intervention on the deck of the *Du Teillay*.

"I believe it was your speech, following that true fellow Ranald's that carried the day. I have been wondering how I shall reward you when I come to St. James's. Shall I ask my father to give you a regiment? Colonel Miss Darthula Maceachan. . . . That is a strange name you bear—Darthula —and one I have not met before."

"It is Deirdre," she murmured, "Deirdre of the Sorrows, of whom Ossian sang. And it is I was the child born in my father's grief."

"Darthula, then, means 'woman of sorrow' in your tongue?"

She had blushed as she corrected him. "It means, sir, 'the woman with fine eyes.'"

Standing over her in his mood of elfish happiness, and looking down at her from his tall height, he had laughed at her blush.

"Ah! but," he added, suddenly grave, "I believe I would have thrown up my hand yesterday in the wood but for those eyes of yours and the daring in them." He shot a glance at the violin in the window. "It will be long months, I surmise, before I take that old friend in hand again," and the sound she was still hearing as she took her leave was the sigh with which he said it.

When she got back to Glenmarisdale House she found Dr. Hay in the dining-room, with its heavy mahogany furniture perpetually stared at by the oil portraits of the family. There was her grandfather, Roderick Maceachan, all peaked periwig and breastplate, and her father, Fergus Maceachan, in plaid and ruffles, with Hector's blue-grey eyes, but sadder, and wanting his impishness.

The chaplain started from the book he was reading over his long-neglected supper between the silver candlesticks. His face was drawn with anxiety. There was no sign, he said, of Hector's return, and what troubled him worse was that Rob Sanderson had not been near the place all day.

"No cattle have been driven up here as he undertook. Miss Darthula, I like it not. You say you can spare Rob Sanderson's presence about the house: I answer that I love my enemy to be where my eye is upon him. Be sure, Mr. Sanderson's at mischief somewhere, somehow."

Darthula tried to cheer him by telling him of the events at Loch-nan-Uamh, but all he seemed to pick out of the tale was the refusal of the Chiefs of the Isles to give their help.

"Fearful news!" he groaned. "Miss Darthula, I beseech you, harken to me! Let us lift the cases of arms together . . . and drown them in the loch. No one will guess what has become of them, and unarmed no one can expect the Maceachans to march. It may be the last chance to avert ruin from your family."

"I perceive," said Darthula contemptuously, "that old men's blood will be running thin! You are a parcel of fears, my dear doctor."

The next moment both their faces went white in the candlelight. A peremptory knock on the front door rang through the sleeping house.

"Who is it," whispered Darthula, "that knocks instead of entering? Let me call down the house servants!"

"Wait!" The chaplain lifted a shaking hand. "Let me spy through the window first!"

Before he could move a throaty voice shouted outside: "Open in the King's name!"

Darthula stole to the window, and raising it a few inches, called out into the darkness, "Who is there?"

"The Elector of Hanover!" answered the voice, and a shout of laughter followed it.

"Hector!" screamed Darthula. "Oh! I will tear your eyes out for this!"

She rushed into the hall to meet her brother as he pushed the door open and entered, saying with a grin, "A very guilty conscience, on my honour! Why, what the devil! Darthula—?"

She was standing crying and laughing at once on the brink obviously of hysteria. Over the bannisters lights glittered and the frightened faces of servants peeped.

"Back to your beds, all of you!" called the Laird in Gaelic; "we do but make merriment. There is nought amiss!" He pushed his sister before him into the dining-room and demanded testily, "What is the matter? What ails her, Dr. Hay?"

"Come, ma'am, come!" remonstrated the clergyman, standing over the weeping girl, who had fallen upon a chair. "We are shamed by you. Is this the sort of follower the Prince has need of?"

Darthula tottered to her feet and threw her arms round her brother. "Oh, Hector! Oh! my brother! Thank God you are returned at last!"

Hector deftly eluded the fervour of her embrace. "Will one of you," he begged, "be good enough to explain the meaning of all this dramatic passion? Somebody, I think, spoke of a Prince?"

"It is the Prince of Wales, sir," said Dr. Hay gravely; "he is here."

"Fred!" exclaimed Hector incredulously. "Fidgety Fred in the Highlands. 'Tis impossible!"

"Not the Hanoverian claimant, Glenmarisdale. I mean your own, your rightful Prince."

"*Charlie!*" Hector sat down heavily upon the nearest chair. "You are fooling me, the pair of you!" He glanced sharply from the one to the other. "I see you are not, though," he said in a different voice. "Tell me all about it."

Darthula, partially mastering her emotion, recounted her whole tale, while Hector sat listening, his hands thrust into his coat pockets, his feet stretched before him, his heels from time to time drumming the floor.

"Well," he said, looking up with a grin of mischief as her breathless voice died away, "I suppose you are thinking this means the Fiery Cross!"

"That," answered the chaplain firmly, "is for the Chief to say, Glenmarisdale."

"Oh! aye! the Chief!" Hector sat up, his grey eyes sparkling with annoyance. "Lay all upon the Chief! Yesterday I might not so much as give an order for a new carpet to my room. To-day you will be putting your lives and those of all the honest fellows in the glen upon my conscience!"

"Your conscience will be white, Hector," said his sister, "if you follow your Prince and your King, like all the chiefs of the clan before you."

"And if I invoke so much as a grain of common sense, I will be held up to eternal infamy, and my portrait effaced from these walls, like that of the erring Doge of Venice."

He had glanced up as he spoke at the family pictures, and now remained for a few minutes sunk in contemplation of his father, who had ridden off to join the Earl of Mar in 'Fifteen, and whose pony had broken his leg and saved his neck by falling with him before he had got further than Laggan on his journey. The future Lord Brounhill's legal dexterity had just saved him from attainder, and he had seemed ever after to nurse the sense of his failure. He had not married till eight years later, and then Fortune had been no kinder. His young wife had died in giving birth to Hector; and, after moving

about for a few years more as a silent shadow in Glenmarisdale, he had followed her, leaving the children, then aged
nine and six, to his brother's unsympathetic tutorship.

This tale of a frustrated life could be read to-night in his
son's eyes as he sat studying the portrait. Then he turned to
the two who watched him. "I take it," he said in a low voice,
"that you both know this is mere *madness*?"

Neither answered a word.

"But it may mean sport all the same!" said the Laird,
springing up with one of his most impish grins.

Darthula suddenly embraced him, while tears of honest
nature rained from her eyes. "Oh! Hector! Hector!" she
sobbed. "I am not wanting you to be hurt, and you my baby
brother!"

He patted her shoulder. "I will take as much care of my
skin as a soldier may without being shot by the Provost-
Marshal for it!"

"Oh! but, Hector," she went on, still crying, "you don't
know! This morning early I saw the Dreamer wake. I am
not knowing what it forebodes!"

"You saw the Dreamer wake?" His most sceptical grin
showed for a moment. "I am thinking that means, little sister,
that *you* needed to sleep. . . . And yet 'tis odd, now that it
comes back to my mind, *I* have seen—or Ned Burke, who
was with me, saw, which is just as bad—on my last night in
Edinburgh. . . ."

"What, Hector? Oh! tell me!"

"'Tis no matter. Nonsense and auld wives' fables! Well,
it is a good thing that our broad-swords have all had their
hilts fitted."

"They have, sir?" asked the chaplain in surprise. "When
was that done, pray?"

"I saw to it myself more than a year ago. There was no
sense in storing up useless blades—was there? And the

emergency, as you see, does not give you much time to make up for past neglects. Naturally I chanted no songs about what I was doing: Macvarish, Donald Dhu, John the Smith and I made a little forge up in the Corrie of the Ravens . . . you know the spot, Darthula . . . you and the rest thought we were away hunting." He cracked his fingers with malicious delight, while Darthula looked a little sour. "How often Brounie has tried to worm out of me the place where we store them! . . . Father, though he had told Macvarish, never would let *him* know, nor would I. . . . Now, you shall learn, too, Doctor. We may need your aid. We have stolen a march on Brounie this time, I trow." He yawned. "Well, I suppose I may have a few hours' sleep? 'Tis I have been walking and crawling for nearly a week, and sleeping, not very heavy, in the heather. To-morrow we must be stirring early."

"What will you do, Hector?"

"I will be gathering my men and marching to guard the Prince at Borrodale. Young Clan Ranald has clearly not a sufficient escort with him. That youth is the sleepy one. You need not be troubling to have me called, Darthula. I shall wake early."

2

NEVERTHELESS, it was Darthula who roused her brother, pale-faced in the first greyness of a grey day, and beckoned him, as soon as he had thrown on a kilt and a shirt, to the window of her room overlooking the lake.

Hector whistled. Along the path running by the western shore of the loch a small detachment of soldiers came marching. There was little sun in the woolly light to glint upon their muskets, but they were already close enough for the red of their coats to be discernible. There seemed to be about thirty of them, led by an officer on a grey horse.

"The fools!" muttered Hector. "How they butt ahead blindfold, without so much as a scout in front or a picket to sweep the hillside above! We could be rolling them into the loch with stones or overwhelming them by the simplest ambush! And that grey horse, what a mark! . . . Nevertheless," he added, "since it is they have surprised us before we have a single man under arms, it is perhaps we are the daft ones!"

Noiselessly, Dr. Hay had stolen down from his room and joined them. "I don't understand," he whispered. "We burnt Sanderson's letters. Who can have given them the alarm?"

"Look!" exclaimed Glenmarisdale. Some two hundred yards behind the soldiers a small civilian cavalcade had come into view. "Who the devil will those be? I am thinking I know that lang-leggit fellow too tall for his pony."

"Why, I believe," ejaculated Darthula, blushing, she knew not why at such a moment, "it will be—"

"Brounie! 'Tis Brounie!" Hector struck his fist on the sill. "No, not the lanky fellow, of course. Yon is Brounie in front in the cloak. Where in hell is he sprung from? I thought him still at Brounhill. I know he aye hopes to catch Master Sanderson napping by appearing unheralded. But at this hour it is strange! And who is the long-legs, Darthula? You were saying you recognised him."

"It will be . . . I think it will be Mr. Duncanson," she answered in an indistinct tone.

"Why he, a' God's name?"

"It was planned he should come in August on a visit."

"With soldiers?" Hector fell silent.

The detachment was nearing the house now, and on an order shouted back at them by the officer the men, who had been marching at ease, came with a precise movement to the shoulder. The halberd carried by the leading sergeant gave a dull gleam of its axe-head as he brought it into position. Darthula shivered, either with the morning chill or at something faintly alarming about this tiny fragment of the enemy's war machine. They might know nothing about mountain fighting, but there was something discomfortable about their very slowness and deliberation . . . they seemed in no hurry at all . . . that made a troublesome impression. They halted in front of the house and dressed their line.

"I will tak' my affidavit," said Lord Brounhill to Darthula before the door, "that ye were not expecting the pleasure of our company this morn. . . . Whaur is your brither?"

Darthula turned her head. Hector, she was sure, had come downstairs behind her to greet the Tutor. But she saw only the perturbed faces of the servants clustering in the doorway.

Darthula made stammering excuse to her uncle. "He will be about the house, sir, to find Macvarish and be giving orders for your reception."

Brounie grunted, and as he prepared to dismount, Rob Sanderson, who had hitherto concealed his presence among the baggage train, hurried forward obsequiously to assist him.

"I will give all orders that are necessar'," said Lord Brounhill. "Let Hector be found without delay." He conferred for a few moments with the officer in charge of the escort, who went off to dispose of his men about the stables and cottages at the back: and then, returning, said sharply to Darthula as he entered the house, "Be showing some civeelities to Mr. Duncanson. Hae ye forgot your behaviour?"

Darthula crossed to the young lawyer, who was standing in silence holding the bridle of his pony, and greeted him cordially. There was no wisdom (so she said to herself to

account for the warmth of her welcome) in making more
enemies than necessary.

"I implore your pardon, Mistress Maceachan," said Allan.
"It was very far from my desires to make my promised visit
here with such a following! However, affairs of State make
hay of private hopes."

"What does it mean?" she asked in a low tone.

"I cannot very well follow it all out. My Lord Brounhill
is a very clam for keeping his own counsel. I set out with
him from Edinburgh some days ago; he had been pleased to
advance the date of my visit to you; and nothing of note,
I think, occurred, until after we had left the New Road and
come down to a place named Roy Bridge. Then, a rumour
reached us." He stopped.

"Rumours fly like bog-lights over this country," said Darthula defiantly, "and they are as worthy of trust."

"It may well be so. I know only that his lordship came to
me, looking sore troubled, and said, 'I must trespass on your
patience to make a detour with me by Fort William, instead
of proceeding by Spean Bridge. I mean to take effective
steps to prevent any folly on the part of the younger members of my family.' Upon that, Miss Maceachan, I besought
him if there were some differ between himself and his family
to let me turn back forthwith, as the presence of an outsider
to your affairs could not but be disagreeable to you."

"Spoken like a gentleman, Mr. Duncanson! But he would
not hearken to you?"

"Miss Maceachan, he replied to me with an emotion that
on my honour I must consider sincere, 'Come you with me,
my man, if you are a friend to the Maceachans. Maybe your
young face will do what my old tongue cannot—wean a mad
girl from ways that will be her own ruin and her brother's!' "
Allan Duncanson repeated these words with such an embar-

rassed sense of their delicacy, and such a fervent anxiety in his deep-set eyes, that Darthula hung her head, feeling her reckless retorts struck from her lips.

"Miss Maceachan," pursued Allan, after a pause. "If you think your secret is safe, you deceive yourself. It is known all over Lochaber that the son of the Chevalier de St. George has landed on this coast. Mr. Sanderson met us at Fort William with full particulars. It was he finally decided Lord Brounhill not to advance farther without soldiers."

"And for what purpose will he be bringing red-coats to my father's House, Mr. Duncanson?"

"To disarm your clansmen, Miss Maceachan. And to take the persons of your brother and yourself back to Fort Augustus, and thence to Edinburgh, as hostages."

Before she could answer old Macvarish, of the silvery hair and gracious face, who had returned soon after Hector during the night, together with the Forester and the ponies carrying the hunting-spoils, came up to her with anguished eyes. "His Lordship, Mistress," he stammered, "is wishful to be speaking with you. . . . He has been waiting in your own room this long while . . . and he with the black spirit on him, too!"

"Go, I beseech you," said Duncanson, "do not provoke him further."

When Darthula reached her room she found her uncle waddling up and down on his short, bandy legs, his hands clenched behind his back. He turned fiercely on her as she entered.

"Hector!" he demanded, his grating voice rising almost to a squeak. "Where is he hiding?"

Darthula looked bewildered. "Has he not been found yet then? Have not the House and policies been searched?"

"Aye, by rascals who knew weel he was not there! He

has taken to the heather. But you shall tell me where he has gone!"

"How should I know, sir? Has Glenmarisdale not the right to betake himself whither he will on his own domain?"

"Glenmarisdale!" The Tutor repeated the title with a sarcastic sniff. "Well," he raised his finger solemnly. "If Hector is awa' to join the Pretender's son, on his own head be it! . . . A wilfu' man maun hae his way: I hae done ma best, I bid you witness it, Darthula, to presairve the lad fra' his ain ruin! Now," he seemed to sweep his nephew from his mind, and to be seized with a fresh access of energy, "I mean at least to save the lands for the fam'ly. You have store of arms hidden in the House or nearby. . . . Whaur are they? . . . Tell me, girl, or I'll choke the life from ye wi' my ain fingers!"

"Arms, sir, is it I would be knowing of arms? Are those matters would be confided to a girl like me?"

"Dinna practise your play-acting wi' me, Darthula. I ken your tricks of old. Your father on his death-bed imparted the secret to the twain of ye . . . mere infants . . . and weel ye hae kept it, even from me that had the right to be acquaint wi' a' sic dangerous matters, aye, I had the right as Tutor, as next o' kin to the pair o' ye . . . and, in the event of accident to Hector, next in order of succession!"

As these last words were jerked out of him, Darthula looked up and gave him a glance of peculiar meaning. He checked himself, and his angry eyes glazed into legal impassivity. "I require your answer," he said.

"Whatever I may know, sir, you shall learn nothing from me. My oath to our father when he lay dying in this very room, was to keep that deposit inviolate for the King or him whom the King should lawfully appoint in his stead."

"Wha' asks ye to do onything different, Darthula?" asked

her uncle in a voice that he tried to creak into mildness. "Ye may keep your oath to ma brither, unauthorised though it were. Lieutenant Henderson and mysel' *are* the lawfu' representatives of the King—there can be nane ither. You may treat the matter as one o' fac', not theory."

"I am fearing I lack the legal training to appreciate that point, sir."

"There is a muckle at stake, Darthula!"

"Indeed there will be, uncle! Honour and loyalty!"

He made a gesture of violent impatience; then, seizing the back of a chair, pulled it to him and sat down in an effort to compose himself. Slowly he clasped his hands and let his head settle down between his hunched shoulders, as he always did upon the Bench before commencing a summing-up. "I will beg for a few moments of your close attention," he said quietly, "the attention of your unbiased mind. Before all things, it is necessar' in this case to rid your intellects o' school-girl fancies and auld ballads. I will not say whether thirty years syne your ideas might ha' been adapted to the necessities o' the situation; it is ony gates not for me to blame your father for his choice. Had it been the will o' the people o' Great Britain to receive back the ancient line of Kings, there had doubtless been an obligation on all law-abiding folk. But the Scottish and the English nations, the Powers of Europe, the course o' destiny—in the whilk, Darthula, we maun trace the fingers o' Providence, aye, the fingers o' Providence—hae declarit themselves against an unhappy family. It has no been ma doing, and I canna help it. To tak' up arms in the Pretender's behoof to-day is to involve our country in a whirlpool of troubles: it is to beat down such prosperity as we hae painfully established. Scotland, that is now a country poor eneuch, will be made a land o' beggars. It is nae doot a fine-sounding thing to be leal to your Prince, a handsome callant, by all I hear! . . . Aye, but ye maun consider, there is an auld woman, worn wi' many sufferings, to whom ye owe a deeper loyalty, and her name is Scotland. . . . As the Apostle saith," he added, fidgeting uneasily at his own rhetoric, " 'I speak as a fule'—in the sole design of appealing to your ain romantical imaginings." He was silent for a minute. "And what do ye answer?" he asked at length.

"That I was never hearing more elegant pleading for disloyalty and cowardice!"

"Verra weel!" He jumped out of his chair. "Gin ye will not yield to suasion, I maun resort to sterner measures!" Before she could understand what he would be at, he had crossed to the door and pulled the rusty, unused key from the lock. "Ye may now," he said grimly, "have a taste of the lot of obstinate jurymen. In this room shall ye be locked, and de'il a bite or sup shall ye be given until ye have disclosed the hiding-place of those weapons! Aye!" he shot at her with a clenched grin, as she started forward indignantly, "if it iss a week I must starf you, I will be haafing your secret from you!"

Before she could stop him, he had slipped out and she heard the key grind in the lock.

"Will you be taking me for a child, then, uncle?" she called after him, stamping her foot, and then broke into a trembling storm of tears, the revulsion from her self-control during the interview.

Presently she dried them, pressing her hot palms against her eyes, and stood listening. The house seemed very still. In a fresh fury, she ran at the door and beat upon it till her hands were bruised. She desisted and there was still no sound. "Hector!" she cried shrilly. "Hector! how can you be leaving me here?"

She faced about and looked at the windows. She was not afraid of the drop, but of the indignity. Still, the familiar room was closing in upon her with an oddly prison-like hostility. She decided at last; ran to the window overlooking the loch . . . and saw that she had missed her opportunity. On the terrace below the house was a red-coat sentinel, who glanced up and shook his head at her appearance. She dashed across to the back window; there stood another sentry. Her uncle had dared to make her a real captive . . . and . . . the thought came chilling to her . . . there was no one in the house, now Hector had so cruelly disappeared, who could withstand his authority.

She was slowly withdrawing from the back window, when her eye caught the dark corner of the old keep up the hill, and a memory she could well have dispensed with flitted bat-like into her mind. Among the legends of the family there was one blood-curdling tale of a primitive Maceachan, who, having been betrayed to his enemies by his own wife, had hanged her by the heels from that tower until ravens picked her eyes.

She forced herself to laugh, as she turned away with a toss of her curls. As if Brounie, the respectable Lord of Session . . . she remembered the unsmiling grin he had given her as he whipped round the door, and wondered if any of their cateran ancestors had looked more savage. But it was the idiot she was surely becoming! Starved to death, indeed! Such barbarous, such Gothick notions, were a jest in this enlightened age. Then she felt sickish as she thought of Coll of Barisdale, the blackmailer, and his notorious engine of torture, Barisdale's "cat." He reigned not many miles away . . . but his methods were for vulgar offenders, smugglers and the like. Yet, a voice that turned her cold, whispered to her: Who was it that was plotting to let loose violence and the sword, to revive feudal strife all through these valleys?

Darthula threw herself on her sofa, burying her face in the

cushions; and lay there, a battle-ground for fear, anger and the sensations of helplessness, while the minutes limped by and the discomfort of a morning passed without any breaking of her fast sharpened in her imagination into a torture of hunger and thirst. She wondered what had become of Hector; if, as she supposed, he had made his escape while he could to join his Prince, she could not in fairness blame him—but he had left her in a sore strait. Once she stole to the window to see if the sentry could be caught off his watch; but he was still resting on his musket below. She saw, however, in the distance groups of his comrades, red dots against the grey and green of the loch-side, peering and scrambling about, tugging to lift boulders, thrusting gun-butts into thickets; and realising that they were searching for the arms, and that their search was anything but "warm," felt a defiant strengthening of her will to endure.

By the movement of the sun it was well past midday when she heard a step that was not the sentry's under her front windows, and ran to see who passed.

It was Dr. Hay sauntering by with a fishing-rod over his shoulder; and though she waved her handkerchief and called to him as loudly as she dared, till the soldier threateningly waved her away from the window, he went on his way down the lawn towards the loch as if he had observed nothing. Fresh tears sprang to her eyes. Deserted by everyone, she felt that now the chaplain, too, was seeking to put himself on the side of those who had seized power in the house. His fishing-tackle seemed to proclaim ostentatiously the peaceful, non-political character of his cloth.

The loch, sparkling in the midday heat, tortured her with genuine thirst; and after watching for a few moments while Dr. Hay pulled himself away from the shore in the rather large boat he had chosen from those by the landing-stage, she was about to turn back into her prison, saying bitterly, "It is he that can fish!" when a thought ran through her like a flame.

It was he that could fish! What was he gone a-fishing for? Palpitating with excitement, she crept back to the pane, and flattening herself into the corner so that the sentry should not mark her interest, followed the Doctor with eager gaze.

Slowly he sculled his big boat past the Island of Graves; and then worked round as though he would cross behind it. There were no soldiers visible now on the shore or in the woods. They had probably abandoned their search and gone to get their dinners. The Doctor and his boat passed out of view.

For a whole hour she stayed glued to her corner in an agony of doubt. Was Dr. Hay quietly fishing, moored to the further shore of the islet beyond the chapel? Or had he crept up the tiny creek in that shore, invisible from the house or the sides of the loch, and was he daring to do—what she scarcely dared hope? She waited the leaden minutes quite unable to move; then inwardly cried her remorse to the frail, indomitable old gentleman for doubting him. For the prow of the boat very slowly emerged from the screen of reeds and bushes at the island's far end; and it was riding deep in the water, and the chaplain was straining heavily at his oars. He had taken his burden on board.

Darthula thanked God, as she stood there with tear-stained cheeks, for her father's inspiration in hiding the weapons of his Clan in mock-coffins laid beside those of his ancestors under the stones of the deserted burial chapel. Superstition kept the dwellers in the country-side from landing without necessity among the graves outside the chapel, much more from peering within at the more ancient vaults. Nor would any search-party easily credit that a Chief of the Maceachans should do such apparent violence to religious reverence and natural piety. But she had been of her father's mind, as she pondered with maturer understanding over what had been almost his last words to her as a child: "They were not ashamed of the arms they bore to serve their Clan or their King in life. Why should they repugn to lie beside them in death? The Maceachans never tire of serving!"

And now the little chaplain had found means to prise up the stones with his own unassisted strength, and to collect the arms unseen, that he might place them in the hands for which they had been kept. He was making toilsomely across the loch for the mouth of a burn which widened at the strath not far from where the cottages were most thickly clustered, forming almost a tiny *clachan* or village. But how snail-like was his progress! At any moment, she dreaded, the yawning sentries round the house might suspect the deeper lading of the boat—which had gone out with only a rod and bait and some empty sacks which she had seen the Doctor throwing about—and a shout might be raised. The gap between the craft and the creek by the houses seemed not to diminish even by inches. Once Dr. Hay had brought his precious cargo to the land, it would be safe. The clansmen would wait for nightfall, or, if challenged, would stream out by daylight to take possession of their broad-swords, and it would need more than a score of silly red-coats to deprive them of their arms.

As she could not help by watching, she closed her eyes and prayed. When she opened them at last, the boat had passed into the creek, and was sheltered from view at the loch-head by the depth of the bank. Dr. Hay was strolling along the shore of the lake, throwing a casual fly here and there; and close by the spot where the arms were moored, well-covered, no doubt, by the sacking, a clansman, who had sauntered down from the houses as the Doctor strolled away from them, was lying on his back gazing at the sky, a picture of detached laziness. He would stay there on guard, she realised, till darkness came. Darthula gave a little sob, and sank down where she stood by the window, overcome with weakness and fatigue.

3

WHEN she came to herself it was night, and her eyes were dazzled by the rays of candles. She closed them in pain for a moment; then reopened them, to see the face of Allan Duncanson close to her own, an expression of anguish upon it. He was kneeling beside her on the floor by the window, she realised, as her senses cleared, and was chafing her hands.

"Forgive me!" he said in tones with a deep tremor in them. "Oh! forgive me! Will you believe that it was not until a short hour syne that I learned how they were treating you? Oh! speak, if you can! Tell me, are you bad?"

She struggled into a sitting posture. "It's I am thirsty!" she said hoarsely, "oh! and hungry, too!"

"Wait!" He sprang to his feet and hastened to the door, which, she noticed with inexpressible relief, stood wide. "I bade them make ready," he said, and "Mary!" he called, using the name of her own maid.

While he waited, looking down the passage, Darthula dragged herself up by the window-ledge and peered out. The moon was bright, and she could not see any sign of the boat or its sentinel down by the creek of the strath. She felt assured that the arms had by now been removed and distributed and sank down upon the floor, feeling weak and happy.

Duncanson was at that moment taking a tray from the hands of the little maid, whose curiosity he checked by a firm word of dismissal. Then he approached Darthula again, after carefully closing the door.

She seized the glass he filled with claret, and drank it greedily.

"Go canny! Go canny!" he commanded. "And, here, sop this bannock in the wine, and take it slowly!"

She obeyed, though not used to obedience.

After her long hours of imprisonment and fear she felt a relaxed contentment in being cosseted.

"How comes it," she asked at length with a pale smile, when her pangs were a little assuaged, "that *you* are my deliverer?"

"I had been here sooner, believe me, but that it needed an hour's argument to lead Lord Brounhill to see that he cannot treat you in this barbarous fashion . . . and to make him surrender the key. I could, no doubt, have set my shoulder to the door; but it is better to avoid effraction while there is hope of persuasion. In truth, I do not believe he would have yielded now, if I had not promised to try reasoning with you." He smiled his grave smile, like one who admits defeat in advance.

"You may be sparing yourself those pains," said Darthula, getting to her feet, and holding out her empty glass, "and you may give me instead another small drop of wine. The arms which Lord Brounhill was torturing me to betray to him have been taken from their hiding-place. They are by now in the hands of those who will know how to use them, and he who would recover them may go gather the dewdrops from the heather-bells. Tell my uncle he is welcome now to know their place of concealment. Let him row to the chapel, and see what watch the dead Maceachans kept over King James's swords! Aye, let him go to the chapel, if his conscience does not scorch him before the tombs of the forbears he has dishonoured!"

She swayed a little, and with a firm arm he set her in a chair. "That would not be a peace-making message," he said almost satirically. "His Lordship will learn the truth soon enough; and though I trust I am a leal subject of King

George, I will not intervene in this process. No, there is but one thing that troubles me, and that is your fate, Miss Maceachan. I fear to think what might have happened to you this day, had I not been visiting here."

"You have grounds for fear, Allan!" she answered, letting his Christian name slip out in the emotion of her gratitude. Her eyes were wet as she spoke, and he seemed to her suddenly tall, not gawky, dignified, not solemn. She could appraise the determination it had required to make head against Lord Brounhill as he had done on her behalf—for a guest so to affront his host, for a young advocate so to thwart the powerful Lord of Session who could make or mar his career. And she felt quite sure that when he had said he would have broken in her door to rescue her if her uncle had been obdurate, he had only said what he would have done, without bravado, but without wavering . . . she realised that for a long while Allan Duncanson had obscurely stood for her as a thing unchangeable in an existence that was turmoil, a rock amid her shimmering phantasies.

"What is to become of you?" she heard his grave voice going on. "I dare not leave you in the power of that man! Miss Maceachan, there is an implacability about Lord Brounhill, when his will is crossed—"

"He will be a Highlander, after all!" she said with a touch of pride. "But what can he do to me? His prize has escaped him."

"He means to take you back to Edinburgh, as I warned you."

"If I consent to go! But what then?"

"You will be his prisoner."

"I shall not! I am of age; he is not *my* Tutor; he cannot restrain me whatever."

"He can gain authority to restrain you as a suspected person. You do not realise the peril of your position. He will have himself appointed your gaoler in his own house. No, I see but one means by which you may be delivered."

"One means?"

He opened his mouth as if to make a formal speech; then shut it, paused, and said simply, "You know, Darthula Maceachan, you have known for months all my feelings. Will you give me the right, here and now, to be your protector?"

"And you are willing," she asked half-bitterly, rising from her chair, "to be fettering your advancement by marriage with a—suspected person?"

He brushed the insinuation aside with an angry gesture, and a shining veil of tears blinded her again. She felt herself trembling all over, and clung to the edge of the table for support. As the tear-curtain parted, she saw his eyes, usually so pale, burning with passion in their deep hollows, and an irresistible delight stole over her; the next moment she stiffened against the acknowledgment that his long, bony face, his long, muscle-knotted hands had such power over her.

"No violences, no affronts," he said, "will be offered, I promise you, against the affianced wife of Duncan of Inveralsk. I know I am driven to make my offer on a sudden and without courteous preparation; but necessity drives me, and . . . and . . . Darthula, no prepared speech could better interpret my heart's devotion than these few words . . . all I find in my power to utter."

She was silent.

"Have you no answer?" he asked sadly after a while. "Is it," a sharpness of pain came into his voice, "is it that I am so hateful to you?"

"You are not to think it!" she cried before she could restrain herself. "But it is I have a different loyalty, and I am telling you no lie!"

"Darthula," he said gently, "have a care not to forsake the substance of life for a kingdom of shadows. And indeed, my dear, what is it that you hope to be doing? If there is to be civil war—which God and sanity forbid—are you hoping, like a new Camilla, to lead a band of Amazons on horseback? . . . You will have your own life to make, whatever King sits on the throne!"

His words fell on her with an almost physical force. She knew that she was being offered something sweet and wholesome, a life of solid joys. Love, home, children, a dignified prosperity—she was not insensitive to the value of such a secured life, after her short existence among the feuds and plots, the thwarted designs, the shifting loves and hates and despairs that so often seethed below the tattered mantle of Highland nobility. And there was more, far more than these worldly goods in Allan's offer—there was his own virility, so compelling in spite of his garb of awkwardness, perhaps sharpened by the very contrast. It had indeed been the secret provocation that had made her in past months shower such mockery upon the staid and slow young lawyer.

But let her yield to it—she felt twisted with anguish at the dilemma—and she turned her back upon the rare, the exquisite adventure that had begun in Beasdale Woods. She would be doing what the Camerons had so indignantly repudiated, staying at home, in Edinburgh it would be, to read her Prince's fate in the news-sheets. And yet what more could a mere woman do? She had been of some service; she might even dance at the Court of a King Charles at Holyrood one day for recompense.

If her brother had taken her with him on his abrupt flight it would be different. But she knew Hector. He would never admit that a woman could be of use in sport or war— he could never forgive her for having been the leading spirit in his rather infirm and timorous childhood. He would tell her mockingly to wait behind at Glenmarisdale while he and the Clan went to fight, and she might as well wait at Edinburgh, with a husband.

As she let these thoughts spin through her over-tired mind, her eyes roved distractedly through the room, and came to rest without purpose on the narrow gilt pier-glass in the wall between the bookcase and the cabinet. It was a dim and distorting old mirror, and suddenly in its black depths there appeared to her in a kind of greenish glow the little image of the Prince, with its stereoscopic solidity and liveliness, that had gleamed in the chaplain's cylinder. Fancy had made the image from some beam of moon or spark of candle-light refracted in the glass, and fancy endowed it with a look of reproachful appeal. Ah! what elegance, what graciousness and radiance it made in the faded grey dungeon of her room! How clumsy of attitude, how sombre of face was the man who waited on the other side of the table for the most impossible of answers!

She was only looking at a blur of light in the surface of the mirror, when she said, "I cannot, Allan, I cannot be your wife! I am pledged, indeed I cannot tell how, but I am pledged to another."

4

THE mid-day sun, as the short cavalcade wound its way along the shore of Loch Maris, strengthened to a scorching heat. It struck gold sparks from the ultra-marine wavelets of the lake, and made a dazzling furnace of the heaven between the peaks, moulding the wrinkles of their surfaces and making Acherontic pits of their shadows. The feet of the soldiers beat rhythmically upon the stony track, striking small pebbles up from time to time round their white gaiters. Most of them had slung their muskets over their shoulders, and occasionally they raised a chorus as they marched.

In the centre of the little column rode Lord Brounhill and the other civilians, with the baggage animals plodding some distance behind them. A tiny rear guard of four soldiers with a corporal closed the line.

There was little talking among the travellers, for each had his own dismal preoccupations. Darthula kept glancing from time to time at her uncle, studying his hunched shoulders and the dour mask with the gashes carved at the corners of his lips into which he had again composed his features. She could not help almost morbidly dwelling on the racial fury that lurked behind this human vizor—she had experienced it a few times in her childhood, but never in such a terrifying blaze as yesterday. The law courts of Edinburgh, she reflected, would be amazed if they knew the immovable Brounie capable of such convulsions. It seemed to her, however, that the mask was drawn and haggard to-day, and she could not, though she chid herself for her weakness, help a feeling of sympathy for the man, or repress a query whether there might not lurk somewhere in him, like mountain streamlets welling from the heart of granite, dashes of tenderness or even compassion. For his country, perhaps? Certainly neither his wife nor his daughter nor his wards had often been refreshed by them.

A week ago, it is probable, Darthula would have had no such compunctions. But within those few days she had had a Prince lean his soul upon hers for strengthening; she had gone in terror of her life and of torture, and had not surrendered her loyalty; she had refused the love of the man she loved who now rode just behind her stirrup-iron. She did not perceive how much of her girlhood she had shed, though she was disturbed at the chords that now vibrated within her.

And Brounie at any rate had not stormed at her or tried

to bully since Allan Duncanson had released her. He had simply said, in his quiet creaking tone, that she must go with him to Fort William, a summons she knew she was too much of a prisoner to resist; and he had then added the surprising remark, "I praise you for having had prudence eneuch to decline young Duncanson's offer of marriage. That is a matter can weel wait now." She had puzzled a little over this change of front, without coming to understand it. However, she had been unable not to applaud secretly his sarcasm with the Lieutenant of the red-coats, when that officer came hurrying that morning to tell him that not a man of the Maceachans was to be found in the village and scattered houses by the loch. "Only women, boys and one or two infirm dotards. The rest are fled, I suppose to some secret rendezvous."

"It is a peety," Brounie had retorted, at his most sardonic, "that your intelligence, Lieut. Henderson, whilk is so effective in discovering that thirty or forty stout callants have fled, fully armed, to join the Pretender's son, was not so effective to forestall this accession to the rebels' ranks. You needna shrug your shoulders, mon. Let me warn you, ye maun be sleeping less sound, and rising earlier gin ye would not be surprised by the Hielander on his ain heath." Henderson had replied shortly that he would lose no time in falling back on Spean Bridge to effect a juncture with his superior, Captain Scott, who was marching with two companies of the Royal Scots regiment to stiffen the garrison of Fort William. Lord Brounhill then agreed to accompany him, since there would be no safety for him alone at Glenmarisdale.

With a curious, self-defeating monotony the road ribboned along the side of the loch, passing over promontory after promontory in a gentle switchback. Each little eminence when reached displayed the unfolding of further capes, so that the low hillock with its dark edging of pines that rose in front of a vast grey mountain at the loch-foot seemed never to come any nearer. It was rather as though with deliberate and malicious magic it lengthened the distance between itself and the traveller by the interposition of fresh headlands and unexpected stretches of woodland. It was only when one looked back to the loch-head that it was apparent distance had been traversed. Glenmarisdale House was now a tiny cube, the half-moon of firs a mere sickle, the burial isle a dark lump upon the water, its chapel a barely visible fleck. Darthula from time to time turned her head to the diminishing mansion, as one not knowing when she would see her home again. Every time she did this she noticed that Rob Sanderson, riding at the head of the baggage animals behind her, was craning his head uneasily about at the rocks above, the road behind, the opposite shore, as though he much disrelished his position. The rearguard, another fifty yards at the back of all, were even more casual and careless than the main body. One or two were smoking short clay pipes, and all were listening to a tale that was being told by a man in the centre of the group; no one made any pretence of watching the road.

After a short rest at the foot of the loch when at last it was reached, the *cortège* resumed its journey in the late afternoon, and entered the narrow and steeply falling defile which ran beside the river on its outlet from the lake.

Rob Sanderson's apprehensions evidently increased here; for, without asking permission, he left the baggage-train and urged his pony up into proximity to the gentlefolk. The soldiers, however, pursued their inattentive way, swinging with easy tramp down the windings of the pass, and whistling or singing as they went. At their head the Lieutenant on his grey horse could be seen riding with the same steady indifference. Overhead the sky blazed; the defile was close and scented with its trees; far below the stream sang what suddenly to Darthula's ears seemed a warning song, though for the soldiers it was only a temptation to drain their water-bottles.

The pass opened out into a little natural amphitheatre. To the left spread a grassy space shut in by a low, heather-covered hill, strewn with boulders. To the right the ground fell steeply amid jagged rocks to the river, and the opposite bank mounted sheer in a clothing of birch and pine.

The sound of marching feet grew dull on the grassy track. Overhead the burst of blue, as they emerged from the defile, was blinding to the eye. Darthula put up her hand for a moment to shade her sight as she glanced around; and in that moment saw a slight, short figure spring up beside the solitary pine on the crest of the hillock. A long Chieftain's feather stood in its bonnet, there was a targe on its arm, a broad-sword in its hand. Taut and alert, it stood, as though crouching for a second on its prey, then waved the sword round its head.

An irregular rattle of musketry broke in answer from the hillside and the boulders, reverberating among the cliffs and leaving curls of smoke among the heather. At the head of the marching column, the officer fell from his grey charger like a stone, shot through the head by chance rather than aim; the soldiery, startled and terrified, bunched together in the middle of the road, fumbling at their slung muskets, while the Sergeants dashed in among them, bellowing confused orders. In another second Darthula was torn from her saddle by Duncanson's arm, and flung down under the cover of a large rock by the roadside to escape the next volley.

It never came. Instead there rose a yell as of fiends, and the whole slope of heather fluttered into tartan. Sword-points twinkled in the sun; pipes squealed out like some maddened beast; and Clan Maceachan flung itself in a wave upon the soldiers. Darthula, crouching under the rock, saw a broad-sword shine wet and crimson, as it came, like a needle through silk, out at the back of a scarlet coat, whose owner toppled back with hands clutching at the air upon the roadway. Then Duncanson covered her eyes with his hat that she might witness no more. She heard, however, the frantic clatter of the baggage-animals as they broke back and fled the way they had come, overthrowing the rearguard of the soldiers and sweeping them away in the general panic. Then a voice, at once familiar and utterly strange, cried above the turmoil, "Throw your arms down then! Line up in the middle of the road! Who is the commanding officer?"

She thrust Duncanson's hat aside, and saw the elder of the two Sergeants advancing, his musket held high above his head in token of surrender, towards Hector, who stood now on a rock close by the road. Mackissock the piper was at his side, holding his mouthpiece ready to play to the attack again the moment order was given; and behind him glowed the war-standard of the Maceachans, which had hung in the chapel of the islet since 1715, exhibiting the golden galley and silver salmon of Clan Ranald differenced by a blue water and two trefoils. It was held aloft by a strange, ragged figure whom it took her a second or two to recognise as Angus Maceachan, Hector's foster-brother, miraculously returned in a day from his hiding of years!

The cowed red-coats were obediently lining up in the middle of the road, with a pathetic mechanical habit dressing their ranks as they did so. Donald Dhu the Forester, with his grim-ridged face and long, druidical black beard, now transformed into a Sergeant bristling with arms, was marshalling them into place with harsh monosyllables. Darthula was relieved that the slaughter seemed less than the shrieks she had heard when her eyes were covered had led her to think. The man she had seen thrust through was lying still where he fell in the middle of the road, while a group of clansmen, squabbling like children, ransacked his pockets. Another was curled up on the turf by the roadside, while three more, less gravely wounded, sat near the same place, with others of their enemies disputing how to render rude first-aid. From away down the gully of the stream shouts and occasional shots announced where several of the soldiers had sought refuge, pursued by the flicker of the clansmen's green, red-threaded kilts. Although she had long looked to see it happen one day, she was amazed at the transformation of the quiet figures with soft voices and slow smiles that she knew so well about the House and farms into these warriors with jutting chins and hotly-gleaming eyes—amazed, too, at the number that had been mustered, nearly fifty Claymores in all, she guessed.

Then Hector caught sight of her, and rushed to lift her from the ground. "Darthula, you! Not hurt, not hurt, are you? I never dreamed you would be letting them carry you along with them—else I might have failed to signal the attack! Though, on the other hand," he broke into one of his most provokingly derisive grins, "I might not. This business of man-hunting hath a devilish fascination! I have played no game yet I liked so well.... What do you say, Macvarish?" The old henchman had stepped up, looking far more dignified than his Chief with his white hair, flowing plaid and splendidly burnished weapons. "Their officer is killed, shot through his head? ... I am sorry for that, devilish sorry! Poor Henderson! He beat me at the golf once at Edinburgh. Make every decent disposition of the body, Macvarish; tell their Sergeant he may take six men without arms to escort it with due honours to Fort William. ... Ah! Duncanson!" He had just noticed the lawyer, who had risen from his cover by the roadside and was phlegmatically dusting his clothes. "You will be no fighting man, I perceive!"

"Without a weapon? No, Glenmarisdale."

"That sounds, I am thinking, as if you hoped to fight another day!" Hector grinned.

"Maybe."

There was a note in his voice which made Darthula feel cold in spite of the sweltering sun, the scarcely subsided dust of the late conflict and her own perspiration. She hastened to chide her brother. "You need not be taunting Mr. Duncanson, Hector, and he your prisoner!"

Hector thrust his bonnet back off his forehead and wiped his brow. "Is he my prisoner? I will be damned if I know what to do with him, then . . . or with my Tutor yonder!"

Brother and sister turned to look at Lord Brounhill, still sitting stolidly on his horse. But suddenly there was a savage diversion.

Rob Sanderson, since the fighting began, had been crouching for refuge at Lord Brounhill's stirrup, almost under the belly of his horse. Now, seeing the eyes of Hector and Darthula turned, as he thought, toward him, he resolved on a wild attempt at flight. Instead of slipping down the gully, he dashed in his panic across the road and started to scale the heather-covered hillside. There as he ran he was seen for the first time by Angus Maceachan.

With a fearful cry the returned fugitive drove the haft of the standard into the heather, and leaving it planted there, made after his enemy. Clansmen and soldiers, friends and foes, stood silent together on the road, all watching the terrible chase as though it were a coursing-match. Rob's short legs, spurred by panic, carried him at a marvellous pace, but Angus Maceachan gained on him with leaps like a greyhound's. High up the hillside at last the factor's breath and strength gave out; he staggered, threw up his arms and fell forward on his face. In two bounds his pursuer was upon him; a dirk flashed like a burning-glass in the heather; an appalling howl and moan floated down the hillside. Darthula clapped her hands over her ears, and went white. There was a roar of exultation from the clansmen, and swords and targes clashed together.

Angus returned swiftly down the hill, striding along on his thin legs, and plucking as he came a purple tuft on which he wiped his blade. Then he grasped the standard once more, and resumed his post as though nothing had happened.

"My brother," said Hector in Gaelic, "that was ill-done, and he unarmed."

Angus looked at him with surprise on his starved face. "Our mother," he said, "died in the snow in Glen Dessarry last Christmas night. Let eagles pick the dog's eyes! Hi, Macvarish, have you a flask?"

Hector with a shrug turned back to his sister. "I dare not approach Brounie," he said.

"What! Is it you have fought and conquered the Elector's troops, Hector, and dare not face an old man who is your captive?"

"No! Not on my life! Speak to him for me, Darthula, please. Tell him—My sorrow! What will you tell him?"

"Ninny! Coward!" Darthula stamped. "Tell him you are grieved to have to put him to alarm and peril. Tell him he is free to depart to Fort William or where he will, with his servants, and to take Mr. Duncanson with him under a safe-conduct that you will provide. And that your sister will be going with you."

"The devil you will, Darthula! But I cannot stop you, whatever! Go, tell him as much then!"

"We will go together."

Both victors quailed before the old man's glassy stare, as they dictated their terms with the demeanour of two children begging pardon for a fault.

"Ye think ye are a mighty man of war, Hector, do ye not?" said Lord Brounhill at length, "because ye have surprised these helpless red-coated loons by the aid of the bandits your father and grandfather trained. . . . But it is of the family I am thinking, my grief! and of the lands of our forefathers, and the position they have built up for us! . . . Now all, all is to be pulled down, to make excitement for a feather-brained boy like yoursel', and this mad slip of a lass who leads ye into all the mischief. However, I am done speaking wi' you. God knows if I hae given warnings eneuch! Ye canna blame me, either of you, if I now tak' the measures needfu' to save what may be left of our family fortunes. . . . Weel, what are we waiting for? But I forgot. I suppose it is for me to ask what ye will do with me, young Alexander."

"I am wishing to do nothing, sir, but to safeguard your journey to Fort William or wherever you may desire to go." He detached the badge of golden heath, with the silver brooch that bound it, from his bonnet. "If you will carry this by way of safe-conduct, Uncle—"

Lord Brounhill brushed it contemptuously aside. "I will shelter behind no rebel's badge!" he said. "Do ye think, ye young fule, that Government will not set its foot on your up-risings and pipe-squealings as upon some poisonous beetle? Or do ye think, maybe, that because ye have laid a cattle-thieves' ambush for a Sergeant's guard, for there was little mair to face ye, your bands will break the regiments of Dettingen and Fontenoy? Hae done wi' your posturings . . . am I free to depairt?"

Allan Duncanson approached Darthula to take his farewell. "Pray," she said, "oh, pray be forgetting my brother's unworthy speeches."

"Hard words break no bones, Miss Maceachan," he answered. "I only hope it may not fall to me to break your brother's bones in cruel earnest some day. Aye, God forfend! But I will look for better times yet, times when a man shall be valued by his civil talents and his power of contributing to the happiness and prosperity of his country, not by his craft in tracking his enemy and slaying him when found . . . especially when that enemy is a brother Scot! But you, Darthula, forgive me if I use that name for the last time, may God counsel you and have you ever in His mighty keeping! Your Uncle beckons me, I must go."

Lord Brounhill had collected his little following; the body of Lieutenant Henderson was being strapped upon one of the baggage-animals, and Hector was giving orders for the dead officer's fine grey horse to be led aside for his personal use, a sight which caused the Tutor to mutter, "Aye, the auld riever's bluid, the auld riever's bluid!" Suddenly there was a clatter among the clansmen, and arms were pointed to the hillside.

A man was coming swiftly over the crest, and, after a few moments, the keen-sighted Donald Dhu announced, "It will be a Macdonnell of Keppoch." Excitement buzzed among the watchers as the messenger drew near, his bright scarlet kilt swinging against the heather. He strode up to Hector, crying *"Fáilte!"* and broke into a stream of Gaelic. In a minute the purport of his news was known. Wild cheers went up; the clansmen broke into dances in defiance of discipline; Mackissock set his pipes to his lips and poured forth a skirl of victory.

"Uncle," called Hector through the din. "It is right that I should be telling you this news. This morning Macdonald of Tirnadris and his men took prisoner Captain Scott with two whole companies of his regiment, their colours, drums, and baggage in a running fight that began at High Bridge on the Spean and ended on the borders of Lochiel. So you see, sir," he could not help adding with his imp's grin, "the cattle-thieves will after all be making head against the army of Fontenoy and Dettingen!"

"Laugh!" said the Tutor, "tak' your fill o' merriment!

I perceive, as weel as you, that the heather is breaking into spots of fire. Tak' heed whom the conflagration shall consume!"

Chapter VIII

THE CLANS

1

THERE was no sound but the smack and splash of the oars as the three boats moved steadily towards the head of Loch Shiel. The sky gloomed, sending dashes of rain to wrinkle still further the steely waves with their frills of darting silver; cloud-blankets trailed their lazy lengths along the purple mountain-walls enclosing the long, narrow water-way. As sombre were the pine woods that clothed the lower slopes, alternating with stretches of barren turf. Here and there a tiny hut clung to the steep cliffs, but human activity seemed discouraged from the spot. There were no roads; since leaving the wooded cleft of Glenaladale half-way up the loch, their last resting-place in Moidart, the Prince with his followers and his guard of Clan Ranald and Maceachan warriors, had moved through a region that might have been cursed by Nature at creation, sterile, threatening and death-stricken at its birth.

From time to time as the uneasy water gurgled under the prow of the leading boat, spray of brackish waves broke over the heads of those sitting in it. Darthula Maceachan, turning her face, where she sat beside her brother, to escape the splashes, found her eyes drawn again to Charles Edward in the stern, beside the ragged and rugged old steersman. In spite of the squalls of rain and the cutting wind that blew from the gap between the huge mountains now dimly visible through rents in the clouds at the loch-head of Glenfinnan, he had thrown aside his hat, and seemed to aspire forward to drink in his native airs. The wind fluttered his pale-brown wig; but with his full lips parted, and his eyes piercing the mountain-chains before him to see by the spirit into the heart of his Kingdom, he appeared armoured against the asperities of the weather.

The rowlocks squealed as the patient rowers swung to and fro; the wavelets hissed like laughing fairies under the keel, lifting the boat in a gentle dance; the muffled outlines of the Prince's three ancient counsellors sitting near him in the stern looked like the figures of decrepit sorcerers. The other four of his knights-errant were disposed here and there about the boat, and Hector Maceachan with a pocket dice-box was beguiling the time by playing his right hand against his left. Once Charles, hearing the dice dropping on the wooden seat, glanced at his young champion with a look of peculiar comprehension.

But the most important person, after the Prince, in the boat this morning was undoubtedly the dapper little man who sat at his right hand, absorbedly sorting papers and docketing them from a tiny inkhorn fastened to his button-hole. It was the same small gentleman who, a few weeks ago, had been accosted by Counsellor Penicuik and Mr. Duncanson in the King's Park, and had inquired if there were any news from France. Mr. Murray of Broughton was now enjoying as Private Secretary the fruits of years of unwearied plotting for his master.

Presently he looked up from a letter, and said, "Old Glengarry, sir, writes to inform your Highness that age and infirmity forbid him to lead his Clan. His brother, Lochgarry, and his younger son will lead it in place of his elder son, Alastair, who is in France. I believe your Royal Highness is acquainted with that gentleman."

"Who? Alastair Ruadh? Yes, I know that dare-devil young Glengarry well. *You* sent him to France, Murray, did you not? With a letter forbidding me to come to Scotland. Yet here I am, you see, for all that."

Murray bent his head deferentially over his papers again. But there was a look of obstinacy in his sharp little face nevertheless.

They were drawing near now to the loch-head. A lovely islet with a crown of pines for a few minutes masked the approach; then there opened up a strip of pebbly beach, and behind it a stretch of vivid green herbage with a swampy look, through which the river Finnan seeped its way. The stream flowed from the most desolate of glens, winding away between the folds of the two gigantic peaks, Fraoch Bheinn and Beinn nan Tom. Not a figure stirred anywhere within the view, and no habitation was to be seen, except a small building with only half of a thatched roof, which might in its time have been either cottage or barn.

For some minutes the Prince, balancing himself with a fisherman's skill, had been standing up in the boat, darting his head like a bird's to right and left, his pale-brown eyes dilating and beginning to start forward in consternation. Turning round to Sheridan, "*Mais où sont-ils donc,*" he demanded, "*les hommes de guerre? M'a-t-on donc trahi?*" The keel grated on the beach as he spoke, and he leapt impatiently over the side without waiting for the boatmen's assistance.

The five and twenty men of the escort, the little handful

of friends made such a minute speck at the foot of Fraoch Bheinn, ranked round the little pile of baggage with a mysterious enwrapped pole in the centre of it, that Charles might be pardoned if he abruptly turned his back upon them, and spurning the shingle with his heel, began to pace up and down the swampy sward. Darthula, watching him from a point of higher ground whither she had walked, entered thoroughly into his feelings. To have come so far, buoyed by so many promises, to have expected to step ashore at this spot chosen for the raising of the Royal Standard amid the acclamations and flashing swords of an enthusiastic multitude—and to find instead, emptiness, desolation, the crying of a couple of curlews circling over the marshy ground and the infinitesimal river! The tiny bodyguard had already made a rude bivouac, wrapped in their plaids. They looked, Darthula recognised, like an encampment of vagabonds, while Charles Edward, as he stalked to and fro in his elegant brown coat and scarlet-laced waistcoat, a little yellow rosette in his three-cornered hat, looked every inch the Royal Prince come to take his subjects' homage.

Of a sudden he caught sight of her as she stood alone, and strode up to her. His face was drawn as she had seen it on the *Du Teillay*, and there was the same boyish disappointment in the pale, wide-opened eyes.

"Mistress Maceachan, *you* will tell me the truth, I know. What does it all mean? Am I being duped, trapped?"

"Is it duped or trapped by your loyal Highland people that your Royal Highness will ever be?"

"Ah! Remember Macleod! Remember Macdonald of the Isles . . . breakers of their plighted faith! And old Lovat, haggling and paltering still!"

"Those were never tricks of the Clan Ranald . . . or of the Camerons either, sir."

"Yes, but what then am I to make of it all?" He swept his arm round the frowning solitude. "I fix this spot, by the advice of the Chiefs, for unfurling my father's Standard and reading his proclamation with my own commission of Regency. I name the date and am promised they will all be there with their powers. . . . Where are they? Not one is present. Not even Clan Ranald! By G—, it is an insult to His Majesty!"

"Sir!" insisted Darthula respectfully. "They will be coming. They are only late."

"Late! Late on my summons! I do not understand such fashions, let me tell you, ma'am!" He began to fidget up and down again.

"Sir, with submission, you must take us as we are. . . . And what a treasure your Highlanders will be offering you, in their own time and at their own pace, oh! believe me, your Highness does not yet know!"

There was a thrill in her voice, there were stars in her eyes, which made him stop and gaze. "I believe you!" he cried, "I believe you! They will come yet! Of course they will come! Oh! Darthula, if only they have all hearts like yours!"

"Look, sir!" she cried, pointing. "Am I the teller of truth?"

2

Down the steep hill-road curving from Borrodale through the black woods there came into view a small body of armed men preceded by a single piper playing a melancholy strain that accorded with the spirit of the scene. "They will be Borrodale's men, sir!" said Darthula.

"Are there no more of them?" asked the Prince. "O'Sullivan!" The Irish captain had gradually edged his way to his favourite tactical position within view and call. "Do you mark that?" said Charles in a heartbreaking voice. "There are not above twenty or thirty men coming."

"Ah! sir!" sighed O'Sullivan, "if only they had let me bring over even foive hundred of your Cousin's Irish boys to make a rale army for you!"

The Prince gave an exclamation in an altered voice. Some hundreds of yards behind the advance-guard, which was all he had yet seen, Clan Ranald's main body was coming steadily through the woods. The splatters of rain had ceased, and the dull light that had begun to shed occasional sparkles on the leaden waters of the loch now glinted on the tips of swords and targes. On the column poured, not marching with the disciplined swing of regular troops, but flowing rather like some irresistible torrent from the hills, the rare flashes on its arms resembling somewhat the foaming of the ripples. On they came, more and more of them, descending in flood towards the valley bottom, and there spreading out in a wide green-coloured pool that would fade at any distance into the green and russet tints of the background.

"Look at them, O'Sullivan! Admire them!" cried Charles enthusiastically. "What would you put their numbers at?"

"A couple of hundred, perhaps, sir. It is hard to count a mob."

"Monstrous! There are not less than four hundred there!"

"Four hundred it is, sir, devil a man less! What an *oye* you have!"

"And not a mob either, if you please! They are a fighting force, every movement shows it to my eyes."

"Incredibly stout fellows, sir! They'll do you credit yet—with a little drilling."

Young Clan Ranald himself, followed by his Major, Alexander Macdonald of Glenaladale, now advanced in front of his ranks, to the foot of the little rise where the Prince was standing. "These are our children, sir," he said, saluting. "We are gladly giving them all to you!"

"Ah! Clan Ranald!" said the Prince, "from this moment I cease to envy the Elector his Guards of Fontenoy!"

"God bless your Royal Highness!" answered Clan Ranald stirred for a moment from his deceptively lethargic manner. "These men will go forward or die. They will never turn back!"

"Faith, and that's poor soldiering, sir!" commented O'Sullivan impudently. "Retreat is often the most necessary part of war!"

Clan Ranald looked him up and down with eyebrows lazily raised, as if some insect had reared itself to fantastic heights from the bog. But before he could speak, if he were minded to retort, the Prince cried out again: "More!" he exclaimed with childish delight; "there come more! . . . Yes, and from the other way, too!"

The day was now clear, though dull; the cloud scarves had retired to the top of the peaks and were beginning to float away even from them. In the better light Charles had descried far up the valley a further detachment of nearly a hundred warriors rounding the colossal flank of Fraoch Bheinn. At the same time some scattered parties from the Cameron country could be discerned labouring along the path on Beinn nan Tom opposite.

"That will be my Uncle Morar's force, sir, coming to join me," explained Clan Ranald. "And those others are Cameron men from Glen Pean and Glen Dessarry. Lochiel is at hand with his main power by his own loch." He turned about and pointed to a narrow defile leading from the shore into the winding glen traversed by the Callop River. "I am wondering we do not hear or see him yet."

"You are sure, are you not," Charles answered, thrown back in a moment into his nervous agitation, "that Lochiel will come? He was very hesitant to the last. . . . We cannot hope to achieve anything . . . but worthy deaths . . . without him, can we, Clan Ranald?"

"Having freely rendered his plighted faith," rejoined the Chief with a proud and melancholy smile, "Donald Cameron of Lochiel is as sure to keep tryst as is the night to fall on him and you, sir, and on all of us at last. . . . May we be offering your Highness some refreshment below there, to fill this time of waiting?"

They descended together towards the ruined barn, and Darthula went in search of her brother.

She found him sharing the rough food of his clansmen, the remainder of whom had arrived with the Clan Ranald. "Hector," she asked, "who will be the keenest-sighted of our men?"

"Ask Donald," replied her brother with his mouth full; and the grim sergeant, being appealed to, gave a croak that brought up from the sitting ranks a boy with yellow locks and reckless eyes, whose panoply of broad-sword, dirk, musket and targe seemed to envelop him like a tortoise's carapace.

"Neil, the son of the Bard!" ejaculated Darthula. "Hector, you will never be letting this child spill his blood with the men!"

The boy overheard her and broke into a splutter of barbarous English.

"And for why whateffer waas she not to pe carrying her sword wi' Himself and a' other shentlemens? Waas she a girl to pe left in her home?"

"You see how it is, my dear," said Hector. "That is the way of all of them when I speak of youth or age or sickness. They have no use, it seems, for their lives, except to throw them away for *Phrionssa Tearlach*. . . . Their whole faith is stayed upon that amiable young spark from the Roman

Corso. . . . I would I could wrap myself in their credulity!"

"Hector!" She glanced at the listening clansman and frowned.

"Well!" he shrugged his shoulders and threw away the remains of his lunch. "What service do you require of Neil?"

"Send him, Hector, to a point from which he can be watching the road to Kinlochiel. Let him keep his piece primed."

"He will blow himself to bits!"

"Na, na!" protested the lad. "She waas fera knowledge-able wi' ta gun!"

"So soon as he is sighting Lochiel and his men let him fire the piece in the air—once. I will then be giving his Highness word that the Camerons are coming."

"Is it you are making the fine courtier already, Darthula! First with the good news . . . and the reward, eh? Are you looking to curtsey as a Countess in Holyroodhouse?"

"I am thinking," answered Darthula, "that he is a young man who has borne suspense and disappointment enough. The more they can be shortened, the better for his health—and his cause."

"Well, there will be sense in that," Hector conceded. "A dispirited Prince would be a broken reed indeed." He turned to Neil and gave the boy precise instructions in Gaelic. Leaving the heavier parts of his armament behind, the lad sprang away like a deer, his gun on his back, towards a fan-tastic hillock, wreathed with bright-green foliage, that rose by the shore and overhung the defile leading to Loch Eil.

Slowly the afternoon hours wore themselves away. The clansmen, strolling or dotted on the turf, took their ease with the magnificent indifference of men for whom the clock had never had urgency. From time to time bursts of music from the pipes rose to lose themselves in the vast sadness of the hills, and once or twice a few groups danced reels to the shouts of their comrades. The Prince, after emerging from the barn, had seated himself upon a stray boulder, and was plainly becoming, as the hours passed, a deeper and deeper prey to dejection.

Darthula could do no more to comfort him; she was almost caught by the infection of his doubt, and wondered if Lochiel had been overcome by fresh scruples, and had halted his powers between Achnacany and the trysting-place.

So listless had her spirits grown that she was taken quite by surprise when a puff of smoke shot up between the twisted trees upon the hillock by the road, and the report of a gun rang out, to be taken up in muffled, majestic thunder among the mountains. Charles raised his head sharply, and Captain O'Sullivan came running out of the barn, his napkin still at his throat, roaring, "Mother av God, we are attacked! Save his Royal Highness!"

Both Hector and Darthula started towards the Prince, crying, "There is no need for alarm, sir! It is our scout who sees Cameron of Lochiel approaching!"

"Is that true?" demanded Charles, springing up with his white face pathetically quivering.

"Aren't you hearing the *pibroch*, sir?" shouted Hector.

There could no longer be any doubt. From behind the hill where the scout had been posted there swelled forth a mighty volume of pipe music, with the blood-whipping rattle of drums for its undertone; and, while the encampment swarmed to welcome them, the Camerons began to issue from the defile. The collected pipers of the Clan marched first with long plaids aswing and pipe ribbons fluttering; then came the thudding kettle-drums; and then the Chief himself on horseback, followed by the great crimson standard of his House, emblazoned with his arms on a square green inset. Behind the flag rippled endlessly the red kilts with their shimmer of dark-blue lines; a serpent without a tail their wearers made as they streamed from the glen, more than twice the number of the Clan Ranald array, their broad-swords bright, the spikes and bosses of their targes gleaming.

Charles's face blazed with excitement; his foot tapped the soil in time to the pulse of the drums. "There is a good number of them without any arms at all, sir," muttered O'Sullivan in his ear, but he paid no heed to the grumbler. His eyes were fixed on the Chief, who had dismounted and was coming across the grass to salute him.

Donald Cameron of Lochiel was dressed to a greater degree than the other Highland gentlemen present in the fashion of the day. His hair was carefully powdered and tied with a black ribbon. Beneath the plaid that flowed from his shoulder was a claret-coloured velvet riding-coat with gold-laced cuffs. His clear, grey eyes were large, with the slightly strained look of a man perpetually harassed by conscience in all his doings. His face was square and sensible; but the lips fell away again into melancholy, which had drawn its lines at the corners of the mouth.

After warm greetings exchanged, he took his stand with Clan Ranald by the Prince, to watch the still unfinished defiling of his men into the open by the loch-side.

"Who are those red-coats?" asked Charles of a sudden. "Prisoners? . . . Prisoners already? . . . And so many?"

"They are the men of the Royal Scots, sir, whom Keppoch and I took between us the other day in the Great Glen."

"Are those not officers walking with them?" said Charles quickly. "We must release them, so soon as we can get their *parole*. I would not have gentlemen I look to see one day serving me in my army feel degraded in my presence. You will see to it, will you not, Lochiel?"

The march-past continued, the column slowing step amid the cheers of the other clansmen, as it wound its way round the grassy space, to form in a triple line across the valley mouth; and after a little while Donald Cameron, glancing at the Prince, who had fallen strangely silent, saw tears stealing out of his eyes and hanging on his cheeks. Their looks met, and Charles in a choking voice faltered out, "Oh! Lochiel, what are you giving me? . . . I had not understood before, I think. . . . When I surmise the fate I may be preparing for these noble fellows—"

"Sir," said Lochiel quietly, "if they fall, I will come back for more. If I fall, my successor will be doing the same. To this end our mothers bore us, to serve our Prince and King."

Unable to speak, Charles grasped the Chief's hand in passionate gratitude. Lochiel started a little, as though disconcerted; then his firm grey eyes shone with a soft light, and uncovering, he stooped to kiss the Prince's hand that held his own. And from that hour he followed his friend, unquestioning, uncomplaining, through peril and pain, to ruin and death in exile.

"See, sir!" was all he said. "Macdonnell of Keppoch's battalia follows close on my heels!"

A continuous roar went up, as the fresh mass of warriors came flooding through the gap, to mingle with the throng that filled the marshy flat to overcrowding.

3

IT WAS no simple matter, with the rude Highland notions of drill, to range the assembly in order for the ceremony of raising the Standard. By the time they were duly drawn up round a small hump of ground not far from the ruined barn, the sad day was already beginning to expire. At sunset a bar of yellow light had torn the sky away down the loch, and was now filling the hollow where the Clans were gathered with a pale, uneasy lambency. Darthula, after joining herself to a knot of civilian sympathisers, gentlemen and ladies, who had ridden out from their homes to witness the spectacle, found that she was too short to see what was happening in the crowd, and climbed the hillock above to the side of the boy Neil, who was cracking his fingers and hopping like a goblin from leg to leg, enthralled at once by his liberty from the ranks and by the sight below him.

She reached the point where he was dancing just in time to see a little procession ascend the knoll underneath—first the Prince, with his yellow-ribboned hat, then the old Marquis of Tullibardine, followed by a stalwart clansman with the Standard furled over his shoulder; then Sir Thomas Sheridan hobbling, and the Chiefs crowding behind him. The Prince walked a little apart from the others, and stood outlined alone, looking down upon his host.

There was a stir in the centre of the group, and the weighty Standard of red, white and blue, already consecrated by the Catholic Bishop, Hugh of Morar, was seen to be with difficulty shaking out its silken folds, like a bird that would escape from a snare. There was no wind, and in the feeble gripe of old Tullibardine it fell together again as though it would collapse. Then the sturdy gillie who had borne it to the spot seized it again, and helped to shake it out with his powerful arms, till the heavy folds rippled and the colours shone clear in the strange, illusive rays of the waning sun. Immediately the Prince uncovered his proud young head, and over the bonnets of the multitude below the sword-blades gleamed out like a storm of sleet, accompanied by a stern roar of cheering, by the impulsive discharge of muskets in the air, and by a mad skirl of all the pipes together.

Darthula's heart gave a great leap. The man who had landed at Borrodale with seven adventurers for his train; who last week in the bare house beside the secret, flowery bay of Kinlochmoidart—enchanted demesne for a Kingdom of Dreams—had held his court with a handful of armed clansmen, while the pipers played before him in the low-beamed dining-room, and the country-folk flocked in to worship, as before some sacred relic; this man had in a month evoked the dark, the tossing and tumultuous sea before her, which still sent its breakers of sound against the barrier of the surrounding mountains.

The Chiefs upon the mound signalled a long while in vain for quiet, while Tullibardine unfolded the parchment engrossed with King James's commission of regency for his son. The old man's cracked voice was inaudible at more than a few paces; but as soon as he lifted his hat to call for loyalty to Prince Charles, the echoing thunder rolled hearteningly round the crags again.

Then the Prince, stepping to the edge of the knoll, raised his hand for silence. A stillness followed in which only the complaining cry of an eagle could be heard, high up among the precipices. The youthful voice floated vigorously over the crowd; Darthula straining her keen ears could now and again make out a phrase from its utterance: "As much to procure your welfare and happiness as to assert my father's right . . . I chose that part of these islands where I knew I should find brave gentlemen fired with the noble example of their predecessors. . . . With the protection of a just God Who never fails to avenge the cause of the injured!"

The day faded fast as he spoke; already the restless mists were wreathing the peaks again and creeping over the floor of the valley; he ended his address as a faceless figure, half drowned in shadow. But his voice had been defiant to the last, and when it ceased the tempestuous roaring broke forth again, more menacing than ever in the darkness.

It seemed but a few minutes later that the red eyes of watchfires were winking through the mists all over the ground, sparks from the furnace that in this hidden spot was preparing a flame to erupt all over Britain.

Chapter IX

CHANGING THE GUARD

1

COUNSELLOR PENICUIK, cloaked and with a cudgel in his hand, came out of his chambers in Mylne's Court just as the clock of St. Giles's finished striking four of the morning, to find that the mists had enveloped Edinburgh. The sight of the white vapours oozing through the tunnel that led from the Court sheer down towards the Nor' Loch did not, however, deter him from his untimely promenade; it only sent him in again to fetch a scarf. He knew it was no use trying to sleep any longer; and he meant to find out, if he could, what was really happening.

Never, he considered, had a capital been so humiliated as Edinburgh during these September days. He could not understand how things had been allowed to come to such a pass. Why had General Cope, after marching off to fight the Young Chevalier, faded away to the north, and left him unopposed to lead his Highland rabble straight down through Scotland upon Edinburgh? . . . Madness! . . . They said Cope was now hurrying back, as fast as sail could bring him, by sea to Leith, to try to save the capital. What if the winds were more sluggish than Highlanders' red shanks?

So thought the Counsellor, standing a while in the mouth of the court, coughing a little in the mist, and feeling for his snuff-box as he listened. The High Street, up and down, appeared to be empty, though one could not see as far as the Castle one way or the Tolbooth the other for the drifting white curtains. It was a very odd mist, so dense for the time of year.

Not denser, however, he thought with a malicious little smile, as at length he began warily to descend the High Street, than the fog in the minds of those who should be defending the city. Archie Stewart, the Lord Provost . . . his game was well enough kent! The more he protested his loyalty to King George, the more plainly he blazoned his treason. Not that a straighter man could have done much with the only resources that it seemed Edinburgh could command. The walls, Counsellor Penicuik believed, were rotten in spite of the efforts the Professor of Mathematics from the University had made to restore them. The Castle garrison, under old General Guest, refused to stir from its lair. The Town Guard was senile. The Edinburgh Volunteers . . . hech, sirs, a braw showing they had made!

Mr. Penicuik had come opposite Parliament Close, and paused to take a peep within. A single light made a blur in a window high up in one of Inigo Jones's Gothic pepper-pots; and a sentry of the Town Guard stood in the square underneath the uplifted hoof of Charles II's stone charger, which seemed to be kicking at his head from the fog. Otherwise the whole place was shrouded and deserted.

The Counsellor, after hanging about a little while, came out again in the High Street, his mind recurring to the shameful behaviour of the Volunteers. Summoned yesterday to the Lawnmarket by the clang of the fire-bell disturbing the Sabbath sermons, they had been invited to march out with

Hamilton's Dragoons to support Colonel Gardiner's squadrons, which were awaiting the rebels' advance at the village of Corstophine some six miles from the city. They had set off bravely down the West Bow; but as they went their courage, moistened by the tears of wives and sweethearts, had melted so fast that by the time the West Port was reached they had nearly all slipped away down the wynds and closes on the route, leaving their captain almost alone. . . . That young Mr. Duncanson, one of the handful who had held fast, had been paler than ever with anger at being made to cut such a figure, and had sworn he would find some other corps to serve in. . . . A braw showing in sooth!

Out of the fog there took shape suddenly a livery-stable coach, its lamps shedding yellow patches on the mist. It had been standing outside a tavern by the Mercat Cross, and as Mr. Penicuik approached it began to jolt slowly down the hill. Who the devil, thought the Counsellor, standing still, was abroad at this hour in a coach?

He decided to follow, keeping it in view, while he reflected that after all the Volunteer lads could hardly be blamed when one remembered the show the Dragoons themselves had made the same afternoon.

At a shot or two from the scouts preceding the advance of the Highland host, they had turned about from Corstorphine and galloped in a mad panic towards Leith, flying along the Lang Dykes beyond the Nor' Loch like a flare of red sparks through the gorse. All Edinburgh had seen their "canter" from the walls—and that was how King George's regulars defended his Scottish capital, sirs!

After that, it seemed, the Lord Provost had had no idea except to despatch one deputation after another to the Young Chevalier's headquarters to try and negotiate with him. Though Mr. Penicuik did not know it, the coach which was going at the slow pace of its wearied horses down the hill in front of him had just brought back the latest emissaries with a simple demand for the surrender of the city; and after setting them down was now seeking its stables in the Canongate beyond the Netherbow. What worried the Counsellor was that you never knew where these d——d Hielanders were. They gave you the glaiks like any Jock-o'-lanthorn! Yesterday they were at Corstorphine to the west of the city. . . . Last night it was reported they were at Gray's Mill down to the south. . . . And where would they be now in this fog? Aye, that was the point!

Mr. Penicuik still followed the hazy yellow lights of the coach, and presently the tower of the Netherbow Port showed black through the mist, which was turning more silvery in the first dour glimmer of the dawn. From the Guard Room of the gate proceeded drunken choruses and altercations—"Gudesakes!" murmured the Counsellor, "it is as weel the enemy does not know the quality of our defenders!"

He quickened his step, and came up under the arch of the gateway in time to hear an angry argument between the coachman, who insisted that he must take his horses back to their stables outside, and the ancient Private of the City Guard who had been left with five comrades to keep the watch while their officer went to bed; and who maintained, as he swung a lantern to and fro, that he had no authorisation to give egress or ingress to anybody. "There was a loon in a hunting-cape out yonder a while syne, said he maun enter wi' a message for his master, a Dragoon officer; but we drave him awa'," grumbled the veteran.

At length the coachman seemed to have quoted some sufficient authority, for keys clashed together, and the old "Town Rat" stooped to unlock the gates. Slowly he and one of his comrades swung back the heavy iron-studded leaves. A grey light flowed into the gloomy archway as the gap widened, dimly defining the Guardsman's three-cornered hat and the Counsellor's beaked nose above his muffler. Beyond the gate a spangled curtain trembled, through which the overhanging shapes of the Canongate houses loomed. The coach thundered with alacrity out of the arch, and its yellow beams swept fanwise and disappeared into the mist.

For a minute the two watchers and the Counsellor stood peering through the open gates into the void . . . one minute too long! A roar, a shriek of pipes, a dance of giant, kilted shadows leaping on the mist; then through its torn ribbons rushed the ambushed swordsmen of Lochiel.

Mr. Penicuik jumped behind a leaf of the opened gate, and squeezed himself into the space between it and the wall with a vigour he had not displayed for years; while the archway filled with the tumult of the clansmen, brandishing their weapons and swarming into the guard-room, whence came yells and the crash of glasses. More followed, pouring through the gate into the High Street, which they filled with a turbid, shouting stream that nevertheless preserved a loose cohesion. Behind, leading a second company, came pipers playing derisively:

> "We'll awa' to Sherramuir,
> To haud the Whigs in order!"

Suddenly Mr. Penicuik perceived a familiar figure hurrying through the archway, and started from his hiding-place to pluck his sleeve.

"Gudesakes!" he panted, "it is never you, Mr. Murray . . . Murray of Broughton!"

The little gentleman jumped round; and in spite of his jack-boots, sword and pistols, seemed relieved to find he had no more formidable challenger.

"Counsellor Penicuik!" he stammered. "You were safer in your home, I think. But we shall not harm you if you make no opposition to us," he added importantly.

"We, Mr. Murray? We? Are you, then, one of the Chevalier's soldiers?"

"I have the honour to be Private Secretary to His Royal Highness the Prince Regent. Follow me, if you wish to be safe, Mr. Penicuik!"

He shouldered his way through the press out of the gate, the Counsellor sticking close to his heels, and paused to speak to an officer of the Camerons on the causeway. The latter waved his claymore towards the Castle. The pipes continued to rage, the dark figures of the Highlanders to stream cheering through the arch. Already the keys of the port had been secured and a new Watch set. Under the pinnacles of the tower the clock, unseen in the murk, slowly, regretfully pealed five through the turmoil.

Mr. Murray took the Counsellor aside on to the pavement. "Things are changed, Mr. Penicuik," he said with a shade of pompousness, "since we last met in Edinburgh."

"Aye. I mind ye were speiring the news fra' France. A bonnie wee bit news you and your frien's hae brought us this morn!"

"Hush! Counsellor! That borders on treason. I presume you wish to keep your robe?"

Mr. Penicuik shrugged his shoulders and sought his habitual consolation. "And wha' may yon cater— yon men of war be?" he asked, opening his snuff-box.

"This is Cameron of Lochiel's power. Look, there he goes himself!" Lochiel at that moment had ridden through the gates, and striking sparks from the stones in the half-light, cantered swiftly up the High Street, accompanied by a wave of cheers and tossing bonnets.

There were lights in many windows now, and cautious heads protruding; but after a Highlander with a dram of whisky on his empty stomach had discharged a musket at random and caused a tinkle of falling glass, most of the candles went abruptly out again.

Back came Lochiel at a fast trot. "Put that man under arrest," he shouted. "I will have no violences or pillaging, do you hear, all of you?"

A profound stillness fell on the marching column, and only the scrape of their feet on the stones could be heard as they toiled upwards, their red kilts dully staining the muddy light.

"Ah!" mused Mr. Penicuik, snuffing himself thoughtfully. "Your Lochiel is a gallant gentleman, I winna say you nay to that. But he little kens whaur he may be driven . . . or in what company, in this civil strife."

His sharp lawyer's eyes gave close scrutiny to the files of the clansmen as they passed. He noted the proportion of greybeards and mere boys, with one or two whom he would have called cripples hobbling stoutly along nevertheless. He remarked the number of bare feet slipping, blue-bruised or even bleeding, over the rough edges of the stones, and was quick to pick out where here and there an antiquated Lochaber axe, a scythe or even a bill-hook supplied the place of broad-sword or musket. Yet these deficiencies, he had to own, were swallowed up in the determination, the blithesomeness, the strength of the spirit that bore the Clan along. The patches were only on the hem of the garment.

"We have all the honourable gentlemen of the Highlands with us," boasted Murray in his ear. "Look, there go Major Cameron of Errachd and Cameron of Torcastle. . . . I am waiting to have word with Macdonald of Glenaladale so soon as the Clan Ranald contingent enters."

"Aye, ye hae a' the chieftains, nae doot! But I note ane thing ye dinna seem to have gained."

"And what is that, pray?"

"The population ò' this capital, Mr. Murray! I dinna hear

a voice to welcome you. Nor a pairson . . . forbye mysel' and yon lost cur in the gutter . . . that has come out e'en for the pleasure of a glisk at ye!"

"Pooh! What signifies that, Counsellor? The citizens of any town are at first afraid of an invader. They will learn to know us better . . . Ah! yonder I think I see Glenaladale coming through the port."

"I know him not. But, tell me, is that no' my young acquaintance, Maceachan of Glenmarisdale, wi' him?"

"That is Glenmarisdale—a shrewd young officer, too. I approve of Glenmarisdale."

"God abune us! What a rencounter! What will have become, I wonder, of his lovely sister?"

"She has marched with us, like my own wife, and several other gallant ladies."

Mr. Penicuik creaked his snuff-box, his little eyes glinting with malicious amusement. "And sae ye hae an Amazonian cohort too! And is that a fac'?"

"I must leave you, Counsellor. I advise you, go home!"

"I thank you. And I wish no harm may befa' you pairsonally, Mr. Murray."

The secretary was politely lifting his hat when it fell from his fingers on the stones. "Wh-wh-what is that?" he stammered, paling as he stooped to pick it up.

A roar like the voice of some deep-throated monster in a lair above their heads had reverberated hollowly through the mist; the marching column had sagged to a standstill.

Mr. Penicuik, not without a tremor shaking his little legs, took snuff with a flourish. "That, my gude sir," said he, "is anither thing that ye hae maybe forgotten. Yon is the voice o' King George, speaking from the Castle Rock. Ye will hae your wark cut out to storm that place, Mr. Murray."

A message came down the halted line, and the advance was slowly resumed.

Mr. Penicuik heard one Highland officer say to another, "They will be setting the outposts at the Weigh House up yonder."

"My grief! Will they not be for rushing the Castle instanter?"

"Not this morn, I am thinking."

"No!" chuckled Mr. Penicuik, as he turned away. "Not this morn, nor the morn's morn, nor many morns to come, by my way o't!"

He escaped up a wynd, and so by many stairs and gardens came deviously home at last to his chambers in Mylne Court. He was gratified to find that his porridge was no less punctual and hot because, since he last crossed his threshold, Edinburgh had been assaulted and taken by storm.

2

MEANWHILE in the turret of the Parliament House where Mr. Penicuik had observed the solitary candle glimmering through the fog on his descent, Lord Brounhill still slept, his head on his arms upon the table. Sleep had overtaken him, without his knowledge, while he laboured to combat with his pen the inertia and muddle of the civic authorities all around him.

To this little chamber, often used as a retiring-room by the judges, he had finally withdrawn after a day of discouraging conferences—in the morning with the Lord Justice Clerk, who had afterwards left Edinburgh for his country house, and then with the Lord Advocate and the Solicitor-General, who had promptly followed their superior; during the afternoon and evening at frequent intervals with the Lord Provost and the members of the Town Council. In none did he find either counsel or resolution, and he had at last betaken himself to this quiet corner to frame careful memoranda calling for the enrolment of fresh and stouter volunteers, for a more active part in the defence by the Castle garrison, and for the preventive arrest of known Jacobite sympathisers.

Further, he had written a long letter to Duncan Forbes, the Lord President of the Council, who as early as the beginning of August had gone north to his family seat at Culloden, in order to grapple with the rebellion at its source and restrain if he could the wavering chiefs. In this he set forth the whole lamentable situation, and begged Forbes to infuse more vigour, if he was able, into the Government in London. But it was doubtful, he reflected dismally, as he stopped to rest his tired eyes and cramped wrist, whether this letter would ever reach its destinatory. Forbes was the only *man* on the Government side, even though too clement by nature; but how could Forbes act at once in Inverness, in Edinburgh and in London? And so reflecting, Lord Brounhill had dropped asleep upon his papers, leaving his candle still burning into the wan, mist-covered dawn.

He awoke stiff and chilled, and went to the window to see what was stirring. As last night, he saw the tip of a sentry's Lochaber axe under the upraised hoof of King Charles II's stone charger. Something, however, about the headgear of this watcher struck him as unfamiliar. He unlatched the window and thrust his wigless head out into the square. The sentinel turned about at the sound and looked at him in equal surprise.

My Lord Brounhill's low forehead puckered with bewilderment. "Wha may you be, fellow?" he demanded. "Ye are no the guard that was posted here last night."

"I am not," replied the Highlander casually. "She waas reliefed. What service will I pe doing your honour?"

From the High Street came a triumphant cry of pipes as the new Town Guard, set by Cameron of Lochiel, paraded in warning to enemies and marauders.

3

UP CAME the full sun at last, melting the mists into the blue
and gold of a perfect September day. Despite the bustle in
the streets—the new guard piping on its rounds, the barri-
cades going up in front of the Weigh House dome at the
head of the High Street, to defy the Castle across the narrow
no man's land of the parade-ground; despite the bands of
Highlanders, peering with ejaculations into the shop windows, clashing their weapons with ferocious shouts and stepping off the pavement to give way to every woman they met;
despite the coming and going of alarmed civic officials in
coaches, a timeless air brooded over the captured city. Normal life was suspended, a blank query took the place of the
future; and in this enforced relief from plans and business the
citizens of Edinburgh had unwonted leisure to survey the
beauties of their wind-swept town, bathed now in the delicacy of its autumnal colouring. The hand of war laid on the
capital had stilled it to a paradoxical peacefulness.

Everyone who could make excuse for it was out of doors.
A large crowd still swayed in front of Holyrood Palace,
staring at the two splendid sentries in Cameron tartan with
spiked targes, who stood below the crown of stone over the
carved doorway; and seeking in its mind to read the riddle
within—the Prince who had been lodged there now for several hours. Many thoughts stirred this assemblage besides
simple loyalties to James or George. Patriots, still resentful
of the Union, dreamed a dream of Scotland's independence
won again; merchants calculated the value of a Court in
Edinburgh and the possible restoration of the Mint; ministers
of the Kirk saw the encroaching shadows of popery and
prelacy blot the sunlit turrets. But all were silent, glancing
each man askance at his neighbour, as though opinion were

a treasure and not to be cheaply sold.

But by mid-day a still larger throng had gathered round the Mercat Cross. Here tongues seemed loosened, for a feeling of relief was spreading. There had been, after all, no bombardment and no storm of the city; it seemed certain now that there would be no sack of it. In spite of their wolfish looks, these Highlanders, it seemed, were, after all, no children of Attila. A little pilfering from the exposed wares on the Luckenbooths, a few truculent demands for "Ransom!" appeased by a dram of whisky or the gift of a bawbee, seemed all that Edinburgh need fear. And as for the women, Trongate Meg had voiced the opinion of her sisters when she declared, "We maun e'en set out to rape these Hielan' men!" Many sentimental glances already followed the flying locks, the bare legs and the gay kilts rippling against the smoke-blackened walls of the old Puritan stronghold.

For the moment the theatreless city, starved of shows, was eagerly awaiting the diversion of King James's proclamation at the Cross. Jovial faces shone in the sunshine of the street, and only here and there at windows appeared the shadowy frown of city fathers and Whig notables.

"Come, father!" cried a sparkling voice; "there is room at the top of these stairs, and we shall see the whole show! Ned Burke keep close by us, and give heed that his lordship is not jostled—is a good thing that we have a Hielander to protect us this day!"

It was Jean who spoke, dressed in silk and ribbons as if for a fête, a wide-brimmed straw hat perched saucily on her head, and the gold bands of her hair shining through a pinner of fine lawn that came down to be crossed upon her bosom. She skipped up one of the worn stone flights of steps leading to house doors over shop fronts, and stood with her mittened fingers on the iron rail, looking over the heads of the crowd round the Cross. Lord Brounhill followed her, his hands, powerless now for good or ill, clasped behind his back, his eyes dull and impenetrable. Ned Burke's carroty head made a mark in the surging throng below as he kept the foot of the stair for his patrons.

"They are coming!" cried Jean, standing on her toes and clapping her hands as the music of pipes floated joyfully up the hill from Holyrood, followed shortly by the grave, melancholy face of Lochiel riding in front of his clansmen. Behind followed the heads of Clan Ranald, Keppoch, Stewart of Ardsheals and other chiefs, carried slowly along, it seemed, upon the river of steel that was forcing its way between the gay banks of the crowd. Last came two figures the sight of which caused Lord Brounhill to utter a snarling exclamation.

"Look!" he growled to his daughter. "Look! Yonder goes your bonnie cousin Darthula a-horseback, exheebiting hersel' to a' this rabble like a play-actress! A proud day for our fam'ly! A gran' show, truly, ye have brought me out to see!"

The people of Edinburgh, indeed, were throwing up their hands with exclamations at the spectacle of two ladies among the armed men, both splendidly mounted and draped in tartan, with white cockades in their bonnets and a bagful of the same at their saddle-bows, to distribute to the recruits they hoped to enlist after the proclamation. One of them, a tall, red-haired beauty, was Mrs. Murray of Broughton; the other, as her uncle had recognised with horror, was Darthula Maceachan.

"Will you tell me so, father?" murmured Jean, her scarlet lips parted in amazement. "And is yon Darthula? Who could have believed it?" She uttered a little scream. "Only look, now, at that savage brute she is riding, rearing himself straight up! I admire at her courage . . . and she such a wee thing to hold the beastie!"

"Courage! Impudence, brazen impudence, the hizzie!

That is if my poor opeenion weighs still wi' you, or wi' anyone else in Edinbro'!"

"Och! Darthula must aye be exhibiting herself, as you
say, to someone or another as an object of interest." Jean
smoothed down the lace on her bosom, with a side glance at
a young man below who was looking at her. "It is nothing
extraordinar'. . . . Oh! father, see the man in the gay
jacket! . . . Herald, do you call him?"

"We'll unherald him, I'll uphaud you!" grunted Lord
Brounhill. "Though," he checked himself gravely, "I am
no that sure ye can behead or hang a herald by ony law."

A silence had fallen in the space round the battered grey
cross. From the stone balcony running round the octagonal
arcading of the monument Roderick Chalmers, Ross Herald,
was reading the proclamation in a voice that boomed back in
confused echoes from the buttresses of St. Giles. At the conclusion he rolled up the red-ribboned parchment and waved
it round his head, inviting cheers for King James VIII. There
was an instant's pause, and then a faint and fluttered sound,
more disheartening than a defiance, drifted across the Square.
Swiftly Lochiel raised his blue bonnet and released the throats
of his men. *"God save King James!"* The roar that leapt
from the ranks behind him hit the Laodicean crowd like a
shot, causing it to sway back and nearly trample its own
members in alarm, though not a clansman had stirred from
his position.

Darthula's fretful charger reared high again at the noise,
and her hair fell with gleams of copper from under her bonnet upon her neck. She pressed forward, however, among
the throng, with Mrs. Murray doing the same upon the other
side of the Square, and boldly challenged all the young males
present to accept the white cockade and enlist for King
James. A forest of hands went up to snatch the ribbons she

strewed like white roses over their heads, and she was loudly cheered.

"Extraordinar' insanity!" muttered Lord Brounhill. "This is high treason, pure and simple . . . nae mair play-acting! Enlisting men for the Pretender, God save us a'!"

"Hoots!" said his daughter composedly. "Do you think there is a man or a lad here that means to go fechting? They only wish to attract the eye of a moderately handsome wench that knows no better than to expose herself to their insults."

"She waves a claymore now, the demented wretch! Do you mark how they cheer, Jean?"

"Aye, and laugh too. Do you hear them laughing? Let us go home! You are right, father; yon is an offensive spectacle!"

4

IT WAS not a long journey, though impeded by the press, back to Advocates' Court. As they turned the last spiral of the stair before reaching their lodging, Jean, who was going first, gave a joyful exclamation.

"Hector!" she cried at sight of a slim figure, wearing a feathered bonnet and a silver-mounted broad-sword, that waited outside the door, and she gave him her cheek for greeting.

"Fortune will be smiling at last!" he said, taking his opportunity with a warmth that made her blush. "I was beginning to think they had orders within not to admit me—or perhaps to admit no wild Highlander at all!" He broke off as the shadow of his Tutor appeared on the wall round the curve of the stair. "Good-day, sir!" he said, saluting Lord Brounhill.

There was a silence. "Have you no greeting at all for me, uncle?" he asked.

"I tauld ye the last time we met—in sic agreeable circumstances as ye will doubtless remember—that I had nae mair to say to you, sir. Ye come here now wi' your hands red wi' the bluid of the King's soldiers. . . . I admire at your nerve. Ye are like to be the curse o' your father's house. Get you gone fra' ma sight!"

"He shall not!" cried Jean, her cheeks more hotly aflame than before. "What, father, you would send Hector away without a glass of wine or a word of welcome, just for your political differ? Think shame to yourself."

She rasped the tirling-pin with an indignant hand, and when the door was opened led the way into the large room without waiting for her father's permission.

Hector jumped in after her, a grin, unseen by the Tutor who followed behind, upon his face.

"Sit ye down, Hector," said Jean coolly, "in your old seat in the window. Tell me all that has befallen you since we last met. . . . Father, are you coming in or staying out? Anygates close the door; we can smell the dinner cooking!"

Her father gave her one of his glassy stares and went out, shutting the door behind him.

Hector sputtered into laughter. "Oh! Jean! Jean! Is it not the misfortune now for the criminal class that you are not an advocate in his lordship's Court? For you would be winning your case every time!"

"I do not like father to be unreasonable," said Jean quietly, seating herself and taking off her hat. "Though he has much to try him these days. . . . You are a trial especially, Cousin Hector; what is it you would be at?"

Hector eluded the inquiry. "It is good to be back here again," he sighed, looking round the grave room with its polished black furniture glimmering in the greenish light from the bottle-glass of the window. Outside the rumour of the mob beat up faintly like waves at the foot of a cliff.

"Yes," he said, "after so many days marching, and counsel-
ing, and quarrelling—"

"And fechting, Hector?"

"Too little fighting for my taste, my dear! But it is pleasant, anyway, to be back in this old room, and it always a
home to me—I cannot quite tell what way, for I have always
been a trial to your father, as you say, and it is he has never
spared to let me know it!"

He was aware that he was not being at all truthful when
he said that he did not know the reason why the grim lodging
in Advocates' Close had the charm of home for him. The
reason sat in front of him in a stiff oak chair, with one hand
tracing out the carving on the arm of it, and the other
dangling her straw hat by the ribbons; and from her shining
hair under the lace pinners to her little arched feet in their
red-heeled shoes, she was a delectable vision, trim, plump
and, with her cool smile, infinitely provocative. It seemed to
him suddenly that for the past two months nearly he had
seen nothing but male faces, gaunt and bearded, or crafty
and courtier-like. Darthula did not count, of course, and
lovely Mrs. Murray was of a disconcerting faithfulness, even
in words and glances, to her pompous little rat of a husband.
. . He let himself relax, the first time really for weeks,
while he murmured, "Everything the same . . . as if nothing extraordinar' had happened! Here I am in the window,
and there are you in your chair, just as we used to be sitting
when we were lad and lassie . . . you looking round for
your tambour as you always did. We only lack Darthula by
the fire-place, keeping guard, the jealous little cat, lest I
should steal kisses!"

"Hector! Will you have done? It is a long while syne you
had any such thoughts about me!" She flushed rosily, but
her eyes danced.

Hector jumped up, but sat down again abruptly as the

door opened and Lady Brounhill entered, cold and formal.

There were salutations without warmth, and his aunt went straight to the chair by the fire, where he had been picturing Darthula, and sat down with the air of a sentinel.

An awkward silence followed. Jean laid her hat on the table and picked up her tambour-work of the crimson apples. From time to time she shot side glances at her mother, as though understanding who had sent her. Hector, with his lips tightly pursed, studied Lady Brounhill's handsome head with the mob-cap and pearl ear-rings, and reflected that it was plain whence Jean got her elegance, though not her charm.

"And have you no news for us, Hector?" asked Jean after a while, breaking the silence as she bent over her needle. "What will you be doing with us all?"

"You I will be taking prisoner," he answered lazily. "Yes, Jean, I shall carry you off . . . to the first ball at Holyrood-house."

"There will be no balls for the present, I am thinking, Hector."

"Indeed, and will there not? A hundred Highland gentlemen starved of beauty since July! And how many hundred Edinburgh ladies dying for a glimpse of our handsome Prince?"

"I would like fine to meet your bonnie Prince Charlie," confessed his cousin, meeting her mother's formidable glance with defiance.

"Will you bring her, ma'am, if I procure the invitation?" asked Hector point-blank of Lady Brounhill; and as she turned her head to annihilate him he added a sigh. "But I fear I will be forestalled. It is you will be commanded. I have seen the list in Sir Thomas Sheridan's own hand."

"What list, Glenmarisdale?" asked his aunt.

"The list for the first levee. Lady Stair's name came first.

and it was struck out and yours substituted."

Jean darted a furious glance at him from under her lashes, and bent her head again over her embroidery. He saw that her lips were fighting with a smile, nevertheless.

"I dinna ken, Glenmarisdale," said Lady Brounhill in a gentler voice, "why my name should come first amang a' the ladies of Edinburgh."

"You must allow His Royal Highness, ma'am, to be judging who is important and who is not, and who will adorn his levees, and who will . . . wrinkle them."

Lady Brounhill put her hand to the coils of her fine hair which by some secret showed no frost upon their black sheen. Then she shook her head dolefully, making her ear-rings click. "I fear, Hector," she murmured, "you will need to be thinking of fechting rather than dancing. It is a peety! Sae many braw young men!"

"Oh! as to fighting, aunt," replied Hector cheerfully, "it is we will come off well enough if we are having the right commander on the day!"

"What may that mean, Hector?" asked Jean.

"It means, coz, that we have two lieutenant-generals who take it in turn to command on alternate days according to a rota. One, whom we all love, is that noble fellow the Duke of Perth, against whom none can say a word except"— Hector's blue-grey eyes showed a wicked spark to his cousin —"except that he will be always speaking 'braid Scots,' and he a Highland gentleman! Heard you ever the like of that? . . . Well, no matter; we are trusting Perth. The other, whom we all hate, and I at least am not trusting, is Lord George Murray, brother to old Tullibardine. Is not that the stick of a martinet, who holds that a few years' service in the King of Sardinia's army hath given him all knowledge of war! On his day it is nought but regulations and reprimands —and that is no way to be leading Highland men. Besides that, my gentleman was colloguing with Mr. Cope at Crieff a week or two before joining us, and hath always been on terms with his other, Whig, brother, James, who keeps Tullibardine out of his Dukedom of Atholl. I believe he has entered our army to betray us . . . and if what Elcho tells me is true, a very high personage will be of much the same opinion. No doubt Elcho is bitter that he is not made lieutenant-general himself; but so the world wags in Court and camp, Cousin Jean."

"You do not seem a very united host, then, Hector."

"The enemy will unite us . . . if they ever face us . . . Madam," he turned to Lady Brounhill, "I am imploring you, do me a favour. Intercede with his lordship to grant me an interview. It is not much to ask of an uncle and a Tutor, and it life or death for me! He will hearken to you, I know!"

Lady Brounhill rose doubtfully. "I will try what I can do, Hector. But I do not think Brounhill will speak to you. He is sair angered . . . and you have given him gude cause, I maun tell you!"

She rustled out of the room, and Hector sprang from the window and embraced Jean.

"My soul, and it happy!" he said, while she, protesting and scarlet, set her lace straight. "And was not that the prodigy of generalship, to get rid of our new sentinel and win that kiss. . . . But, Jean, do you think my Tutor will be letting me have some of my money?"

"I think you are mad to suppose it, Hector!"

"My grief! But I *must* have it. It is mine! My men need to be fed and they deserve to be paid."

"Cannot your Prince look after his army, then?"

Hector shrugged his shoulders. "Our commissariat, our treasury is chaos. The chiefs are tending their own people . . . and I would not be ashamed among them. Dr. Hay, whom I have left at Glenmarisdale, has promised to collect what rent he can and transmit it to me."

"That is illegal, Hector! You are still a minor!"

"How," he asked, with a return to his old affectation of fatuity, "is it metaphysically possible for me to be at one and the same time a minor and a major? For it is Major I am, let me be telling you, in the regiment of Clan Ranald."

"But the law, Hector—"

"Law! The sword will be the law now! But I need a larger sum, and why should not Brounie disgorge? I tell you, Jean, he is on the losing side. Your Hanoverians will never stand to face us. I am thinking it would be a wise insurance on his part to give me cause of gratitude to him—to-day. Ah! That will be him coming."

He sprang back to his seat in the window as Lord Brounhill entered, followed by his wife. Brounie looked from him to Jean, who was blushfully conscious that she still looked slightly disordered. "Gang to your room!" he said briefly. "Gang to your room! Do you hear me? I will send for you when I need you."

Jean gathered up her embroidery and went out with a worried look, after giving Hector her hand to kiss.

"You, sir," said Brounie, as soon as the door closed. "I will thank you first not to press your attentions on my daughter."

Hector gave another shrug. "It will be the first time, then, sir, I have had reason to think it would be unpalatable to you if—"

"I hae no desire to see Jean wed a penniless proscript, if that is your meaning."

"As to pennilessness . . . it is you can remedy that, uncle!"

"It is likely! But I didna come back to you to hear your impertinences. Whiles you have been here there has been a messenger come to my private entry wi' news that may concern you. General Cope is landed the morn at Dunbar wi' his army. Now ye will hae opportunity to try your claymores upon regular troops. Dinna come to me to conceal ye from justice after the rout!"

"I will be coming to you, sir," said Hector, tightening his sword-belt with an automatic gesture, "but only to ask your permission to take Lady Brounhill and my cousin to the Prince's first ball at Holyroodhouse."

As he spoke there came an angry roar, followed by a crash and splintering of glass in the street below. The continuous murmur of the crowd turned to shrieks and a frantic hubbub, which died away as the people rushed for shelter. Lady Brounhill screamed and fell into a chair with her hands over her ears.

"The Castle is firing on the town," said Lord Brounhill with grim composure. "Yon are the balls awaiting your bonnie Prince Charlie!"

Chapter X

GHOSTS AT HOLYROOD

1

THE music of strings in a minuet rose tremulous against the black panelling of the picture gallery in Holyroodhouse. From the two immense wrought-iron grates wood fires breathed smokily upon the fluted pilasters of dark oak and the candles in their sconces. Fireglow and candle-beams in contest made an unearthly flicker upon the pallid faces of the monarchs of Scotland in their long array. From their frames they seemed to fleer at the assemblage that disported itself upon the waxed floor with a subdued and nervous gaiety.

At the doors the bearded Highland sentinels were like the intrusion of gnarled oaks into an Italian parterre, and beyond them on the broad stairway similar live statues were rudely ranked with torches in their grasp.

"I am nigh feared to enter, Hector!" said Jean, who was coming up the stairs on her cousin's arm.

"For why, my pretty coz? My soul! You will be as becomingly dressed as any woman we will meet, and prettier than all of them."

He looked at her with a spark of passion, and she glanced

in her turn with open admiration at his slight, alert figure in gold-buttoned jacket with a falling lace *jabot*, across which the Clan Ranald tartan rippled from his shoulder. His face, she thought, was browner and thinner than it used to be; the eyes showed larger and more excitable. His brows still stood out like smudges under his freshly powdered wig, and there was still a strip of black plaster on his chin, which he profanely called "Colonel Gardiner's last prayer." It covered the scar of the sabre-cut, now a fortnight old, which had been given him by the old Dragoon, before yielding his life in a final transport of Puritan piety to the axes and dirks of the clansmen on the field of Prestonpans.

"I would have saved his life," Hector had several times declared, "had he not demanded with blows to be martyred! It was Angus would be dirking him. I would have loved to take him back to be disputing with Dr. Hay!" And upon that he would laugh with a high-pitched, extravagant note such as was frequently heard these days in the Highland camp, and along the darkling corridors of Holyroodhouse. It was the laugh of victors who could scarce believe in their own good fortune, and were almost frightened at the ease of their victory. None had hoped to see the Elector's well-drilled scarlet lines crumble as they had done into panic-struck ruin and flight within eleven minutes after the Highland onset—Johnny Cope arriving first at Berwick with the news of his own defeat.

It was hard even now for the conquerors to know to what they should attribute their triumph. To the rawness of the English levies, said some, the seasoned troops being on the continental front. To the inability, others opined, of men trained in the clockwork of barrack-yard drill to withstand the flexible fury of the Highland assault, twisting their bayonets on its targes and groping for their undefended bodies with its stabbing-dirks. To the natural inability of the Eng-

lish to stand up to the Scots—a popular theory with the rank
and file. To the superb organisation and disposition of the
Highland host hinted Quarter-Master-General Colonel
O'Sullivan. To the infectious glamour of Prince Charlie's
boyish daring, slipping and sliding over the ditches, and waving his men on with the Gaelic shout, "*Greas ort! Greas
ort!*" * was the conviction of the ladies.

Only here and there an officer or a sergeant who had seen
active service in this or that army upon the continent ventured to whisper to some other veteran that a main factor in
the victory had been the steely nerve and swift decision of
the Lieutenant-General, Lord George Murray, who had
led the Highlanders by night waist-high in wet through what
was believed an impassable marsh, and had flung them at
dawn upon a surprised enemy who had barely time to re-
form front in this new direction. But it was not in the
Prince's hearing that anyone would have dared to stress this
element in the glorious victory of Gladsmuir by Prestonpans.

Lord George was at the moment standing before one of
the great fire-places in the picture gallery, wearing a neat
peruke above the Murray tartan. A tall man with a well-
drilled carriage, a head held arrogantly erect, thick eyebrows
over shrewd, reflective eyes, and a sensitive, lightly ironical
mouth. Around him were clustered several other officers,
with a little the air of a claque. They manifested loudly their
enjoyment of his conversation, which could be seen from the
quiver of his lips to be sarcastic. Yet about Lord George, too,
hung the atmosphere of victory, expressed in a brightness of
the eye, an alertness and briskness of bearing.

"Where is the Chevalier?" whispered Jean, gazing with
awe round a gathering splendid beyond anything in her experience. "That's no him, is it, yonder, by the fire-place?"

"It is not, indeed," laughed Hector, "and I am thinking the

* "Make haste! Make haste!"

Prince would be very little pleased at your mistake. He is not arrived yet."

"And what will I do then, Hector?"

"Make the most charming curtsey in the room. What else?"

"But would that not be high treason?"

"No worse than your presence here! I suspect you are not the only one of our guests to-night who will be shaken by inward tremors. Only look at our old friend, Counsellor Penicuik, yonder, how he slinks along by the wall!"

"Indeed, I wonder," said Jean, "that my father allowed me to come in the end."

"It was he had no choice!" Hector smiled with delighted malice. "He desires a pass to retire to Brounhill till these bruilzies are done. I was asked by Secretary Murray whether I would be guaranteeing my Tutor's good conduct. What think you of that?" His vibrant laugh rang up towards the shadowy ceiling. "So I made your company to-night the price of the requisite testimonial. Do you know, Jean, I am thinking that at the back of his mind was the idea that should we win the last game it would be no ill thing to be having one member of the family on the winning side . . . and was not that Highlander's calculation?"

"You do ill to mock him, Hector! Father has no purpose in life but his duty to the family."

"But is not that the way of all of us? We will be making a dream, a crazy dream out of some material thing—a bit of pasture-land, the feather of chiefship . . . or a crown . . . and we will be eager to give our happiness and our lives, to wreak havoc on a city or a continent, aye, and some of us to commit any crooked crime, to attain our ideal! . . . There is enough of the political! Look, they will be taking places for the *contre-danse*! Shall we step out? . . . No, stay a moment! Here comes the Prince, I am thinking."

There was a stir round the doors. Highland ladies and
Edinburgh tradesmen's wives, clergymen and card-sharpers,
Jacobite officers and Hanoverian spies, nobles, merchants and
lawyers, the whole mixed assembly that the ignorance or
policy of Prince Charles's Court admitted tag-rag to its re-
ceptions on the passport of a decent dress, began to surge in
that direction till held back by the sentries. Through the
doorway a phalanx of gentlemen and officers in full-dress
could be seen slowly ascending the stairs. Hector, standing
on tiptoe, made our Lord Elcho's peevish handsomeness,
Colonel O'Sullivan, pompous and florid, with his red hair
frizzed in curls, the old Marquis of Tullibardine limping on
his ebony stick, Lord Kilmarnock, Lord Lewis Gordon, and
Lord Nithsdale, recent prized accessions to the Cause. . . .

"Here comes His Highness," he told Jean. "No, by
G——, it will be just Darthula!"

Entering the ball-room thus in the midst of her private
court, Darthula, in spite of her minuteness, looked entirely
the queen. Her slight figure in white satin was outlined
against the crimson ground and the green and black lines of
the tartan *arisaid* draped back from her shoulders and over
her hips. The white rose gleamed among the coppery ring-
lets of her coiffure, and her eyes, brilliant in their wide, white
ovals, stood out with an almost crepitant vivacity. For the
instant she seemed the only live person in the long, gloomy
gallery that fought with such sullenness against the effort of
wax-tapers and silken dresses to brighten it. Even the spectral faces of the disapproving kings seemed to fade for a moment from the walls. And the aged leader of the orchestra,
one of her devoted slaves, postponed the opening of the
contre-danse to play a favourite Highland air of hers. Jean
felt a second's unexpected exquisite detestation of her cousin.

"Is not that the grand entry, eh?" Hector turned to Jean,
laughing sardonically. "And, behold, coz, it is she will be

coming to greet us as pleasant and condescending as if we were somebodies!"

Darthula, indeed, with well-timed tact, had freed herself from her courtiers at the doors. Her curtsey was too enchanting—and where respect was due too respectful—to leave any of her train aggrieved at their dismissal; while the other guests had no time to accuse her of stopping the ball before the prelude to the *contre-danse* duly struck up.

"At last, Jean!" Darthula came rustling towards her cousin with a welcome that shamed her late feeling. "I have been waiting for the day when you would come to pay your homage where all our family are properly belonging!"

"You forget, Darthula, my mother is Lowland."

"My dear, this will not be a Highland raid! This is an uprising of all that is loyal in Scotland."

"I brought Jean here to dance," grumbled Hector. "Not to listen to these eternal politics!"

"Very well, child!" Darthula tapped his cheek with her fan, to his discomposure. "It is you shall be having your treat! Stand up on the floor—and if nobody will be admiring you, they shall all admire your partner. Dance away, my man!"

Hector made a profound bow. "We are grateful for the permission—*your majesty*!"

Jean gave a little jump. She felt as if sword-blades had suddenly struck sparks near her head. She gazed from one of her cousins to the other. Darthula's eyes were blazing: Hector had risen from his bow with a bitter sneer on his face.

"And am I not to dance at all to-night?" Jean demanded after a moment. The tension broke, and Hector, with some lazy witticism on his lips, led her out upon the floor.

Darthula remained where they had left her, driving her nails into her slim palms, until in a second or two Lord Elcho, outdistancing competitors, bowed before her, murmuring,

"May I presume to claim the privilege?" He glanced sharply up at her face from under his half-closed lids, and added, "I hope, ma'am, you have not taken a sudden distaste for Terpsichore?'

The next instant he could have sworn some trick of the candles had illuded him, so radiant was the smile with which she walked out on his arm.

"I wonder," he murmured as they sought their places, "if I could prevail upon you, Mistress Maceachan, to put in a word, if opportunity offers, with His Royal Highness, on behalf of an officer of mine in his Life Guards, who has incurred the totally unmerited displeasure of Lord George Murray?"

The violins thrilled and sobbed; the dancers bowed and crossed each other with elegant motion beneath the ironical eyes of the ancient kings. Suddenly a chamberlain entering rapped upon the floor with a white wand. "His Royal Highness, the Prince Regent!" he cried.

The dance broke off, and the guests jostled each other into two lines down the sides of the room. The band gave out "The King shall enjoy his own again," and in a moment Charles entered the picture gallery from his private apartment, accompanied by Lochiel and another important, newly won supporter, Lord Pitsligo. He wore white powder tonight, which, with his pale, flowered vest, gave him an ethereality against the sombre panelling of the room. It was almost as though the stately chief and the thin old aristocratic scholar escorted between them nothing but a wraith, an insubstantial apparition gleaming in blue sash and Garter Star, with falls of soft lace covering the wrists of the sensitive musician's hands. But the feature of the Prince's dress which struck the female onlookers with consternation was that his trews of Stewart tartan disappeared at the knee into jackboots with serviceable steel spurs on their square heels.

"Will he be sleeping in boots?" whispered one. "An unco

strange ball dress—do ye no find it strange?" asked another
"He tak's but sma' pains to pleasure us!" bridled a third
"Leddies, he doesna think of us at a'," tittered a fourth
"There is one here he has eyes for!" murmured a fifth, slyly
pointing her fan at Darthula, who stood conspicuous in her
white satin at the farther end of the gallery.

But at this moment, at any rate, it seemed true that Charles
had eyes for none of them. Listlessly swinging his diamond-
clasped bonnet of blue velvet in his fingers, he let his melancholy gaze wander without recognition over the assemblage;
and appeared rather to seek out the eyes of the painted kings
upon the walls—as it were a living ghost giving challenge to
dead ones—than to be paying heed to the friends, flatterers
and enemies crowded upon the floor to watch him.

So he stood while the band played through the pathetic air
of the old song. As it finished, a cheer was started, and taken
up with a volley of hand-claps; then some lady was seized
with the inspiration of casting the flower she was wearing at
the Prince's feet. Her example was swiftly followed by the
others—white roses and cockades, ribbons and favours fell,
like a shower of snowflakes about to melt, round his spurs.
Still, amid this ecstatic homage, he stood emotionless and
dreaming; while behind him in the shadow the two grandees,
swathed in their plaids, took on the look of figures of destiny,
enwrapping a riddle no mortal might resolve.

The cheering died away, as if discouraged, and at last
Charles with a little shiver, appeared to come to himself. He
sent his charming boyish smile round the gathering, and
acknowledging the fresh plaudits it evoked, walked slowly
the length of the room with his two attendants. In a moment
or two, however, the smile wavered off his face again; the
cloud came back; and his eye seemed restlessly to be searching for a particular face.

Near the long windows at the end of the gallery Darthula

was waiting; and as she curtsied in her turn at his approach, his forehead cleared and his lips relaxed. The rose that had starred her hair fluttered circling to the boards before him. He stopped and put out his hand. There was a second's pause; then Lochiel, with a troubled brow, stooped and handed the flower to him. His fingers closed tenderly over it, and with bent head he turned and entered the State apartments on his right. A whisper went rustling round the room before the band struck into a gavotte.

2

THE dance proceeded, but Darthula did not stir from her place by the window. No one dared break in upon her privacy, though many eyes gleamed in question or in envy towards her. And out of the tumult in her mind, as she let her own eyes rove over the ball-room, there emerged first, with an apparent inconsequence, a sense of the changefulness of the Court scene. New faces everywhere to-night! Where were the Seven Men of Moidart? O'Sullivan, indeed, could be seen and loudly heard; Tullibardine and old Sir Thomas Sheridan were warming hands together at one of the fires. But rough Sir John stayed in the camp in King's Park, training the Prince's cavalrymen, and no one seemed to remember to summon him to Court. Francis Strickland the Prince had likewise removed from about his person to a military post in deference to a protesting letter from King James, who dreaded the Englishman's influence on his son's religious principles. The intrusive little cleric, Kelly, was on his way to France with highly confidential dispatches. Poor Æneas Macdonald was in permanent disgrace for spreading discouragement, it was averred, among the party; and wished he was back in his counting-house at Paris. There were new gods already at every turn of the palace corridors—Perth,

Lord George Murray, Elcho, Pitsligo, who could remember all their names and titles?

Loud cries came from the centre of the ball-room. The party was losing a little of its ceremony, and the courtliness of minuet and gavotte was giving place to reels danced by the kilted Highland gentlemen. Darthula saw her brother's lithe form exuberant among the rest, and his taunt to her struck back like a whip. *Your Majesty!* She had not such sluggish ears as not to have overheard the titles of "Princess of Wales" and "Queen" that had flitted derisively about the ante-rooms and vestibules of Holyroodhouse on her passage, ever since the night soon after Gladsmuir, when the Prince had placed her on his right hand at a small banquet in the palace; and even more noticeably since he had made her ride by his side, with his staff jingling fifty yards behind, round King's Park and through the Hunter's Bog one afternoon after a review of his troops . . . though all the time he had only soliloquised on his difficulties with his officers and his desire to undertake the immediate invasion of England.

Well: those sardonic homages did not sting her much. They were proof, at any rate, that no one even in the extreme of jealousy was daring a baser insinuation—indeed, if any man had, she knew Hector would have made a corpse of him by now. Nor did she acknowledge to herself that she should have been presumptuous to entertain such a dream. Once upon a time the Maceachans had been Kings, too. They had ruled the Great Glen to Inverness and all Knoydart to Loch Hourn. So Ewen the Bard had sung to her in her childhood and she harboured not the least doubt of it. The Stewarts were a new family compared with the children of Hector, the son of Astyanax, the son of Hector of Troy.

It was not the sense of disparity in birth that had prevented her in fact from entertaining for a moment such a vision. Certainly she was not so unworldly as to think that Charles, trained in the maxims of St. James's and Versailles, would judge her his equal. But there was something that mattered much more. It was her intimate, unanalysable conviction that Charles Edward would never be her lover truly, or any other woman's. Fascinated and enthralled by him she was, and owned it to herself. But the form of surrender to himself that he demanded, absolute and unreserved, had none of the tenderness of flesh and blood. Sometimes she was reminded, as she analysed her thoughts of him, of the devotion of the nuns in the French convent where she had been schooled towards their mysterious, inaccessible Beloved on the Altar. . . . The sacredness of his person to her exalted enthusiasm removed the comparison from profanity. . . . At other times she would frantically stretch out the arms of her soul and find them close upon . . . impalpable air. He remained smiling and alluring, provoking and inspiring; but aloof, a messenger from other spheres, never to be touched to love, she believed, in his heart or soul by any woman . . . or perhaps even to friendship by any man.

She doomed herself to human frustration, she knew well, in yielding to his fascination. His was the lure of the spirit that inhabits high places, that leads the feet to the edge of precipices, and then with vertigo draws the victim to the abyss. But she was powerless to resist the attraction. It beset her with the spell of her native clouds and cliffs, as the expressed burden of its melancholy chants, as the promise of a fame for which it was worth while to abandon earthly felicities. She would never now be anything in her life; but after her death she might become a legend. . . .

The revelry in the centre of the room was growing more boisterous. Champagne had been served, and spirits were flicked into a wilder exhilaration. Claymores were clashed overhead, and others laid down for sword-dances on the black oak boards. Loyal choruses mounted with passion to the ears of the disdainful monarchs overhead.

Suddenly the doors from the State apartments opened, and Lochiel stepped forth. He smiled kindly as his eyes fell on Darthula. "Where is Glenmarisdale, cousin?" he asked. "His Highness commands his immediate presence."

"He will be over yonder, dancing, Lochiel. There is no trouble, is there?"

"Set your mind at ease! The Prince designs to honour him. A delicate and difficult mission to the north. . . . I may not tell you more now."

As Hector a minute later passed her, following Lochiel to the presence, he signalled to her with a rueful quirk of his eyebrow, which expressed at once his boredom with honours and the end of their petty quarrel. She knew that it would be useless to wait and bombard him with questions when he issued from his audience. That was never the way to elicit his news. She walked down the room to the main entrance amid deferential salutations, and learning that her cousin Jean had gone home in a sedan some time ago, descended to find her own chair. As she passed down the great stair she heard the voices singing overhead:

> "Then look for no peace,
> For the wars shall never cease
> Till the King shall enjoy his own again."

3

NED BURKE was waiting for her in the court with his chair. "This iss the last time I will be haafing the honour of bearing you," he said, as he closed the door for her.

"How comes that, Ned? Is it you have inherited?"

He grinned. "My sorrow! and my expectations that could be carried in a mite's mouth! But no! I haaf at last the opportunity to follow my Prince!"

"You will be enlisting, Ned? Noble fellow! Alack! we have not so many Macleods as we had hoped!"

He scowled. "And is not that the black shame on the Clan? But I'll no' be joining the ranks. My clansman, Macleod of Muiravonside, Advocate of this city, iss appointed aide-de-camp, and he hath promised to take me with him as his servant. I will be liking it finer than carrying your fat Whig madams that haaf neffer a bawbee to give you for trink money. And there will be plunder, too, I am thinking."

"For shame, Ned! And you a Highland gentleman!"

"Ach! It wasna in my mind to rob any shentlemens! Only the English, when we cross the border!" He grinned again as he took up the poles.

It was a short journey to the White Horse Inn in the Canongate, where Darthula shared a lodging with Secretary Murray and his fair wife. She was about to mount the outside stair in the inn-yard to her door when a short man in a kilt rose from the shadow where he had been squatting, tottered a little and saluted her.

"Who are you?" she called to him over the wall of the stair, a little startled.

"A messenger!" he replied in Gaelic, "who craves speech with you, lady." His voice was husky, almost whispering. In spite of its deference, there was an insistence about the tone that displeased her.

"I am not knowing you," she said. "You will be a gillie, will you not?"

"Perhaps the lady is knowing this!"

He reached up and put a knot of ribbon into her hand. She turned towards the lantern over her door, and uttered a little exclamation. She was holding, faded and with a rusty spot on it, a favour of Clan Ranald tartan, fringed with gold, which she recognised. . . . It brought back Lady Stair's saloon on a thunderous night, and a gallant young figure swinging through the door, head high, with this ribbon held in his closed hand over his heart. She wheeled back towards the messenger. "You will be Glengarry's servant? Why does he send this?"

"Because he cannot come himself . . . he cannot write . . . it is he needs your help, lady. . . . He is the prisoner of the Sassenachs in London."

"What is this stain upon the ribbon," she demanded fearfully.

"What should it be but the blood of Himself?"

"Alastair's blood!" Her voice trembled. "He is not . . . dying?"

"Prison is dying to a Macdonnell! . . . It is not his family that can deliver him; it is you, lady! If you turn me away, it is you will be giving sentence of death on Himself!"

Darthula drew a key from her reticule and unlocked the door.

"Enter!" she said, "tell me your tale!"

She went inside, and the little shadow hopped, limping, up the stair and followed her.

Chapter XI

CAPTIVES OF A STAR

1

BROTHER and sister crossed each other in the Prince's ante-room the next morning.

"Darthula!" exclaimed Hector. "What are you seeking here?"

"Secret for secret!" she answered bitterly. "Should not you be telling me first what mission was given you in these rooms last night? You went to the camp with Clan Ranald instead of sleeping at our lodgings, and so I am knowing nothing of what I greatly desire to hear." Her tone spoke her resentment at his growing secretiveness and independence of her counsel which had once been his sole guide.

"I am going, if you will be curious, Darthula, to Inverness."

"To Inverness? What work has the Prince found you, so far away?"

Before Hector could answer or refuse to answer, Murray of Broughton came through the gilded doors from the presence-chamber. "His Royal Highness gives you audience, Mistress Maceachan," he said in a sharp tone, and Darthula, knowing Charles's impatience if anyone kept him waiting, hurried straight through to his drawing-room. The

Secretary closed the doors carefully and was walking away, turning over a sheaf of papers in his hand.

"For what will my sister be having audience, Mr. Murray?" inquired Hector.

"How should I know, Glenmarisdale?" replied the Secretary in an absorbed tone. "She sent a prayer to be received early this morning." He looked up with his sharp little smile. "I have more discretion, I hope, than to intervene between the Prince and a lady!"

He slipped through the little door into the picture gallery before Hector could question him further.

The Laird of Glenmarisdale stood alone in the antechamber, while his eyes began to shine with suspicion. Suddenly he made a step towards the folding-doors as if he would break in upon the Prince's conference with his sister. Then he stopped, still hesitant; shrugged his shoulders, and swung about on his heel. But with his hand on the little door to the picture gallery he paused once again, irresolute and troubled, before passing through and taking the sentry's salute.

"And what brings you abroad so early, Darthula?" asked Charles Edward, rising from his writing-table on Darthula's entry and strolling to the fire-place. He turned and faced her. "You are not here to scold me, are you, for sending Glenmarisdale away?"

She perceived from his manner that this was to be an hour in which Court etiquette would be suspended—though it was always needful to be wary, for he would fly like a bow released to full Royal dignity on any irritation.

She sank into the chair he indicated with eyes watchfully fixed on him, in spite of her smile. "I am not knowing yet, Abbé," she said, using the name she had chosen for him when he told her he hated to be "sired" in intimacy, "why the boy is sent to Inverness at all."

"You shall hear," he said frankly. "I have made him one of my ambassadors to the hesitating Chiefs—I hoped you would be pleased at the honour done him. . . . Well, smile, if you are!" he added with a touch of petulance. "Yes, that is better! Macleod of Muiravonside goes to wrestle with the Chief of that ilk in Skye, and, if he can, to prevail upon Macdonald of the Isles. Your brother is to coax Lord Lovat."

"The old spider!"

"Yes, I begin, Darthula, to distrust even him. It is a Dukedom for himself, not a crown for my father, that he is seeking." Charles sighed with the note of discouragement that always touched her quick sympathy. "And there is another thing Hector is commissioned to do. . . . I give away State secrets in handfuls to you, my Muse, do I not? Well: we must drive that fox Duncan Forbes from his lair at Culloden. He does me more harm with his tongue and pen than all the Elector's regiments—so far. So Glenmarisdale carries also a warrant to the Frasers to attack Culloden House and bring the President a prisoner to me here. Lovat has been begging for weeks in his letters that the warrant should read 'alive or dead,' but I will have none of that. I am not the assassin of my subjects, and I fear I know how the warrant would be executed if I made it out in those terms. . . . There is the honourable trust I have placed in your brother, Darthula." He smiled his most candid smile. "Now, how are you going to show your gratitude?"

"It will be by asking another favour, Abbé!"

Charles leaned back in the arm-chair, where he had placed himself, and laughed for several moments. "You are *impayable*, Darthula!" he declared. "Ever the unexpected! Well: what can you want now? I can give you nothing, you know. One Mr. Murray controls my business and another Mr. Murray commands my army, and I may do nothing but affix the seal where they point their fingers."

"Abbé, this will be no light matter that I am asking you. There is a faithful friend of yours in sore trouble. It is Alastair Macdonnell, Young Glengarry."

"And what has befallen him? Is he not in France?"

"He was coming from France, with a piquet of the French King's Scots Regiment to join your flag, when he was taken at sea and clapped into the Tower of London, some three weeks since, I learn."

Charles sat up with an irritated look. "Why was I not informed of these troop movements? . . . Where is my intelligence? How come you to know these events before I do?"

"His messenger reached me last night, sir, and he worn with the speed of his journey from London."

"Why you, Darthula?" His glance was cold.

She coloured a little. "He honoured me by turning to me as to an old friend."

"Hum!" His voice sounded disagreeable. "Why does he not turn to his family?"

"Because, Abbé, in this strait it is not they who can help him. For five hundred pounds, he is assured, he could buy his escape from the Tower. But my sorrow! Old Glengarry has not the money at command."

"That I believe," mused Charles, leaning back and staring up at the magnificent wreathed ceiling. "They are a faithful family! His Uncle Lochgarry, his young brother Angus, a gallant boy, are among the best of my officers: my Glengarry regiment is a fine one!"

"Why! then it was poor Alastair Ruadh was wise in bidding me make appeal direct to you! You will be helping him, Abbé, of course you will."

"If it is feasible. It is not so much 'of course,' child, as you think."

"Oh! Abbé, must Darthula be kneeling to you?"

"Why are you so anxious about this man's fate?"

She threw her head back proudly. "Because he is your loyal servant. Even in prison he has been collecting intelligence for you."

"Of any value? I doubt it!"

"Of that you shall be judge, sir. His message for you, as his servant brought it to me, was this, and I was bidden to insist that he had it from a servant of Lord Tweeddale that was laid by the heels in the same prison for some treasonable handlings. 'Lord George Murray props himself on a strange staff these days!' . . . Why, sir, will it be a cipher?"

Charles had leaped out of his chair. His manner, his face were completely changed. His eyes had darkened; his lips were compressed to a thin scarlet line. He strode to the writing-table and jangled a small bell.

"Bid Mr. Secretary Murray attend me," he said to the officer who appeared, "and to bring the pieces of the staff . . . he will understand."

"My grief! What will all this be?" cried Darthula as the officer withdrew. "Is it bad news, Abbé?"

"Not for me!" retorted Charles grimly.

In a few minutes Murray of Broughton slipped into the room carrying in his hand the two broken pieces of a staff like a shepherd's.

"Shut the door carefully, Murray!" said Charles. "I have discovered our Judas!"

"It is Lord George, of course, sir?"

"Why, Murray, I did not think you suspected!"

"It is not my way, sir, to speak without proof. But the man who stands by Cope in August and by us in September is not a man who will ever have my confidence."

"Miss Maceachan brings proof, Murray, that your instinct was sound."

"Indeed?" The little secretary arched his brows suspiciously. "I claim no more than the instincts of fidelity, sir."

"Tell her how this staff came into our possession."

"Some days ago, ma'am," said Murray, turning to Darthula, "a man of Stewart of Appin's regiment fell into a quarrel with a rough shepherd-like fellow upon the causeway of the Canongate here. They fought, and the stranger's staff was broken. He took to his heels, and wrapped inside the stick our man found this note, which he had the good sense to bring to me." Murray unwrapped a tiny piece of soiled paper.

"Read it, Murray!"

"It runs, 'My dear brother, words will not be taken as proof of your good dispositions to the White Horse.'"

"'The White Horse,'" interrupted Charles, "the Elector's crest, you understand!"

Murray resumed. "'But all may be pardoned, yea and honour follow, if on the next encounter in the field you keep your word and bring your regiment over to our side.' There lacks any signature," he concluded, folding the paper.

"That we can now supply," said Charles, with his lowering look again. "Mistress Maceachan has had a message, too, from London—from a source in a highly-placed household. It is 'Lord George Murray props himself on a strange staff these days.' I see the whole intrigue. James Murray the Whig, the mock Duke of Atholl, corresponds with Lord George through these shaggy messengers. By G——, I will hang the rogue higher than Haman in the Lawnmarket, for all Edinburgh to take note!"

"Sir!" cried Darthula, in distress, "I am begging you, be not precipitate. . . . Oh! I am sorry I ever brought that message from Glengarry. It is I have an instinct, too, sir, which tells me there is something amiss here. I am not believing Lord George is false!"

"Your brother, ma'am, if he were with us," slipped in the secretary, "would be of His Highness's mind in the matter, I dare be sworn."

"Of course," said Charles impatiently. "There can be no shadow of doubt. Do not insist, Miss Maceachan, I command you! This is a matter for men, and soldiers. I may not know the laws of war, as Lord George so frequently is pleased to remind me, but I know the law for dealing with spies and deserters, eh, Murray? I will confront him forthwith with these proofs of his villainy. Send for him, Murray . . . yes, and for his brother, old Tullibardine. It will be a sore stroke for my old friend, but he may learn the truth as well now as later. . . . You, ma'am, I did not signify your audience was ended. I shall need your witness."

Darthula stood with her hands pressed together in anguish. She knew Charles could as well be restrained as a maddened horse, when galled by the spur of suspicion. She had never joined in her brother's and the secretary's constant carpings against Lord George. An intuition she trusted more than these enigmatic messages told her that the disagreeable, self-opinionated soldier was upright . . . and that Charles could not dispense with his aid.

She was still casting desperately about for means to dissuade the Prince from rushing on a precipice of which none could see the depth, when Lord George entered the room, followed by the old Marquis, and both bowed gravely to their Royal master.

"Lord George Murray," said Charles with an icy hauteur, "I will be brief in what I have to say to you. For the sake of your brother here, one of my oldest and most trusted friends, I grieve with all my heart that I must say it. But the safety of my gallant army and my father's crown are dearer to me than all personal bonds. You are a traitor, sir!"

Lord George's tall form stiffened, and Darthula wondered

that even a Prince dared face his look.

"It is useless to protest, Lord George. Here is the letter we have intercepted from your other brother with the enemy. Read it, Tullibardine, my old comrade. . . . This man is to abandon me in the next battle we have to fight. It is arranged. It is not I who accuse; but they who confess!"

The two grandees pored, with bewildered looks, over the dirty little piece of accusing script, and asked a question or two. Then:

"Sir!" cried the aged Marquis, "sir! you are most shamefully abused! My brother James, whatever his misfeasances, never wrote this!"

"You see, William," said Lord George, contemptuously letting go his hold on a corner of the paper, "to what base accusations and what self-confessing forgeries our brother James will have exposed us by his tergiversation. Your Highness, I do not know who wrote this letter, nor whence it comes, nor how it fell into your hands; but I have never corresponded with my brother, the titular Duke, since I came to your Standard, on my honour as a gentleman and an officer."

"I give you my *parole*, too, sir," said Tullibardine, with the moving dignity of his age. "I go bail for my brother George's fidelity with this head that has so often slept for you on the hard ground, and that would so gladly fall into the headsman's basket for you."

"Ah! Tullibardine!" murmured Charles, his face running with tears. He shook his head hopelessly.

"What, sir," cried the old man. "Do all these years of service go for nought? Am I to be doubted at the finish?" He plucked his sword from its sheath; made an effort with feeble hands to break the blade; then cast it at the Prince's feet.

Charles quivered, and put out his hands as if to ward off a blow.

"I demand to know more!" exclaimed Lord George with a sudden vehemence. "This letter is anonymous. Who are my traducers?"

Charles motioned Darthula forward. "Tell him what you know, Mistress Maceachan!"

Lord George started. "Is it this lady will be made judge of a gentleman's honour?" he asked. "Or of a woman's?" he added under his breath, but audibly.

"George!" remonstrated Tullibardine, his delicate, worn features flushing.

Darthula went slowly white. "I have a brother, Lord George!" she said at last.

"A brother, who, I understand, most obligingly absents himself to Inverness this afternoon!"

"Tullibardine," said Charles in a choking voice, "call the officer of the Guard! Your sword, Lord George!"

Darthula threw herself on her knees at his feet. "Stay, sir, stay," she sobbed, "I implore you! My name, my reputation, what do they matter? Is it I shall be the cause that your friends fall from you? Better you run me through with this sword upon the floor! We have been deceived, deluded . . . I am not knowing how! But his lordship here, however low he may stoop in his passion to strike at a woman's honour, will be guiltless of treason. Let him keep his sword, sir. God knows how sore you may need it in the days to come!"

"Sir!" pleaded Tullibardine. "You hear Miss Maceachan repudiates whatever charge you looked to her to substantiate! Darthula, you have a noble heart! Burn that noisome paper, sir! It is a united Army of which you must be leader!"

Charles, totally overcome, had walked into the embrasure of one of the crimson-curtained windows. Abruptly he turned back into the room, crumpled the incriminating letter in his hand, and hurled it into the flames upon the hearth.

"She intercedes for you, Lord George," he said. "I cannot persist. I will believe we are abused by some machination of our enemies. Prove me right in the future! Prove me right! Tullibardine, my dear comrade, take back your sword!" He stooped himself, and returned it to the old nobleman, who kissed the hand that did so.

"Mistress Maceachan," said Lord George, after a pause, with pedantic self-justification, "has imported into some hasty expressions of mine, when smarting under a shameful calumny, a meaning they will not bear."

"Enough, brother, enough!" said Tullibardine with a weary gesture.

Lord George settled his chin obstinately into his stiff collar. "May I assume, sir," he asked the Prince, "that I have the honour to enjoy your full confidence again?"

"I have said, General, that we make a fresh start, and forget what is past."

"Indeed! I would have thought sir that Gladsmuir was a memory a Prince might have cherished!"

"I have not forgotten Gladsmuir. I am not an ungrateful nature . . . to those who do their duty by me."

"I shall seek to do so in the future, sir, as in the past—perhaps with better hope of success if your Highness will be pleased to translate the confidence of which you speak into a willingness to let my counsel weigh with you in determining the lines of our military operations."

"Lord George, I have never been averse from receiving advice from my military commanders, nor ever shall be."

"May I assume that that is equivalent to a gracious undertaking on your part, sir, not to be committing the Army to important steps for the future without summoning your Council of War?"

"Oh! as you like, my lord!" Charles dismissed them with a weary gesture, and turning his back to the room rested his head against the marble mantelpiece.

"Oh! Abbé," cried Darthula, as the doors closed behind the two Atholl lords, "was not that the noble deed? Forgiveness and trust become a Prince!"

2

CHARLES whipped round, and she recoiled at his look. His eyes flamed a murderous dark blue, and the Cupid's bow was again wiped from his lips. "Forgive!" he cried. "What do you mistake me for? Trust? Do you suppose I did not know that the letter I was forced to destroy was genuine? That this prim poker, who stands here taunting me in every word of his mock-submission, is in concert with my enemies? He is on both sides . . . as he hath always been. And on the battle-field, mark what I say, he will be found sold to the highest bidder! Can you not read his devilish game? He has wormed himself into the command of my Army, and makes of it a counter to bargain with my enemies. They must pardon him all his treasons to them, because he may still give them the supreme prize of all—my head. And I must endure his treacheries and his insolences, because, if he chooses, he can put me on my throne—to be his puppet, he hopes, while he plays Mayor of the Palace!"

Darthula's brain spun. That these tortuous thoughts should lie behind the open forehead of her "Abbé" seemed to make the world unreal.

"But if that is the truth, sir," she stammered, "why, why will you be placing your fortunes in the hand that can crush them?"

"Why? Why? How dull you are sometimes, Darthula! On paper I may be Commander-in-chief . . . Regent of the Three Kingdoms. In fact I am the prisoner of my own subordinates. I have an Army I cannot command any further than the chief officers please. There is not a Chief who does not claim the right to withdraw his power on the lightest movement of pique or imagined injury. There is not an officer without one foot in the camp of the other King at Windsor!"

"Abbé! Abbé! Is it you will be saying so?"

"Well," he softened a little. "There is a handful I may trust. Lochiel will never betray nor the old man who has just left us . . . nor Clan Ranald, I think. Nor . . . nor your brother, of course." He seemed confused by an odd embarrassment as he alluded to Hector. "But still," he seated himself on the edge of his writing-table, and began to play with a blood-coloured seal that lay upon it, tossing it up and down as though it were a ball, "I can only command by yielding. Yes, so long as they will go forward, I will humour them . . . While they are still willing to fight, they shall fight in what disposition they prefer . . . After all, they may carry me with their wavering wills to the Throne . . . And then, then, my dear, there shall be a reckoning . . . a severance of the sheep from the goats. If there are scaffolds on Tower Hill it will not be for the Generals who have been shooting their balls against me . . . it may be for some who have led charges under my Standard."

He said this almost gaily, swinging his spurred foot to and fro, and tossing and catching the little silver-mounted seal with its blood-coloured spot. And as Darthula listened a shadow seemed to fall across the splendid apartment with its tapestries and its paintings; it was as though the October sunlight streaming through the long windows had been suddenly stolen. There passed shadowily through her mind, steeped in history books, a defile of the servants and intimates of the Stewarts who had been overtaken in the midst of their favour by doom. Strafford's head glared at her fancy . . . and the eyes of Darnley, in whose bedroom, not many yards away, Charles Edward had slept last night.

"What are you shaking for?" asked Charles lightly. "Come to the fire and warm yourself. Young Glengarry, I doubt not, was well-informed by Tweeddale's man. But there is plot beneath plot here, I suspect."

"Then, Abbé, you will be finding the sum needed to secure Alastair's release, will you not?"

Charles's look narrowed. "That is another story. My Treasury, my dear, has nothing in common with the Widow's cruse of the Scripture. Five hundred pounds, the fellow said, did he not? That is preposterous, you know!"

"For the delivery of a Chief, and he a loyal, a gallant servant?"

"The best way to deliver him, and to set all other wrongs right, is to march upon London and make myself master of my capital . . . Do you not agree that the proper course lies there, my Muse?" He glanced at her sharply from the chair into which he had thrown himself, but she was conscious of doubt behind his look.

Strained as she was by the scene she had passed through, and depressed by his hardness, she struggled to rally her forces and meet this new demand from his changeful nature.

She sat a moment, her brow lined by perplexity. "Will it be true," she said at last, hesitating, "what they say, that there are no less than three armies barring the road to London against you?"

"Three armies!" He puffed out his full lips contemptuously. "Have you been talking to Lord George Murray, as well? Doddering old Wade, who lurks behind the walls of Newcastle, afraid to move out! My fat cousin Cumberland, still stiff in the joints from his drubbing at Fontenoy, and seasick from his passage across channel, who seeks, I am told, to collect a mixed horde of foreigners, Dutch, Hessians, the Lord knows who . . . even a few Englishmen perhaps . . . somewhere in the Midlands. And then the so-called camp in some village. . . . Finching or Finchley . . . outside London, a mob of untrained volunteers, I believe . . . Am I to fear any of these or all of them—after Gladsmuir? Darthula! In an enterprise like this we must risk, risk, risk everything, go on risking, to snatch the palm! Besides," he concluded inconsequentially, "I am sure of a great expedition landing from France within three weeks at latest, so that by the time I cross the border I shall be vastly superior in strength to all my cousin's wretched foreign mercenaries."

Darthula felt herself carried away by the rush of his words; but she tried dutifully to stem them. "What will be the other course that is pressed upon you?"

"To stay cooped up here in Holyroodhouse, an ineffectual phantom among the ghosts of my ancestors! They would cut my Crown in two, by G——, and leave me the beggar's half—Scotland!"

He had risen in his fretfulness and now stood upon the mat before the fireplace, swaying his long slim form to and fro upon his toes. A sudden gust of autumn wind piercing the crevices of the windows at that moment made the fire whimper and caused the crimson curtains to belly out into the apartment . . . For a second she had the most fantastic of notions, that with another such puff of the wind he might dissolve and be carried in an eddy of smoke up the chimney, so frail, so elusive he appeared.

Yet that frailty, she knew, was deceptive. Charles Edward's Army knew something of his wiry strength. All the way up from the Western coast, over the ghastly Corrieyai-

rack Pass, by the road Marshal Wade had so obligingly built
for the invaders of his master's dominions, the Prince had led
the march on foot with his tireless mountaineer's stride . . .
It had been a jest among the hardened clansmen the day he
tore a heel from his brogue, that perhaps he would now have
to show a little mercy on them.

But this fount of energy in so tenuous a frame, from
whence did it spring? From hope and excitement! Once
quell them, and what would be left? Might he not collapse in
spirit and so in body, to the ruin of the whole enterprise?
She remembered what he had said at their very first meeting
of his hatred of repetition, of doing over again what you had
once done successfully. He had conquered Edinburgh, won
a victory in Scotland. Was it likely he would be content to
lie down on so short a bed of laurels? And if, thwarted, he
gave way, where would the rest of them be? Grumblers,
plotters perhaps, loyal followers exasperated by his perpetual
claim of a divine right to silence opposition—to all of them he
was more necessary than they to him. Were he really to
vanish like a wraith according to her recent fantasy, then
into what pit of ruin would they not, every man, be plunged?

They had chained themselves to his Star—she with the
rest. They must accept him on his own terms; they could
not compromise so late as this by asking him to be other than
he was . . . Just for a minute did another picture rise before
her alluringly? A life of security in a settled society, an adoring husband, awaking and gratifying the passion in her nature, children and every solid happiness? It whirled away
as the newly-risen wind gave another impatient shake at the
casements.

"Abbé," she said, looking up and steadily facing the doubt
in his eyes, "it is you must go to London . . . to be getting
that new hat you spoke of!"

He gave a sigh of relief, which cruelly brought down on her the weight of her responsibility. "You are convinced, Muse? You have no doubt?"

"No doubt in the world," she bravely lied.

"Yet every trained soldier among my council—"

"Abbé," she taunted him, "if you are not taking the road over the border soon, I will be riding on before you."

"March with me, that is all I ask!" He had crossed to her and caught both her hands in his tense, almost painful grasp. "March at my side, and I will go to London! You alone, Darthula, can lift me out of those fearsome moods when the whole centre of my being seems to dissolve, and I am driven to doubt if there be any real core to me at all. Sheridan is always telling me I drink too much wine when I am in my black moments—but what can I do when I am left alone, with no one by me who truly divines my needs? I have only to look at you, and behold me strong and purposeful again!"

"Is it I go with your Army on campaign?" said Darthula doubtfully. "That will be another matter than travelling behind you to Edinburgh."

"Where is the difficulty?" he asked petulantly. "You shall be attached to my suite. I will give you a bodyguard of your own—"

She shook her head laughing. "My sorrow! What would tongues say? And my brother away to Inverness!"

"If I command," he said, slapping his hand down on the table, "there is no one shall be so presumptuous as to whisper!"

"Abbé, not even you can be changing the nature of man and woman!"

"Well, but you will not be the only woman to travel with us. Murray of Broughton brings his handsome wench of a wife, I know. And probably other ladies will follow their lords . . . I must have you," he reiterated almost with fury.

"I need the inspiration of your countenance, I need your help and support. Without you I will not march into England or anywhere—that is flat!"

"I am thinking now," she answered soothingly, "I can foist myself upon the Murrays as travelling-companion." She smiled to calm him, but her heart was like a stone. "I need the inspiration of your countenance . . . I need your help and support." The one thing he had not said was: "I need your love." Had he done that, defying formalities and the opinion of Europe . . . why, her heart swelled with a mingled rapture and bitterness, she would have carried him triumphantly through the world in arms to his throne! As it was— she gave the lightest of sighs, hardly ruffling the ribbon at her bosom, and said simply, "It is I will be at hand when you need me."

He had already, presuming after his fashion on her assent, seated himself at the writing-table and drawn a clean sheet towards him, on which he was now beginning to write with pursed mouth and shining eyes.

"What are you writing, Abbé?" she asked, not daring to look over his shoulder.

"General orders," he said briefly, "general orders for an advance across the border."

It was on the tip of her tongue to cry: "And your promise, not an hour since, to Lord George, to take no decisive step without your Council of War?"

But she knew it was useless . . . and besides her mind was made up. He must act by his nature, and they must bow to it. Alike he and they were the captives of his Star.

BOOK TWO

THE SCATTERING

1 7 4 5 - 1 7 4 6

Chapter I

ET TU, BRUTE?

1

A COMPANY of travel-worn men and women sat at dinner in a deserted mansion in Derby. The curtains had been stripped from the windows, the arras from the walls; pictures had been removed, carpets rolled up, ornaments packed for hiding by the servants of Lord Exeter, the owner of the house, before their flight. Upon the bare mahogany table the meal of a few simple courses was served from a collection of china hurriedly brought together and not even matching. There was, however, abundance of wine, and silver candelabra, offered by a Jacobite gentleman of the town, shed light on the blithe face of Charles Edward at the head of his guests.

He was blithe in spite of the traces of physical fatigue and spiritual effort, which, since he led his army out of Edinburgh a month before, had refined his countenance, thinning the plumpness of the cheeks and enlarging the brilliant eyes. Darthula Maceachan, from her place at the table, could see the same look in them as had glowed there a few hours before, when in the December dusk he had led his men into the Mid-

231

land town on foot amid the hollow clashing of the bells, rung
for him by a politic order of the corporation. He had been
oblivious, she knew, as she saw him pass in a glare of torches,
scarcely a person was in the streets to welcome him, that
hardly a cheer went up, since his Highlanders had no breath
left after their rapid march to supply the gaps in English
loyalty. In his mind he was entering London under emblazoned arches, the flowers raining round his feet, the pavements and balconies filled with applauding figures.

And he had, Darthula thought, every right to look blithe-
some. His great gamble seemed already a success. He had
taken the fastness of Carlisle with scarcely a struggle, and
slipping, with the elusiveness of a marsh-light, through the
clumsily manœuvring armies that sought to bar his passage,
had penetrated unopposed to the very heart of England. The
exhausting marches of the last few days had wholly baffled
their most formidable enemy, the Duke of Cumberland, who
was now groping for them to the west while the road to
London lay uncovered before them. It had been a piece of
strategy which only the tireless mobility of the Highlanders
could have accomplished—and which (Darthula was forced
in justice to own) only the skill of Lord George Murray
could have conducted so faultlessly.

Lord George was not among the invited guests to-night,
though his easy-going colleague in the command, the Duke
of Perth, was present, laughing and jesting in his broad Scots.
Darthula had seen Lord George, too, ride into Derby, his
face gloomy, his lips drawn together as though he were
whistling. He had glanced with a sarcastic cock of his heavy
brows at a little knot of enthusiasts who had mounted the
white cockade and come out to raise a thin cheer. She had
been furious at his behaviour, but yet she felt that he should
not have been omitted to-night. It was, she hoped, only
fatigue and responsibility that were weighing on the chiefs

and other officers, who spoke so little and so subduedly—the three kinds of wine which the Prince's servants had managed to provide ought soon to raise their spirits. Except for Colonel O'Sullivan, resplendent in fresh curls, white breeches and silk stockings, a sight which had obviously not pleased the Prince, they had come to the impromptu dinner-party in their marching clothes, with barely time to wash away the dust and mud of the journey; officers like men had to travel light on marches like those they were making. She herself was still in the riding-habit of green cloth which she had worn on the road, and the other two ladies present, Lady Ogilvy and lovely Mrs. Murray, were no better adorned. There was excuse for all if their tongues were slow to be loosened.

Mrs. Murray's husband, however, was not among the depressed ones. "I take it, Miss Maceachan," he said in his dogmatic manner to Darthula, who was his left-hand neighbour, "that our task is more than half accomplished. I doubt if Cumberland will come after us with a speed to overtake us: I doubt indeed if he has any desire to face the broad-swords of Gladsmuir. What is there, then, but the rabble of Finchley between us and the capital? We are in sight, by my way of it, of the rewards we have earned." He smiled at her significantly. "I think there are a plenty Scots ladies would well become English titles. Maybe we shall be seeing more than one fair new Countess."

"Mr. Murray!" Lochiel leaned across the mahogany over a pool of primrose candle-light. "Mr. Murray," he asked in his grave, courteous voice, "have you any better intelligence concerning our English friends? I must say they seem more at home in the toasting and speechmaking: in forming associations and swearing to pledges, than in honouring those pledges when the moment to take to the saddle comes."

Murray looked a trifle annoyed. "I misdoubt, Lochiel,

that the very speed, the irresistible onrush of our advance, has taken our English sympathisers somewhat by surprise. They have barely had time to muster themselves."

"Oh, come! Mr. Murray," expostulated Lochiel, with a spark of irritation in his luminous grey eyes, "they have had ample time for preparation if they were in earnest. The Usurper has equipped several battalions of militia in these parts: except for the gallant gentlemen who formed themselves into a regiment for us at Manchester, we have not, that I can see, enlisted a man since we crossed the Border!"

"Well, Lochiel," confessed Murray, "I believe, when all is said, our chief succours from the southern portion of this island must be looked for among the gentry and loyal commonalty of Wales."

"Wales!" eclaimed Lochiel. "We are leagues from Wales, man! Must we turn aside thither to recruit our strength?"

Before Murray could think of his reply the pipers who every evening attended the Prince's dinner entered the room, and marched round the table playing "Lochiel's Salute," for they were Camerons to-night. As they disappeared, the Prince turned to Lochiel with an affectionate smile. "There is your answer, my friend," he said to the Chief, who looked a trifle embarrassed at having been overheard. "We shall turn neither to the right hand nor the left: we shall march straight forward to London to finish our work. What is there to stay us? With that music in my ears I cannot think I need any other troops for the task in hand. Gentlemen, drink with me to the Clans!"

He stood up, a glass of crimson burgundy shining in his hand, and drained it with slow enjoyment to the end. While the others chinked glasses, and cried the toast, the voice of bagpipes was heard again without, and was taken up as though in answer all over the town, where the retreat was being played by the various regiments. The heartening sound provoked Colonel O'Sullivan to demonstration. "To His Royal Highness and victory!" he shouted, drawing his sword, "Next week in London!" The Highland Chiefs caught fire at his rich, rolling voice; they unsheathed their claymores, and the jewels in the hilts glinted as the Ferrara blades struck with a silvery sound together over the candelabra. Clan slogans resounded in deep voices: "Dh'aindeoin co theireadhe!" ("Gainsay who dare!") cried Clan Ranald; "Dia's Naomh Aindrea!" ("God and St. Andrew!") said Keppoch; "Geal is Dearg a suas!" ("Up with the Red and White!") said Menzies. "God bless your Royal Highness!" murmured old Sir Thomas Sheridan, with moist eyes.

Darthula thrilled. In spite of the gloom and gauntness of the stripped room, the draughts that pierced the uncurtained shutters like daggers, here glowed a circle of loyalty and faith. Here hearts were united; here hope shone starry through the winter's night. And outside all around the devoted Highland Army filled the English town: in the houses of the gentry officers pored over their maps or wrote their orders; in cottages, hovels and stables, wrapped in their plaids on boards, or burrowing, for warmth into straw, lay the Highland men, scantily fed, ill-clothed, lean and taut, their brogues in thongs, their feet blistered or bleeding with the late forced marches; but their spirits keen as the weapons they so assiduously ground and polished. For them indeed neither toasts nor homages; their reward permission to return to their mountains, their huts, their starveling fields; until called again to leave wives, children and their tiny store, to give their limbs and lives . . . for what? . . . For Kingship. . . . *Was it worth it?*

Darthula started as the question thrust itself, like a sword-blade, into her mind. She did not realise how her senses had been sharpened by watching for weeks the privations of the rank and file, how thin the tissue of mere romanticism had worn under the stress of her own fatigues and efforts. She felt a doubt, and asked herself a question. Asked it, and lifting her eyes to the figure of Charles Edward, radiant in the halo of candle-light at the head of the table, answered joyfully, proudly that he was in truth well worth it.

As she did so, she saw that his eyes were upon her, too, darkening to a blue veil behind which brooded a thought she had never seen in them before. Her blood tingled at it, her sight went cloudy as she felt nervously for the stem of her wine-glass. The tall cornices of the room, the flickering candles, the bearded gillies at their service, the tall, tartan-clad forms of the Chiefs dissolved; she was alone in a swirling mist, through which shone two deep sapphires, piercing into her soul . . .

Slowly, like a wave running up a beach, the voices, the clink of plates and glass returned to her. The Prince, after a jesting debate whether he should wear Highland dress or an English uniform on his entry into London, rose, and led the way across the hall into a drawing-room with the same chill, abandoned air as the room where they had dined. A wood fire sent leaping flames up the chimney beneath a carved mantelpiece from over which, as a line of nail-holes showed, the mirror had been removed.

One by one the Chiefs and officers went up to the Prince, as he stood before the fire, to take their leave before returning to their duties. Almost every one seemed to have some difficulty to put before him, and he listened to each in turn with a smiling reassurance. Sometimes he called Murray of Broughton forward to produce a paper or give information; once the Secretary intervened unasked; and Keppoch, who was in audience, turned on him with a rapped-out retort. In a moment the Prince had the Chief gratified and beaming.

Darthula observed that those who went up to Charles hesitant or anxious came away relieved; those who approached in confidence left him with a swing, almost with a swagger. He was at his best, she realised, to-night, imparting to all about him his greatest gift, his unconquerable spirit. His whole entourage was catching the full flame of his sacred fire.

The room was emptying. Lady Ogilvy made her curtsey and departed with her husband. "Mr. Murray," said Charles, "there will be no more work for you. I give you to your lady for to-night."

For a second Mrs. Murray hesitated, glancing with a little question in her look at Darthula; but her husband touched her almost imperceptibly with his elbow, and made a signal with his sharp eyes towards the door. They withdrew, and Darthula became aware that, except for old Sheridan, who was snoring like a wearied hunting-dog in the chair he had been allowed to take, she was alone with the Prince.

2

WITH eyes like a school-boy's he put a finger on his lips and blew out all but one candle on the mantelpiece. Then he beckoned her to follow him through the open folding-doors that led into the shadowy back-part of the long *salon*, where a mass of furniture had been piled together and covered with cloths. It included a sofa, and Charles drew her down on this beside him.

"At last," he said in a low whisper, "I have you to myself! You need not be uneasy; you can hear that our excellent *chaperon* is at his post. We shall not wake him unless we are very noisy. . . . Ah! Darthula, this is my night of nights! If I have a star, as you so often tell me, it stands at the zenith. London is ours for the trouble of stretching out hand to take it. So far the star has brought me . . . but who is the star? It is you, Darthula, my guide, my encourager, my support!"

"Oh! no, no, Abbé," she answered, with soft vehemence. "'Tis not I am deserving your gratitude: it is the men, the men who have done all, and for whom there will be neither crosses, nor titles nor lands. 'Tis perhaps in the order of Providence; but do not, at least, deny them their thanks."

"Ever a poetess, Darthula!" he answered in a slightly mocking tone. "I assure you, though, I do not forget the Clans. More than once I have thanked them to their faces. In due course they will also, doubtless, have the honour of hearing from the lips of my Father, the King himself, that they have done their duty, as we looked to them to do. But do not let us confuse the peasant's lot and the Prince's, the gentleman's station and the hind's. Without their leaders these nameless heroes of yours would sink into forgotten graves at the foot of their mountains. Without the King the Chiefs would have no guiding-star, no cause for which they could manifest their valour. . . . And, Darthula, but for your fearless soul and your bright eyes, he who to-day holds the King's place could not have led them to the verge of triumph. . . . What reward can be great enough for you?"

"You know," she whispered, "that I am desiring no reward but continuance in your service, *Phrionnsa*."

"So that," he moved a little closer to her on the sofa, "if I were to ask more from you, you would be ready to give more, admirable girl?"

"What I have to give you is simply said. It is—my all. I am withholding nothing from my Prince."

"But is there nothing you would withhold from Charles Edward . . . from the man?"

She could not affect to misread the throb in his voice, and her whole nature was thrown into a tumult. He had asked: could she give? Her pride revolted. She was not the stuff of which a Royal leman could be made. She could not stoop to be an equivocal Countess at St. James's, she whose ancestors had been Kings in the Great Glen.

She felt his hand on hers, his breath in her ear. "Crown me!" he was whispering. "Crown me on this greatest night of my life!"

She tried to temporise. "Abbé, forbear!" she murmured. "This will be no hour for thoughts of love! Private joys must follow public victory!"

He broke in with an intense exasperation. "There may be no victory if I am never to be granted what every hind may enjoy! Do you take me for a walking statue—to be continually presiding at Council, acknowledging salutes on parade, tramping, tramping over your endless leagues of heather, endless miles of stony road? And then when the day's toil is accomplished, my recompense is to compose the quarrels of those who should sink their personal differences and ambitions in my cause. . . . Am I never to be just a man? Never to know a little peace, a little consolation? Never to bathe my wearied spirit in beauty and in love?"

She felt her will wavering. When had she ever denied him anything for which he pleaded in that tone? "I am afraid . . . afraid," she said in a sobbing breath.

"What do you fear? Darthula, a Prince's necessities are understood by all reasonable persons. I will encircle you for your protection with honours . . . with such high honours. . . ."

"They will be honours! What you will never be able to restore to me will be—honour!" She sat in silence with hanging head.

"Is that your only scruple?" He had drawn away from her a little on the sofa.

Was it? In the bleak, dark apartment there rose before her the face of Allan Duncanson, with its hungry eyes, with the sense of coiled virility behind its hesitant bashfulness. It was almost as hallucinatory in its vividness as the little image of the Prince that she had seen in the glass at Glenmarisdale on another night of fateful decision. She detested herself for thus facing about; then felt that sudden dead-locking of a divided will that prevents all further thought or struggle. She sank back exhausted against the coarse cloth draping the sofa.

"Darthula!" insisted Charles, "that is your only scruple?"

As she made no answer he took her silence for assent. "I think," he said, "it might be removed. Wait! Let me reflect!"

He rose from the sofa and began to pace to and fro, silent in his brogues, in the adjoining room. She lay back, thankful for the respite, tears she could not check running down her cheeks. It seemed to her that hours had passed when Charles wheeled swiftly, and came with his lithe step, in which there always seemed something of the motion of a gracious young tiger, back through the folding-doors into the room where she waited.

"Darthula," he said in a low, vibrant voice, "you have often told me you are the daughter of kings."

She could not repress a wan smile. "You cannot expect me, sir, to be disbelieving the records of my House."

"I do not ask you to disbelieve them," he answered astonishingly. "I am asking myself whether they are not indeed worthy of credit. Could I bring myself to that faith . . . then you could be mine with no scruple of honour at all."

The whites of her eyes flashed in the gloom with amazement, as she stammered, "Do you know what it is you are saying, Abbé? You can never be meaning—"

"Why not?" he breathed defiantly. "A Highland King is as good as a German or Italian Princeling for lineage. . . . My ancestors have married subjects. What a King has done a King may do again."

She still sat staring blankly at him. "You would be marrying me . . . making me your *Queen* when the time comes?"

"I have said it. What Queen more gallant could Scotia demand? Ride with me to London, Darthula Maceachan, as my promised Princess in secret. In London I will proclaim you to all the world."

"It is impossible!"

"Am I not the man for whom the impossible comes true?"

"I cannot give an answer now."

"You must," he declared with a terrifying intensity. "Once pledged we need not deny each other! Refuse me to-night, and I tell you I shall go mad!"

"So," she cried, "you are not, after all, to be respecting me? What signifies all this talk of Queenship then?"

Before she realised what had happened, he had, with a bound like the young tiger to which she had been comparing him, snatched her into his arms. She struggled as though against a hoop of fine steel. Then his kisses were stifling her murmurs . . . cold lips which seemed to suck the strength from her. It was like being plunged in the spray of an icy fall—more than once out of some wild impulse of daring she had risked that at home, bathing in mountain streams before the clemency of summer had tempered the keenness of spring. Her sensations now were of much the same kind, fearfully multiplied. The icy waves were dashing round her, against her throat, her eyes, her hair. It was a breath-taking ecstasy, shot with pain . . . but an ecstasy in which desire seemed struck suddenly dead.

Her bosom was still panting when the Prince's grasp abruptly relaxed, and she saw that his head was turned from her in a listening poise. . . . In the garden which ran from the back of the room where they were down to the river, they could hear a step, and it not the regular foot-fall of a sentry. From the drawing-room long windows opened on stone steps that led to the lawn, and these back windows by oversight had not had their shutters closed when the house was abandoned by its servants.

Charles, without moving, peered through the panes, but the night outside was too black to reveal the trespasser. The foot sounded on the steps outside the window, and they had the eerie sense that they were being looked at by the unknown. But they, too, were not discernible from without, for the single candle in the front room threw but a faint glimmer into the back part. There was a pause, and then came the rasping sound of a knife-point inserted into the window-catch.

"Call the guard, oh! call the guard!" whispered Darthula to Charles, who stood with an odd rigidity, his arm round her. For answer he only clasped her tighter, as if enjoining silence.

The windows burst open, letting in a cold draught, and a figure could be dimly seen groping its way forward through the piles of swathed furniture. It did not observe them, where they had withdrawn into a corner, but came cautiously forward towards the candle-light in the front room. Darthula hardly kept down a scream when she made out the sheen of a dirk in its hand.

Suddenly Charles spoke. "Well, Glenmarisdale," he said, "I divined somehow that it was you. Is it thus you force entry into my presence?"

Darthula did not this time stop a cry as Hector whirled round between the folding doors and faced them. The sound woke the old tutor slumbering in his arm-chair in the front room. "God save His Royal Highness!" he stammered confusedly; then tottering to his feet, stood with fallen jaw.

"Major Maceachan," said Charles quietly, "has returned from his mission to the north . . . and brings me his news without waiting. Sir Thomas, you are too late from your bed. You may retire now. Glenmarisdale will be my guard."

Sir Thomas blinked. Hector was dusty with travel, his breasts were heaving, he had the naked dirk with which he had forced the window in his hand. The Prince was unarmed.

"Oh! be easy," laughed Charles. "We had an alarm of eaves-droppers, but it is over. The guard, I must complain, is very remiss."

Sir Thomas bowed, and was retiring when the Prince called to him.

"How many years have you known me, Sir Thomas?"

"Why, sir, I think you were some five years old when I first set my blessed eyes on you."

"And we have known good times and bad times, triumph and failure together, have we not, my dear old friend?"

"That has been my great honour, sir."

"And never in fatigue or disappointment, or when your personal views were in jeopardy, or when appearances of things have been distorted against me, have you ever had a doubt of me, have you?"

"Sure, sir, I am no madman to harbour such a thought!"

"I thank you. I am always thanking you in my heart."

He held out his hand to kiss, and the old courtier backed out from the room.

"Is your Highness's Italian comedy over?" demanded Glenmarisdale roughly as the door shut.

"Hector!" his sister broke in, regardless of etiquette. "How dare you take that tone? How dare you be breaking in here like a thief? Have you lost your senses?"

"I am where I have a right to be! I returned to find you absent from your lodgings. Mrs. Murray disclosed the shameful truth to my questioning. I am demanding satisfaction whether he be a Prince or no. Our family honour is as precious as his—"

"I do not deny it, Glenmarisdale," said Charles. "But

your honour stands in no danger of soiling."

"You would have me be believing that? You sent me to
Inverness that you might have your way of her unhindered.
. . . I find you alone with her in this dark room, midnight
past. . . . Do you take me for a child, sir?"

"You *are* a child!" Darthula rated him. "You have mis-
construed all! On your knees, and be begging pardon for
your madness!"

"Be so good, if you will, as to attend to me," said the
Prince. "I believe I am competent to decide on affairs of
honour, being at this moment honour's source in this kingdom. There may be something in the accidents of this rencounter that seems to condemn me. It is appearance only—
good God, one cannot observe all the fashions of etiquette in
the hurly-burly of campaigning! *Honi soit qui mal y pense!*
I pardon your intemperateness, Hector, seeing that you are
fatigued and surprised. Moreover, it is my purpose to clear
away all doubts and give you entire satisfaction in public at
to-morrow's Council."

Darthula gave a cry of dismay. "To-morrow, sir! No, no.
I implore you—"

"It has become needful now, Darthula," said Charles in-
flexibly. "Think on the future! Can I any more than your
brother endure that the faintest shadow should rest on your
name? And so for the present, Glenmarisdale, leave us!"

"Leave my sister with you, ——," he used an abominable
Italian word.

Charles stepped forward with hand upraised to buffet him.
Hector lifted the dirk, and Darthula rushed between them,
and fighting like a wild-cat, bit deep into her brother's hand
to make him drop the steel.

Charles, with his royal composure regained, shrugged his
shoulders, saying, "I deemed, Glenmarisdale, that you had
taken up those arms to defend our body. Darthula, you had

better go with this boy now. I tell you, my dear, that to-morrow all shall be made crystal clear." He bowed and kissed her hand.

Outside in the garden there sounded murmurs and the clink of weapons as the guard, who had belatedly discovered the open window on their rounds, approached the spot.

Hector held out his bleeding hand. "Such are the wounds I will be gaining in your service, Charles Stewart," he said; "*Non obliviscor!*" Turning, he slowly left the room with his head sunk low. Darthula followed him, despairingly weeping.

3

SHE passed a night of sleepless suffering in the lodgings they shared with the Murrays. On their way thither Hector had refused to speak a word to her; her entreaties, her tears of sorrow at the hurt she had done him in her frenzy, her attempts at reasoned argument met the same wall of contemptuous silence. He locked himself in his room, leaving her imploring on the threshold; and early the next morning she heard him descending the stairs, but could not catch him before he had gone out into the street. She could not think what purpose of black anger he was meditating.

Soon after nine arrived an aide-de-camp commanding her attendance at Exeter House in an hour's time. She had no choice but to make ready and go. Charles received her immediately and was adamant in his intention to announce his proposed marriage to the Council at mid-day. "My faith!" he cried blithely, "the Chiefs will be honoured that I choose a daughter of their nation!"

"It will be the very way to disunite them," she remonstrated desperately. "Do you suppose that none will be jealous because their own families have not been chosen?"

"Your family, at least," he laughed, "shows little appreciation of the privilege! But we will calm that mad boy of yours. You gave him a shrewd bite yestere'en, my little wild-cat! You would be a better bodyguard, I am thinking, than a file of Grenadiers!"

She broke into sobs, and he tried to soothe her with tender rallying. "And now," he said, "I must ride round the quarters; it will cheer the men to see me about betimes and thinking of them. . . . You see, I am always learning lessons from you!" He picked up his blue bonnet and set it on the grey wig he had taken to wearing, and she followed him down the wide oak staircase from the upstairs drawing-room, where he had received her.

Through the open door she could see his horses waiting in the sunshine on the drive; then two shadows fell on the steps of the little pillared porch, and the sentry outside saluted as Lord George Murray and her brother entered.

She stood still, with a painful jump of her heart, on the bottom step of the stairs, one hand grasping the heavy knob of the balusters. The white bandage on Hector's hand seemed to sear her eyes.

Charles greeted the visitors smiling. "You are welcome, Lord George. For what purpose do you seek audience before the Council?"

"I trust your Highness will agree with me," answered the lieutenant-general, whose face was grave, "that it is time to decide what we must be doing."

"Doing?" asked Charles, surprised. "Is it not decided? Have we not agreed to march to-morrow, after sending out parties to secure the road against surprise?"

Lord George shook his head. "I for one, sir, never assented to any such line of action, and I am sure I am not alone in disapproving it."

"Disapprove? Disapprove what, my lord?" Charles's voice was rising in irritation.

"I disapprove the project of an advance."

"You wish us to linger more days in Derby?"

"I am not at all in favour of lingering, sir."

"Why, then, I confess, my lord, I cannot read your meaning."

"My opinion is, sir, that we should use no delay at all in commencing our retreat."

"*Retreat?*" Charles's eyes rounded in school-boyish perplexity. He forced a laugh. "Sure, you jest, my lord!"

The General frowned austerely. "It was never my way, sir, to jest about the grave concerns of life. Least of all where your Highness's fortunes and safety are involved."

"Why, then," Charles clutched at a madly whirling straw, "I must suppose this is some strategic feint you have planned. *Reculer pour mieux sauter*—ha?"

Lord George pursed his lips in their whistling way. "I will not deceive your Highness into thinking that I see to-day the prospect of advance, after whatever movements of manœuvre. No, sir, my sole concern, my urgent concern, is to bring yourself and your army off safe, if I can, by immediate retreat into Scotland, from the enemies that are gathering in irresistible force to crush us."

"Turn back from London!" ejaculated Charles in a whisper of consternation. "Can I hear you aright? What have we to fear to-day that we had not to fear yesterday?"

"I was full of apprehensions yesterday, sir, as indeed I have been since we entered England. The failure of our friends on this side of the border to rise—doubt of the strength of the enemy that hangs on our flank to menace us—the certainty that we must, with numbers that diminish instead of augmenting as we march, assault a great armed camp on the north of London. And to this has now been added news brought me by Major Maceachan here early this morning, which forbids me to hesitate an unnecessary hour in pressing retreat on your Highness. . . . Major Maceachan has not always shown so worthy a sense of his duty to me."

"Major Maceachan has brought you news!" Charles's eyes blazed darkly. "Why, sir," he turned on Hector, "was I not informed of it so soon as you reached Derby last night?"

"I presumed to wait upon your Royal Highness for that purpose," replied Hector with a devilishly sardonic look, "but had the misfortune to find you . . . otherwise preoccupied." He lifted his bandaged hand to his mouth.

"And what may your precious information amount to, sir?" asked Charles after a pause.

"I beg your Highness not to make light of it!" interrupted Lord George almost peremptorily. "Major Maceachan gleaned, as he rode along to join us, that Cumberland had reached Lichfield on our flank with a force of nigh on 8,000 men . . . and that there is another army—he could not learn under what commander . . . Ligonier or Hawley—across our advance at Northampton. Sir, we risk being caught in pincers too strong for us."

"Preposterous!" cried Charles. "You invent armies from the air, the pair of you! They have not so many men in the kingdom to bring against us!"

"Well, sir," said Lord George, settling his obstinate chin into his stock, "I am disposed to credit Major Maceachan's informants."

"Glenmarisdale, my former friend," said Charles in a low, entreating tone to Hector. "Think well what you are saying! Are you bringing us the truth?"

Hector had been staring moodily behind the Prince at the figure of his sister, standing like a statue upon the stair. Now he turned a terrible, frozen face upon the Prince. "I have brought your Highness the best intelligence I could gather," he said in grating voice. "I am willing to repeat it to the

Council. They shall judge of its value."

"Aye," cried Charles, "I appeal to the Council! They shall make short work of this folly . . . if it be not worse!"

"Your Highness," said Lord George in a cutting tone, "is not pleased to be complimentary to our devotion! But I am very well content, too, to lay my case before the Council."

There was a little sighing gasp behind them, and a rustle of skirts. Darthula had bowed forward, and, as it were, toppled in upon herself. She lay, white in a swoon, in a heap upon the stair.

As the short brightness of the December day faded, and the snow-streaked hills round about the little town began to stand out gaunt in the gloaming, wild rumours began to run about Derby. They increased and grew wilder when the Council, which had been sitting since mid-day at Exeter House, broke up in a dissolving throng of melancholy, anxious, and here and there shame-stricken faces. The chiefs were glum, the officers reticent. But in the hall of the Prince's residence old Sir John Macdonald, usually so taciturn, was heard uplifting his gruff voice in defiance of discretion to a couple of perplexed Highland officers lingering for orders.

"Poltroons! Namby-pamby babies!" boomed the man of Moidart. "Running from their own shadows! Well, *sang de Dieu*, you may mark my words! You will none of you ever see London now till you traverse it in the hangman's cart!"

"Old Shonnie has been at the clar't wi' his dinner," tittered one of the Highlanders behind his hand to the other.

"As for Lord George Murray," pursued the irrepressible veteran, "I expect it of him—a barrack-ground soldier, always frightened of numbers. But for what need that young spark Glenmarisdale have backed him so venomously? . . . Ah! there is something below the surface there. His Highness knew it well. *Et tu, Brute!* Those were his words to young Maceachan. . . . One of you two is a Clan Ranald man, is he not? . . . You have a pretty coxcomb there, *sacré nom d'un Nom! Et tu, Brute!* Those were the Prince's words, for I heard 'em myself!"

Chapter II

GREAT DAYS FOR THE MACEACHANS

1

THE January wind howled, razor-edged, up the wynds, and swept like the sword of an invading army round into the High Street of Edinburgh. In his coffin-shaped study in Advocates' Close, Lord Brounhill was bent over his desk, his back to the slit of window through which could be caught a glimpse of the grey, ruffled Firth, the wintry fields beyond, etched with black dots upon white, the plaintive ghosts of the Highland hills hanging on a snow-laden pall. The wind moaned beseechingly round the room and in the chimney, but the scratch of the unrelenting pen went on till close upon mid-day.

Then the servant announced, "Mr. Duncanson."

The judge looked up from his writing, and sat for a moment with the glassy look by which he masked surprise.

Instead of the black-clad legal figure he had anticipated, he saw before him a young Highland officer in the dark green kilt and plaid of the Campbells of Argyll.

"I barely recognised you, Mr. Duncanson," he said at length in a slowly grating tone.

"I have secured a lieutenancy, my lord, in the Duke of Argyll's Militia. I am doing what so many others are at this emergency, following my Chief's standard to the war."

"To the War!" Lord Brounhill frowned. "I grieve to hear this news. I had other plans for ye, Mr. Duncanson. I had hopes that it might very shortly be in my power to advance your prospects substantially in the law."

"I profess my gratitude to your lordship. It seems, sir, that your benevolence must await a more favourable opportunity."

"Aye, young man!" broke in the judge testily, "but golden opportunities once neglected, ye ken, will not return at our beckoning. I had designed to place ye very near me, and I may soon have powers of patronage far beyond the openings that appertain to a mere Lord of Session. Sit ye doon, Mr. Duncanson." He rose from his chair and waddled over to the starveling fire, which flickered feebly on the wooden lines of his face. "I will be plain with you, for I know you are to be trusted," he said at length, turning round to face his visitor. "Ye ken, I suppose, that Duncan Forbes grows, wi' every day that passes, into waur odour wi' the Government?"

Allan Duncanson lifted troubled brows. "I am surprised to hear you say so, my lord. His indefatigable zeal, his exposure of his person to peril in the heart of the enemy's country at Culloden, where he hath taken his seat for more effectual dealing with the rebels—"

"Or for more effectual shielding of them," interrupted Lord Brounhill in a voice like a felled branch crackling.

"What an extraordinar' suggestion, my lord! Only a few months syne in the autumn my Lord President was imperilling his life on the battlements of his mansion, resisting the attack of the Frasers. He had been shot, too, but for your own ward Glenmarisdale, who struck up the musket of Lord Lovat's bravo—you surely know all this?"

"I know nothing gude of Hector Maceachan," said the Tutor with a stony look.

"They cannot reward Forbes for such devotion with disgrace! What reason have they for dissatisfaction. . . . Government, that is?"

"I have confidence in you, Mr. Duncanson, and I will open all to you. Duncan Forbes is aye for exhibiting clemency to the rebels."

"Clemency may be no bad policy, my lord."

"I will tak' leave to differ from you there—and in the interests of Scotland itsel'. It is aye a grand temptation to a Government situate as ours is, to purchase allegiance by pardoning those who have offended, at the expense of those who hae borne the brunt o' the day on its behalf. That is neither justice nor gude policy. It holds out no promise of peace for the future."

Duncanson glanced up sharply. "I should have supposed," he said, looking Lord Brounhill in the face with a cold, pale eye, "that placed as your Lordship is, you would have seconded any movement towards amnesty—for family reasons."

"Ye read the Scriptures, Mr. Duncanson?" asked Lord Brounhill, unperturbed.

"I endeavour not to fail in that duty, according to the measure of my opportunities."

"Then ye will not have failed to read that 'every branch that beareth not fruit He taketh away,' John, chapter fifteenth, sub-section second. And ye will have read, 'The soul that sinneth, it shall die,' Ezekiel, chapter eighteenth, sub-section fourth. There ye hae the exposition o' the Divine Law on the matter before us. By what natural justice, either, I pray you, suld a whole fam'ly be uprooted for the misdoings of one, twa rotten members? Shall the great House of Maceachan o' Glenmarisdale, older far than Clan Ranald of a royal lineage anterior by centuries to Stewarts o Guelphs, shall it be sacrificed to the madness of a stripling not twenty years of age, lured to his doom by a crazy wenc wha has played to him the part of a sorceress rather than sister?"

"I would respectfully put you in memory, Lord Brounhil that you were latterly pleased to honour me with a propos that Miss Maceachan should give me her hand in a treaty o marriage."

"I proposed it to your father," agreed Lord Brounhil taken aback by the steel in his tone. "I did not weel know at that date what black maggots were breeding in my niece brain. I will beg you henceforth to put Darthula clean fro your head. We maun remake our projects. As I see the li o' the land to-day, a far more favourable combination i within the scope o' Providence. Hector will be attainted fo his share in this wicked rebellion—there exists no power i these Isles that can save him—"

"Mistress Darthula!"

"She, too. The doom is set. But I hae hopes that the estat may escape forfeiture, thanks to my loyal efforts in Hi Majesty's cause. It may be resettled upon mysel' and th heirs o' ma body—by a special provision, on the heirs ma *or female*. I am no likely to procreate a son at my time o life. What say ye, then, Inveralsk, to becoming the husban of the heiress o' Glenmarisdale . . . aye, and son-in-law t the new Lord President of the Council?"

"Say, my lord! I say . . . that I wish your lordship th advancement you look for."

"I am sanguine."

"It would appear so. But I pray you, leave me hencefort out of your calculations."

"How, Mr. Duncanson! I never knew you, before, as one to quarrel wi' your ain bread and butter, to turn your back on your fairest prospect of advancement."

"I would not willingly be so unreasonable. But your lordship forgets that Mistress Darthula may have made an impression—"

"Forget it!" said the judge indifferently, lifting himself up and down on his little legs by his heels, with his skirts raised in his hands from before the fire. "What! isna my Jean a winsome lass eneuch? She wad be fairer in my sight, I'll uphaud you, were I a lad, than yon little Hielan' cat wi' her hungry een." He wriggled his high shoulders, as though seeking to rid himself of a discomfort.

"They are eyes," said Duncanson softly, "that I can well believe would haunt any man who did her wrong. I would be sorry to have the memory of them, like a burden, upon my soul when I came to die."

"Mr. Duncanson, what is a' this unprofitable talk? Wha' spoke o' burdens upon the soul?"

"What does your lordship suppose is to become of your niece?" asked Duncanson bluntly.

Lord Brounhill very slowly uncrumpled his hands below their tiny wrist-frills, as though to demonstrate their perfect cleanliness. "Can I tell? Can I penetrate the designs o' Providence? Darthula has made her ain bed . . . on the heather. She maun lie thereon."

There was a silence in which the wind from the north again raised its imploring moan in the chimney.

"At least," said Duncanson after a pause, "your lordship, if you are raised to the dignity of Lord President, will be in the position to do for her all that in law can be done."

"I admire at you, Inveralsk!" said Lord Brounhill harshly. "Would you have me bend my high office to fam'ly interests?"

Allan Duncanson rose with a shrug. "Perhaps I may be permitted to speak with you again, sir, on these topics?"

"Aye, reflect weel! Go canny! . . . I wad not hae you of a different nature, gin ye are to be my son-in-law." He began to collect papers from his desk. "I will be awa' now to the House o' the Lord Justice Clerk, to the Council o' War to be holden there by His Royal Highness, the Duke of Cumberland and His Serene Highness the Prince of Hesse. . . . And now I bethink me, the Duke holds levee the nicht at Holyroodhouse. I will mak' your presentation wi' ma daughter's, gin ye will accompany the twa of us thither. If ye are sae dooms set upon making this campaign, I will at the least bring ye into the sun o' the Commander-in-Chief's presence; it may be profitable to ye."

"I am obliged to your lordship." Allan Duncanson bowed.

"Oh! have nae fears! I will elevate ye, Inveralsk, wi' my ain fam'ly . . . gin ye work ma will! These be great days for the Maceachans! Wha kens if the superiorities and jurisdictions o' Clan Ranald himsel' may not pass to a new Chief that has held true in adversities and vicissitudes to the lawfu' King o' these realms?"

Allan Duncanson stood for a moment looking through the narrow window at the pitiless, winter-bound landscape. Along what ice-covered roads, over what snow-laden passes, was the rebel host at this hour painfully pursuing its retreat to the north, heartened perhaps by its recent resounding victory over the pursuing General Hawley at Falkirk, yet dashed in hope, it must be, that the issue of fresh success was only retreat . . . yet again retreat. With them was the boy Glenmarisdale, scarcely ignorant now, surely, that he had engaged himself and his family in a ruinous adventure. With them was Darthula, facing in her slight, little person the cold, the hunger, the exhaustion of such a march through Scotland in the fiercest grip of winter, comfortless, hopeless, with not one bright ray to gild her future beneath the leaden skies of the retreat.

Great days, truly, for the Maceachans!

2

LORD BROUNHILL, wigged and robed, took a chair to the Lord Justice Clerk's house. There were plenty of people in the High Street, despite the cold wind and the powdered snow on the steps of the gables. The causeway was dotted with red-coats, and outside the Luckenbooths he observed a group of the Prince of Hesse's Hussars in their fur caps and tasselled boots, who were combing their long fair locks in front of a mirror, watched by curious bystanders.

Arrived at the Lord Justice Clerk's residence, he walked upstairs into a room filled with uniforms and civic gowns. The Prince of Hesse was listening to a communication in German from Lord Crawford, his liaison officer with the British troops. Brounhill noticed the English Generals Albemarle, Ancrum and Brigadier Mordaunt; the Colonels Ligonier, Sempill and Barrel; Lord Mark Ker in Dragoon uniform, the red and sullen face of the now superseded Hawley, the defeated of Falkirk. All these and a throng of others were chatting in low tones, waiting for the arrival of their Royal Commander-in-Chief; and Lord Brounhill had only time for a brief word with Lord Milton, the Justice Clerk, in his red robe, before an orderly officer announced "His Royal Highness," and all the soldiers present stood to the salute.

Into the room, with a pigeon-toed step, his hands joined behind his back, his head hanging forward, as though pulled by the ball of his corpulent belly, rolled a young man with a pear-shaped head, tapering from the base to a narrow forehead plastered with carefully-powdered curls. His cocked-hat was thrust to the back of his head, his nose pointed sharply and inquisitively, with the large, protuberant eyes close in to each side of it. At the moment they were dull and distrait, as though the Duke were immersed in reflections of his own; the slab of the lower lip protruded with a ruminative movement.

He answered with a negligent nod the salutes of the military, the bows of the legal and civic functionaries; and seating himself at the head of the table looked round with an impatient air for the others to take their places. There was a shuffle and a clink of scabbards and spurs as the Council found its seats.

Cumberland sat for a moment drumming fat, white fingers on the table; his nails were long, pointed and polished. His A.D.C. placed a paper of agenda before him on the green cloth; he glanced at it a moment with his lower lip distended, and then flipped it away. For a moment he sat still, his coarse double-jowl creased over his neck-cloth. Then suddenly, without compliment or preliminaries, he said sharply to the Justice Clerk in a guttural voice:

"Well, my lor-rd, and what is the position?"

Lord Milton, a trifle disconcerted, played with a pen.

"Don't you know *anyt'ing*?"

"Your Royal Highness," answered the Justice Clerk with dignity, "it scarcely appertaineth to my office to advise upon military matters. We looked to be enlightened by your Highness's officers."

"My officers!" Cumberland heaved up his heavy shoulders, and the corners of his mouth creased in dismally sardonic lines. "Gadzooks! My officers have but one opinion. The war-r is as good as won! Eh, Hawley?"

"I believe, your Royal Highness," mumbled Hawley sullenly, "that the rebels suffered more heavily in the engagement at Falkirk than has ever been acknowledged. They are thinned, too, by desertions."

"Desertions!" snapped the Duke. "They are always deserting, according to the news . . . but their army never grows less. What can you expect when the whole of Scotland is a br-reeding-ground for r-rebels?" He glowered challengingly at the Scottish dignitaries round the table.

Lord Milton leaned forward with an indignant sweep of his red sleeve. "I venture to hope that your Royal Highness underestimates . . . cruelly underestimates . . . the loyalty of this Kingdom! I think . . . I think . . ." he faltered, as the dull, bulging eyes seemed to look through and through him.

The Duke's gilt-buttoned waistcoat heaved in a rasping chuckle. "You t'ink, my lord, you t'ink! . . . Well, gog's wouns, I am *asking* you what you t'ink! You know the Highlands? You are acquainted with the Highlanders?"

Lord Milton saw a slit of escape. "You are a Highlander yourself, Lord Brounhill," he said. "You can better tell His Highness of their mind!"

Cumberland, out of the corner of his eye, peeped at the wooden face of Lord Brounhill. "A Highland judge!" he exclaimed, pulling the corners of his mouth down again in dismal sarcasm. "Well: let us hear the Highland judge by all means. . . . Speak, Highland judge!"

"I am a Lord of Session," said Brounie in a sharp tone, "and it is true that, having for years had the care of a Hieland estate, and been the chief support o' loyalty to King George in those parts—"

"A fine tr-riumph, you have made of it!" jerked out the Duke. "Well?"

"I say," continued Brounie, as calmly as though he were addressing his Court, "I say the war is *not* yet over. The spirit of the Hielands remains unbroken, and your Highness has harder battles to fight than any you hae encountered in the Netherlands."

"Gog's wouns! Here is fr-rankness from my lard!" mur mured Cumberland, rolling his eyes up under their lids, ami sycophantic tittering from his subordinates. "Well, si well?"

"To overcome their army, which is still in being, and still it may be, gaining accessions of strength among the Clans, i may be necessar' to fight twa, three more engagements i the style of Falkirk."

"No, no, my lord!" the Duke cut caustically in, rollin his great pear-shaped head from side to side upon his shoul ders. "I beg to cor-rect you there. We shall fight no furthe engagements in the style of Falkirk—saving your pr-resence General Hawley! There will be only one battle mor-re."

"After which," continued Brounie, "it will be your Roya Highness's task to see that the rebellion does not recur."

"Zooks! I t'ink you may tr-rust me for that!"

"Your predecessors, sir, hae tried clemency . . . we ha known the voice of clemency upraised in this place! It ha failed. This time, the harrow maun be driven over the Hie lands, and the auld soil in whilk revolt was bred broken u for ever . . . and re-sown."

The dull, protuberant eyes came round with a slow revolu tion to the judge's face, and rested there, scrutinising weighing.

"It will be appropriate," went on Brounie passionlessly "to show nae mercy to the Chiefs of rebel Clans. They maui expiate their sin wi' fu' penalties, one and a'."

A little shudder ran through the Scottish members of th Council at these words; Cumberland sat still, his eyes fixe on the speaker, his head slightly turned to catch some infor mation which one of Lord Brounhill's colleagues was whis pering into his ear behind a lifted hand.

"Their superiorities and jurisdictions," pursued the un moved voice, "maun be abolished . . . in cases where pru

dence does not dictate that they suld be transferred. Their
arms must be ta'en from them . . . in airnest this time; their
kilts and their tartans clean forbid for a' time. Let them dress
like other reasonable and peacefu' subjects."

There was an incredulous gasp at this proposal, and someone was heard to cry, "What would Maccallum More say
to that!" but Cumberland's harsh voice broke in.

"Gog's wouns!" he declared, "I have found a man after
my own hear-rt in Scotland . . . one man, and he a
Highlander!" He fumbled an instant below his billowing yellow waistcoat, and produced a snuff-box, set in
brilliants. "Lord Br-rounhill," he said, "pray will you do
me the honour?"

Jealous eyes watched while Brounie dipped unmoved fingers into the box and snuffed unresponsive nostrils. Cumberland snuffed his own, long, inquisitive nose, making the
nostrils palpitate voluptuously. "You have heard the policy
of the Government, gentlemen," he said. "There shall be
such a chapter of judgment as shall dr-rive your caterans
back into the holes and lairs of their mountains, not, I t'ink,
to stir forth again. . . . You desire to say somet'ing, Major
Wolfe?"

"I was only recalling, sir," answered a young officer with a
keen, up-curving nose and vivid blue eyes, "that these men
are your Royal father's subjects, with whom we must one
day learn to live in peace."

"Hum!"

"And," continued Wolfe boldly, "that they are some of
the best recruiting stuff for our Army in these islands."

"Ha! . . . We tr-rifle time, gentlemen! Your Serene
Highness, I depart for Perth to-morrow morning, *Ich gehe
nach Perth, morgen früh*. I beg you will concentr-rate your
forces there with all reasonable dispatch, to follow up the
r-rebels with me."

"It will be well," suggested Kerr, the Dragoon, "to diminish the start they have of us!"

"I am in no hurry, my lord. I mean to take my time and make my r-roads. So, I shall bring every soldier well-fed, and every gun well-mounted to the decisive field." He rose amid a general rustle and clicking. "Your Serene Highness, my lords, and gentlemen," he said, "I hold levee in Holyroodhouse to-night. I shall be happy to receive you all."

There was a murmur of humble thanks as the Council broke up. Cumberland signalled to Lord Brounhill, who came with his bandy dignity unhurried toward him. "Keep me informed, my lord," he said, "of all that happens in Edinburgh during my absence . . . and of all else that you can ferr-ret out! I have told you you are a man after my own hear-rt. . . . You speak on a different note from that old woman Donald. . . . Duncan, what is his name? Duncan Forbes, then. The time shall come, I t'ink, when we shall remember Lord Br-rounhill. For the Highlander who is ready to exter-rminate his fellow countrymen . . . and send his own nephew to the scaffold, it seems . . . why, that is the Highlander for me!"

He was rolling with his pigeon-toed step out of the room, but near the door stopped in front of a great, dusky oil-painting, one of the Justice Clerk's chief treasures, depicting the Rape of the Sabine Women. Flames of burning houses filled the background; in front young warriors were writhing, bleeding from sword-thrusts, and women in the grasp of ravishers struggled and cried for deliverance with contorted mouths. Cumberland stood for several minutes examining the details, while a peculiar gleam lit his dull, dark eyes, which seemed to protrude more than ever. He fished for his snuff-box again, and inhaled another pinch with a gloating movement that made his great belly quiver.

"An excellent piece of paint," he said at last to his host;
"the school of Salvator R-rosa, I t'ink it is."

3

THE MUSIC of an English regimental band, loud with brass
and kettle-drum and the jingling of the bells that crowned
the pole thumped by a shivering negro drummer on the stones
of the colonnade, floated up with the sound of a challenge
into the picture gallery in Holyroodhouse. From the two
immense wrought-iron grates wood fires breathed smokily
upon the fluted pilasters of dark oak and the candles in their
sconces. Fireglow and candlebeams in contest made a mocking flicker on the faces of the monarchs of Scotland in their
long array. In their frames they seemed to curve contemptuous lips at the red coats, lawyer's black and Presbyterian
bands, at the heavy expensiveness of Whig dames and the
puritanical primness of clergymen's wives upon the floor
below.

At the door stood two sentinels in gaiters and pipeclay,
with the mitre-caps of Grenadiers upon their powdered
heads, shouldering their firelocks in rigid attitudes. They
brought the air of the barracks, of the guard-room even, into
the assemblage, and more than one guest looked as if doubtful whether he might not leave the room under arrest. This
did not abate the cheerfulness of Counsellor Penicuik, who
hobbled from group to group, full of the praises of the new
black snuff that the Hessians had introduced to Edinburgh
nostrils, and offering pinches of it right and left. The Counsellor bowed with a special deference as Lord Brounhill in
his scarlet robe, his three-cornered hat under his arm, entered with his lady, brightly rouged and carrying her handsome head higher than ever. Behind followed demurely Lord

Brounhill's fair-haired daughter on the arm of Mr. Duncan son, wearing his Campbell tartan.

They approached the dais that had been set up at the far end of the room, where the Duke of Cumberland waited attended by A.D.C.'s in silk stockings and ushers with white wands, to receive the guests as representative of his father King George.

"Lord Brounhill and Lady!" cried the usher. Brounie bowed with his puppet-like jerk, and his wife turned a glowing cheek to the perfunctory kiss of royalty.

"Mistress Jean Maceachan: Duncanson of Inveralsk!" cried the usher again. Cumberland saluted Jean with a faint flicker of interest in his eyes and let her pass on. Then suddenly he stiffened, and pointed a podgy, white-gloved finger at Allan.

"Pr-ray, sir, what is the meaning of this dress?"

"It is the uniform of the Argyllshire Militia, your Royal Highness," answered Allan, drawing himself up.

"Ar-rgyllshire Militia! What the devil is that?" demanded the Duke over his shoulder of an A.D.C.

"It is Clan Campbell, your Royal Highness, under the command of his grace the Duke of Argyll."

"In r-rebel uniform?" snarled Cumberland.

"May it please your Highness—" began Allan Duncanson, flushing.

"Hold your tongue, sir! Who bade you speak? What am I to understand, Lord Br-rounhill, by this offensive masquerade? A man entering here in the garb of the Pr-retender's army! Call the guard!"

Brounie was aghast at the failure of his presentation. However, he preserved his wooden equanimity and retorted in his harshest tones, "I dare assure your Royal Highness of the perfect loyalty of this gentleman, as of that of all Maccallum More's great Clan."

Cumberland's sardonic smile began to flicker upon his fat face. "So you answer for them, do you, my little fighting cock? Well, if you assure me that this is the type of High-lander that will cut its fellows' t'roats with alacr-rity, why, you know, I take your word for it. . . . Pass on, sir, and prove yourself better than your dr-ress. . . . Watch him out of the palace, all the same, Colonel," he added in a low voice to the A.D.C. "The fellow may still aim at planting a dirk in my side, or blowing my br-rains out with a pistol in the courtyard. . . . I tell you I know the br-reed!"

It was a gloomy little procession that went home through the freezing night in single file of sedans up the hill to Advo-cates' Close. Allan walked beside Jean's chair, which was last of the three. As they passed by the Abbey sanctuary she lowered the window, and said in a soft voice, "Mr. Duncan-son, I must speak with you. I fear my father has no kind in-tentions any more towards Hector and Darthula."

"I fear you say sooth, Miss Jean," he answered sadly.

"Ah! I ken by your tone I can trust you! . . . You are, I am sure, the pivot of my father's new scheme for rebuilding the fortunes of the family. Is it not so?"

"In a measure, yes."

"And I, too, am to play a part. Is *that* not so? . . . I ken from your silence that it is so, Mr. Duncanson. Well," she paused a moment and her warm little breath made a wreath of smoke in the cold air, "you may condemn me as un-maidenly, Mr. Duncanson," she went on in a small, sobbing voice, "but better be thought forward than proved false. Whatever power my father may have over my hand, my heart is bestowed, where it cannot be recalled."

"I thank you for your candour, Miss Jean. I will go about as straight with you. My heart has been your cousin's for two years. It may break now, but it will not be transferred."

"Oh! I bless Providence for your words! I am gey glad I had the courage to speak to you . . . Allan!" Her tiny mittened hand rested an instant on his, which he had placed on the window-ledge, then was swiftly withdrawn. "We will be allies, will we not, to help in all ways in our power, to succour poor Darthula, and . . . and . . . Hector?"

"You have my pledge, Jean."

"I cannot believe my father, angered though he now be, would, in the last resort, leave them to their doom. And he has, it is clear to see, influence with the Duke of Cumberland."

"I cannot say," replied Duncanson philosophically, "that that is an advantage I seem likely to enjoy myself."

Chapter III

TO CULLODEN

1

A THICK mist, turned by the northern stars to a veil of glimmering pallor, curled over the wild uplands between Inverness and Nairn, as it were an army of phantoms with streaming fingers. In places it swirled so close that a man could see but a few yards upon his path; in others it was thin enough to show the arms of whin and broom bushes pearled with night moisture. Now a long lane would hollow itself out—till it yielded a hint of black mountain forms in the distance; now a rent would open overhead through which the cold jewels of the firmament glittered in their setting of jet velvet. Then the phantoms would close in again in a mocking reel, while a puff of freezing wind made a crackle in the bushes.

There was a nodding motion in the branches and bracken, a marching roll in the coils of vapour—a nodding and a marching, bonnet-feathers that fluttered, kilts that flapped, starlight gleams on points of steel. An endless serpentine column, approaching from Inverness, wound through the linked hands of the dancing mists, bodies wrapped against the cold, heads bent against the icy stabs of the wind, feet brushing the dead fronds of last year's heather that would never bloom again.

"Halt!" said a voice in front, and "Halt! Halt!" a sigh wavered down the column to where its tail disappeared into the fog. As if struck by a cannon-shot, the line seemed to slide into collapse, the wearied men dropping down to sit with heads in their hands, or falling flat in drowsy exhaustion. A few scrabbled with their fingers, or slashed and dug with their sword points, among the bracken and the brown, powdery heather, if by chance they might find green shoots of spring that could be chewed to stay their hunger.

A little group came from the head of the line and asked for "the Major."

"Well?" asked Hector Maceachan moodily, unwrapping his plaid from his mouth.

"The maan says he iss lost, Glenmarisdale!" grumbled Donald Dhu, whose black beard sparkled with drops. He shook his broad-sword menacingly at the frightened guide from Inverness.

"The scoundrel says we are lost, son of Allan!" repeated Hector as the tall chief loomed up.

"I am much of the same opinion," drawled Clan Ranald.

The guide murmured something in Gaelic about waiting for the day.

"Just what we dare not!" said Clan Ranald. "Glenmarisdale, come you with me, and let us be our own scouts this time."

They disappeared together into the mists ahead, and were quickly out of touch with their men. After cautious progress for a considerable while, they found themselves descending a steep slope, their feet sinking into soggy moss and heather. "It must be the river down yonder," said Clan Ranald, pausing. "We have turned east!"

"There is something else," said Hector. "I am seeing your features!"

"I am seeing yours, Glenmarisdale. It is the day: we have been too slow."

The next minute Hector, who was standing a few yards to his commander's left, threw out his hand in a gesture of warning and fell flat in the heather. Clan Ranald dropped immediately beside him, and both pricked their ears.

Close to them they heard through the mist the click of a musket brought to cock. Then a tough London voice roared out, " 'Oo comes there?"

The two Highlanders suspended even their breathing. The next moment they saw, looming through the fog, the shadow of a soldier, his three-cornered hat, coat-skirts and bayonet dimly outlined in the sick light of the coming dawn.

" 'Oo comes there?" he bellowed again, and stood a moment intently listening. Then his shadow dwindled as he turned away and disappeared. The two chiefs lay still, not daring to move.

They had been there about ten minutes when the chime of a church clock floated up to their startled ears from below, and they realised that they were on the very outskirts of the little town of Nairn, round which Cumberland's army lay encamped. At once a voice called from their right: "No. 4 Post and all's well!"

"No. 3 Post and all's well!" roared the sentry close by them.

"No. 2 Post and all's well!" wailed a voice farther away to their left.

"Back!" whispered Clan Ranald in Hector's ear. "Back! On hands and knees!"

With the practised motions of deer-stalkers, they turned noiselessly and wriggled on their bellies through the heather.

They had gone perhaps a couple of hundred yards when

another sound stopped them. It was a rumble and a throb which at first they took for a burst of distant thunder over the Moray Firth. Then they looked at each other and understood. It was the pulse of drums beating to arms in the English camp round Nairn.

"Better watch than Johnny Cope kept!" said Clan Ranald. "It was the pretty jest to dream of surprising them this night!"

"It is the day," said Lord George Murray in a voice like a knell. The chiefs and staff officers crouched about him under shelter of a grey dike-wall could not gainsay it; they could see each other's figures clearly. There was a freshness in the air, too. The wind blew on a rising moan and was tearing the fog into strips. Overhead, through the faintest of grey veils, the stars glimmered palely towards extinction.

"Gentlemen," said Lord George, while his plaid fluttered and he held his bonnet down against the wind, "what is your opinion? Should we not turn back instanter?"

"Where is his Royal Highness's column?" asked a doubtful voice.

"More than half a mile behind," said the general; "they will not keep up. Our plan has miscarried."

There was a moment's dispirited silence, then a protesting murmur. "Let us press on natheless," urged Hepburn of Keith. "What if the red-coats be awakened? They may be presumed to be for the most part, in their own phrase, 'drunk as lords' with celebrating their Commander's birthday all yestere'en."

"Let us trust our claymores!" said another gentleman volunteer; "they have never betrayed us yet!"

"I acknowledge your valour, gentlemen," said Lord George sadly. "But we must not fight at every disadvantage. Lochiel, what is your counsel?"

Cameron's anxious brows drew together. "We should retreat," he said with evident pain, "according to my advice.
No man was stronger than I for attempting this surprise. It
could have been done by night; but it is now too late. . . .
It grows lighter every moment."

"You hear, gentlemen!" said Murray, nodding gloomy
assent, and there was a dejected rustle through the council
which showed that the verdict was accepted. It was followed
by a movement to disperse.

Suddenly Clan Ranald felt his arm gripped as by a claw.
He turned and saw Hector Maceachan with eyeballs glaring
in the pallid light. "Son of Allan!" he cried in a high, cracked
tone. "They will be for turning back! Do you hear, my
Captain, they will be slinking away?"

"Are you surprised?" demanded Clan Ranald. "You
yourself, with me, heard the English drums."

"Drums!" exclaimed Hector. "Is it the drums of the Sassenachs we will be fearing now? We could still overwhelm
them in one charge! Retreat is ruin! Retreat is infamy!
. . . Withhold me not, Son of Allan, for I will speak to the
council!"

"Hold your peace, Glenmarisdale! On your allegiance!"

"Glenmarisdale," rejoined Hector with a furious glance,
"will be owing no allegiance to Clan Ranald, save what we
freely tender. I now withdraw it! My lords, chiefs, gentlemen," he thrust his way, wildly gesticulating, into the midst
of the dissolving throng, "hear me, I have the right to be
heard! I, the Chief of Clan Maceachan, am speaking; I say
this deed of shame *must* not be accomplished!"

The Highland gentlemen paused, and, concealing their
astonishment, gave ear with grave courtesy.

"Must we always be retreating at the crucial hour?" demanded Hector. "We retreated at Derby—ah! my sorrow!
I well know why—we retreated after Falkirk . . . and now,

now this is our last opportunity, our single hope! . . . Lochiel, my kinsman! . . . Keppoch! . . . Hepburn, you who spoke so boldly but now! . . . Will none of you be hearing me?"

"You are overwrought, Glenmarisdale," said Lord George not unkindly. "You must bow to the will of your chief and your superior officers." He moved towards his horse.

"Go back, then, niddering chiefs!" cried Hector, his arms raised in the air. "But as sure as I stand here and there is a God above who listens, I am seeing at this moment the headsman, and he standing in his mask upon the path you tread. . . . Yonder he is . . . and now there . . . and there!" He pointed and laughed with a terrifying note.

"Come away! He is fey!" muttered Lord Kilmarnock.

"There is death on his face . . . and I am seeing my own in his eyes!" said Macgillivray of Dunmaglass, the yellow-haired colonel of Clan Chattan.

With a sudden swish of plaids and brushing of hurried footsteps the chiefs scattered like dead leaves blown by a gust of winter wind.

A command was cried; the waiting clansmen tottered to their feet, faced dispiritedly about, and began to shuffle back in the direction of Inverness, whence they had come.

"You shall be giving me the satisfaction of a gentleman for this!" declared Clan Ranald to Hector, his languor banished, his fingers furiously playing in his sword-hilt.

"Content you, Son of Allan! It is blood enough you will be seeing flow before that sun sinks!" answered Hector. He pointed to the Eastern sky, livid behind the contorted mountains that rose, range beyond range, across the ravine through which rushed the River Nairn. A single red streak like a dripping sword pierced it, the point toward Inverness. "Blood enough!" repeated Hector.

The wind whistled loudly now upon the backs of the re-treating army. It threatened to sweep the bonnets from their bowed heads, and made a whirl of their tartans. They plunged on over the jade-coloured carpet of heather and moss, through the undulating waste on which the whin-bushes chattered together. Here and there premature tufts of broom had had their too impetuous petals sprinkled on the ground by Winter's returning assault, and the tattered brogues and bare, browned feet of the warriors wearily, heedlessly trampled the golden hope of spring.

Suddenly over a swell in the moorland came a thud of hoofs that galloped on the matting of dead nature, and a horseman dashed towards them, bare-headed, his red and blue plaid streaming from its jewelled shoulder-brooch.

"Here comes His Royal Highness, Lord George!" cried Lochiel warningly. Murray looked up and reined aside as Charles rode full tilt into the group of the staff.

"My lord!" he gasped hoarsely, "what does this mean? I cannot credit it! You have taken it on yourself, sir, to dis-obey my orders! You have ordered the retreat of my army! Are you insane, Lord George?"

"Sir," replied the General doggedly, "necessity will not wait on any Prince's orders. This withdrawal was unavoid-able! Every superior officer in the column assented to it."

"A set of d——d traitors!" shouted Charles, beside him-self. "*Madre di Dio!* If I had but one loyal regiment of Guards to cut you all to pieces!"

"For G——'s sake, young man," retorted Lord George in a contemptuous voice, "forbear to go on saying what you will regret all your days! A Prince should control the mo-tions of his spirit!"

"And you will read me a lecture, you who sold me at Derby, who sold me at Falkirk, who—"

Lochiel rode between them, his face like a winding-sheet. "Sir," he said, "*I* counselled this retreat. Will you repeat those words to *me*?"

"You, Lochiel, you! Why, then—" Charles abruptly spurred his horse round so that his back was turned to them. They saw him sitting with his head bowed, his hands clenched on the pommel, his body shaken with sobs.

"March the men on, Lord George, for G——'s sake!" said Lochiel, and riding up to the Prince threw a supporting arm around him.

The dreary shuffle of the retreat continued, while the bleak day widened on crag and morass, lying inhospitable under a scowling sky. From the Firth the bitter wind, with the promise of snow in it, blew and bit at the Highlanders' bare hands and legs. As Hector Maceachan passed the Prince, now watching the defile with wildly staring eyes, he turned aside and pulled his plaid over his face as if he dare not look.

Now the former leading column had amalgamated with the second column that the Prince had accompanied, and in a single, sagging serpent, the host climbed on to Drummossie Muir. Beneath them now in the piercing, bluish light lay Inverness, a mass of grey roofs pricked by the needlepoints of steeples, with the square of its castle aloof by the thread of the river. Behind, dark mountains, their heads streaked with late-lingering snow, huddled together like watchers, and on the vaporous bosom of the Firth two guard-ships made white flecks with their curving sails.

"For G——'s sake, sir!" said Lochiel to the Prince, "command the pipes to play! Let us unfurl standards and march with some heart back to the town! Sir, a smile from you, if you can smile over the cracks in your heart, would be worth a *corps d'armée* to us in this hour!

A smile of a melancholy, ethereal beauty stole across the Prince's tragic face at these words: "Noble Lochiel!" he murmured. The next moment he had spurred to the head of the line, and wheeling with his usual finished horsemanship, presented to each regiment as it approached a gay, inspiring countenance.

A sound of ragged cheering went up, which thickened and deepened. Banners began to flap out against the cruel blast, and everywhere the preliminary drone of the pipers mingled with the huzzas. In a few minutes they burst into full sound, a weird confusion of music, for each clan was playing its own march against the others; but there seemed all the more spirit and fierceness in the cry for that. Stern idealism burned again in the tall and narrow Celtic foreheads as in good heart and restored order they trod upon the high plateau of Drummossie, defying their foes and their fate, until below in a hollow to their right there appeared the grey, castellated cube of Culloden House with its central tower, rising in stately solitude among its sparse plantations and park walls.

An order came down the line to wheel to the right, for it had been decided to camp at Culloden instead of marching on into Inverness. The column curved away, descending the slope, and suddenly the rustle of feet on heather gave place to a squelching noise.

"Incline our regiment to the left!" cried Keppoch in warning—unnecessarily, for the agile Macdonald clansmen had anticipated orders and reformed themselves loosely on the edge of the bog.

"Yon is dangerous ground!" commented their Chief to his Major. "We will do well to beware of it, if we fight here to-morrow."

"This would be the left, Keppoch," replied his second-in-command. "The Macdonalds hold aye the right of the battle-line."

They descended towards the parks of Culloden House, whose owner was now in flight in Skye.

2

In the bedroom of the great house to which he had retired
for an hour's sleep before riding round the bivouacs to see
if his starved men were being fed, Charles Edward stood
looking through the window. Underneath, the lawn was
starred with daffodils, writhing their delicate necks in the
churlishness of the wind. Beyond stretched a low wall with
stone pillars guarding a gateway; and from the gate the road
wound up and away towards the desolate rim of the moor,
backed now by a purple sky with grey clouds fleeting
through it.

For some minutes he stood there brooding, wondering
what Fortune's next blow would be. Had his star forsaken
him? He knew that the players in the gaming-houses of
Rome and Paris always submitted stoically to the goddess
Luck. When she was favourable they could not do wrong;
when she frowned there was no course but acquiescence.
He had always despised that paralysis of resolution, but here
it was creeping over himself!

Wearily he rested his forehead against the pane. The wind
screeched and rattled the sashes, as if seeking to enter and
rend him. As he stood thus drooping he might have been a
stone angel mourning over the tomb of his House. Thoughts
whirled through his head—Murray's treason, the desperation
on the faces of the clansmen when they received the order to
retreat this morning, the lengthy list of desertions that the
muster-master Patullo had reported yesterday and the day
before. It was turning colder; in the fireless bedroom his
fingers were going blue; still he lacked strength to move.

Where was faithfulness? Where was hope? Darthula!
. . . Yes, she could console; she could inspire, but she was
gone from him. She had never spoken to him since the Black

Friday at Derby . . . he remembered her eyes now as he passed her on the stairs, as if unseeing, when he came out from that disastrous council. At the moment she and all of her name had been hateful to him. She might have understood! . . . If she had not left the army at Glasgow and sought her home without her brother, he might not have entangled himself at Bannockburn with the black-eyed wench—Walkinshaw's daughter . . . Clementina, that alluring piece of ugliness who provoked and exhausted him so madly. Ah! he wished his Muse was with him to-day.

Then he scourged himself. Leaning on a woman! Was that the part of a prince . . . of a soldier? Where was his hardness? Let him seek support where a soldier should, among his still faithful men!

He could see them now pouring into the fields beyond the wall to make their camp. Fires were being lighted, and clouds of smoke rolling in the wind. Foraging parties were coming in with sacks of meal, and a few with carcasses of cattle slung between them. . . . Some at least of the poor fellows would have meat; that was good!

But it did not seem to be enough. He moved across the room to where a smaller window gave on the road along the shore to Inverness, and after a single glance stood rooted in dismay. The road was black with figures moving all in one direction, towards the town—more, far more of them than could be required for victualling parties. His army was melting away. He groaned, for he knew the limits of Highland discipline. Nothing would bring them back, crazed with hunger as they were, but their own loyalty perhaps if they heard the cannon. . . . He could not blame them. His commissariat was execrable, and they were famished. . . . Struggle was useless! Fate held him in her grip!

He was about to throw himself upon the bed when his keen, hunter's eye fancied it caught movement upon the moor two miles away. He drew out his spy-glass. Minute figures, he could now make out, were scurrying along the sky-line, and . . . yes . . . a rider on a grey horse made a galloping speck upon the brown curve. Scouts had been left up there, he knew, to watch any movement of the enemy from the direction of Nairn, but the English were not likely to stir to-day after yesterday's potations.

What could be agitating the scouts? He watched through the glass for several minutes until the tiny figures disappeared over the horizon. They did not appear again, and he looked down to the lines of his army round the house. In heaps they lay about wrapped in their plaids, sleeping the sleep of exhaustion in every contorted attitude, like corpses shot or hewed down—an army annihilated. He, too, was utterly fordone. His lids drooped leadenly, and he sank, dressed and in his boots, upon the bed.

While he thus slumbered, and his bedroom grew darker through the approach of a thick, blue, snow-laden cloud, drifting up from the Firth over the moor and the parks, Darthula Maceachan arrived at the west door of the house by the road from Inverness. Old Macvarish, the henchman of Glenmarisdale, happened to be crossing the stone hall with its garnishment of stags' heads at the moment when she dismounted from her pony, and stood gazing at her in silent astonishment. Her appearance was the last thing he had expected, for, like all the clansmen, he knew of the bitter quarrel that had parted her from her brother—since Derby not a word had passed between them—though no more than any other clansman did he ever discuss it. Nor did he now manifest his surprise, but simply walked forward to salute her, with his sunny smile.

"Can I speak with Himself, Macvarish?" she asked as she entered, and again he did not give a flicker of his courteous eyes at the significance of her words. "Is my brother sleeping?" she added, "if so, I would not be having him roused."

Macvarish replied that the Chief was not sleeping; he was playing cards with his foster-brother, Angus Maceachan, the Standard-Bearer.

Darthula smiled wanly. "I need not mind disturbing him from the cartes. Pray fetch him, Macvarish!"

"Be pleased to wait in here," said the henchman, opening with the dignity of a proprietor the first door to hand, which gave, fortunately, on an unoccupied room, a small corner-parlour hung in faded red damask.

As Darthula stepped inside, a moan arose as if from all the ghosts of the ancient house stirred to protest. It was, however, no more than the voice of the wind at the corner of the mansion, which uplifted its plaint thus whenever the door was opened. Darthula shivered in the fireless chill, and drew her riding-cloak closer round her.

As she stood waiting while the room steadily darkened under the shadow of the imminent storm, she reviewed the motives that had led her a week ago to decide to make the journey from Glenmarisdale to Inverness, with a single boy for attendant, in order to see her brother again. She was even now a little puzzled at the sudden breaking down of her wall of revengeful resentment, at her abrupt resolution to forgive. Possibly the chaplain, Dr. Hay's, sad face whenever Hector had to be mentioned between them, might have had a little to do with it—if he had presumed to lecture her on Christian charity, how she would have flown at him! But by saying nothing he had no doubt made her a little ashamed.

Yet it was no such external influence that had moved her one morning when wandering in the wood below the upper falls which was just clouded with the shy green of spring. She had come there to nurse the ache made by the empty shrine in her heart, and had been gazing at the great cone shaped peak that towered above the falls still wearing its wintry snow-cap. Suddenly there had come upon her the vision of Hector as a child one January day at this very spot kicking off his tiny brogues to trample defiantly in the snow, whereby he had given himself a rheum of which he nearly perished. And in that memory her heart had melted, while at the same time her ears had drummed with the sense of urgency. She must embrace her little brother again before . . . before what? She could not define the peril she feared, perhaps dared not, since he might any day, she knew, be involved in a great, a decisive battle with the oncoming English host. Anyhow she had set out for Inverness immediately, and thence had made her way to Culloden House, where, she had that morning learned, soon after daybreak, the Macdonald brigade had encamped with the rest of the army after its ineffectual night attempt upon Nairn.

There was another convulsive moan from the wind as the door opened, and Hector stepped diffidently into the room. On his worn, unshaven face she saw the very look of half-fearful entreaty he used to show as a child when he had deserved punishment and doubted forgiveness. In an instant they were locked in one another's arms, their tears streaming together.

"Why," she said at length when they had grown a little calmer, and were sitting side by side on a sofa, "why are you here, Hector? Oh! why did not you attack at Nairn?"

"We lost our way and were surprised in our turn by the dawn. I was for falling on the red-coats nevertheless, in the hope that they would be too drink-sodden to withstand us. But the other Chiefs would not have it so. My loss! there goes the Prince's last hope . . . my last chance of atonement!"

"Torture yourself no longer, my poor darling. You have been a good soldier."

"Always . . . except in that hour of madness. But, Darthula, Darthula, I should have been telling the truth that day! I repeated mere country gossip about the strength of the English and their movements. . . . I believe we could have slipped through on the road to London with security. . . . But I was wanting nothing then except to make *him* suffer. . . . Since then I have been watching the long, unravelling of the fatal ball I helped to unloose. . . . But, my grief! my sister, one cannot always, by any effort, undo the wrong that one has begun. One can only be paying the price."

There was a violet flash through the window of the little parlour and a thunder-clap; then a fusillade of hail-stones beat upon the panes drowning Darthula's voice as she tried to speak. For some minutes they sat regarding each other's shadowy figures in a gloom like night.

Then, swiftly as it had come, the storm passed; the squalid daylight crawled back again into the room with its blood-red hangings, and he could see the tears running down her face. "We will be sharing the burden henceforth," she said in a choking voice, "and from now on we will be holding nothing back from him that he demands of us."

Her brother did not answer. He was leaning forward listening. Then he sprang up and ran to the window. Down the slope leading to the pillared gate at the east front of the house he had caught sight of a soldier riding at full speed on a grey horse. It was one of Fitzjames's French cavalry piquets, and he shouted as he came, awaking a tumult among the clansmen bivouacking on the slopes. Sentries called; sergeants ran to and fro; the men sat up groaning and rubbing the sleep from their glued eyes. The messenger galloped through the gate.

"What is this?" cried Hector, and dashed out into the hall. The officers who had been drowsing there were leaping up, buckling on their swords, and crying questions to one another. The next moment Lord George Murray, trim and alert, appeared in the midst of the confusion.

"Rouse His Royal Highness at once!" he called. "The enemy are on the Muir!"

Darthula with thudding heart stood clinging to the doorpost of the little red parlour, while the wind rose and fell with the same eerie whisper and menace.

Chapter IV

DRUMMOSSIE MUIR

1

THE Macdonald Brigade marched up towards the moor with a gallant swing in spite of fatigue and still unsatisfied hunger. Clan Ranald held the van; Keppoch followed in the centre; the Glengarry Regiment, led by its chief's brother Lochgarry, brought up the rear. The massed pipes of the conjoined Clans moved in front, playing a defiant march.

As they emerged on to the plateau, the Clan Ranald standard, with that of the Maceachans beside it, fluttered out in the steady blast off the Firth. Suddenly Clan Ranald, who was leading the brigade on foot, exclaimed to Hector, who was just behind him, "Glenmarisdale, what are those Atholl men marching across our front for? Go forward and bid them make way!"

At this moment one of Lord George's mounted *aides* scampered toward them, waving an arm and shouting.

"What the devil can this fellow want?" growled Clan Ranald. "I cannot hear him. Bid the pipes forbear awhile, Glenmarisdale!"

Hector spoke to the pipe-major, and the gay, defiant tune

wavered into silence. The pipes of the Macdonalds were heard no more that day.

Meanwhile the Captain of Clan Ranald was expostulating with the *aide*. "Remain here upon the left, sir? You will surely be misunderstanding your orders! The right of the line belongs to Clan Donald—it is our place of honour!"

"I entreat you, Clan Ranald, to waive the point to-day," answered the anxious *aide*, who fully appreciated the disaster of the situation. "It is a positive order from the General, and be sure there is no affront intended. His dispositions require it."

"What is amiss, Clan Ranald?" demanded Keppoch and Lochgarry, who had hurried to the front on finding the line thus checked.

"We are ordered to remain here on the left!" Clan Ranald told them glowering.

"Impossible!" asserted Keppoch. "We are holding the right by constant privilege."

"Gentlemen!" pleaded the staff officer, "the enemy draw nearer every minute. I implore you take your appointed positions in the line!"

"My grief! Atholl takes the right, look!" exclaimed Lochgarry furiously. "This will be one of Lord George's pretty plots to seize the precedence! And, see, the Camerons deploy beside the Atholl men. Sure, Lochiel will never be lending himself to this dastardly affront upon gentlemen, his friends!"

"Seek the Prince with me, Lochgarry!" said Clan Ranald. "Keppoch, hold my place here. Do not you be stirring till I return!"

"But, gentlemen," pleaded the anguished *aide*, "will you leave our line in the air? For God's sake form upon the left of Clan Chattan in the centre yonder! You may dispute your claims of honour afterwards."

The chiefs did not listen. They were already bounding

towards the spot where they had discerned the Royal Standard carried behind the Prince, who was advancing, escorted
by his Lifeguards in their blue uniforms with red waistcoats,
in the interval of his two lines. At his back the regiments
of the second line, the Duke of Perth's, Lord Ogilvy's, Lord
Lewis Gordon's, largely composed of Lowland volunteers,
were slowly massing, while behind them the towers and
steeples of Inverness stood faintly outlined on a dreary purple haze.

Before long Clan Ranald and Lochgarry were back with
faces sullen as thunder. "There is no remedy," said the
former curtly; "His Highness entreats us yield precedence
for the day. He hath made a promise, it seems, to Lord
George . . . the feckless boy! My sorrow! This is an ill
beginning for our fortunes. Murray could not be playing
Cumberland's hand to more advantage if he had been paid
to do it. Glenmarisdale, wheel your Maceachans to the left
—someone must be leading!"

"Is it I must be heading disgrace?" answered Hector
sulkily; but he went off and begged rather than dared command his men to turn left. The emaciated standard-bearer,
Angus Maceachan, showed especial signs of mutiny. They
moved draggingly off at last, accompanied by the staff officer,
who kept darting anxious glances to the front.

The Macdonalds were finally aligned with their left tip
some two hundred yards from the edge of the hollow in
which Culloden House glimmered grey in the uneasy light.
Two of the Prince's six little field-guns had been brought
into position on their flank, their amateurish gunners peering
over the earth-stuffed wicker gabions that protected them,
as if doubtful, with good reason, of their ability to get the
range of the advancing enemy.

Abruptly, Keppoch uttered a curse. "Look! Lochgarry,
look how we are disposed! Yonder d——d bog straight be-

fore us, across which it is impossible to charge! And on our flank, beyond these futile pop-guns, smooth turf for the Sassenach horse to ride round and envelop us! 'Tis we must stand here to be shot and ridden down without a blow struck!"

"And they will be saying," interjected Hector with a bitter laugh, "that we would not fight—from resentment!"

"Gentlemen!" cried the staff officer, who had been sweeping the moor in front of them with his spy-glass, "attention! There come the English!"

Silence fell on the line of ragged, hungry and discouraged men as they craned forward to see.

2

COMING out of a dip in the plateau less than a mile away, the Highlanders could see a number of crawling lozenges, black against the heaviest storm cloud of the day, which was lowering up from the Firth behind them. On the misty waters moved a flock of food ships with their attendant gun-boats, like lazy gulls. Presently on the left of the advancing English line there was a quicker, undulating movement of one of the dim rectangles, and Lord George Murray, who had his spy-glass levelled where he sat behind his Atholl men on the Highland right, looked anxious. "Cavalry moving to outflank," he said. "Yonder they go down towards the river."

He glanced restlessly at the long sheep-park walls of grey stone, descending to the stream, on which the right of the Prince's line rested, with a dike like a lean horn curving out in front. "Those walls will be a snare rather than a protection," he snapped. "They may serve to mask any manoeuvre."

"The walls," objected Lochiel, who had come across to confer with him, "suffice to check cavalry, whatever."

"If it were only cavalry," growled Murray, bending forward in his saddle and peering more intently.

By a freak of the April weather the sun had at that moment broken through the clouds that lay over Inverness, and now sent its rays upon the English as they came on with the storm at their backs. Against this black curtain every regiment and every uniform were made suddenly clear.

The dark lozenges had changed to scarlet threads as the company columns deployed into line; and within a few minutes the threads had become ranks of soldiers in three-cornered hats, hair-powder, red tail-coats and gleaming white gaiters. Like the levers of some polished machine, the legs rose and fell as the line moved forward with its ponderous goose-step, the halberds of the sergeants flashing in the watery rays that were filling the field with a spectral glory. Here and there the yellow mitres of Grenadier companies varied the black hats; the King's and regimental colours fluttered from their staffs; the mounted officers paced behind the lines on their heavy chargers. The whole force moved with unrelenting deliberation, like a great engine, unhurried, unperturbed; and the continuous mutter of the drums, the thin crying of the fifes was as the roll and creak of the mechanism.

Rumbling and clanking between the scarlet battalions were the numerous guns with their caissons, the drivers flogging their beasts over the soggy ground.

Some four hundred paces from the Scottish array the whole line halted with a ripple and glint of steel. The sergeants ran to the front and began to dress the ranks. At that moment between the first and second line, which was approaching over the rising ground behind, a dimmer wave of scarlet, a stout figure on a grey horse was discernible, with stars that glittered on its coat. Dismounting near a large boulder, by climbing which a better view of his enemy could be obtained, Cumberland applied his glass to the study of the Highland host.

To his barrack-square mind it was more like a mob than an army. It surged in a ragged line still lit by the last beams of the sunburst, which threw up the crimsons, greens and yellows of plaid and kilt, the crosses and hereditary blazons on the standards, the blue bonnets with their white specks or sprigs of golden broom. A stir and rumour ran through it such as no English sergeants would have tolerated; men often broke rank to go to the rear, or move up and speak to some friend in another group.

But the heavy-faced man staring through his telescope did not make the mistake of his predecessors, and despise their indiscipline. He snapped to the glass, and briefly instructed his *aides* to ride along his lines and repeat once again to every regiment his reiterated instructions. "When the rebels charge thrust at the man *to your right*, whose side will be exposed. Any man disarmed by fixing his bayonet in the target of the man in front of him will be court-martialled." He paused, and taking a pinch of snuff added, "Bid them to forget defeats: I am leading them now. The enemy have sworn to cut the t'roats of every pr-risoner they take, and I will shoot every man who hesitates or turns his back. Therefore it will be better to be bold and win the victory. There shall be plenty of plunder afterwards."

The *aides* scattered with the ferocious message and the Duke climbed awkwardly to the saddle of his grey charger again.

Meanwhile, Lord George Murray was still apprehensively studying the long, sinister horn of crumbling stone that curved across his right front. The English Dragoons, ponderous as effigies with their enormous boots, massive stirrups and great pistol holsters, had gone jingling and slithering down the steep slope towards the river bed, and now a fresh cloud of troops was moving off in the same direction with a speed very different from the pace of the English march. The failing light shone on dark-green kilts and Orange ribbons, and in a lull of the English drums a screech of pipes went up like a witch's curse in the darkling air.

"The Campbells!" ejaculated Murray, striking his knee. "The cursed Campbells! Traitors, and the spawn of traitors!"

There was a dull boom from the middle of the Highland line. The Prince had sent an order to his puny artillery to fire upon the English. The two little guns in his centre puffed smoke, and those on the left by the Macdonalds took up the cue.

Lord George shrugged. "And that is useless, too," he said; "the balls will fall short." He turned again towards his nagging cause of anxiety. "Your Grace," he said over his shoulder to the Duke of Perth, who had ridden up from his place on the left to ask why they did not attack, "your Grace, the Campbells have gone down behind the walls there to the river. They will be meaning some mischief. I think I will advance Menzies to line that cursed dike."

"We havena' too mony men for our charge, my lord!" objected Perth.

Lord George pursed his lips with their whistling motion. "At any rate, then, Ogilvy's Regiment behind us must move up and line the dike when we advance. See to it!" he commanded Ker of Graden, his chief of staff.

"I will send a messenger," said Ker, but at that moment came an interruption.

The tiny Scottish guns had been laboriously discharging ineffectual shots from behind their gabions in the face of the English line, over which the thick cloud was now drifting like some evil genius of the air, with his tattered mantle trailing across the dim firmament. Now at the signal of bewigged *aides-de-camp*, cantering with the elegance of riders in a mounted minuet to the various batteries, the English guns un-limbered and matches sputtered.

At the same moment the storm burst upon the faces of the Highlanders in hail-stones mingled with sheets of icy rain. Their standards were in a second turned to limp rags clinging round their staffs; while the men, pulling down their bonnets or lifting their plaids over their heads, cowered, not before the English who were hidden from them by the veil of sleet, but before the elements.

Then, on top of the painless pelting of the hail, came the roar of the English guns and the crash of the cannon-balls, trundling through the ranks, knocking men over in knots right and left, shattering limbs into bloody splinters, cutting bodies nearly into halves. The little rivulets, filled with dancing hail-stones that runnelled the pale moss-carpet of the moor, turned crimson in a minute. A shot struck one of the two cannon on the Highland right, setting fire to the gabion. A column of yellow flame shot up into the hissing sleet, and showed the face of Lord George, pale and with softly whistling lips, trying steadfastly to peer through the smoke from the guns that now still further hid the enemy.

As swiftly as it had broken, the squall whirled off through the second Scottish line; harmlessly tossing now the limbs of whin-bushes and trees upon the moor, and soaking the hun-dreds of stragglers from the Prince's army who were toiling up the road from Inverness in hopes of arriving in time for the battle.

As the sleet thinned away, the opposing armies could be seen in patches through the smoke wreaths. The Highland line was filled with the still or writhing forms of the victims of the cannonade, their tartans faintly fluttering, while from the back of the line little jets went constantly forth, clansmen carrying dying or supporting wounded comrades to the rear. From the survivors went up a prolonged growl of fury as the men fingered their useless broad-swords, and Gaelic cries began to shrill from right to left demanding the charge.

Lord George looked over his shoulder. "We should not be waiting much longer," he said. "This cannonade is ruin to us. I marvel his Royal Highness will not be sending the word to attack."

3

"Why does Lord George not give the word to charge?" demanded the Prince in a high-pitched tone that had yet a ring of steel in it. He was standing up in his silver-chased stirrups gazing with dilated eyes at his unmoving front line, while behind him his gay Lifeguards were ranked, with the rain-drops dripping from their hats. The English cannonade had raked the ground round him, but O'Sullivan for begging him to retire out of range had only been savagely snubbed. "Why does he not charge?" repeated the Prince. "I will send another messenger! Major Maclachlan," he looked to a tall *aide* mounted on a fine black horse, "you are well mounted. Ride like the devil to Lord George, and give him the order to attack with the whole front line *at once*!"

Maclachlan saluted and dashed off in a spurt of fiery zeal. "Now!" said Charles, "perhaps we shall set the dance going!" Another ball spattered his staff with mud and his bonnet was whirled off by the wind of it. "And I must get my head wet with waiting, too!" he cried with shrill hilarity.

"Why in G——'s name," ejaculated Lord George, biting his lip till a bead of blood came, "do we get no orders? Cumberland is playing nine-pins with our men; they will not stand it. Ker, look back through your glass! Do you spy no messenger coming?"

"I can see nothing, my lord, but a black horse, straying riderless . . . it drags a man, I think, by the stirrup."

"Gallop yourself to his Highness, Ker! . . . No, it is too late! There goes Clan Chattan without orders. I knew they would not wait!"

Unable to endure any longer the tormenting, the irrational delay, Macgillivray of Dunmaglass, the commander of Clan Chattan in the centre of the line, had stepped out waving his claymore in the air. A ripple of raised hands ran down his clan as the men scrugged their bonnets down tight upon their brows; then, as their leader rushed forward, his corn-coloured locks taut behind him in the wind, his standard-bearer close at his heels, the Mackintoshes, in a torrent of red and dull green, broke away from the line, and with pipes frenziedly skirling and high Gaelic yells rising in the chill air against the continuous thunder of the enemy's cannon, streamed after their banner. The rest of Clan Chattan followed, dragging with it all the centre.

"I must go, Murray!" shouted Lochiel to the general. "The Camerons cannot be left behind!"

"Go, and God strengthen your arms!" cried Lord George in answer, the responsible look of the Commander peeling off his face, to reveal a blaze of savage exultation. "We are coming, too! Forward, men of Atholl! Charge!"

In a maddening clamour of pipes, drums and voices, the whole Highland right, like a tide bursting a breakwater, plunged out and raced across the strip of ground that parted them from the immobile English regiments.

Lord George was spurring his horse to take the lead of the Atholl Brigade when he reined in with an abrupt oath. He had seen the grey horn of stone that curved across the right of the advancing flood topped suddenly with heads; the barrels of firelocks glinted; and an irregular volley of musketry swept the Highland flank and sent it sagging in upon the centre.

"The Campbells!" he cried in a fury, "the Campbell curs!" The next instant a tall young officer in the dark-green tartan appeared over the adjoining wall and began to pull away the piled stones with his hands, aided in a moment by a score of others.

"Where is Ogilvy?" raged Lord George. "Did no one carry my message?" and, infuriated by the coolness with which the lank young officer proceeded at his work of demolition, he drew his pistol and discharged it straight at Allan Duncanson—fruitlessly, owing to the agitated wheelings of his charger. The beast's curvettings brought his face to the rear, and beads of sweat broke out above his heavy eyebrows as he saw a solid mass of English Dragoons pour through another breach in the wall further back, and charge upon Ogilvy's advancing men. The Prince's second line stopped in confusion.

With a despairing groan, Murray turned his horse, and galloped forward with drawn sword to cast himself upon the English bayonets.

The storming Highland mob were now within fifty paces of Barrel's and Monro's Regiments, ranged in three ranks with the front one kneeling. They bristled with bayonet-points, and had the added protection of wooden beams planted with *cheveux-de-frise* dug into the ground in front of them. The Highland men, after a scattered discharge from their muskets, flung them away and drew their broadswords.

"Load with grape!" said an English artillery officer in the centre.

"Steady, the 37th!" cried Colonel Monro. "Hold your

fire till you see the whites of their eyes!"

"Dunmaglass! Dunmaglass!" roared the yellow-haired Macgillivray, as with his broad-sword twirling in snaky flashes round his head, he leaped clean over the *cheveux-de-frise* ahead of his followers.

"Sons of the hounds, flesh yourselves!" came the deep, musical voice of Lochiel in his Clan slogan.

"Fire!" cried the commanders of Monro's and Barrel's simultaneously.

Red arrows of flame spat the length of the English regiments from the muskets, and upon that the grape from the guns swished with searing impact into the Clans. Blue-black smoke, acrid with the smell of salt-petre, masked the English line again from view, while all the front of it was laden with the fallen Highlanders, as though some crate of many-coloured flowers had burst and strewed its contents in the mud and soaking moss.

For a second more the red lines showed firm as the smoke-curtains of the volley lifted; then, as though struck by a hammer, it bent, buckled and split asunder. In spite of artillery, musketry, planted scythes and bayonets, the remnants of Clan Chattan, the Camerons, the Atholl Brigade and the rest had charged home upon the scarlet ranks and dashed them to fragments. Where Monro's and Barrel's had stood a minute since, the English left was now a whirl of confused combatants, basket-hilted sword clashing on musket-barrel, target taking and twisting the point of frantic bayonet. Crimson seams opened on powdered hair, lopped hands flew, men fell cloven through neck and shoulder as the claymores sang and swung. "Victory!" chanted Lord George Murray in ecstasy. "It is Gladsmuir again, my children!" His hat and wig had been struck off by a ball; his face was mud-spattered; his horse's leg was gashed by a stone flung up from the bullet-ploughed soil; but there was only triumph in his mien.

In a few minutes a swarm of red-coats and twinkling white gaiters was fleeing back upon the regiments of Sempill and Wolfe in the second line, and a quiver ran through even those sternly disciplined ranks at the sight of their panic-stricken comrades.

Then through the thinning smoke-wreaths Sempill's men were aware of a huge figure like an equestrian statue, holding aloft a cocked hat and thundering in an enormous voice: "Stand firm, Englishmen, for your homes, your liberties and your r-religion!" As if galvanized by the terrible voice, by the glower of the dull eyes above the bulging, marble jowl, Sempill's wavering ranks stood together and trembled back into firmness. Swiftly their Colonel seized the moment and gave the word to fire.

From Sempill's, from Bligh's on the left of the Highlanders, from Wolfe's, which had been wheeled forward to take their right flank, a concentric fire blazed out which at this short range was annihilating. Lochiel fell forward on his face, hit in both ankles, and was dragged away by his standard-bearer and his henchman; Lord George Murray went down with a crash under his shot charger; Macgillivray stood for a moment as if doubtful whether to turn and rally those of his Mackintoshes who were fleeing back from the hell of the musketry, or to join the thin spray of those who were tossing themselves in vain now upon the steady bayonets of Sempill's triple line. As he hesitated, another discharge of artillery cut him to the ground, his yellow locks streaming among the dead heather.

4

"God!" exclaimed Charles Edward, "ah! dear God!"

He had ridden forward with his staff in despite of O'Sullivan's remonstrances till within a couple of hundred paces of the conflict, and now sat as though stupefied in his saddle. In place of what he had confidently looked to see—the triumphant advance of his Army—he beheld a field littered with the dead and crawling with the wounded bodies of the shattered first line Clans. To the right Ogilvy's men were desperately resisting the sabres of the English Dragoons, while the Campbells, like green and orange wasps, were swarming through the gaps they had made in the park-walls and delivering triumphant bursts of musketry. He saw the great rent in his centre which Gordon's and Glenbucket's Regiments were striving in vain to fill; and then, turning despairing eyes to his left, beheld the Macdonalds standing still, not a musket answering the galling fire from the Royal Scots opposed to them.

"Ah! God!" he said again, "what has come to Clan Donald? Have they betrayed me?"

O'Sullivan laid a hand on his bridle. "Come away, sir! Withdraw! For the love av Jesus! Your safety is all that matters now!"

Had the Prince known it, the Macdonald ranks were at that moment a scene of angry confusion and divided counsels.

"Charge, Clan Ranald, charge!" vociferated Keppoch, "do not be waiting for orders, man! The day hinges on us now!"

"No man can charge through a bog!" raved Clan Ranald, shaking his broad-sword in a hand palsied with fury. "My grief! Why must they be posting us here to make us impotent?"

"Do not be reviving that coil now," pleaded Lochgarry, running up to the other two Chiefs. "We must charge, or our men will go mad!"

"Try then!" said Clan Ranald bitterly. "You will be up to your knees . . . to your waist . . . in mud in a minute!"

"I am done with you all!" shouted Hector Maceachan suddenly. "Clan Ranald, farewell! Maceachan will fight alone!"

"Come back, Glenmarisdale!" commanded the Captain of Clan Ranald sternly, but the Maceachans paid no heed to his order. With Mackissock playing "Sons of Hector" with defiant fury, and Angus Maceachan holding their banner proudly aloft, the little Clan followed its boyish Chief across the field towards the centre.

"My loss!" murmured the Captain, " 'Black dawn when Maceachan from Clan Ranald's side shall fall!' "

"Here come the Sassenach cavalry!" cried Keppoch. "Do not be giving me to the dogs, my children!"

Glengarries and Keppochs were sliding in a huddle towards the rear, as a great mass of English dragoons swept round the smooth turf on the edge of the morass and bore down on their flank. Keppoch stood alone, his scarlet and pale-green tartan fluttering, his broad-sword held up as a rallying-point.

"A sitting bird!" sniggered a young Cornet on the flank of Cobham's squadrons. "But there is no grace for rebels, eh, sir?" and he discharged one of his long pistols. Keppoch sank forward on his knees. "Forward!" he choked. "Claymore! Claymore!"

"Winged, by Gad!" said the subaltern and let fly with his second pistol. Keppoch dropped dead upon his face. . . .

In a few moments Clan Donald had melted in rout.

Meanwhile Hector with his little knot of Maceachans had halted towards the right of the battle-field. He had found no place for a stand yet; everywhere his eye had caught none but flying men, and no evidence except of ruin. Every second live bodies, whole or wounded, driven by the panic of the Gael, as frenzied as his valour, rushed past or hurtled against him. And as he stood buffeted and bewildered, he heard in front an infernal drumming, and saw, breaking through the dissolving wisps of the musket-smoke, the whole English line at its stiff parade step, its colours lifted triumphantly to the breeze, its mounted officers pacing processionally.

"Follow me, Macvarish!" he cried. "We'll be dying for our Prince!"

"Whateffer for, Son of Hector?" pleaded the ancient henchman, catching at his plaid. "Come awa', and live for your own folk!"

"Run then and be saving your own bones!" retorted Hector, savagely shaking off the arm that had so often lifted him in childhood to the old man's shoulder. Without looking back he rushed at the head of his little band towards the enemy.

"A wilful maan must have his way!" sighed Macvarish, and began to run after his Chief on his stout old legs. The advancing English paused to deliver a volley; a ball entered his brain; he spun about clutching his head, and sank down with a look of severity on his aged features which they had never shown in his lifetime.

The same volley mowed down the Maceachans like a scythe-sweep. Little more than half the Clan were left standing. Angus the standard-bearer fell, grazed by a bullet on the scalp, bringing down Hector with him under the weight of the heavy staff, and in an instant they were trampled by the gaitered feet of the enemy wrestling with the remnant of the Clan for possession of the Standard. At last Donald Dhu, the black-bearded Sergeant, slashed the silk from the pole, and ran off with the precious folds clasped to his body. "Come on, men!" shouted an English officer, "Tally-ho and away!" and headed a rush after the saviour of the flag.

The movement of the battle passed over Hector's unconscious body, for he had struck his head against a stone when he fell. When at last he came to, violently sick, he found himself looking at the dead face of the boy Neil Maceilein, son of the Bard, still clutching a dirk in his small hand. Angus Maceachan had disappeared; there seemed no company but the dead of his household and his people. A bubbling sound came from his right, and he perceived a small well that rose from a spot near the sheep-walls, and trickled across the field of the struggle. A racking thirst seized him, and he crawled on hands and knees, his broken claymore swinging from its wrist-knot, towards the spring. Then he recoiled at finding it tinged with red. Over its brink hung a head of corn-coloured hair, the head of Dunmaglass, who had dragged himself here to die.

Hector was trying to struggle to his feet, when he was enveloped with savage shouts. A cloud of Campbell militiamen came rushing through the broken walls, shouting their slogan, *Cruachan!* They beat him down with their claymores; stripped him naked, and left him for dead by the well.

5

THE sounds of battle grew fainter, as the pursuit rolled away towards Inverness. The slaughtered Clans lay in stiffening piles; here and there the corpse of a red-coat, the green of a Campbell flecked the jade moss. There was a tumbled heap of these latter near the dikes, as though some struggle without quarter had taken place at that spot. The ground rustled and shook with the tramp of Mordaunt's Brigade, the English reserve, following up the fighting front over the moor. Then a hush fell again, while the biting afternoon wind under the purple sky crooned and whistled, mingled with faint sobbings and moanings. Curlews piped, as they circled over the field, and the little well bubbled unceasingly.

Then came a rapid step, pausing to search among the slain and wounded, and Allan Duncanson at last recognised with a gasp of horror the slim white body of his friend. He had caught his men bearing off their trophies, and had recognised the brooch with the Maceachan crest. He felt for Hector's pulse, and his fingers were rewarded by a faint beat. Then he examined the wounds; there were cuts on the arms, and an ugly jagged wound in one shoulder. The cold air and the tatters of his shirt, which the Campbells had not troubled to slash away, had caked the blood in a purple crest, stemming the hemorrhage. "I might save him still," Allan thought, sitting back upon his heels, "if I could convey him to a farm, a hut, any place of safety."

So intent had he been that he had not observed the trampling of horses and clink of bridles approaching. Now he looked up with a start to see the frowning face of Cumberland himself looking down upon him from the midst of his splendid, powdered staff.

"What are you doing, sir?" demanded the Commander-in-Chief, "staying to plunder before the pursuit is done, ha?"

Allan saluted. "No, your Highness; tending a wounded friend."

"So. You are one of the Campbells, are you not? You have showed yourselves cunning foxes to-day. I am pleased with you! To what r-regiment does your fr-riend belong?"

"Sir, it is Maceachan of Glenmarisdale, one of the enemy Chiefs."

The Duke's brow blackened, his eyes bulged glaring. "So! You would save a r-rebel's life, would you, Mr. Campbell?"

"Duncanson of Inveralsk, if it please your Royal Highness."

"You do *not* please me, Duncanson! Use your dirk to despatch this carrion, quick!"

"I am no flesher, your Royal Highness!"

"I'll make butcher's meat of *you*, my fine man! You d——d are every one of you mutineers!"

One of his officers murmured in his ear. Allan caught the words, "Duke of Argyll."

Cumberland sneered. "Pr-rotected, eh? We'll change all that in Scotland, by G——! After all," he heaved himself up in his stirrups, and looked down at Hector's limp form lying like the pierced St. Sebastian of an Italian church in his friend's arms, "after all, I believe the dog is dead." He fished for his snuff-box while his eyes wandered gloatingly over the gashed body of the boy. "A-ah!" he said, inhaling with a quivering contentment, and turning his horse rode on.

As his staff followed, the youthful, blue-eyed Major Wolfe paused and said to Allan in a low voice: "Well done, sir! In your place I had answered the same. He can command our commissions, not our honour! Hasten to get your friend into some house, if it be not too late."

He spurred on, and Duncanson looked about him with a failing heart. He did not dare to lift Hector on to his shoulders for fear the wound should break out again with the jerk of the movement. Yet to leave him here was to leave him surely to die. Then, close under the grey horned dike he saw a pile of corpses, red-coats and Campbells, heaving and rolling over. From underneath them crawled a ghastly figure, the gaunt form of Angus Maceachan, stripped to his shirt, his face a mask of crimson below his bald skull, who rose slowly to his feet and came towards him.

"You haaf safed Himself," he stammered hoarsely. "You canna pe a Campbell at aall, she * waas thinking! Take you his feet, she his head. She would pe his prother. We will pe carrying him through ta wall to ta hut yonder together!"

* I.

Chapter V

FAIRY PRINCE

1

In the small farmhouse of Gortuleg, some twenty miles from Inverness, Lord Lovat dozed in a wooden arm-chair. He had but a single hard cushion to support his bulk, and the blue and gold flames of the wood-fire before which he sat flickered on the buttons of his waistcoat where his immense belly drooped towards the blaze. The doze became a slumber, a slumber filled with grunts, mutterings and sharp little cries of protest. Once, at about ten o'clock, his gillie, wearing the russet and green hunting-tartan of the Frasers, with his dirk-hilt gleaming in his stocking, peeped in to see if the Chief was not yet ready to sup. Finding him asleep, he silently laid fresh logs on the fire and stole out again without disturbing him.

Upstairs in a bleak little sleeping-chamber a small girl of about ten, with a Fraser tartan shawl wrapped round her shivering shoulders, was peering defiantly out through the window-panes, instead of going to sleep, as she had been told to do, in her box-bed. This was the daughter of Mr. Thomas Fraser, Lord Lovat's factor, to whom the house belonged.

Mary was not willing to stay in bed like an obedient girl because she knew that at night the Silent Ones made their rings and danced their dances in the drear, marshy hollow that dipped below the windows of the house. The stars glittered to-night, waking a stagnant gleam from the pool in the centre of this sloping hollow—it might, Mary thought, be the lantern of one of the Little People waiting. Above the marsh shadowy moorland rolled away to where, beyond the distant sheen of Loch Mhor, a line of mountains rose as if cut in black cardboard against the more distant spangles. Round the hollow ran the path, palely glimmering in the starlight, that led up at last between two white pillars to the door of the house.

Mary knew very well that she ought not to be standing thus with bare feet on the cold, knotted oak boards, to watch for the fairies. Her trouble was that if she waited in her bed she always fell asleep and did not wake till dawn was pouring through the uncurtained windows; and by then the Silent Ones had all danced away! To-night she had been able to keep her eyes open till her mother and the two maids were safely occupied in the kitchen downstairs. They were getting the supper of the terrible Macshimi, whose ogrish belly —filled, she was sure, with the soft flesh of babies—and whose hard, twinkling little eyes always terrified her so much that she had no need to be told to observe her manners when he was in her father's house. And now, being awake, she would watch . . . and watch . . . until the Silent Ones showed themselves.

Noiselessly she lifted the three-legged stool that was the only other furniture of the room from the bedside to the window, and sat herself down upon it, her nose pressed to a white blob against the foot of the pane. Never mind if she did take a rheum! She would watch . . . and wake . . .

and wake . . . and watch . . . her little body shook with an anguished yawn. . . .

She woke with a jerk, to find her teeth chattering, her limbs a-tremble. Ach! She had gone to sleep again! But not for long, surely! It was still night. She peered again long and carefully through the window, moving her head from side to side . . . and then stopped dead.

There they were! Aye! there they were! She could not be wrong! She brought her face, with its wide-opened mouth, so close to the glass that it frosted and she had to rub it with her shawl. They were not just men, these seven shrouded riders, so slowly passing along the rim of the enchanted hollow, with their horses' heads drooping. . . . They were coming up through the pillars towards the house —that frightened her a little. . . . But no! There was one at the head of the line, now unwrapping his magic mantle, the sight of whom made her draw a breath of delight. He must be the Fairy Prince, with the long feather in his bonnet! . . . aye, he was as bonnie as the Prince in the storybook . . . so tall, so slim, so fine upon his horse! . . . Ach! but why was he so sad?

Below in the bare parlour Lord Lovat gave a gasping groan, and with a convulsive effort heaved himself out of his chair, to pitch forward, almost, into the flaming logs. He saved himself by setting one hand against the overmantel with its stag's antlers, while with the other pressed to his neck, he sobbed, "Jesu, mercy! Mary, pray! Lord have mercy!"

The watchful gillie rushed into the room at his cry. "What ails you, Macshimi?" he exclaimed in Gaelic, throwing his arm round the old man's quivering shoulders. "What ails you, O my Father?"

"I am dead! I am dead!" babbled Lovat. "My neck, Simon, my neck! Ah! the fearful stroke!"

An affectionately respectful smile broke over Simon the gillie's bearded face. "You have been dreaming, Macshimi, that is all! Dreaming here in your chair by the fire!"

"Am I safe, am I safe?" quavered the old lord, his white fingers clawing the henchman's shoulder, his stomach shaking like a jelly.

"Why, my father, you are here in your own house, in the midst of your own domains! I am at your side, with sword and dirk, ready with every drop of my blood to protect you! All is peaceful . . . and the collops for your supper will be burning!"

"Supper?" Lovat stared at him vacantly. "Ah, yes, my supper!" He wiped his wet forehead with his wrist-ruffle. "Oh! Simon, I have had an ill dream! . . . Why, what is that?" He started back from the chimney-piece in a fresh fit of trembling. "I heard a cry! A cry in the night!"

The gillie bent his head to listen. A thin cry sounded indeed from upstairs. Simon smiled. "It will be the wee maid who sleeps above." He listened once more, and his grave smile deepened. "She is calling to her mother; she says the Silent Ones are approaching the house. She, too, has been dreaming, Macshimi!"

"The Silent Ones!" Lovat's little eyes, still rounded with terror, rolled vaguely. Then he gave a terrific start. "I hear horses! . . . They are at the door! . . . See who comes, Simon!"

The gillie padded lithely out of the room. Lord Lovat stood harkening, with his head thrust forward over his swollen bulk, as if his life hung on it. He heard voices murmuring by the house-door; then Simon returned leading a short, squat, carroty-headed Highlander.

"Here, Macshimi," said he, "is the servant of Macleod of

Muiravonside, bringing, he says, an urgent message from his master."

"Macleod of Muiravonside?" said Lovat with a perplexed look. "Ha! Do I not know you, my man?"

"Ned Burke, Macshimi. I will haaf had the honour of bearing your lordship in my chair in Edimbro'."

Lovat blinked at him. With his Macleod kilt, his broadsword, dirk and targe, he looked anything but an Edinburgh chairman. His clothes were muddied, and his coat torn, as though he had been in some conflict. "What do you wish of me?" demanded the Fraser Chief.

"My master, Muiravonside, waits without. He bade me ask you, Macshimi, will this house of yours be safe to receive him with four other shentlemen . . . and one guest of high degree?" Ned lifted his eyebrows with an unmistakable significance.

"A guest of high degree?" Lovat's jaw suddenly dropped. *The Prince!* . . . Here at my door, at this hour of the night? Who attends him?"

"Four shentlemen, as I waas telling you, Macshimi . . . and that would be all."

"Then . . . his army?"

Ned Burke raised his arms in a rueful gesture. "They beat us at Drummossie."

"No!" wailed Lovat. "No! It cannot be! For the love of Jesu, man, think again! Think on my grey hairs, and tell me it is not so!"

"Macshimi, we will be hoping to rally at Fort Augustus—"

"Rally! Rally a drove of asses! I read all in your whey face. You are routed! . . . Dolts! Poltroons! . . . Ah! dear God, I am ruined and forsaken! . . . Simon, do you hear? These cowards are in flight! Chop off my heid! Chop off my heid! My dream! Simon, my dream! Ah, Jesu! My dream!"

"My lord," said Burke. "You are keeping your Prince outside your door!"

"Take him away! You have destroyed him among you with your swithering, craven counsels! Take the boy away, and do not bring the shadow of the axe upon an honest nobleman's house, d'ye hear me?"

"Lord Lovat!" cried a high voice, "I did not look to hear such words from your lips to my father's son!"

Charles Edward had come without a sound into the room, his riding-cloak thrown back to show his white face and his eyes tinged with blue despair.

Lord Lovat cowered, pressing his finger-tips together like twisting snakes. "I would not turn you from my doors for bite and sup!" he mumbled. "I served your father, and *him* I respected. But the lives and goods of half the gentlemen in the Hielands now stand forfeit . . . and the forfeit, sir, lies heavy on your heid."

"My Lord Lovat," answered the Prince, "I have seen my faithful subjects fall around me this day in hundreds. I sought to share their lot, but fate refused me. I saw no reproach in any eye glazing with death upon the field . . . I needed to come here to find it!"

Lovat darted an evil glance at him. "My son, the Master of Lovat! What have you done with him?"

"The Master," interposed Sir Thomas Sheridan, who had limped, stiff with riding, into the room on the Prince's heels, "was marching to join us, but failed to arrive, alas! in time for the encounter."

"It is *you* that are saying he was marching to join you!" retorted Lovat sharply. "He had no orders from me but to protect my territories and maintain the King's peace in my borders."

There was a murmur among the little knot of the Prince's followers who had edged their way into the room behind

Sheridan. Lord Elcho's sardonic laugh was heard.

"My lord," said Charles, "we are here . . . but seven of us in all . . . dropping with fatigue and famine. We have suffered a reverse, and we hope to retrieve it. You will not deny your Prince a shelter for the night?"

"I would not be failing in due hospitality to any gentlemen travelling these muirs by night," growled Lovat. "I will entertain you and your train as well as my poverty permits, and, if you will, you may repose yourselves here an hour or twa. . . . But no longer! . . . Get you gone before it is day, I enjoin you all! You, sir, find passage to France, if you may! Your lingering in Scotland can but add the death of many to the ruin of all. . . . Get you gone, sir, and may God forgive your rashness in coming to our land to tear it asunder!"

"My lord," said Charles, stung beyond restraint, "it is barely a month since you wrote to me at Inverness . . . I bear the letter about my person . . . assuring me of your readiness to sacrifice yourself, your family, your clan, every living being and every chattel over which you have domin- ion, to my cause and my father's."

"The de'il I did, young man!" snapped Lovat. "I hope, if you have the letter you speak of, you will restore it me be- fore you are away with your friends to-night. It is a recom- pense you may fairly think you owe me for my hospitality. . . . As to the sentiments you are pleased to impute to me, if they were uttered, it was on your own showing a month syne! Many things have happened since then. One is that, as this fellow tells me, you have been hunted like hares by Cumberland's Dragoons upon Drummossie Muir!"

He turned, forcing his bulky way through the Prince's followers to the door of the room, and could be heard in the passage shouting orders to the servants to prepare food for the visitors.

As soon as he had gone Charles sank down, as if unable to endure more, in the arm-chair in which the ancient Chief had lately had his terrible dream. Sir Thomas Sheridan hobbled over to lay a fatherly hand upon his forehead, while Ned Burke knelt and placed the wooden footstool Lovat had kicked away in his tremors under his feet. The other gentlemen slowly left the room—Lord Elcho with his nostrils pinched in savage discontent, O'Sullivan with the stupefied pout he had worn since the moment when the line broke at Drummossie, Muiravonside and a Captain O'Neill, the inferior officers, whispering anxiously together. The Prince's entourage numbered now one less than the train that had sailed with him to Moidart.

After a while Ned Burke brought him a plate of the minced collops that had been cooking for Lovat's supper. Charles appeared to take no interest in the food, but he looked curiously at Burke's kilt and appeared to be measuring him with his eye. He said nothing however.

Presently Sheridan, who had limped from the room for some time, came back with a decanter of Lovat's best burgundy, which he had coaxed with difficulty out of the reluctant peer. He touched Charles on the shoulder. "You must eat, sir," he said softly. "Sure, we all need that you should sustain your strength."

"I have no appetite . . . indeed, my friend, I have not to-night."

"Then at least let me beseech you take some wine!" The old tutor filled a glass with the glowing burgundy. Charles watched with a spark of interest, and drained the glass as soon as it was handed to him. "Fill it again, Sheridan," he commanded.

Sir Thomas complied after just a second's hesitation. It went the way of the first, and Charles sat up with a spot of colour in his haggard cheeks. "I must work," he said. "Leave the decanter beside me here. I want Muiravonside . . . if he has supped. Do you know if the gentlemen have been looked to? Have they had a bite and a dram?"

"Sure, your Highness needs not to trouble himself about any of us!" answered Sir Thomas cheerfully, though his voice creaked with hunger. "We shall be well enough provided for, every man of us!"

" 'Tis well," said Charles casually. He lifted the decanter again, and refilled his glass, staring into the fire. "My old friend," he said, as he wiped his lips, "the time has come for us to part."

"Faith, I hope your Highness is not asking of me that I should desert you . . . after so many years?" There was a tremble in the fatigued old voice.

"Yes," answered Charles, "you can no longer help me. . . . I will take that fellow O'Bourke, Burke, what is his name? His coat is too short for me, but I will wear his kilt."

"And where will you go, sir, so very ill-guarded?"

"To France! I have had enough of treasonous friends!"

"Sure, that's a hard word to speak, sir!"

"You know it is true, Sir Thomas! You heard that old Falstaff of a Fraser upbraid me to my face, but now! Ah! *Madre di Dio*, if I had but axe and block at my command to-night!"

"Faith, sir, your cousin, the Elector, is like to spare you the trouble, I'm thinking!"

"Then there is Murray! . . . Not my poor Secretary. . . . Where is he, I wonder? It is ill weather to rise from a sick-bed and flee. . . . No, he is not capable of betraying! I mean Lord George, who has played with me in his hand like a captive fly, till he judged the hour come to crush me! And the Macdonalds, all the Macdonalds, who stood aside in concert with Lord George to-day, to deliver me to Cumberland!"

"I hear one of Clan Ranald's Chieftains, at least, died bravely for you, sir, to-day. Young Maceachan."

"Ah! Is Hector dead? . . . He made reparation, then, and I forgive him."

"I am wondering," hinted Sir Thomas, "what may become of Glenmarisdale's sister—if your protecting arm is withdrawn, sir."

"His sister? She is in her home!"

"No, sir. She arrived at Culloden an hour before the battle, and saw her brother."

"She came to Culloden House?" Charles turned his head sharply. "And I did not see her?"

Sheridan made no answer, looking at the floor. Charles let his head fall on his chest again, and murmured, staring into the fire, "My Star had forsaken me already then!"

There was a silence; then the Prince, rousing himself, said gently, "Go and rest yourself while you can, old friend. Let Muiravonside come to me now—with materials for writing."

In a few moments the *aide* was seated writing from dictation which Charles delivered between sips of the fast-dwindling burgundy in the decanter.

"This is to Cluny Macpherson," he said. "There is no other Chief left with a power that has not been shattered.

> *Dear Sir,—You have no doubt heard ere now of the ruffle we met with this forenoon. We have suffered a good deal; but hope we shall soon pay Cumberland in his own coin. We are to review to-morrow at Fort Augustus the Frasers, Camerons, Stewarts, Clan Ranalds, and Keppoch's people—*

"What are you staring at, Muiravonside? For God's sake, man, write!

His Royal Highness expects your people will be with us at furthest Friday morning.

"No, I will not sign it," said Charles abruptly. "Set your own name to it, Muiravonside. . . . Is that done? Now, I charge you, soon as you are fit, take horse again and carry that missive to Cluny. I will ask you to leave behind your servant, O'Bourke; I may have a use for him."

"Burke, sir, is at your service as much as I myself. May God keep your Royal Highness safe!"

"Amen. I thank you, Muiravonside."

The *aide* was about to leave the room when Lord Lovat pushed his way in, without ceremony, walking with the aid of his black stick, and saying, "Well, sir, are you rested? 'Tis time you were on the road, believe me, for your own safety's sake!"

"Show his lordship that paper, Muiravonside," said Charles.

Lovat took the letter, carried it to the candles on the table, and by the help of a large magnifying glass which he drew from his pocket, slowly deciphered it, seeming, from the motion of his crumpled lips, to be chewing over every word of it. Then he laid it down on the table, and restoring the glass to his vest-pocket, said, "Do I rightly understand from this, sir, that it is your purpose to go to Fort Augustus, there to seek means of renewing this desperate conflict?"

"My letter, my lord, I believe makes its meaning clear to those who read it with attention."

"Then, sir, I entreat you leave me out of your calculations. No Fraser will rendezvous with you at Fort Augustus."

Charles shrugged his shoulders indifferently. "You know, sir, I have no power to compel you. Be so good as bid my suite to be ready to ride in half an hour. . . . Muiravonside, away with you! I wish you a safe ride!"

Lovat had gone to the window and opened it a few inches to peer out into the night.

"The mists are rising," he said.

"The better for me!" answered Charles. "They are my kingdom. Let the fellow O'Bourke be sent to me."

Lovat gave him a long, crafty and inquisitive look; then went slowly out of the room, sucking one of his splayed thumbs.

So soon as Ned Burke entered Charles bade him close the door with care. "Now, O'Bourke!" he said.

"Ned Burke, if it waas pleasing your Royal Highness."

"Well, Ned," the Prince smiled. "What is the most sacred oath of a Highlander?"

"Upon his dirk, your Royal Highness."

"Draw yours, Ned! . . . Kiss it, and swear to be true to me and never to betray my counsel."

The squat little Highlander complied without hesitation.

"Now, Ned," proceeded the Prince. "We leave with the gentlemen in half an hour for Invergarry, as we planned. There we part with them. I will take your clothes . . . so many of them," he glanced humorously at the dumpy figure, "as I can put upon myself, and we shall set out alone, we two, to find a place of safety for me. You can guide me to the coast?"

"Faith, I will be doing that as easily, sir, as I could carry your Highness from Castle Hill to the Cowgate."

"Noble fellow! Not a word to be spoken, Ned, of our design, in this house or after we leave it! Remember your oath!"

"I haaf kissed my dirk!" replied Ned briefly.

There was a knock on the door. "Enter!" cried Charles. "Go, Burke, make ready!"

The ex-chairman rolled on his thick legs from the room, as Lord Elcho, thin, peaked and with the dissatisfied dints still showing on his nostrils, entered. "The gentlemen all await your Highness," he said, bowing. "I doubt, though, if Sir Thomas's strength will let him bear more riding to-night."

"My poor old friend!" cried Charles. "Where is he, Elcho? . . . Lying down in the back-room? I will go to him myself. Await me, the rest of you!"

He hurried out of the room, leaving Elcho tapping an impatient boot upon the boards. He glanced at the decanter, and shrugged irritably to find it empty. Then the tattoo of his foot abruptly ceased. He was staring at the window. In the little opening Lovat had made a short while ago he perceived a hand scrabbling on the sill. His fingers went to his sword-hilt, and he stood ready to strike or raise the alarm. The hand now fumblingly pushed the sash a little farther up. Slowly there came into view the point of a powdered wig; then a puckered forehead; then one hard little twinkling eye.

"Macshimi!" gasped Elcho in bewilderment, as the old Chief raised himself into full view, and with difficulty forced one gouty leg over the sill, levering himself by his crooked black stick on to the floor of the room.

"Macshimi!" whispered Elcho, "what is the meaning of this? Is there any danger at hand?"

Lord Lovat stood puffing, his hand on his heart. Then he murmured hoarsely, "I have heard! I have heard!" A chuckle broke from his heaving waistcoat which nearly choked him. "I overheard it all!"

"Eavesdropping, Lord Lovat, on your Prince, in your own house!" asked Elcho austerely.

"Aye, my lord, aye!" Lovat began to dust his velvet coat. "It was bitter out yonder, but it was well I did so. Now I know all! The rendezvous at Fort Augustus! Dust thrown in all your eyes! He means to slip away alone and leave you at Invergarry!"

Elcho took a step back. "I thought so! Ah! the d——d cowardly Italian!"

"Hush! he comes back!" Lovat set a finger to his lips. "Go with him now! Take your own measures for your safety! I know what I will do. They will never catch me."

Elcho smiled revengefully and hurried out to the door. Old Sheridan was being assisted into his saddle.

Lovat remained, leaning on his stick and listening. The trample of horses' hoofs was heard and grew fainter.

From upstairs came the child's shrill cry. "See, mother, oh! see! They will be away, the Silent Ones!"

"Simon!" called Lovat in a hoarse whisper. "Hither, Simon! . . . Have my litter brought round without delay! I am going, Simon, where I will never be found!" He clutched the gillie's arm with eyes wildly shining. "You know the place, Simon," he murmured in the servant's ear. "On Loch Morar! The island on Loch Morar! I will baffle the red-coats. . . . I am too old a skulker for them! Let the d——d younker go to his doom—he has betrayed us all! But they will not catch me, Simon, they will not catch me!"

Chapter VI

THE TOKEN

1

ALREADY the heather was tingeing the slopes round Loch Maris with pale purple. The days had lengthened; the lake was a burnished shield in the summer dawns; the white clouds between the tips of the peaks sailed across gashes of dazzling blue.

But the glen was silent, and the grey House was silent. No boats moved by day upon the loch; no figures sat or strolled by the water-side; no smoke went up from the chimneys. A passer-by would have observed in the cluster of houses on the strath or in the scattered farms along the lake-side only women, children and a few very old or crippled men. The whole place seemed deserted and dead.

Yet all the while it palpitated with an intense and secret life. All around, in the hills, in the rocks of the water-courses leading down to the loch, in the recesses of the woods, men were hiding, many of them wounded, all emaciated. In the first weeks after the scattered return of the remnants of the Clan from Culloden there had been night after night some rude funeral rite performed over a grave scratched hurriedly among the pines or behind the boulders in the heather, where some survivor, dragged helpless from the massacre, had paid the deferred price of his loyalty. The mourners returned furtively to their caves, to their holes concealed by screens of heather, to the sheilings on the highest and least accessible stretches of the surrounding mountains. There they waited in dour or religious patience for their women and children, who, stealing out by night, or risking their errand by day under pretext of tending a herd or visiting a sick female relative, brought them the scanty store of food by which they lived.

It was still not too scanty for subsistence, for none of Cumberland's parties had yet pushed thus far, burning and exterminating. Yet every week some fresh ghastly tale crept up to this still unviolated retreat—Lochiel's Castle at Achnacarry plundered and burnt, Kinlochmoidart laid in ruin, Borrodale a blackened husk, Morar unroofed, and its Laird dwelling beside it in a herdsman's bothy. Everywhere the flocks had been driven away to feed the conquerors, the meal confiscated, the ripening corn-patches trampled. Well might the lurking remnants of the Maceachans thank God that there was yet food for their families and roofs to cover them.

Glenmarisdale House itself stood blank and shuttered before its sombre half-moon of fir. No inquisition along the loch-side would have extorted the hiding-place of the boy Laird and his sister. Any spy searching for them on behalf of the troops patrolling the country-side in all directions from Fort Augustus, would have presumed that some inaccessible cave or secluded bothy in a fold of the mountains was sheltering them. Yet in fact—seeking safety in audacity —Darthula had brought the shattered form of her brother back from Culloden to the House itself to nurse him. Knowing he could not face the exposure of a cave or a hut in the heather, she had hidden him in an attic room, leaving the shutters of the lower stories fastened. Their food was all cooked by Dr. Hay, an old campaigner, beside the hut of branches he had built himself in the woods behind the House, lest the sight of betraying smoke should arise from the chimney.

Hector's recovery was in good measure due to the visits that Dr. Archie Cameron had been able to pay him before transporting his own wounded brother, Lochiel, to a refuge with Cluny Macpherson in Badenoch. But the miracle had been, rather, that Hector had been brought alive off the battlefield.

Allan Duncanson, after depositing him in a hut not far from the place where he had fallen, which was found to be already tenanted by six or eight wounded Highlanders, had left him there in charge of his foster-brother Angus, while he went towards Inverness to seek a surgeon. In the thronged and panic-stricken streets of the town, he had run across Darthula herself, searching for any fugitive Maceachans who could give her news of her brother. It had soon appeared that it was vain to hope to secure the services of a doctor, since the whole town was fast becoming a hospital, the needs of which far outran the medical assistance available. They managed, however, to furnish themselves with some brandy and linen for bandaging, and set out to retrace the difficult way to the moor, passing not without obstacles through the rear-guards and posts of the English on the field of battle, thanks to Allan's Campbell tartan and officer's shoulder-knot.

When at last they approached in the dark to the place where the hut should be standing, they were appalled to see a red palpitation in the sky, and, drawing nearer, to find only the charred walls, still shooting out flames. There was not a living being in sight, and certainly none of the wounded in the hut could have escaped perishing in the conflagration. They stood together in silence, with hearts that seemed to lie cold at the bottom of their being, and Darthula clung to Allan's hand for support.

A last hope that was scarcely a hope came to him. "There is a farm not far from here," he whispered, "Balvraid. If any survived, they perhaps found refuge there . . . at least we may gain some news. Darthula! . . . oh! Darthula!" he pressed her hand, unable to find words to speak his suffering or his sympathy.

It was not far across a few fields to Balvraid, and when they tapped cautiously at the door it was opened by . . . Angus Maceachan. Darthula threw herself with a cry on his tattered breast, and in a swift torrent of low Gaelic he consoled her. He had Himself . . . alive, he believed, though very weak. Darthula produced the brandy-flask, and Angus, pouncing upon it, led them to where in a dark room Hector lay unconscious on a rude bed, covered only with an old plaid. Angus had laid a hot brick to his feet, and now tried, but unsuccessfully, to force some drops of the brandy between his teeth. They lit a candle, and bandaged the cut the Campbells had given him on the scalp and his slashed arms as best they could, and then stood watching him in silence.

Presently Angus, turning to his difficult English out of politeness to Duncanson, explained what had happened. Some half an hour after they had gone a party of red-coats and Argyll men had approached the hut, and one of the less badly wounded men inside it had had the imprudence to fire upon them.

"She didna' wait," said Angus grimly. "She waas knowing well how it would pe wi' ta *saighear ruadh* * and ta Campbells t'at would pe outdoing ta one ta other for ta De'il's fafours! She took Himself in her arms and ran. . . . Her

* Red soldiers.

legs waas lang, or Himself will haaf peen burnt wi' ta rest."

"Burnt!" ejaculated Allan.

"Aye, Inferalsk! Ta hut waas burnt, wi' ta men inside her. And ta piper o' ta Campbells waas marching up and doon playing 'Maccallum More's Salute' to droon ta scraiching of ta Hielant men within."

"Horrible!" said Allan Duncanson, shuddering.

Angus turned back to Darthula, and reverted to Gaelic. It was concerted that Darthula should watch by her brother's side for the night, and at earliest grey of dawn, if it seemed possible to move him, he should be carried on straw in one of the farm-carts, which the owner of Balvraid would drive himself, down by an unfrequented moorland track to a ford on the river below. There Angus promised to meet them with three other Maceachan clansmen, whom he pledged to collect somehow during the night, to bear their Chief away into safety through the wild hill-country beyond Nairn.

So it had been done, though Darthula, looking back, could still not understand how. The first night of the journey especially she had thought Hector must have passed away in spite of the almost feminine tenderness with which the clansmen had handled him. But a shepherd, crossing the moorland with his flock of horned, diabolical-looking, black-faced sheep, had met them, and taken Hector into his turf-hut, where he had lain two days half-conscious, relieved only by the constant washing of his cuts in pure mountain-water and changing of his bandages. After that, slowly returning to consciousness, he had been able to endure the remainder of the journey and, thanks to Dr. Cameron's skill, had at last, it seemed, turned the dark corner.

2

ENFEEBLED by loss of blood and wasted, he was now creeping back to a shadowy life in the dim attic-room with its sloping roof, where the rats could be heard by night gnawing in the silent chambers below.

He lay in a state of complete passivity, obeying all medical orders, showing no interest in what went on about him, lending only an inattentive ear to the reports that filtered through to Glenmarisdale about the state of the country—the burnt and desolated houses, the spread of starvation as flocks and crops were ravaged, the rumours of orgies in the Duke of Cumberland's camp at Fort Augustus, prisoners tortured and women made to ride naked in pony races for the sport of the conquerors. He seemed to care no more for those rumours that the Prince was flitting from spot to spot in the Islands, hotly pursued, but never overtaken, by English men-of-war, red-coats and parties of Campbell militiamen. He would listen to these tales, murmur, "Aye, aye, will it be so?" and fall again into his passivity, which had a curiously expectant air about it.

"What are you listening for, my dear?" Darthula asked him one day, laying a hand on his knee. He gave a faint start, and turned a face that looked, in the beam of light from the high window of the attic, like the face of a little old man towards her.

"Listening?" he murmured. "Will I have been listening?"

"You have no fears, have you? I promise you, they have not tracked you here. There will have been no stranger in Glenmarisdale since the beginning of June, more than six weeks ago—Angus has kept the most careful watch. And if there were any spy lurking in our borders he would be seeing by every token that the house is empty, and be told on every hand that we are away to the hills together."

Hector's teeth gleamed in a ghostly likeness of his old whimsy. "As in fact the House *is* empty, little sister. 'Maceachan's power has passed from the lake.'"

"You must not be saying so, Hector! It will be your illness makes you think it. Will one defeat daunt the sons of Hector?"

"It is one . . . and the last, Darthula. And I, here in this shuttered, deserted mansion, where the teeth of rats and mice are the only voices, I am but the unquiet ghost of my ancestors. . . . Perhaps as ghost I may be scaring away the Sassenach bumpkins when they come to take me, but I am not holding it very probable."

"They will not be coming . . . and they shall not come, not at least until we have had time to convey you to the cave in the Ravens' Corrie."

He tapped his wasted legs. "It is I would make sorry work of it in the heather! I shall never stand on Fraoch Bheinn or by the White Stones on our own Peak again . . . and the deer would be gathering round now to mock my impotence, and they goring me while I lay a-dying. . . . Charles Edward will be more fortunate than I"; a sharpness as of jealousy crept into his sighing voice. "He still has his strength. I wonder where now he skulks."

"I would I knew that, too!" said Darthula softly. She looked up at the tiny window cut in the slope of the roof, and at the strip of blue sky that gleamed through it. The white ovals of her eyes shone for an instant in the dusty shaft that cut its way through the gloom of the attic, and her look was sharp and curious, like that of a bird peeping between the bars of its cage.

Her thoughts, at least, were birds that could fly free, and she sent them wheeling and peering among the grey, shadow-drowned isles, with their fairy bridges of gold and silver

trembling by sunset or moonlight across the water to the
mainland. Her spiritual counterpart seemed to follow her
winged thoughts across them on tip-toe, searching and
straining its gaze in vain. But at least her Abbé was still safe;
she must have had rumour of his capture if he had been taken.
Surely she would have known it by a sword in her soul, even
if no message had come through lips of flesh and blood!

But even while she sank back, letting her fancies flutter like
circling doves in and out the recesses of the isles, she heard
her brother's voice saying, "I am sometimes ungrateful to
Allan Duncanson for picking me off the moor—yet I ought
not to be. It is strange for a Maceachan to be owing his life
to a Campbell. . . . Well, 'tis you must repay the debt!"

She started violently, her meditations shattered. "Is it I
repay him? How shall that be?"

He grinned with a flash of his old provocation, but the grin
came ghastly from his discoloured lips and sunken cheeks.
"That will be for you to be finding out," he whispered, for
his strength could still not endure long conversation. "I shall
never be in a condition to show gratitude to my conquerors.
. . . No, I shall never repay my debt to Allan Duncanson.
Never . . . never!"

"Hector, what is it you will be listening for—again?"

"Was I listening?" he murmured, sinking back on his
couch with his eyes closing.

"So at the least you always appear to be, dearest!" she
said, rising and laying her hand on his forehead.

"I vow I did not know it," he yawned. "I have no taste
for sentry-go these days. I had rather sleep . . . and go on
sleeping."

"You shall sleep for now, at any rate," she told him. "I
will be fetching your dinner from Dr. Hay's hut."

He opened his eyes, and their black pools for a second
trembled with their former blue-grey impishness. "It takes

more commissariat planning to feed me here," he said, "than all our army could boast. . . . Faith, 'tis I am the preposterous ghost!"

"Lie back upon your pillow, and do not you babble foolishness." She adjusted, to the best of her power, the coverings of the box-bed upon which he lay uncomfortably enough, and went away with a rustle of her dress, itself ghostly, down the wooden attic stair to the lower part of the house.

She was dressed in a short and ragged tartan skirt, with her legs bare, and no covering for her head except her old plaid, which she could pull over it if the weather grew foul. In fact, she had made herself like the daughter of one of the humbler clansmen, in order that if she fell into some unsuspected ambush she might run less risk of recognition.

Now as she made her way downstairs through the darkened house she was thinking of that debt to Allan Duncanson . . . how it grew and how it became more and more impossible to pay it. Not that he ever presented his bill. He had taken leave of her at Balvraid farmhouse to return to his duties with an unemotional stolidity that had almost aroused the old Eve in her to a jet of annoyance. But for Hector's unconscious body in the next room she would have said something sarcastic . . . ah! how little she could unravel the tangle of her nature and her desires even after the purging she had gone through these last weeks!

But of one thing at least she was sure. There could be no thought of Allan Duncanson for her; he could throw out no noose that would catch her while she remained dedicated to that other devotion . . . pledged twice over now, since she had vowed to atone for her brother's wrong at Derby. She would withhold from Charles Edward nothing that was hers . . . and again it struck her that her existence in this bare, grey house was growing curiously into the likeness of that of the nuns who had tended her youth in their bare, grey convent; an existence barren except for its vigil, always tending a lamp of hope before a hidden shrine, a shrine which might at any moment blaze forth with manifestation of the Awaited One, but which meanwhile stayed dumb and impenetrable in the twilight of watching souls.

3

WITH these thoughts enclosing her mind like a haze, she went went about one or two tasks necessitated in the lower part of the house by Hector's and her concealed living in the attic; carefully hiding again each domestic vessel she disturbed, except the porringer and jug she meant to carry to the doctor's hut to bring away Hector's dinner in. She tied these into a corner of her plaid to hide them, unbolted as silently as she could the door at the back of the house, and stepped out into the sunshine, which dazzled her after the dimness inside.

She got no farther than the doorstep, where she paused, struck still like a statue. Only her ragged green skirt fluttered in the fresh breeze that blew down from the falls. Her eye had caught out of its corner a speck of white on the corner of the grey step. There lay a sprig of faded heather, held down by a little lump of gleaming white stone.

Her heart beat; her blood pulsed; a mist came over her eyes. She had not a second's doubt whose token this was. *He* had come again! He was back again in the neighbourhood . . . and he needed her. Where was he hiding?

She stooped to pick up the withered piece of white heather and the stone that held it in place. So soon as her fingers touched the gleaming surface of the stone, the answer to her question came to her. There was only one hill in the vicinity of Glenmarisdale that displayed stone of this colour and

exture. It was the solitary cone above the upper falls of the
Maris, often called by the dwellers round about the Peak of
the Necklace. Seen from the falls in clear weather, it displayed a half-circle of dazzling white stones, running, it
seemed, round its crest like an ornament, though in fact they
were on one side of it only. Just underneath the White
Stones was a tiny cave, known to those who had climbed
over the mountain. In this cave, it must be, Charles was lying
hid . . . alone or with one or two faithful friends—the
latter most probably. . . . He had found some messenger to
deliver his secret summons during the night; she pictured one
of his companions stealing down the lower slopes at twilight
to deliver it, perhaps, to a boy seen driving cattle home.

If Charles's associates were not enough, if he had needed
to send for her as well, then there was something no one else
could do for him. She must not palter with the summons,
nor hesitate over it. (She was glad to find such confirmations
in conscience for the impulse that was even now making her
limbs fidget with the desire to be bounding along the path
towards the falls and the foot of the peak.) For a moment
she hung doubtful on the doorstep. Should she return to
Hector and tell what had happened? No! she said resolutely
to herself. An instinct warned her that he would object; he
would dispute and agitate himself—to no purpose. For just
as a soldier might not linger with a sick brother or father
when the drum beat, so she might not in honour and loyalty
reject this call. Had she not vowed to withhold from Charles
Edward nothing . . . nothing that he asked?

Hector must be left, but he could be left in safe keeping.
There was Dr. Hay, who would bring him back his dinner
and remain to take her place by his side. And there was
Angus Maceachan, who would redouble the vigilant watch
he already kept on all the paths leading to Glenmarisdale

House. On any alarm these two could find help to convey
Hector to the cave prepared for him in the Corrie of the
Ravens.

She turned and kissed her fingers in silent farewell to her
brother. Then she lingered an instant, gazing on the familiar
grey walls and high-pitched, half-thatched roof, austerely
irresponsive even to the sheet of mid-day sunshine that was
bathing them. They stood peacefully enough, however,
with the deep blue waters of the loch sparkling and lapping
the shore behind. A pigeon trilled on the stone dovecot below the chapel in the north wing, its voice blending soothingly with the sough of the firs, which floated down with a
sound like the beating of the ocean on a distant beach.

Darthula turned her back on her home and ran up the path
to the woods to meet and warn the chaplain.

Chapter VII

IN THE HEATHER

1

Private Cooper of the 48th paced on his sentry-go, and
wished with all his heart he were anywhere else. He hated
this country by day, and by night he could not abide it at all.
In the day it was glum, unkindly, always the same, with its
endless, great hills and waste lands crossed by tracks that
they had the impudence to call roads. There was not a cottage in it that you would give to a pig-man in his native
Dorset—and when you said that you were saying something;
and there was not what you would rightly call a public-house
in the length and breadth of it. You could not get beer at
the hovels they called inns, not if you threatened—and did—
burn the roofs over their heads. That was Scotland by day.
By night—

He shivered as a blast of wind came moaning up the glen,
flapping the skirts of his coat. It blew a roll of cloud over the
moon, which had been making ghosts of the peaks at the head
of the pass, and waking a glimmer like that of an evil eye
from the tiny loch at their foot.

The night was darker now, and it had been dark enough
before. Glen Cosaidh was narrow and steep, shut in on either

side by black mountain walls, from which tiny falls roared
like voices as they discharged themselves into the torrent
pouring down its middle. Cooper was posted at the glen-
head. He stood in the fork made by the main stream, which
just here curved to the south wall, whence it was fed by a
cataract through a cleft, and by a minor rivulet that flowed
through a deep gully of rocks from the *lochan* almost closing
the issue at the northern corner.

He was the most advanced man in the chain of sentries
going from here to the foot of the glen, and was cut off from
the next man by the narrow but deep bed of the lesser stream.
Across this rill a watch-fire blew smokily in the wind behind
some rocks, and this fire, too, formed the end of a series,
built at intervals of some four hundred yards along the whole
length of the confined valley. From time to time Cooper
could see the head and shoulders of the sentry who paced
between this fire and the next below; but for the greater part
of his walk this man was hidden by the grass-covered rocks,
the lumps and hillocks that broke up the floor of the glen.

Private Cooper considered that the intervals between the
watch-fires were too long, and that he ought to have been
given a companion in his isolated station between the gully
and the top of the glen. It might be all very well as it was,
in daylight, when you could see what was coming at you.
But by night—particularly a night like this, when the moon
was darkened and the wind was veiling the fires in smoke—
you might be sprung upon from the gully or from the bed of
the main stream, or by someone crawling down from the
mountain-side under cover of these mounds and broken
humps of rock, and knifed before you could even challenge.
They had not enough men in the detachment to double the
thickness of the chain of sentinels, he knew; but still he had
been given too much ground to watch.

Not that he knew exactly what it was that he feared as he

paced up and down. But you might look for anything at the hands of these people . . . people who, whatever you might say, had brought their troubles on their own heads. He had at first thought the Dook was precious hard in bidding the lads spare none of the rebels, whole or wounded—but by G—— he had learnt better since! It was like facing wild beasts, fighting them; they had none of the manners of the Frenchies—not they! Why, at C'lloden, Private Cooper had seen a chap rolling on the ground, and had spared to bash his brains out with his musket-butt, and what had he got for it? Damme if the man hadn't stabbed him in the calf with one of their little knives just as he was aiming at another of 'em, and made a flesh wound from which he still sometimes limped a little! (They were ugly things, those little knives they called dirks. So quick and quiet they did their work!) And someone had said afterwards that the fellow who did it was a gentleman!

Well, that might be their d——d Scotch way of looking at it, but to his mind a gentleman was as gentle did—their captain, for instance, when he had let them loot the old 'ooman's house in Inverness. They had not got much out of it, but a couple of snuff-boxes and a silver bowl; still the captain had claimed nothing for himself—*that* was gentlemanly. By now Private Cooper had realised that hunting the rebels was just like chasing cats or baiting rats with terriers. They were not yuman really, and it consekently didn't matter what you did to 'em. If they had souls to go to heaven, then he knew nothing of his Bible.

D——n! Here came the mist again, creeping up the glen from the big piece of water below there like a moving wall! Private Cooper had had some experience of the mist of this country. When it came on heavily you couldn't see the length of your arm! This didn't look like being as thick as all that, but it was bad enough. Already the watch-fire across the streamlet was fading out of view, turning into a faint reddish glow on the white curtain. He hoped they would double the guard if it got real bad. Otherwise no man would be able to see the next, and they would have to rely on shouts, which seemed at such times to come from anywhere and were deadened by the fog.

You couldn't tell one thing from another in these b——y mists. Some of those rocks would look just like men crawling towards you. Only last night a comrade had let off his musket at one of them, and how they had jeered at him round the fire afterwards! But better to waste a bullet than have your throat cut . . . yes, better to be over-cautious than to let the Pretender's son slip through. That was what he and his comrades were there to prevent, a great chain of them—so they told him—stretching all across the country and watching the heads of every inlet from the sea, so that the fellow could not possibly get through the cordon. That is supposing he had come back to the mainland, which no one really knew for certain.

It would be a bad thing, all the same, to let the Pretender's son get through. A matter of a thousand lashes, if they didn't make a hanging charge of it. Whereas any man who caught Charlie would receive a reward, the figure of which made Private Cooper feel warm for a moment even on this dank night, with its penetrating wind.

His walk had brought him up to the edge of the gully again. He looked across and tried to see the other man through the mist, which had thickened considerably in the last few minutes. Instead he suddenly saw the yellow haze of a lantern and the shape of several hats defining themselves. Visiting Rounds, by G——! He stiffened to attention and shouted his regulation challenge to the officer across the rivulet. The lantern light thinned and vanished. He would be free to his own devices for half an hour now; he wondered if he dared light a pipe. Better not, he concluded, and facing about he resumed his pacing.

His mind was still running on that fabulous reward—he would like to earn it, by G——, he would! Though what he could do with all that money up here in this God-forsaken country he could not think. . . . There was no Christian booze . . . and no Christian women either. Prim as parsons . . . at least when there was anyone looking on. They had had some sport with them, all the same. At Fort Augustus the Dook himself had come out and looked on. That was gentlemanly, too. He seemed to enjoy it more than anyone else. Lawd, how he had roared to see them trying to ride races on ponies, wearing only the shifts their mothers had borne them in! . . . It had made Cooper himself feel a bit queer at first, until he had remembered that they were not real girls . . . only a sort of brute like the animals in the fields, and it did not matter what you did to 'em. . . . He had availed himself thoroughly of that liberty since, but somehow without much satisfaction. . . . How this d——d wind sobbed and whined, as if someone was hurting it.

He paused for a moment, peering down into the bed of the larger river, now a trench of swirling mist. If it wasn't for the row it made, you might easily step into it without knowing. Not easy to see anyone who might be trying to crawl along it, either. . . . No, they had had no sport, he reflected as he resumed his pacing towards the shut-in head of the glen, since they left Fort Augustus and came up to this lousy hole, all the way along that gashly stretch of water down there. Loch Quoits, or whatever they called it—who could twist his tongue round such names? Anyway, here they were, encamped beside it, too few of them for the business that was set them, and likely, in his private opinion, to fall off the edge of the world if the mountains were not standing round to stop them. Brrr! How cold it was, and they called it summer up here!

He turned slowly and had gone some fifty paces towards the streamlet, when he stopped short with his jaw stupidly fallen.

Right in front of him on his path stood a woman, laughing at him. He had taken her for a moment to be a sperrit, so silently had she risen from nowhere; it had given him such a turn that he had not even brought his musket to the ready, or given her a "Who comes there?" Where had she sprung from? Out of the gully or from between the hillocks? And what did she want anyways? She was standing there, barelegged, jabbering away at him softly in their outlandish lingo, as if there was nothing whatever to be frightened of!

"Speak English!" he growled surlily, "and say who you are, or I'll fire! *Comprenney?*" He dropped into the jargon he had used on sentry-go in the Low Country. "*Voo fusilier!*" he said, levelling his musket threatingly. She clasped her hands over her ears and crouched down as if in terror at his gesture, whereat he reluctantly lowered his piece. D——n it! he didn't want to shoot a woman, even a Scottie. And this was such a little thing! . . . This ought to be remembered to him for decency, and for the forgetfulness of one or two things he had done to women at Fort Augustus, of which he was not at all proud.

"Can't you speak English?" he asked her, "and tell me who you are? We're at war, you know! You can't go traipsin' over the country like this at night without givin' account of yourself. Be quick now . . . I oughtn't to be parleyvooin' with you at all!"

She seemed to be seeking for English words. "She waas going to Donal' yonder!" she murmured at length.

"Ho yes!" chuckled the private. "I dunno who Donal'

may be, but this is no time to be visiting him. Couldn't you do it by daylight, my dear? But I s'pose," he chuckled lewdly, "you had your reasons!"

She was a tidy-looking little piece, now he came to look at her as well as he could through the mist-wreaths, and a flame of virtue suddenly shot up in him. "Disgustin'!" he declared, shouldering his piece. "It's the guard-tent for you, my gal!" He was about to call out for word to be passed to the Corporal across the streamlet, when a sudden thought struck him, and he lowered his musket again. "Come here!" he said in a low tone, "no, closer!" She obeyed. "Do you know, by any chance," he asked her, "where *he's* hiding? You know who I mean . . . the Pretend—Charlie, what d'ye call him? There's a heap of money in it for me *and* you, if you just slip me the office like in a whisper!"

She shook her head uncomprehendingly, and then put a hand into the tattered plaid at her bosom. Cooper stepped back and brought his bayonet against her breast. "None o' that, you little b——!" he snarled. But she had only drawn out a small stone jug, of the kind he knew whisky was carried in, and was holding it out to him in a friendly fashion.

"Whisky, eh?" he said, "whisky for Donal'! I could do with a dram, even of that stuff; I'm fair perished with cold. Here!" He looked through the mist towards the next post and listened. "I'll chance it! Come here, Highlan' Mary!" He slipped behind a tall green-grown mass of rock, and she obediently followed him.

"Prime!" he said, smacking his blubber lips as he handed the little stone jar back to her. "And now," he suddenly seized her round the waist, "I've had Donal's drink, can't I have summat else you were keepin' for him? Don't struggle, you little fool!" He had already ravished her cold mouth, and "By G——," he said, thickly on fire, "I b'lieve you're a proper lady all the time!" He was crushing her against the rock, when suddenly he stopped and turned his turnip-shaped head.

He had heard a sound in the gully of the streamlet—the chink of metal, a sword or something, striking against a stone. He started forward, opening his mouth to yell . . . made the silliest gurgle in the world, and stood leaning stupidly against the rock.

Across the gully, the next sentinel came to the edge; peeped round a jagged point that obstructed his view, saw nothing but mist; listened and heard nothing; then turned about and disappeared again.

Noiselessly the little Highland woman writhed from under Private Cooper's limp arm, looked up into his face . . . and struck him with the back of her hand upon his sagging mouth. Then she flitted away into the mist.

2

ABOVE the fleecy fog-bank that choked the glen from one end to the other the moon was bright upon the dark mountain walls and silvered the threads of the falls that runnelled them. Up the stony course of one of these streams six figures moved, like shadows cast by the moon. They were already high above the mist-muffled camp of the red-coats, and after scrambling round a huge overhanging rock, they paused as if by unspoken agreement to cast themselves down and rest behind its concealment.

At length one of them sat up, and the moon-rays glistened upon a patch of silver in a strong black beard. "Well, sir," he said, "you are through the Sassenachs' line at last—myself, I can hardly credit it!"

A slim figure that had been sitting on a stone, panting, with its head in its hands, looked up and gave a low laugh. "Does your nose yet itch, Glen Pean?" he asked of a short and stocky old fellow with a ragged beard protruding like a challenge.

"It will be a wee yeuky," grunted Cameron, the farmer of Glen Pean, who had acted as guide to the party along the river-beds of the valley and up the water-course of the northern mountain-side, where they were now crouched.

Charles Edward chuckled again. "Still flying your danger-signal, Mr. Cameron? I warrant you mine was ready to itch while we lay in the water down yonder listening to Miss Maceachan colloguing with the sentry. What did you say to him at the last that silenced him so efficaciously?" he inquired of Darthula, who was lying huddled a few paces away from the rest of the party. She made a vague gesture without replying.

"It iss time we were moving, sir," said Glen Pean, "there will be far to go before daylight."

"Without a dram?" protested Charles. "Glenaladale, I invoke you! Our delivery merits that we should toast it in Glen Pean's golden nectar."

"I am of opinion, sir," replied the soldierly, black-bearded gentleman, "that none of us will be the better for having spirits taken at this moment. We shall require clear heads, unless I err, for the climbing yet before us."

"Pooh! A single dram will give us heart and not rob us of any of our wits!" exclaimed Charles. "Eh, Borrodale, eh, John?" he asked roguishly of the two younger men who completed the party. One of them was the son of old Angus of Borrodale, the other the brother of Major Macdonald of Glenaladale, the middle-aged officer, who had been the Prince's chief support in all his wanderings since he returned to the mainland.

When the Prince addressed them the two boys were engaged in a muttered dispute, and Charles inquired what ailed them.

"He says, sir," answered young Borrodale sulkily, "that I have his dirk taken whiles he slept last night. What for would I be needing a second dirk?"

"It is not the dirk, my lads, but the flask that we are needing!" Charles Edward rallied them.

"Oh! Mistress Darthula had *that*," answered John Macdonald, "to wet the sentry withal."

Still without speaking, Darthula handed the stone flask to the Prince, who carried it to his lips. "*Slainté!*" he said, and then paused ruefully, weighing the bottle in his hand. "Someone has had a thirst!" he said, "but 'tis no matter." He drank and handed the flask round the male members of the party. It came last to Glen Pean, but the gnarled old gentleman-farmer, instead of raising it to his lips, handed it back to Charles.

"By no means, Mr. Cameron!" protested the Prince. "The last drop is yours by every right in the world!"

"If my Prince," said the harsh old man simply, "will be the last to touch my flask with his lips, I will be treasuring it in my family for aye."

"Glen Pean," murmured Charles, "you shame me! Give me the flask. To you and to your children, Mr. Cameron, long life, prosperity, honour . . . and I shall remember you when I come to St. James's."

Suddenly through the layers of fog blanketing the glen below a bugle screeched faintly, and the fugitives with a single movement turned their heads.

"What does that mean?" whispered the Major. "Will they have found out something?"

"They have found something!" said Darthula, speaking for the first time in a hoarse and trembling voice. "Oh! God! yes! they have found it! Linger no longer! Come away! Come!"

Without waiting for leave or instructions, she had slipped

back into the bed of the rill and was leading them on and upwards at a rapid pace. Glen Pean, their appointed guide through this piece of country, followed, with his beard bristling.

He took the lead again, however, as they turned west to travel along the flank of the hill they had ascended. The full moon was a bright ball now above their heads, throwing lanky shadows of them upon the rocky slope they were traversing. Presently a louder voice than that of any of the little torrents they had already crossed made itself heard; and after a few minutes they found themselves upon the lip of a deep gully, through which plunged brawling downwards a rain-swollen stream that sent up a mist of spray to wet their beards. A score of yards below them the torrent went over a flat rock in a fall of which they could not gauge the depth, though the roar which came up from far below added to the dizzying effect of the water slipping smoothly over the polished slab on the verge of the precipice. A few yards above them large boulders in the bed of the stream broke it into foaming channels, and promised a perilous passage, as by rude stepping-stones, to the opposite bank. A single birch-tree, ravaged by the spray and the winds, quivered on the middle one of these jagged rocks.

"Is that our bridge?" inquired Charles with a wry whistle. "Now I wish, Glenaladale, that I had a double dram taken!"

Glen Pean, without a word spoken or a moment's hesitation, had begun the crossing, stepping from point to point with the sure-footed agility of an old mountain-goat. Charles, who should have followed next, stood for a moment doubtful. The fumes of the whisky he had taken troubled his head, making it spin as he heard the roar of the fall, and felt his gaze drawn fascinated to the reel of the water over the slab into the abyss. Swiftly Darthula Maceachan stepped in front of him, planting her lithe feet on this stone and on that; then, turning in the middle with her hand grasping one of the lower branches of the birch-tree, smiled at him to follow her.

He accepted the challenge, and made his first steps with sufficient agility. Then, by ill-luck, he set a foot on a stone coated with thick green scum just below the level of the water.

It was as slippery as ice. His foot slid from under him; he fell, clutched at the treacherous stone with his hands, and felt them, too, slide over its slimy surface, while the waves buffeted and blinded him; for two eternal seconds he was falling through chill water towards the abyss. Then a jerk stopped him, and he was held by his long-grown hair.

Darthula, as she saw him lose his balance, had flung herself forward on the middle rock, still clinging to the branch of the little birch-tree, which bent forward with her, and had seized his locks just in time. She swayed under the drag of his tall body's weight; the branch cracked; she felt herself, too, sliding forward, breathed a despairing prayer . . . and was clutched round her ankles. Old Glen Pean had waded back nearly waist-high through the water, using the stepping-stones as handholds now, and securely caught her.

For a moment or two the living chain swayed precariously above the bottomless fall; then Glenaladale, wading out from the other side in similar fashion, caught the Prince under the shoulder, and shouted instructions at him, through the roar of the water dashing over them both, where to plant his feet and where to get safe hand-grip. In the shock of the cold water and the peril Charles had recovered all his faculties. Watching Glen Pean and Darthula as they moved from rock-hold to rock-hold before him, and following their movements, he gained the farther bank, and was pulled up by them over the rocks to the top of the bed. There his knees fell suddenly shaking, and he collapsed a moment among the stones of the ridge.

Suddenly he caught hold of Darthula's browned fingers and kissed them. "Twice to-night," he murmured, "twice this night you have saved me!"

"Be thanking Glen Pean and Glenaladale, sir," she swiftly retorted. "But for them we had fallen to death together."

"I thank them," said the Prince. "I am always thanking them!"

"We must be awa', sir!" said the old Cameron gruffly, after touching his bonnet. "The day iss upon us; the enemy alarmed; and I would haaf you safely stowed in Glen Shiel ere sunrise."

In silence the whole party proceeded on its way, and by the time the day broke in misty rain they were hidden in a hollow of a deep ravine beyond Loch Hourn, screened by a roof of long heather and birch bushes.

3

AFTER only a few hours' sleep Charles woke and bade young Borrodale, who was keeping the watch, go and repose himself, so authoritatively that the boy could only obey. The Prince then seated himself where he could look through the screen of branches, and watched the clouds wreathing their shapes round the peaks in the dreary light, until the rain slowly ceased and ever and anon the sunbeams struggled to burst through, glinting among the leaves on the gold threads in his long locks and his soft reddish beard. So he sat alone in his kingdom.

Abruptly a crash of branches behind him startled him to his feet, and Darthula, white-faced and with staring eyes, hurled herself into his arms.

"Save me, oh! save me! Charles!" she sobbed. "He is after me!"

"Who is after you, *mon ange?*" he asked soothingly, holding her to him and smoothing the hair that had fallen over her forehead. "There is none here to harm you, you know. You have been frightened by a dream."

"No! no! I saw him! He will be aye shooting his head over that rock down there . . . the Sassenach sentry!" She shut her eyes and shivered all over.

He kissed her heavy lids with the gentlest touch. "It is a shame to wake you, wearied little thing; but woken you must be if you are still in the tremors of your nightmare. There is no red-coat here, do you hear me, Darthula?"

She opened her cloudy brown eyes wide like a child. "I was seeing him," she said.

"A dream that lingered in your fantasy, beloved! Your eyes were mocked."

"Eyes? I was hearing him cock his musket!"

"I must scold you!" he jested. "You are the bravest of us all, and yet you surrender to these childish notions when all danger is past."

She broke into stormy weeping. "I cannot bear it . . . He looked at me so foolishly . . . so foolishly . . . like a pig that is stuck. . . . I had to do it; he heard you in the stream-bed!"

"*Madre di Dio!*" whispered the Prince, "and you did not shrink from that either?"

In a few minutes he had comforted her and dried her tears. "Come you and sit with me under my tree here!" he said. "We must not waken the old gentlemen. They must be sorely tired not to have heard your flight through the bushes. Now, sit beside me here upon this hummock. It is my throne . . . do not smile, it is, God knows, all the throne I have in the world . . . but there is room on it for two. Listen,

Darthula! While you slept I watched and I thought and I remembered. Yes, I was thinking how, thirteen days ago now—and what days they have been!—you left your brother and all upon my summons; and with what skill you led us, through the net of the Campbell men that was enmeshing us, out of your own country; and how, last night, you twice preserved my very life, once from the red-coat and once from the fall. . . . But the mind is so strange that I flew away from the thought of how you thus many times saved my body, to think how many times you have saved my soul."

"I am not understanding—"

"Poured new life and courage into me, gave me true counsel, enabled me to continue the struggle. . . . And every time I have turned away from you or been parted from you I have run on disaster, and so I am resolved I will be parted from you no more. Who has done for me what you have done, Darthula?"

"I have done no more than was the duty of any Scottish woman. Mistress Flora Macdonald in Skye, by what you yourself have told me, has deserved at least as well as I at your hands!"

"Oh, Flora Macdonald," said Charles idly, peering out at the patches of blue that were melting the morning mists. "Yes, she is a good, brave creature, to whom I gave a lock of my hair, and whom I will not forget all the days of my life, believe me." He turned back to face Darthula with eyes alight amid the unkempt hair that covered his face. "But Mistress Flora could never mean anything to me—"

"More shame to you, sir, that can say it—"

"Anything to compare with what you have come to mean in my whole life. . . . Do not turn away! What are you crying for?" Abruptly he seized her and twisted her round to face him. "Darthula! you will always doubt my faith, because you will never let me prove my love—"

"Let me be, Charles!" She guarded her mouth with her hands. "Let me be: you know I will never be yielding . . . thus!"

"Can you not love, then, except in a Queen's bed? We are man and woman when all is said!"

"I have told you I can never be your Queen!"

"In God's name, then, what do you seek? Oh, Darthula, tell me, for my heart is sick . . . and you will take nothing that is in my power to offer. . . . Now, I know, indeed, that I am a beggar Prince!"

He saw with triumph a gleam of relenting and compassion in her tear-drowned eyes, and clasped her passionately to him. . . . The branches behind them rustled, and the dour faces of Cameron and Glen Pean appeared.

"Well, Mr. Cameron?" said Charles, masking his annoyance in good-nature. "Are you, too, wakeful?"

"Sir," said Glen Pean, "I will be asking you to-day to be finding another guide."

"That is sore news . . . and sudden, too, Mr. Cameron. Will you not carry your kindness a little farther, and bring us all to the safety of a ship in Poolewe or some other northern harbour?"

"I will be passing, sir," answered the old man stiffly, "beyond the borders of my own country. I couldna' be of aid to you farther north. Forbye, I haaf my own concerns, my family, left all in peril, that I might do my duty by you—"

"And nobly you have performed it, Glen Pean!"

"I thank your Highness."

"But who is to be my guide, if you forsake me now?"

"Mistress Maceachan, peradventure, will be taking the task upon herself. . . . She, it seems, haas no ties to recall her whateffer!" There was a sour and hostile look in the old farmer's eyes as he turned them on Darthula.

"Be so good as to rouse the other gentlemen," said Charles

with dignity. "We must take counsel of this matter."

As Glen Pean dived back into the undergrowth, Darthula caught the Prince's sleeve. "You see how it is," she whispered agitatedly. "You must have read in his face all he dared not say! It is I who should be leaving you this moment. I see incalculable woes impending if I do not. They will be falling from you one by one!"

"Send you away? It would be confessing their suspicions to be just! I will not do it! . . . Ah! Glenaladale, my friend, what are we to do? Here is Mr. Cameron tells me he can travel with us no further from his home—and in sooth I cannot blame him! What is your advice?"

"The first necessity in my opinion, sir," replied the Major, "is to scout for vivers. Glen Pean and myself should be able to procure provisions somewhere in the vicinity. At the same time we may gain intelligence. Your Highness, I presume, would wish still to be seeking Poolewe, if perchance the French ships are still in the loch there awaiting you. The way will be by Glen Shiel . . . and from thence we must be taking another guide, for neither I nor my brother have travelled the country to the north. Nor have you, I think, Borrodale?"

"I will be bringing you to Glen Shiel," said Cameron reluctantly. "I canna come one step further."

"Can you help us still, Miss Maceachan?" asked Charles suddenly.

Darthula paused a second, and then answered dutifully, "I will be knowing the country of the Mackenzies well enough, sir. I have been the guest of Lord Seaforth at his hunting parties, with my brother."

"You see, Glenaladale," said Charles, "how blest we are by fortune."

Chapter VIII

HOMECOMING

1

ANOTHER dawn saw them staggering with fatigue as they looked down into the sombre green gash of Glen Shiel with its crests of purple rock, winding away to the west, it might seem, to the very rim of the earth. To the east opened the tumbled and jagged peaks of the Glen Moriston country, a haunt of outlaws and of scanty hill-top flocks watched by shepherds as shaggy as the sheep and as fierce as the men.

Charles Edward surveyed this desolation in the eerie dawn-light with a shudder. "One would think," he murmured, turning to Darthula with his imaginative brown eyes disquieted, "one would think we had surprised the secrets of creation! Is this corner of the world not yet made, or has it been abandoned to ruin by a dissatisfied Demiurge? What say you, Glenaladale?"

"I say, sir," retorted the Major with a touch of impatience, "that I see small need to be troubling ourselves concerning the Demiurge and his secrets. We will be having our own secrets to guard, and those of the enemy to surprise. There will be famine, too, to stave off, for there is

346

scarce a crumb left in any of our sporrans."

"Glenaladale," confessed the Prince, "you are my head-piece!"

"Meanwhile, sir," pursued the Major, "Glen Pean begs you will now be pleased to licentiate him. He hath made a hard five miles with us this last night, at your bidding, past the point where he hoped to be able to turn back."

"Why, of course, he is free!" said Charles, and walked across to the old farmer, who stood leaning on his staff a few yards away among the rocks overhanging the valley.

Darthula, watching Charles from where she sat on a flat stone to rest herself, thought that by now he must be changed enough from his true outer man to baffle any pursuer's recognition. She thought she had never seen among the tramping pedlars or broken outlaws who from time to time traversed her own country so squalid a figure. There were rents to his coat, his shirt was in tatters, his kilt encrusted with dirt. His bonnet had been lost at the passage of the waterfall the night before, and his matted hair hung almost down to his black-rimmed eyes. Facing him old Glen Pean, resting on his rough and knotted staff, with clothes equally stained and torn, looked like some bushy sheep-dog of the hills.

"Sir," the first of these scarecrows was saying to the other, "the King will not prove himself ungrateful for all you have done for his son; and I myself look, Mr. Cameron, to spend some merry nights at St. James's in your company, telling over past perils, and pledging you in red champagne, to avenge our hours of thirst on these hillsides."

"Your Royal Highness's commands to Court," replied the aged farmed simply, "shall aye be obeyed by myself and my family. And were your Royal Father, sir, to think well enough of my son for a cadetship some day in a regiment worthy of a shentleman's son—"

"Mr. Cameron," said Charles, "it is a happy thought! A

commission in the King's Foot Guards! It shall not be erased from my memory."

The breeze of the mountain morning carried away their voices, a feeble chatter, among the clefts and corries, and their rags fluttered as Cameron bent to kiss the Prince's hand.

As Charles turned back to rejoin the others a brace of grouse rose from their bed of heather on a ledge about his head, and soared upwards, black specks against the faint blue that was coming over the slit of sky that over-arched the glen. He followed them with eager eyes. "If we only had a fowling-piece now!" he exclaimed excitedly. "I have never seen such opportunities for sport as during these weeks when I have never had a gun in my hand! That has been the tragedy of it!"

"The grouse, sir," remarked Glenaladale, rather grimly, "would have been of use for food as well as for sport, had we had the means of killing them with safety to ourselves."

"Ah, Major!" cried Charles, tightening his belt with an exaggerated gesture. "Do not remind me that I have a stomach, man!"

A few minutes later the party, without Glen Pean, was creeping cautiously down towards the glen, where a solitary white farmhouse began to glimmer in the rising sun, while the brawl of the river Shiel came up to their ears as they descended.

As they crossed the uneven floor of the glen, bent almost double amongt the rocks and hummocks to elude observation, it was on the tip of Glenaladale's tongue to remark that they were treading on the very ground where twenty-seven years befor the Clans had fought another of their losing fights for King James; but he forbore from raising ill-omened memories. Having discovered a safe hiding-place for the Prince on the opposite slope above the little farm, at a spot where, amid a wind-ravaged tangle of birch and hazel, a hollow

opened under a great stone, Glenaladale and young Borrodale left him, to make their way to the hamlet of Mhalagain
lower down the valley, in quest of provisions.

Charles rested beside Darthula in the hollow of the rock,
while young John Macdonald posted himself nearer the edge
of the trees whence a better lookout could be kept. In
thoughts and in snatches of sleep they passed away the hours,
while the July sun rose blazing into the sky, filling the valley
below with a shimmering heat, and sending golden arrows to
search them out between the branches that sheltered them.
Thirst began to gain upon them, outpacing their hunger;
and the trickle and song of the stream running through the
glen mounted to them in the quiet with an increasingly
tormenting note.

About midday Darthula woke from a troubled sleep, in
which she had seen the face of her brother turned to her in
anguish, and saw Charles lying outside the hollow on his
back, with his hands under his head, staring up at a patch of
sky that showed between the tops of the birches.

For the moment she fancied he was asleep, but suddenly
he startled her by speaking.

"How strange it is," he said, "to lie here and watch the
great clouds pass overhead between the tree-tops! They are
like mighty ships of war or merchant-venturers. I have been
sailing with them into strange seas of ice and oceans of Indian
heat. . . . That is the purpose of life, Darthula, to be sailing
and seeking, never to rest content with what is yours or stay
in the corner that is your home. For that is to be dead alive!"

Darthula smiled faintly. "Will you be saying that of St.
James's and your Three Kingdoms when they are won?"

"A Kingdom may be made an Empery, Darthula, and there
is France to conquer, the old dominion of my Crown, whose
lilies still bloom upon our arms lest we should forget. . . .
Yes, France! I will repay her one day for her niggardly aid

and cowardly betrayal. . . . But look at the ships, Darthula, look at the ships! There they go by, full sail, and oh! that my soul might flee with them. Freedom! . . . Freedom! . . . If ever I come to be king, my people, too, shall be free . . . free in their thoughts of God, free from the tyranny of great lords and little ones. They shall obey me only, and that because of the love we will bear each other. . . . Ah, Darthula! do not you think that God Almighty hath made this person of mine for doing some good yet? There is no climate can break me down, no fatigue that can daunt my spirits. I say not this to you to vaunt myself, for it is the Lord's doing and marvellous in my eyes. I am not as other men, and they can no more imprison me than they could yonder clouds. They drive me from sea to land and from thicket to cave; but they will never be rid of me; and when they think I am farthest away from them and lap themselves in security, then will I come again, like a thief in the night, for my own. For my hiding-place, Darthula, is in the hearts of them that love me. I know it: do you remember how that allagrugous old fellow that lately left us was for treasuring the whisky-flask from which I had drunk as it might be a holy relic? So long as that flask is preserved in his house and in his family, there am I in the midst of them. . . . Again I tell you, I say not this of private vanity: It is God Almighty that hath appointed to me my destiny, and granted me the strength to accomplish it!" He turned over on his side with a groan. "Ah, God! how my head aches and my eyes smart!" he said fretfully.

"Let me seek some water to bathe your forehead; then you will sleep perhaps."

"No. It is not safe to move from here. And who can sleep under this scorching sun and plagued with these villainous mitches? What a fearful country is yours . . . it breeds nothing of worth . . . only the bravest men and loveliest women in the world. . . . From Scotland, Darthula, will I take my Queen to be crowned, and you shall be glittering like a Madonna of Naples with diamonds!"

She laid her hand upon his burning forehead. "Will you be dreaming, Charles, of coronations and jewels? Recollect where we are, what lies before us!"

He raised himself feverishly upon his elbow, and stared through the silvery trunks of the birches at the sun-broiled hillside opposite. As though at a magician's touch the lodes of quartz in the purplish rocks above were glittering like diamonds. It was as if to their eyes, as they lay chained in hunger and thirst and sweltering discomfort, there were being displayed in mockery all the jewels of the world, wealth incalculable, the treasures of a kingdom, to be plucked and gathered by the stretching forth of a hand! Mirage of grandeurs, cruelly exhibited to the hunted Prince in the midst of this stern and barren country that grudged him the barest means of life, and was prodigal only of the outpoured blood and Sisyphean labours of its sons and daughters. Charles sighed. "What is the good," he said, "of fastening our minds upon *ces misères*? If I am fixed where I had as lief not be, I can at least carry myself off on wings of the mind. I tell you I am no man's prisoner—not even my own! God, Darthula, do you suppose I could have done what I have done, if it were my way to take account of what common minds call reality? I have defied reality all my days!"

Shortly afterwards they were interrupted by the return of the Major and young Borrodale, bearing some butter and a piece of cheese, all the provisions they had been able to find. They bore also the crushing news, learned in the inn of Mhalagain, that the French ship which had been waiting at Poolewe had sailed away again in despair of the Prince's coming.

Darthula had never at the worst time so far felt such a

leaden depression as settled on her at this announcement. Extenuated by the heat of the close little copse where they were lurking, tortured by thirst—once she had believed herself thirsty when her uncle shut her for a few hours in her room at Glenmarisdale!—surrounded by a cruel and inhospitable desert of rock, she was prepared to lie down and surrender. She could see from the grimness of Glenaladale's black-bearded face that he was almost as deeply afflicted as herself, while the two youths looked blankly at one another.

Then Charles gave a cheerful laugh. "If this is so," he said, "let us in God's name return with what speed we may to Lochiel's country! There every man is our friend, and we may at least find subsistence. God prevents us from sailing at Poolewe for some wise purpose . . . who knows what turn in our fortunes is at hand?"

So saying, he stretched out his hand to the provisions, and began to divide them up among the little band with jokes that made the young men smile. Glenaladale's forehead lost its puckers, and Darthula felt her heart throb high with loving admiration for the Prince. It was so often in disaster that he seemed to shine forth thus bright and undismayed—how irresistible, how perilous in such moments was his fascination! They had all begun to eat, recalled to the fact of their hunger by Charles's invitation. But soon all perceived that they had been tempted into an error. Both the butter and the cheese were heavily salted, and their throats already burned as if with sores. There proved to be only a few drops left in young Borrodale's leather flask; and they dared not in the broad glare of the afternoon venture down into the valley to drink from the stream, for the two who had crept to the inn of Mhalagain in the morning had been warned that for the past few days patrols of the red-coats had been passing at intervals up and down the glen.

No remedy appeared but patience and silence. The end-

ess afternoon hung poised, it seemed, without moving over
heir heads. They dozed and woke to see the same blinding
shimmer through the boughs, to hear the same mocking song
float up from the river below. They slept again in their
perspiration, dreamt of plunging into cool streams, and woke
once more with throats so swollen that they could barely
whisper to one another, to see the sun no further, as it looked,
towards the west. They lay now or sat brooding each man
over the worst injuries he had received in his life and the
choicest means of vengeance, Darthula haunted by insistent
visions of a triumph in Edinburgh, a coronation in London,
while the bells pealed and the guns thudded in her suffering
head. She scourged herself for her truant fancy, but could
not subdue it . . . her inner resistance to Charles's demand,
he felt, was weakening and crumbling.

Her fantasies were broken by an oath from his cracked
lips. "I will take the risk myself," he declared, "and go down
to draw water. Give me your leather bottle, John! I can
bear to be parched no longer, and Mistress Maceachan is ill."

"That would be madness, indeed, sir!" objected the Major
firmly. "There is a worse thirst than this I will be reminding
your Royal Highness, when your dried lips and tongue are
exposed upon the top of that city-gate in London, howeffer
they call it! As for Miss Maceachan, she chose a soldier's
lot of her free will and she must be abiding by it."

"I am not complaining, Glenaladale," murmured Darthula
hoarsely, "and I beg you, sir, be patient till evening!"

Again the suffocating hours resumed their crawl, and
presently Darthula heard Charles utter a long sigh like that
of a wearied child. She stretched her hand out unseen
through the bracken to touch his, and was startled at the convulsive clasp that met her fingers. She realised what agony
he was repressing beneath his gorgeous, air-borne visions.

After a while his grip relaxed, and she understood that her

touch was slowly soothing him. For a long time they lay still thus hand in hand, till a heaven-sent coolness stole through the air, as the vertical rays died off the hillside, and the sun began to pour itself away in molten streams of gold through the western cleft. It was as this change began that Darthula had a pricking sense of being watched. She turned her head back towards the dimming heart of the copse. The two lads were sleeping fast, buried in the bracken, but Glenaladale had raised himself on his elbow and was steadily regarding her and the Prince. She could see the silver patch in his beard, feel his eyes, enigmatic in the gloom, resting on her, and a tremor went through her. Then, with a return of her old defiant mood she tightened her clasp of Charles Edward's hand. She would not be thus watched and speculated upon.

Reluctantly the purple faded from the rocks, the green from the slopes, and a veil of greyness fell over the glen. By a common unspoken accord, the fugitives broke from their shelter, and plunged stag-like through the shadows down to the stream. For minutes there was silence while they drank, some cupping their hands, others lying flat and lapping.

At last Charles sat up and stretched his limbs with delicious relief in the coolness. "Shall we be upon our way?" he asked. "It is dark enough, is it not?"

Glenaladale gave an exclamation of dismay. "By G——!" he said, fumbling at his kilt, "I have dropped my sporran! It held forty *louis d'ors* of your own, sir, you will be remembering, in a little purse."

"We must bear with the loss," said Charles, shrugging his shoulders. "After all, it has been the goodwill of my people, not money, that has aided us so far!"

But there was a murmur of dissent from this judgment. The purse contained all they had, the Highlanders objected, and they could not hope to travel penniless. Besides, forty golden louis was a sum that only a madman would leave lying in the barren glen. "Of what use will she be to the mountains?" demanded John plaintively.

"My good friend, Glenaladale!" remonstrated Charles. "How many hours have passed since you told me it was better we should all perish of thirst, as we seemed like to do, than expose our heads to be rotted on Temple Bar? And now—" He gave another shrug.

"Where there is grave reason, sir," answered Glenaladale, "a man should be ready to risk his head. I could *not* leave such a treasure lying to be picked up by the first comer; I would be thinking my brains lost, and I with my head still on my shoulders!"

"Go, then, in God's name!" said Charles, seating himself wearily upon one of the great stones in the river-bed. "You will never find your purse, but you will perhaps lose all our lives."

They seemed not to heed his annoyance, but after a short colloquy arranged that the major and young Borrodale should retrace their steps in search for the missing money. The others waited hidden under the steep bank of the stream, grateful at least for the coolness, while the grey veil overspreading the glen turned misty in the evening, and the last embers of the sunset were smothered by accumulating purple clouds.

Of a sudden John Macdonald, who, according to his wont, had been keeping a sharp look-out up and down the valley, with his head concealed in the bracken fringing the bank, turned and made an emphatic gesture to them to crouch down. In a moment he came wriggling towards them on all fours, hissing, "*Saighear ruadh! Saighear ruadh!* The redcoats! the red-coats!"

All of them burrowed as deep as they could into the reeds and under the rocks on the water's brink, hoping that the dusk which now filled the river-bed would aid in their concealment. Presently steps came by along the road over their heads, and holding their breath in to the point of stifling, they listened.

"A b——y waste of shoe-leather," said a London voice, cutting the dewy stillness of the twilight.

"None left for the cooks soon!" answered another, and there was a guffaw.

"Silence, men!" said an officer's voice, and the tramp of the little squad passed on, diminishing down the glen.

When at last the Prince and his companions crept out of their concealment, John observed that if they had gone on their course without the delay imposed by searching for the lost purse they would have run straight into the arms of the patrol up the valley. Charles gave one of his school-boyish grins in acknowledgment.

"Maybe," said Darthula, "the gait they are going, they will be capturing Glenaladale lower down the road, though!"

But the fear was unfounded, for the major and his companion soon came into sight, peering over the edge of the bank. It appeared that they had found the sporran, but rifled of its contents. Suspecting the boy whom they had paid for provisions on the hillside earlier in the day, they had gone all the way to his father's house and at last extorted restitution. They had made a return by a different track on the hill, and thus they, too, had escaped the patrol traversing the valley.

"So you may be pleased to see for yourself, sir," said Glenaladale sententiously as he secured the buckle of his sporran again, "that prudence and providence seldom work a man harm. Had we abandoned our money, we should only have thrown away our lives as well—and deservedly, if you will have my opinion of it!"

"You are *impayable*, Major!" laughed Charles, clapping

him on the back. "I confess my error, and now *en avant, mes amis! Vive la compagnie!*"

2

DARTHULA believed herself to be the first to wake as she sat up in the afternoon of the next day among the heather on a hill above Strathcluanie. The promise of the dawn, she realised, had not been fulfilled. As they had staggered, leg-weary and famished, after another night's march, up to this place of concealment between two rocks, the mounting sun had been spreading a soft, ethereal gold over the marvellous amphitheatre of peaks, which swept round to the west to hide the mouth of Glen Shiel, and merged eastwards in the sullen pinnacles and crumpled precipices of Glen Moriston. In the valley below, bathed in unbelievable peace and seren-ity, lay the long lozenge of Loch Cluanie, its silver changing to a cobalt blue as the sun's rays strengthened; while the white walls of roofless Cluanie House at the loch-head gleamed against the sooty finger-marks of its recent burning. Every-where around them was rich magenta heather and metallic green bracken, tinged with a bronze frond or two prescient of coming autumn, and an air at once keen and bland blew round the enchanted circle of the hills. Just in front of their hiding-place the grey bones and forlorn antlers of a deer's skeleton protruded through the heather.

For a minute or two the spectacle kept sleep even from their heavy eyelids. "Do you know," murmured Charles to Darthula, "that there are moments when your horrid land seems to me almost beautiful? You will be laughing at me for saying so, but in all sincerity I think it!"

She shot him a grateful glance, and "I suspect," he mur-mured, "that this is more of your witchery!"

Once again, as they stood thus with their heads intimately together, Darthula was conscious of the major's troubled glance scanning them, and she hastened to throw herself down in the heather for sleep. The others followed her example without a word spoken, young Borrodale accepting the first watch with a nod.

Very different was the aspect of Nature now when she awoke painfully stretching her stiffened limbs. A thick black cloud had stretched forth its fingers over the cone of the grim mountain that guarded the pass to Glen Shiel, and the air was heavy, dank and thunderous. John Macdonald was keeping guard in place of young Borrodale, and Glenaladale had disappeared. John explained that he had already been off upon one scouting expedition, and had now crept forth upon a second. From the first the major had brought back only bad news. The red-coats were circling round the valley on the slopes of which they were resting; and even as John spoke the sound of two or three musket shots came from behind the ridges at the head of Glen Cluanie, reverberating hollowly among the further peaks, now drowned in sombre haze.

Presently a heavy shower fell, drenching the fugitives to the skin, despite their efforts to shelter themselves in the heather and bracken. The thunder muttered round the watching mountain heads, and the lightning flickered in the strips of livid sky between their cruel points. Depression gradually conquered all the four who lay fidgeting in the heather, hungry and exhausted, but unable to take any step before Glenaladale's return.

Darthula began now to feel seriously alarmed about the Prince. She could no longer doubt that he was ill. The glitter of his eyes, the stomachic trouble from which he was clearly suffering (brought on no doubt by his persistence during the past night in drinking against their advice from almost every rill they passed), his restless tossing to and fro all looked like signs of incipient fever. She exerted herself to woo him out of his melancholy, and succeeded in bringing a smile or two to his face. Yet even this had its disadvantages, since his lips had been so cracked by the heat of the preceding days that they hurt him if he laughed. He groaned and looked down upon the barren valley, now heavily over-shadowed by the clouds behind which the taller peaks had already disappeared.

"To what end," he suddenly asked Darthula, turning eyes that almost glared upon her, "do I persevere? What is it but to endure day after day of these torments, living like a beast of the field . . . no, not so well . . . lured by hope that ever recedes and is never fulfilled? Ah! Darthula, but for your blessed presence I could believe I was in one of those lands of hateful enchantment of which Ariosto tells us, and, like his paladins, subjected to some spell of strong delusion from which I cannot free myself. . . . And when sleep does come to me, if only you knew my horrid dreams! I am journeying ever, on and on, through these dismal scenes, ever mocked by that false display of jewelry upon the crags which you and I have noted so many weary times. Or if I do not dream of crag and precipice and dread holes in caverns where secret torrents thunder to devour me . . . why then, I am flying on horseback through fields of battle covered with dying and groaning men—"

"They will be groaning, *Phrionssa*, because they cannot fight and die again for you!"

Once more the thunder gave its giant, ghostly mutter among the Western hills, and Charles, dropping his head, was shaken by such a passion of sobbing that she feared the two boys whispering together round the point of the rock where they crouched would hear him and become spectators of his moment of weakness. When at length it passed, he lay still upon the ground like a man weakened by a stroke of illness.

During the afternoon they scoured every sporran, pouch and napkin they carried for fragments of butter, meal or cheese from past meals, and had at least a moment's sardonic amusement when they set forth on a flat stone the crumbs they had been able to collect for a royal repast. One torture at least had ceased with the rain showers: they could drink from the hollows and runnels of the rocks, though Darthula had to entreat Charles to be careful.

The following hours brought more bursts of heavy rain, but no sign of Glenaladale's return. And when at last the sun began to sink in tatters of sad colour impaled upon the morose peaks towards Glen Shiel a fresh torment danced up from the heather in the form of clouds of midges, stinging and irritating in a continuous devil's dance. The Prince began to tear desperately at his flesh with his over-grown nails, and Darthula was compelled to restrain him, and to teach him how to profit by her own experience, and to lie still under a bed of torn-up bracken and heather that covered him wholly but for his mouth and nostrils.

Here, as though buried and forgotten in the scowling wilderness about him, Charles lay as still as though he were dead. From time to time heart-breaking sighs of despair came from his living shroud of green and purple—sounds which it terrified her to listen to; she had never in all her acquaintance with him seen him thus brought low. It was as though the relatively trifling annoyances of this day of inaction had acted as the last straw on a load that had finally broken a spirit which not danger, defeat, hunger, fatigue or the ignominious life of a hunted hare had hitherto availed to quell. She was at her wits' end to know what to do, and at length went to John and Borrodale to beg them to seek for Glenaladale and hasten, if they could, his return.

They were both glad of any excuse for movement; and after watching them creep cautiously off in the dusk she returned to Charles and put her hand through the heather to feel his forehead.

"For God's sake sing to me!" he said. "Sing as you used to do in Holyroodhouse . . . and save my wits from madness!"

"I dare not be singing!" she answered. "I would be heard!"

"You need not lift your voice! Put your mouth to my ear, and croon as softly as a lullaby!"

To satisfy him she sang in a voice that was little but a whisper an old love-lilt of the isles, with its burden of loneliness and the wild, dissevering sea. Then, she hardly knew how it had come about, so distrait were her thoughts, she found she had dropped into some poor, rough verses of her own that she had been making ever since she heard of the death of the child Neil, the son of the Bard, upon the field at Culloden:

"Split is the sapling by flame from the clouds,
  Amid the green-glancing boughs of the forest its brown leaves
      hang shrivelled.
They have smitten thy youth, while the gnarled oaks stand
      rooted in pride;
And all the Glen laments with the tears of eventide,
When the cattle steal down to drink the sad waters of Maris."

Suddenly Charles interrupted her in a hoarse and hurried whisper. . . . "You must take me away," he said, "yes, right away from these places! Darthula, Darthula, I offered you my hand when I was a Prince and you might have been a queen . . . and you refused me. Do not say you will refuse me now when I ask you to share beggary, exile, the shell of a life as empty of substance and of hope as that cage of bleached ribs yonder which has haunted my eyes since we came to this place of purgatory. . . . For I have abandoned my dream of being one day a king."

Darthula felt as if her hearing were stunned. Between the grandiose dreams of yesterday and this abdication the gulf was too precipitous. . . . What had opened it? . . . Could one ever tell with Charles Edward?

"You cannot, *Phrionssa!*" she stammered. "This will be the dejection of illness."

"No. It is deliberate . . . irrevocable. What does the world offer to a prince but treason masked in adulation, self-interest that parades as loyalty? Why, even last night these men were ready to risk my head rather than forgo a few paltry guineas!"

"Ah! it is unjust you are now, and it not worthy of you! They may be over-provident—that is not the same thing as treason!"

"I would not be ungrateful . . . but I cannot read the strangeness of their minds. And I cannot renew the struggle on these terms. Listen! Let us steal away, you and I. We can make a pretext for escaping them and go our ways un-hindered—together."

"Go! Go whither, Charles?"

"To Glenmarisdale. I have planned it all. You have a chaplain there; you have spoken of him to me. He shall marry us—"

"Impossible!"

"I say it *shall* be! Then, with your brother, if he be suf-ficiently recovered of his wounds, we will make our way to the coast and find a ship to take us to America."

"America!" Her brain whirled. "What could you be doing in America?"

"Make a new life in the wilderness there! It cannot be as forbidding as the wilderness here. Man at least will not be so inclement to us. They say the savages are noble beings. Perhaps we will found an empire there among the red men that will outshine the effete kingdoms of this old world! With you I can do that or anything. Without you every prospect darkens and appals my soul. I know that I am a prince who can no longer utter a command to anyone. But refuse me, Darthula, and I swear by the Holy Cross I will walk straight down this hill and deliver myself over to the red-coats."

He raised himself on his elbow, scattering the bracken strewn over him, and even in the failing light she recognised in his looks as in his voice the mood of obstinate determination in which she had long known it was hopeless to contend with him.

What answer could she make? Tell him his purpose was insane, and that if he persisted she must leave him? . . . It was insane of her even to frame the thought. She knew she would not leave him, either now in his illness and destitution . . . or even if he bade her accompany him across the ocean. She could not help a wry smile as she reflected that it was loyalty to her Prince which had brought her to this pass, and that now he proposed to strip himself of all that could give him further claim to that loyalty; yet the bonds were only drawing tighter still!

Yet, after all, was his plan so crazed? There was usually a streak of insight in his wildest phantasies. He had made his throw for kingship in Europe, and been disastrously beaten. What hope was there henceforth for him or any of his party, for Hector or for herself, in Scotland? In a new world new hope might dawn. . . . She had always, she felt, been guided to give him good advice so far. What if she were to win salvation for him by saying yes now? Oh! she had been so long resisting him, and at such a cost to herself. Why resist any longer? Could the poor little sliver of iron for ever resist the great magnet? The lodestone rock pulled out the fibres of ships to their ruin, but this looked more like delivery than destruction. For a second the immense weight of responsibility seemed to bow her shoulders almost physically; then some inner pillar of her being collapsed and she yielded. Her decision chimed with his question, "Do you mean to forsake me now that I am nothing and have nothing?" She held out her arms and let him take her into his.

For a bare second she felt an ecstasy of fulfilment; then his clasp relaxed, his body sagged, his head fell backward with a little groan. She laid him down and gazed terrified into his face so far as she could make it out in the cloudy darkness. She saw the whites of his eyes glimmering; felt his limbs and they struck cold. Was he dead? Dying? Or had he only swooned?

She sat back upon her heels, distracted. She could not think what she could do to revive him. A cold thought clove its way into her mind like an axe. *Is he not happier if he is dead now?* She repelled the notion with violence, and stumbled to her feet to find water with which to bathe his temples. As she did so she heard with immense relief low voices coming up the reverse slope of the hill, and ran to meet Glenaladale and John Macdonald, who were returning together.

With the major's guidance it was not a long matter to bring Charles back to consciousness by fanning his face and bathing it. It soon appeared that he had only fallen into a faint, though he seemed extremely weak and lay back shivering on his heather bed.

Presently Glenaladale drew Darthula aside. "It would be well," he said to her, "if we could find him a dram of spirits to recuperate his powers. Can you be helping us in this matter, Miss Maceachan?"

"What would you have me do, Glenaladale?"

"Make your way to the little inn at the bridge below there.

They should have whisky, or be able to tell where it may be gotten, if at all, in the neighbourhood. I would not be setting this task upon a woman, but that I fear to deprive His Highness of even one of his guards at this moment. We are not safe from hour to hour against surprise." As Darthula was silent, he added testily, "You may trust him to us, I am thinking! We be three pretty men to cope with twice the number of red-coats whateffer! If you will go to the inn you may also perchance be gleaning intelligence that will be of use to us."

"I will go, Glenaladale," answered Darthula dutifully.

At that moment Charles's voice was heard, asking with a feeble querulousness what was being debated. Darthula went over to him, and kneeling beside him, told him of her errand. He acquiesced as soon as she mentioned spirits, murmuring, "A dram would save me at this moment!" Then, drawing her head down, he whispered in her ear, "Do not forget . . . it is a compact between us . . . so soon as occasion serves . . . you and I together; the Prince disappears, your husband stays!"

A dawn of weeping mists was struggling to light when Darthula returned wearily to the hiding-place with the aim of her mission unfulfilled. At the poor little inn by the bridge, when she reached it after difficult journeying in the dark, they had told her they had no spirits to give or sell. After long argument they had indicated the whereabouts of a cottage up in the hills behind the inn where a secret still had been for some time in working, and Darthula, in desperation, had set out to climb and find it. But she had missed the direction, and after three hours or so of wandering in the dark she abandoned the quest and turned back. As she crossed the glen amid the first hints of the coming day, she had nearly run into one of the English patrols, and had been forced to lie hid a long while in some bushes before she dared proceed again upon her way.

Glenaladale met her as she came slowly up to the refuge between the rocks and, taking her arm, helped her to sit down. Her eyes went at once to the heather bed where she had left Charles lying: it was empty.

"Where is His Highness?" she asked in an exhausted whisper. "How is he faring?"

Glenaladale seated himself beside her with an almost fatherly air. "Mistress Darthula," he said gently, "you must be nerving yourself to hear news that cannot be of the most agreeable to you. His Highness hath departed."

Darthula sat in silence staring at him. Her great eyes, filled with stunned bewilderment in their blood-shot ovals, seemed to swallow up her face. The elderly soldier quailed before the piteousness of their challenge. But he stiffened himself for his task.

"I must confess to you," he said resolutely, "that it is I have played a stratagem upon you. But it was done in your own interest and the Prince's."

"What have you done with him?" The words, coming from between her parched lips, were barely intelligible.

"I have placed him in the keeping of men of trust, who have sworn to give their lives for his if necessary, and to bring him unharmed to a place of safety."

"What men?"

"Men in hiding here in Glen Moriston."

"He could not even walk!" Darthula uttered a sharp wail.

Glenaladale smiled a trifle grimly. "He seemed marvellous well recovered when he heard the news they had gleaned."

"What news?"

"That the Frenchman had returned to Poolewe after all, and had sent two officers ashore with money to seek him, and to bring him safe back to the Court of his cousin, who will be waiting to embrace him at Versailles."

"Who are these men, Glenaladale, tell me?" demanded Darthula, beginning to take hold of herself.

"I will not be telling you that, ma'am, now or at any other time."

"And what will I have been doing that you should insult me by mistrust?"

"I am asking your pardon." He doffed his bonnet respectfully. "I am not doubting your loyalty. I were base to do so, after what I have seen. It is you have shamed us all by your courage and resource, if you will let me speak my mind on it. But I have seen these last days . . . other things impending, to which I dare not be a party. You have no father, Mistress Darthula. Your brother is my friend. I believe I have done honestly by him and by you in seizing the opportunity to deliver you from mortal peril."

"Mortal peril!" Darthula flushed. "Would you be knowing, Glenaladale, the nature of His Highness's intentions towards me?"

Glenaladale turned away his face. "I would know nothing. That regards you and your honour solely."

"It is you have impugned my honour, and His Highness's! You are a gentleman, Glenaladale, and so I confide to your trust our secret. The Prince has asked me to become his wife."

Glenaladale turned his head sharply, and looked long at her with frowning perplexity on his brows. "You will be telling me the truth when you say that?"

"By the memory of my father, I swear it is the truth."

"Then it's doubly glad I am to have parted you! Such a design were ruin to the cause for which we all have fought, and so many of us have bled!"

"I will be asking you to tell me one thing only, Glenala-dale. The Prince . . . was he going willingly from here to leave me?"

"He was going with the gaiety of a boy freed from the dominie's class. I was amazed to see his weakness vanish on the moment. I saw hope come into his eyes again; I think he was feeling the Crown hovering once more upon his brow. I must be speaking the truth to you, howeffer it may hurt your pride. He showed no regrets whateffer."

"It is I am very glad, then, my friend, that he is going again to his high destiny."

"What would you be doing?" The Major started up as she rose to her feet. "You cannot go after him! You will never find him."

"I am not going after him. And I will not be staying with you. Farewell, Glenaladale, it is home I am going."

3

THE fourth dawn from that one rose again in drizzle and mist, with the hills visible only as shadows and the heather hung with crystalline raindrops; and through it Darthula moved alone, crossing the last pass that separated her from Loch Maris.

She had had speech of no man since the late evening of the day before, when she had approached a cottage at Muir-laggan near the desolate head of Loch Arkaig. The tenant, a ragged man in a Cameron plaid, had come out to meet her, waving back his wife, who stood in the doorway; and though he had fetched her a draught of milk, he had shown himself suspicious and surly—she thought through fright. When she persisted with questions about the state of the country, and whether he had heard any news from Glenmarisdale, he broke into a sort of agitated fury. "Is it I that can tell," he asked her in Gaelic, "for what reason you will be questioning me? Here have been two of your sort already—one wearing our own tartan of the Camerons, but speaking the English of the Sassenachs, and one in the kilt of Glengarry, who would know of me about buried gold. My sorrow, am I the man they would be telling of gold hid in these lonely places? Get you on your way in peace, and trouble me no further. If you are coming again, the dog shall drive you forth."

Darthula could make nothing of his talk about buried gold; she desisted from her inquiries, and made her bed in the heather at the mouth of Glen Pean. The next day she had resumed her walk with dragging legs and aching head, till all sensation left her limbs, and she had let herself fall under a rock for sleep. She had a confused consciousness of terrible travels during the night, travels through air and fire and over bottomless gulfs, during the passage of which she clung for safety to the rock that was sheltering her, and in doing so realised for a second, though only for a second, that she was sleeping alone on the hill-side of a pass.

On rising, she had tried to eat the remnants of her one meal of yesterday, tied into a corner of her plaid, but could not face food. She resolved nevertheless to press on, till she reached her home. After about an hour she had the relief of finding that she had gone over the head of the pass and was now going down-hill between the mist-curtained walls on either hand. Presently the mist began to glisten silvery, and then to shimmer with a faint golden haze, showing the effort of the sun to burst through. The gold gained on the silver; she felt a warmth for which she was unutterably thankful, striking on her chilled limbs; and the chattering of her teeth stopped.

Then suddenly, as though at a signal-bell in the theatre, the mist thinned like lifted gauzes, rolled up, and disclosed a stretch of deep blue water that quivered blindingly with golden spangles. Beyond, a promontory clothed with dark pine came down to the water's edge, and she recognised, with a lightening of all her heavy being, the foot of her native loch. For a second she stood with hands pressed together, gazing round in feeble rapture; then, with a groan, dropped behind the nearest large stones. That brief survey had revealed to her what her first glimpse had missed. Not far from one of the tiny islets adorned with coronals of pine-trees near the exit of the loch a boat was floating, and in the boat sat four figures in red coats with muskets in their hands—English sentries, lazily watching, but still watching the issue from the lake.

For a few moments, huddled there, she was overwhelmed with terror. The chattering of her teeth broke out again, and, as she watched with terrified fascination the sentries on the loch, there stole over her an eerie consciousness of a fifth standing just behind her. She had not heard his approach, but she knew he had come; and she dared not look round because she knew, too, that he had a dirk still sticking in his throat, and a rivulet of a darker red than his coat flowing down to stain his white breeches.

After a time she succeeded in banishing this spectre by repeating to herself again and again the consoling words Charles Edward had used when she told him of her deed of war. She could now see that one of the soldiers had taken off his red coat and was fishing with a line. Clearly, then, these four were alone, with no immediate fear of visit from an officer. She summoned her wits. She could not approach her home by the path along the side of the loch; she must strike back again into the hills, and wind her way till she could come down to the House from the woods behind the loch-head, if indeed that approach were still unguarded.

Midday saw her still creeping painfully along watercourses and through clefts in the mountains bordering the north side of the lake, a circuitous journey that increased the distance of the direct route along the shore by half as much again. She was safe, she believed, up in these fastnesses from sentries and patrols; the enemy she feared was collapse, the final break-down of her strength or swirl of her consciousness into delirium. She rested a good while in the early afternoon in a wood that filled a hollow some five miles from home, forced herself to consume her fragments of food, and drank from a rill that sang through the trees.

When she raised herself to proceed, she came after about half an hour upon the ashes of a fire among rocks, with objects strewn about it. As she drew near she saw a plaid of Maceachan Clan Ranald tartan twisted up, a broken sword-belt, and a half-broiled piece of meat spitted on the ramrod of a gun and devoured by maggots. Near the fire there was a crimson smudge across the grass, and she shuddered away from it, recognising that there had been a conflict here, some of her clansmen surprised evidently while trying to cook a meal. It followed that the enemy had pushed thus far to-wards the loch-head, and that she had been mistaken in thinking that she was safe even in these secluded windings of the hills by her home.

Panic grew on her as she resumed her laboured march. If the whole loch had been surrounded, what had happened to the house? Were they still waiting to surprise its inmates after closing all the issues from the loch and the glen? If so, she might still arrive in time to give warning. Or had they already attacked Glenmarisdale, and, if so, what had been her brother's fate? The terror of this thought, as the shadows began to lengthen along the vast walls impending over her, and to fall across the hollows and passes she traversed, be-came an insupportable addition to her physical fatigue. It shaped itself in her imagination as a sharp wedge splitting her brain, and the pain it sent through all her head gave her once more the alarming sensation of walking above the ground, with no balance of her own and no support to cling to. As the twilight drew on in the deathly silence of the high places, the peaks on either hand seemed to be rocking from side to side with a sort of solemn motion, like tall, shrouded Fates taking whispered conference together. Thunderous voices cried out at her from the depths of folded ravines as she tottered by, and now the whole west between the high pinnacles seemed lit by one huge, threatening conflagration.

Below her now stretched a dark wood of familiar outlines. By passing through it she would emerge above the half-moon of pines that screened the back of Glenmarisdale House. As she approached the border of it, she picked up a branch that had been torn down in a gale, and used it for a staff to support her paces.

On and on she passed into the depths of the wood; the firs blackening funereally as she penetrated nearer to the heart of it, and making an opaque curtain at ten yards' distance. There was scarcely any light left now, but she knew the narrow path that wound over the soil browned by fallen cones, and contrived to keep her feet upon it. She moved at a snail's pace, but some force within her bore her slowly on, and it seemed that all feeling of fatigue had passed from her numbed limbs.

Suddenly she received a violent blow on her head. She had hit it without observing against a branch overhanging the path. A livid radiance spread over the wood, sharply defining the trunks and branches of the firs, and the texture of the cones striking up through the littered soil in which they lay half buried. In front of her, across her path, appeared a fallen tree, and, as though in a cradle among its twisted roots, Darthula saw the white form of a naked baby. For an instant she thought confusedly that it was a child slain and cast out by Cumberland's men after some outrage on a cottage. Then, as she stared at it, filled with horror and pity, the streaks of blood upon its forehead and running from the nostrils told their tale to her. She opened her mouth to shriek, but only a faint sigh came from her exhausted lungs. In a moment the Apparition and the weird light that had bathed it, vanished, and she was alone in the wood and it was night.

For quite a long while she must have lingered in the fir plantation in a state of shuddering collapse, for, when she emerged at last from it behind the house, a large moon had risen which showed the ruined tower of the Maceachans. The plash of the falls seemed wonderfully peaceful and re-assuring after her terror. For a minute or two she stood listening to its homely music, broken now and again by the soft hoot of an owl in some trees just over the stream. Then she climbed down the easy slope to the river-brink, and drank with a peculiar enjoyment the water of Maris.

Infinitely refreshed, she made her way at once towards the paddock behind the house. She was surprised to find the rude gate of saplings, through which she had ridden one morning centuries ago to meet a violin-player in the woods of Beasdale, torn from the leather thongs which served it for hinges, and trampled down with broken bars. A cold twinge of fear went through her at the sight, and with sweat on her brow she turned aside to the byres where their cattle and horses had been stabled for refuge. She hardly needed to peer into the darkness of the stalls, pungent with the odours of stale dung and fusty hay, to realise that they were empty. . . . The cattle taken! Then the house had been raided! With a sob and a cry, Darthula ran, stumbling through the hummocks of rough grass, until she rounded the horn of the moon-shaped fir-wood just behind the house.

The mansion stood silhouetted under the bright orb against the misted waters of the loch, uplifting to the moonshine, like the grin of a death's-head, the rafters of a burnt-out roof.

As Darthula, with tottering steps, drew nearer, she saw everywhere in the silvery blaze the black smears of conflagration, especially at the window-frames, now reduced to charred and rotting fragments. One chimney stack still stood; the other had crashed down inwards, increasing the destruction. Nothing else had escaped, it seemed, but the massive outer walls.

Darthula peered through the gap of the back-door, which had been wrenched from its hinges and had disappeared. The moonlight streamed down ghastlily upon the well of the wooden staircase, which lay in a heap of embers and ashes at the bottom, with half-consumed beams from the floors and ceilings above protruding from the pile. High up on one of the walls glimmered a cracked mirror that had not been displaced from its position in what used to be her own room, and had escaped further damage in the caprice of the flames.

Darthula recoiled with a groan. There was nothing to seek inside Glenmarisdale House, even if she could have forced a way through the wreckage. She circled the ruin like a homeless bird, and then saw that the chapel wing, as they had been wont to call it, was still partially roofed. It had evidently escaped the worst of the conflagration—perhaps through a veering of the wind. She found a broken window of which she was able to raise the sash, and crawled over the sill into the room which had been used as the library. She stumbled over volumes strewn upon the floor, and pulled herself up with a new and acute terror. Hitherto she had been appalled at the wrecking of her home, filled with agonised questionings about her brother's fate; but now, standing alone in the darkness of this room that had been spared, she found herself listening with a heart that thudded, while her spirit quaked with the sense of some fearful, overshadowing presence.

She tried to reason with herself. Nobody could have lingered in the house during the burning. Who could have dared to steal back since? Hector, certainly, whether he was dead, a captive, or in some hiding-place of the hills, was not here, she was sure. Had any servant or clansman from the little *clachan* crept into the house again to seek refuge? It was not credible. . . . And yet, she knew she was not alone. This deserted but partially unruined wing had an occupant. . . . Dr. Hay! Why had she not thought of the chaplain before? . . . Hector had been left by her in his keeping, but God knew what had befallen the pair of them since then. Could Dr. Hay be lurking somewhere in the dark? It seemed impossible, but she must make sure.

She moved softly out of the library into the passage. Through the slit of a narrow window she saw the little turret stair winding upwards. It was the way to the chapel. Who could be in the chapel at this hour? Why should she go there? Yet already her feet were drawing her up the stair, her fingers groping against the cobwebby walls as she felt her way. Now the chapel door appeared ajar at the stair-head, with a pallid light streaming from within. Three times she lifted her hand to push the door open, and each time her fingers fell from the panel, so dreadful was the terror that seemed to pour through the crack with the cold moonbeams.

Then with an effort of all her being she flung the door widely inwards. . . . *Dr. Hay was in the chapel!*

The place had been pillaged. In the strong moonlight it could be seen that the furniture had been broken and strewn about, the communion table stripped and overturned, the lock of the aumbry shot out by a musket in hope of hoarded treasure. But these details did not enter into Darthula's consciousness. Her staring eyes saw only the dark object that hung by a rope from the central beam that used to hold the great brass chandelier. It was Dr. Hay, his hands bound behind his back, his neat powdered wig still on his head, his black silk stockings still on his slender legs, though his shoes had been torn off for the sake of their silver buckles. With a shriek Darthula reeled from the doorway, fell slipping down the turret-stairs, and did not stop till she found herself, she hardly knew how, upon the terrace fronting the loch. For a moment she saw it and the trailing mists across the lake; then it seemed to lurch up and hit her, and she swooned away. . . .

A multitude of voices were murmuring in her ears; she was passing through a crowd of vague faces and trying in vain to pluck at Hector's coat as he paced slowly before her down a lane in the midst of thronging phantoms. He was following a black figure with a flash of light on its shoulder that from time to time took the shape of an axe-head. In vain she sought to catch her brother, who kept ever ahead of her however frantically she tried to pursue him, floating through the air propelled by pushes of her foot against the ground. Always he eluded her, while the axe-head flashed and grew larger every time she made a clutch at him. Then its edge fell, slashing her with a cruel pain in her leg, and she woke with a convulsive jerk of all her members, to find herself still lying on the terrace in front of her ruined home. In the grey dawn light a red-coat was standing over her, who had just pricked her with his bayonet in her bare calf.

The next moment a sergeant appeared, running up from the loch-side, who swore at the scowling, low-foreheaded brute and stooping over her said not too unkindly: "Mistress Maceekan a'n't you? We were looking for you to be back sometime! You must come along of us now, I'm afraid, Miss."

As he helped her to her feet she saw the shrouded head of the Dreamer of Glenmarisdale, aloof at the foot of the Loch.

Chapter IX

"H.R.H."

1

"You are Mistress Dar-rt' . . . Dar-rt'uly . . . I cannot make head or tail of such a name . . . in any case Mistress Maceachan, sister to the notor-rious r-rebel, Maceachan of Glenmar-risdale, whom I have sent in chains to London to stand his trial for High Tr-reason. Are you not that woman?" Cumberland looked up sharply from his desk in the bare room, furnished with a few maps, in a corner of Fort Augustus which had escaped blowing up at the hands of the Highland Army a few weeks before Culloden. At the sight of Darthula standing before him his eyes bulged forward, and he dipped a fat finger in the snuff-mull on the table before him while he studied her.

She might, he thought, have been painted as a figure of Death, so pale was the transparency of her face, so haggard her cheek-bones, so despair-stricken her enormous eyes in their violet hollows. Silvery threads ran across the tangle of hair upon her forehead. Had Darthula been permitted a mirror in her barrack-cell, she might even in the wreckage of her life and hopes, have spared a tear for the obliteration of her beauty.

But the Duke seemed to find a singular fascination in this figure apparently risen from the grave to confront him. Slowly he gathered up another pinch of snuff and savoured it with dilated nostrils. Then in a voice that came out like dough under the roller, he said, "You have my permission to be seated, Mistress Maceachan."

"I prefer to stand!" Her discoloured lips seemed hardly to move; the voice was like the sighing of a ghost.

Cumberland chuckled. Her defiance, which in a Highland man would have stirred him to fury, seemed to him as amusing as the claws of a kitten—he would have laughed while a kitten bit and clawed his gauntlet, until the moment came to swing it by its tail against the wall. Therefore he now rose ceremoniously from his chair, leaning his hands on the desk, while his lips curled downwards in his ruefully sardonic smile. "In that case," he said, "you will compel me, too, to stand thr-roughout our interview. . . . It seems to me that that will be very uncomfortable for us both, Mistress Maceachan. . . . So: that is better!"

She had sunk wearily upon a chair and he seated himself again. "I should have thought, had you asked me," he said, "that you had been on your feet quite enough these last weeks. Come now, where have you been . . . while we wanted you so sorely? Seeking *al fresco* delights . . . hey? hey? . . . But *where*?"

"That I will not tell you!"

"You were pleased to say, *Madam*?"

"I will not tell your Grace."

He gave a little smile at this extortion of a title. Then, playing with the snuff-mull, he said, "If you will not tell me where you have been, it is a confession that you have somet'ing to conceal. Why have you chosen to wander in these hor-r-rid mountains of yours?"

"What has your Grace chosen to make of my home?"

He hunched his enormous shoulders with another rueful leer. "What did you expect, Miss Maceachan? War with r-rose-leaves and sugar-plums? We did not, I conceive, begin these civil broils."

"Where is my brother?" demanded Darthula abruptly.

His eyes bulged. "We seem somewhat to traverse normal procedure, do we not? In summoning pr-risoners for interrogatory, 'tis I am wont to do the questioning. . . . But do not be embar-rassed, pray! Few rules would not bend before Miss Maceachan!" He half rose again, and made a bow, wagging his nose over the table like a fish hovering over some succulent weed. "And I will tell you this, ma'am," he went on, "your br-rother is in a very evil place and in a very evil case, and it would be a sisterly act on your part to do what you may to deliver him. He is by now in the Tower of London."

She leaned forward, a flame leaping into her tired eyes. . . . "What can I do, your Grace? Tell me, oh, tell me!"

"What can you *do*? Ah, yes! That is the question," he answered tantalisingly. He took up a quill, pressed it against the desk, and then walked over with his pigeon-toed step to the window, where he stood rocking up and down on his heels, looking out at the steely glint of Loch Ness, and at the mighty hills with their tranquil lower slopes of green that lined the Great Glen. "What can you do?" he repeated mockingly, coming back to his seat again.

"Tell me, oh, for the love of heaven tell me, your Grace! I will do anything! Anything!"

"I don't t'ink you mean it, ma'am."

"Try me, and see! Oh, before God, I will do all that honour permits!"

"Is that all?" he snorted contemptuously. "Then let me tell you, ma'am, you don't seem to r-realise the seriousness of the situation, not at all, not at all!" He glanced at her keenly out of the corner of his eyes, to watch the effect of the strain he was putting on her. He seemed satisfied, for leaning forward, with arms folded on the desk, he said brutally, "Forfeiture and banishment, they are inevitable! . . . But I pr-resume, Miss Maceachan, you will agree that life is sweet . . . even in exile and pr-robable penury?"

She inclined her head tragically, but said nothing.

"I had really been r-rash enough to hope," he grumbled, "that I should be fortunate enough to receive some encouragement from you, Miss Maceachan, after my clemency! Do you r-realise that for months now this r-room has been filled with petitioners, mothers, widows, wives, children, pleading for some token of mercy for those near and dear to them who had been taken with arms in their hands against His Majesty . . . and I have spoken no word of hope to one of them . . . not a single one?" He closed his mouth with a grim compression. Then, smiling again, "Admit," he said, "that you are most singularly favoured, Miss Maceachan!"

She lifted her head and looked steadily at him. "There will be some motive for that singularity, your Grace!"

"Undoubtedly. Oh, undoubtedly! Your penetr-ration is most exact. We should expect a return, naturally, for such an unusual mercy . . . and one of such dangerous example."

"I am waiting to learn its nature, your Grace."

"Well," he said dubiously, "I do not know." He unrolled a map upon the table, and beckoned her to approach. "I marvel," he said, as though changing the subject, "that a delicate female like yourself could endure to tr-ravel afoot in such a r-rough country as this. I think you must have had bird's wings to help you over these mountains. . . . Come! I am interested to know how you accomplished it at all. Tr-race me your itinerary with your finger-nail. It will be enough."

Darthula drew back. "It is as I thought," she said in a hopeless tone. "The price of my brother's life will be that I should betray my companions?"

"Who spoke of companions?" he inquired blandly. "It was your own itinerary, I tell you, that intr-rigued me. You need not speak a word of anyone else!"

"But it will not be my movements at all, but the movements of those you believe were with me, that concern you in all this!"

He shrugged his shoulders. "Well, if you will be such a very explicit young lady . . . believe me there is gr-reat virtue sometimes in being blind to the implications of a situation . . . if you must needs be so unnecessarily explicit—"

"You ask me to betray my companions . . . and that will soon be said."

He lifted his head slowly. "Companions, no! *One will do.*"

"I am not understanding your Grace."

"Oh, yes you are!" he jerked back with jovial brutality. "You have been in the company of the Pr-retender's son, we know it."

"And is not that a fine assumption, your Grace! What would His Royal Highness be wanting with a poor girl like me?"

"Guidance! . . . And what else," he leered at her with hideous sarcasm, "you yourself know best, m'dear! . . . Come now. I will put my cards upon the table . . . they will not lie there long for you to shilly-shally over, let me warn you! I will tell you what I will do and what I cannot do. I can procure your br-rother a merciful pardon from His Majesty, basing my plea upon his youth, his inexperience of the world, and the total unpremeditation of his most unnatural act of r-rebellion." He glanced at Darthula with a sudden crafty gleam. "I am assuming that it *was* the mere r-rash impulse of youth and the plausibility of a Jesuitical adventurer that misled him. Were evidence pr-roducible to show that your brother was a party to plans laid beforehand to invite the Pr-retender's son to come over and seduce my father's subjects, then even I could not save him from his mer-rited doom. But, assuming that by the aid of skilled counsel, and perhaps some of your famed Highland witnesses," he chuckled, "it could be pr-roved that he was led astr-ray by a wave of enthusiasm, then I think I could procure the remission of the sentence of death and the substitution of one of banishment. . . . From that I could by no means pr-rotect him nor from the forfeiture of the estates."

Absorbed as she was by his statement, Darthula's attention was distracted for a moment by the slow opening of a door behind his back, leading to some inner apartment. No one appeared, and the door remained open as if someone were listening within.

"So," concluded the Duke ponderously, "you now know all. . . . Tell me, where is the Pr-retender's son skulking?"

"Where is he skulking then?"

"You'll not answer? Not for your br-rother's life?"

"He owes it to his Prince!"

"Hum! You have no love for your own then?"

"I am not fearing death very much this day."

"So! You do not fear death. . . . Have you no fear of indignity?"

"I will only be suffering indignity by my own complaisance. Think you the things you have done to the women of Scotland are their reproach and not yours?"

Cumberland seemed stung. His eyes protruded over purpling cheeks and he banged his fist upon the desk. "'Fore God, ma'am, your insolence grows excessive! R-remember who you are! You are no longer a Highland lady, the petty queen of your barbarous tr-ribe! You are no more to me

than one out of half a hundred wenches I have gathered in
from their wretched huts to this camp, to br-ridle their sedition, and to make amusement for my men withal. . . . And
I can do the same with you!"

The door behind his back swung open, and Darthula, staring as if at a ghost, saw her uncle walk out from the inner
room.

The Duke swung round and glared at him. "We did not
summon you, my lord!" he said.

"Your Royal Highness did not. I entered in the exercise
of my discretion."

"I bade you wait within in case I had need of you, Lord
Br-rounhill!"

"Your Royal Highness has sair need of me. You are gang-
ing the way to defeat your ends. Reflect, sir," he added, facing valiantly up to the scarlet colossus, "there is a muckle
hangs upon this conference!"

"I have half a mind to order the pair of you to be flung
into the lake!"

Brounie raised his chin haughtily. "I wad beg your Royal
Highness to pretermit the use o' sic language to me, a Lord
of Session and a gentleman of untainted loyalty!"

"Well, well, my little bantam!" As always Cumberland
seemed amused by the small judge's spirit. "What o' God's
name do you expect me to do with this wench?"

"Permit a member of her family to attempt the force of
persuasion. . . . There is nane other can gie us the information of whilk we stand in need."

"Persuade her, then, by all the devils, if you t'ink you can.
. . . But, if you fail, as sure as I command the King's armies,
she shall suffer for it as though she were one of the camp
trollops!" He picked up his hat. "I go now for half an hour
to inspect hutments. You Highlanders must learn to make
your conqueror-rs more comfortable, by G——!"

He jingled out of the room with his awkward step, and Lord Brounhill, left alone with his niece, held out his arms to her with a wooden simulacrum of affection. She recoiled behind a chair.

"Darthula!" he remonstrated, "hae ye no embrace for your uncle?"

"That, sir, will be depending on the character in which you present yourself."

"It is onygates a character, Darthula, to which religion, nature and reason bid you pay dutiful heed."

"Are you here, uncle, as the Tutor of Glenmarisdale, the protector of my poor brother and our broken Clan, or as the creature of the Sassenach? What way is it that I find you in Cumberland's camp, and in Cumberland's confidence?"

"What a hantle of idle questions have we here!" exclaimed Lord Brounhill fretfully. "For being what you are pleased to call 'the creature of the Sassenach,' I have ever, as you weel know, been a loyal subject of King George. And I am here now to assist His Royal Highness in the pacification o' this unhappy country, and to plead for what gude terms I may hope to get on behalf of its misguided inhabitants. But my politics need not concern you either at this moment. There is but one thing for baith of us to consider, Darthula, and it is by what means we may presairve all of our fam'ly and its fortunes that your brither's madness has left us."

Again a pathetic little flame of hope crept into her despairing eyes. "Hector! You will be having a plan for saving the boy, sir?"

Her uncle made an almost contemptuous gesture. "There exists no power in the twa kingdoms can save that child o' calamity. . . . It boots not for you to greet and moan, Darthula! . . . Hector maun dree his weird. Himself hath asked for the rope, and it shall be gi'en him."

"The rope!" cried Darthula through her sobs. "They will

not be daring to hang the Son of Hector like a common man!"

"Are ye so parteecular to claim the axe?" sneered Lord Brounhill. "Rest assured, then, he shall hae the rope and the knife, too, and his heid shall be rotting on Temple Bar—my sorrow!" he cried with a sudden sharp note of anguish, "the heid of Maceachan o' Glenmarisdale!" He turned aside, and Darthula, her indignation turning to amazement, beheld him press his hands to his eyes and bring them away wet. In a moment he was his wooden self again.

"Darthula," he said quietly, "eneuch o' lamentation and recrimination 'twixt us two. We maun stand together now, to save the heritage o' the Maceachans."

"What will there be left to save?" she moaned.

He shook his wig angrily. "Hae ye nae sense? The estate maunna be adjudged forfeit! There maun be a Maceachan still to reign by the waters of Maris!"

"He will be dead—the Son of Hector!"

"He will be living still, whateffer—the Son of Hector! Stand you by me now, and I will prevail upon Government to resettle the lands o' Glenmarisdale upon my ain self and the heirs male o' ma daughter, Jean. So shall our fam'ly be saved . . . the name, too, maybe, for young Duncanson can change by deed to Maceachan on his marriage day."

"Allan Duncanson is to marry your Jeanie? He will not! And what will this tale of yours be? *He*"—she pointed to the door by which Cumberland had gone out—"he was telling me that he could save Hector's life, but not the estates."

The glassy look came into Lord Brounhill's eyes. "He kens naething of what he says," he answered. "I hae been in correspondence wi' the Lord Justice Clerk and the Secretary o' State—did you think I wad not explore every means whereby to save my nephew? I could get but one answer. 'He is for trial: the law maun tak' its course.' Darthula," he took an anxious step towards her, "do not you yield up your secret to Cumberland! The promises of that man are egg-shells. You ken where the Pretender's son may be taken. Tell it to me now, whiles we are not overheard! . . . I will mak' a bargain wi' His Royal Highness so firm that King and Parliament shall not break it!"

"I will not!"

"Has the man not betrayed you? Has he not ruined this puir land and rin awa', leaving it to its doom? Many of his followers are saying that to-day, I'll uphaud you!"

"Failure will be his sin. Sorrow's me! A fallen prince has few friends, I am thinking!"

"I was neffer his friend—"

"Nor any man's that could not bring you 'siller'! I will tell you nothing . . . shame that you are to our House! And I will never be speaking word to you again, James Maceachan!"

Lord Brounhill raised his hands in the air with a scream of fury. "The curse of our fathers be upon you!" he cried, breaking, to Darthula's astounded ears, into Gaelic, which she had never in her life heard issue from his lips before; and she stood almost unable to recognise him, while invective flowed from his lips like the rushing of a storm-swollen torrent from the hills.

"A very edifying family scene!" said the voice of Cumberland in the doorway. "Worthy Master Judge, you do not seem to have a better way with my pretty pr-risoner after all! Now perhaps you will condescend to let me make one more poor attempt on my own account." He pointed sternly to the inner room. "Leave me alone with your niece; and this time—shut the door!"

For a second Darthula thought that Brounhill would spring upon one or the other of them. Then, with a sound like a beast in pain, he tottered off into the room beyond, slamming the door behind him.

Cumberland walked coolly across and drew the bolt. "And that is the way to tr-rust a Highlander," said he.

He turned and saw Darthula lying upon a chair, her head fallen back in a half-fainting condition. He rang the bell upon his table.

"Send for wine!" he said curtly to the orderly officer who presented himself, and when it was brought by a corporal he poured it out for her with his own hands. "Dr-rink!" he commanded; "I shall not poison you!"

Darthula handed back the empty glass, a little revived.

"I will never," said Cumberland, looking down at her thoughtfully, "deny your high spirit, ma'am! Why will you Highlanders not give this loyalty to *us*? I pr-romise you we would make you a better return." He laid his great hand softly on her shoulder. "You have suffered a great deal, my poor child!" he murmured.

Darthula's tears flowed again. She felt weak as a baby, and the note of sudden sympathy in the voice that had been so harsh seemed to pierce her. "I will only have been trying to do my duty," she sobbed.

"That is the sign of a noble mind!" said the Duke. He pulled a chair up close to hers and sat down beside her. "Let me have the honour of taking your hand," he mumbled, and raising it to his lips imprinted a cold, damp kiss upon it. "Do you know," he went on in a voice more thickly embedded in dough than any he had used before, "you have made a pr-rofound impression upon me. . . . I want to know you. . . . I wish you would make it possible for me to know you . . . much better . . . much more closely than I do at pr-resent. . . . Don't, pray, withdraw that charming hand . . . your conqueror-r implores. . . . Do you know, strange little mountain witch, that 'tis I am fast becoming your pr-risoner?"

She tried to withdraw her hand, gazing at him with eyes wide in horror. His eyes seemed to be starting out of his head; his bull-neck had reddened. "Don't look so shy!" he urged her throatily. "You have been loved by one Pr-rince already, but what a fellow! 'A king of shr-reds and patches,' as the play-writing man, Wycherley, says . . . a r-runaway mountebank! Let yourself be loved now by a real Pr-rince, who can do somet'ing for your present distress and make you happy for the future!"

"You . . . you call yourself a soldier?" she whispered.

"Your countr-rymen should know if I am!" he jerked out with ferocious joviality.

"And are you not knowing there is not an officer in all the army of King James would make such a proposition to a helpless woman?"

"Truly? . . . Zooks! They must be without eyes! Or is their blood so fish-like? Come, Dar-rtilly, or whatever your name is, enough of coyness! It is all in the game, I know, but you have made your sign of r-resistance, and may now surrender with honours of war! . . . Don't be foolish! T'ink what I can do for you!"

"What can you do for me?" The words were a taunt, but he took them as a token of willingness to bargain.

"Set you free, here and now! Save your br-rother's head! . . . And, yes, if that is what wor-r-ries you, perhaps you shall have your lands back, too." He glanced through the window at the serene, watching hills. "All you Scots weigh your deserts in solid gold, do you not?" he joked.

"And a ship and escort to send back Prince Charles safe to France?" asked Darthula.

His eyes narrowed. "Beware, Dar-rtilly! There are some subjects on which I do *not* jest! . . . But come now—and remember your estimable r-relative in there seconds all I am saying—you are going to whisper in my ears . . . only half a dozen words . . . they will never be r-remembered against you or traced to you. . . . Just the few words I need to put me on the right tr-rack. That is all . . . unless," he leered, "you like to whisper, too, that you love me just a little, Dar-rtilly!"

"It will be a fine bargain for me, I am thinking. My honour and my Prince's life for a villa in Windsor Park . . . and the title of countess! Will you not be forgetting the title of countess?"

"Anyt'ing! . . . Anyt'ing! . . . so you will be r-reasonable now for five minutes!"

"Diamonds too?"

"You will find me generous if you are *complaisante*."

"Why am I thus honoured? I am not a German . . . I am not a barrel of fat. . . . My fate! Is it I am to be mistress now to a Hanoverian duke? . . . What an elevation! And yet," she stood up, curtseying, "I decline it—flesher!"

Cumberland rose slowly from his chair, and set it back with deliberation in its place against the wall. Then he rang the bell, and the orderly officer entered again through the folding doors and saluted.

"Are the men having r-races for the Scotch trollops this afternoon, Mr. Molyneux?" inquired the Duke courteously.

"I . . . I believe so, your Royal Highness," answered the young officer, blushing.

"So. . . . Then, Mr. Molyneux, you may take this woman and t'row her in with the herd!"

The lieutenant stared at him, incredulous.

2

THE sunset that had been bathing the mountains of the Great Glen in the tint of spilt raspberry juice against the ghost of a light-blue sky had slowly faded in the silence of Glen Moriston. The only sound was the gurgle of the river rushing round sunken boulders as it raced in the cold, pure air to its junction with Loch Ness. The heather-clad slopes on the southern side of the Glen were turning from magenta to embrowned greyness, while the scowling peaks above them were merging into still more sinister shadow. The pass above Inverwick Forest showed as a darkening gash in the mountain wall. Still the watcher stayed at his post behind a rock in the heather, motionless as the stone against which he leaned, and, like it, losing form and colour in the gathering gloom.

He did not move an hour later when he was surprised by the sound of a pony's hoofs coming through the forest, and then scrambling in the stony bed of the stream; but his ears were alert, and his eyes searched the shadowy gulf of the glen below with the sharpness of an eagle's. A moon had risen now which was shooting a pale glimmer over the night scene. The hoofs seemed to check; then broke out again to the right of him in a duller drumming and swishing, which betokened that the invisible rider, whoever it might be, was mounting the slopes towards the spot where the wild, bearded sentry waited. Still he made neither stir nor sound; he only slid his musket barrel over the top of the rock behind which he crouched, in readiness to fire if a foe should be disclosed.

Louder came the noise of the pony's feet, climbing cat-like the steep rising from the dip below him. He crouched lower as its form rose into view, with wild mane tossing. . . . Then, with a yell of terror, he fell flat on his face, dropping his gun. On the creature's back he had discerned for an instant a slim figure all white and glimmering in the moonshine, which could only be that of a *beanshith*.* The watcher cried aloud in Gaelic for the clemency of the Silent Ones, and lay trembling behind the rock.

A high voice came to his ears, speaking his own tongue. "Is that a true Highland man who lies yonder?"

Quavering, the bearded giant called assurances of fidelity and submission.

"I am no *beanshith*," came the reply; "nor am I one of the Silent Ones, as you appear to dream. But you, man, whoever you are, cast your plaid out to me hither, and do not be raising your eyes till I bid you. So shall you save a woman from the bitterness of shame!"

Still in the belief that he was commanded by a fairy, the man plucked off his plaid, and rolling it with shaking fingers into a ball, flung it as far away from him as he could over the top of the rock.

There was a pause of some moments; then, "You may rise now," continued the voice, "and look, that you may bear witness and your children's children, to the infamy of the Sassenach. Rise, I tell you!"

Unwillingly he lifted himself in his shirt and little kilt, and peered, fearful, over the rock. Before him stood a small, slender girl, draped from her shoulders in his heavy plaid, with only her bare feet shining in the silver glamour that bathed her. In one hand she held the bridle of the pony. "You will not be one of the Little People?" he faltered at length. "You will be a woman?"

"That they could not take from me!" she answered bitterly. "Ah! but it was I gave them the race they did not look for when I leapt the fence on this good beast and made for the woods! They could not overtake me, and God sent their bul-

* Banshee.

lets wide from the mark! I have come through the pass
yonder from Fort Augustus"—she pointed to Inverwick
Forest—"and now, my little Highland friend," she said,
stroking the pony on its neck, "you may return to those that
own you." She slipped off the rope bridle, and, turning, it
trotted away on a sure course towards its home in Fort
Augustus.

She turned to the man. "Of whose people will you be?"
she inquired.

"*Na Siosalaich*. Hugh Chisholm is my name."

"Where do you dwell?"

"With the eagles," he answered simply.

"Are you a man without the law?"

"Without the law of the Sassenach."

"It is what I, too, will be. I am sister to Maceachan of
Glenmarisdale; our house is burnt and Himself the prisoner
of the English. Will you aid me?"

"I will lead you to my captain."

"Who is he?"

"Who is he?" answered the man evasively. "Will you be
pleased to follow me, lady?"

His gun over his arm, he led the way upward through the
heather; traversed a cleft filled with stunted trees, the roots
of which hurt her bare feet as she followed, and then turned
abruptly aside and helped her down a rocky path into a hollow where a camp-fire glowed like a great ruby, its smoke
passing up secure from observation against a grey wall of
stone.

He had given a cry like a night-bird's as he issued from
the trees, and the four men down in the dell sat still, watching
as he approached with his charge. Darthula saw by the firelight that one of them was broiling on a ramrod part of a
sheep cut off from a carcass hanging from a tree nearby,

while two more were sitting above a tumbled pile of clothes counting coins, and the fourth sat with his musket over his arm, regarding the on-comers with an authoritative intentness. To him, the evident captain of the band, Hugh Chisholm explained how he had encountered Darthula on her flight from Fort Augustus. The captain rose and doffed his bonnet. He was well enough dressed, with a face of bold, hard features marked by thick and swarthy eyebrows.

"I am Patrick Grant of Craskie in this country," he said in Gaelic, "and we are eight in all who have taken oath to one another. Our purpose is to be revenged upon the *Saighear ruadh* for the burning of our homes and the slaying of our beasts. . . . To-night the red Duke will see another sign by the road to Fort Augustus, is it not so?" He turned to his companions with a smile that made Darthula shiver under the wrapping of Chisholm's plaid. "I know of you, Mistress," he went on, "and more, maybe, than you think for. . . . Will you eat with us?"

"I will be grateful to you."

He looked her up and down respectfully. "We will be able to give you clothing, too, this night. . . ."

Once more he turned to his associates with the same hard glitter in his eye. "He was a small man," he said dryly.

The man cooking the mutton, a morose-looking fellow, growled something to him across the fire.

"Have no fears, Son of Gregor," replied the captain. "Lady, I will be enforced to put you upon oath first. Raise your hand! Now pray that your back may be to God and your face to the devil, that all the curses the Scriptures do pronounce may be upon you and upon your posterity if you discover to any person, man, woman or child, aught of what you see, hear or otherways observe while of our company. . . . Enough! Now these are your sworn comrades." Ceremoniously he re-introduced her to Hugh Chisholm; then presented Alexander Chisholm, Donald Chisholm and Gregor Macgregor.

This done, Grant led her to a small cave in the rock-wall, where she could dress unobserved, and laid down inside it the heap of clothing she had seen before the fire on her arrival. She found that he had been right in saying that the clothes and shoes of this man, whoever he was, would be very little too large, and she was thankful for the chance that thus provided her. It was when she was turning over the coat to put it on that she had a shock. For, holding it up to the ruddy flicker of the fire outside the cave, she saw a bullet-hole just below the shoulder, and as she examined it her fingers came away damp. She put the coat on, however, after only a moment's hesitation; she was growing numbed to horrors now.

The outlaws courteously offered her the best cut from the meat they had been broiling, and brought bread from their bags and a flask of whisky. She ate a little, leaning up against the rock outside the cave; but sleep was swiftly conquering her. She dropped off without noticing it, after dreamily watching for a while the harsh faces gathered round the blaze, attentive satellites to the glittering eyes and boldly carved features of Patrick Grant, who himself from time to time kept glancing at Darthula with a curious look.

It was grey dawn when she awoke to a sense of bustle, and saw the man who had gone out as sentry come running down into the dell, crying, "The Paymaster! The Paymaster!" All sprang up, seizing their muskets, while Grant trampled the embers of the expiring fire. "Stop you here!" he said roughly to Darthula, "and be remembering your oath! See nothing! Hear nothing!"

3

DESPITE Grant's warning, Darthula could not close her hearing to two shots that came presently to her ears from over in the direction where she had first met the watcher of the band. She was, however, too worn out to move from the ground; nor, when the outlaws filed back looking dourer than ever, and carrying with other spoils a small military chest such as could be strapped upon a saddle, did she stir or pay particular attention. She closed her eyes while the chink of coin being counted made a furtive sound, and only reflected with dreary bitterness on the woe of the time that made bandits out of men she judged to be by nature simple crofters or small farmers. Craskie was a farm which she knew, and Grant would be a gentleman in a small way of living.

The men did not disturb her rest, except courteously to bring her food, and by nightfall she felt refreshed, and dared to ask the leader his plans.

"If you are well enough to walk," he answered, "we will be taking you in an hour or two to a place of safety in Coire Doe, where we shall meet my other companions and take counsel."

"I am not knowing," said Darthula, "whither I can go then, or where I may have friends still living to assist me."

"You will perhaps be finding the answer to your questions in Coire Doe," he answered, giving her again the peculiar look she had noticed the night before, and refused to speak further except in curt, evasive words.

After supping, as on the evening before, they set out and crossed Glen Moriston at Torgyle Bridge. Then, turning west, they made their way by an easy path, for which Darthula was thankful, along the river up the Glen. But at Ceannacroc they made another abrupt turn to the north and

entered the gloomy ravine of Coire Doe. Here climbing began, with slope after slope to be traversed, rise upon rise to
be surmounted, the stones slipping under their feet, the great
rocks glimmering to the moon, as in some endless country of
a nightmare.

Darthula battled dully on, though with less strength then
ever before when fighting with the mountains. No spark of
hope would any longer kindle in her heart to sustain her.
Her feet were hurtful, her breath scant; and she was amazed
at the patient gentleness of her companions, who held out
their hands, imbrued with the recent blood of two men slain
in ambush, to guide her over difficult places; bore her on their
backs across torrents; and stayed their march without a word
of impatience when she begged for rest. Sometimes she wondered vaguely why they should be taking such tender care
of her.

The country into which they were passing under a baleful
moon might have served for a picture of Hell. It was a region
of barren rock-strewn faces and chasms, sweeping round the
rims of vast, scoured bowls, and rising into cones so dreary
that they might have repelled an eagle. No sound could be
heard in the eerie silence but the scrambling of the outlaws'
feet among the stones and the distressed breathing of the exhausted girl.

Painfully they descended a precipitous slope into a desolate hollow, strewn with fallen rocks, at the foot of a high
mountain face. As they threaded their way among the
boulders two men rose, as it seemed from the earth, and
saluted Patrick Grant.

In his ceremonious way Grant presented them to Darthula
while she sat with her head in her hands resting upon a rock
as John and Alexander Macdonald. "You now know all my
band, your brothers," he told her.

"Were you not saying there was an eighth?" she asked listlessly.

He paused for a moment, looking at her with eyes that gleamed in the moonlight.

"There will be an eighth," he said, "and I will lead you to him now. Come!"

He held out his hand, and helped her up a few yards of the slope below a tall peak opposite. A group of three colossal boulders appeared, looking rather like a table of stone that had been spilt open by a thunderbolt. Through this crack in the middle, as they drew near, a faint flicker of firelight rose and sank. The soft voice of a rivulet fell also with a delicious soothing upon Darthula's wearied senses.

Still leading her by the hand, Grant passed round a tall rock that barred the opening into the cavern. The voice of the stream came louder, trickling through the further recess, and a man sitting brooding on the other side of the fire raised his head and stood up. "Is it the messenger from Cluny and Lochiel?" he asked.

"*Charles!*" cried Darthula, gazing at the tall, red-bearded figure as if it had been a spirit.

"I have brought her to you, *Phrionssa!*" said Patrick Grant, "she whose name you have been speaking in your dreams. Say, did I do wrong?"

Charles made a stride round the fire and caught her swaying form as it sank. "Darthula! Darthula!" he groaned, as he scanned her ravaged face, "what have I done to you, beauty of Scotland?"

Chapter X

INTO THE MISTS

THERE was a stir of dawn in the foreboding autumn air, though the moon still shone upon the misted foot of Loch Arkaig. A few yards from the shore whereon the little ripples unceasingly broke and parted, as they had done for æons and shall do for æons yet, the view was hidden by a silvery curtain, against which the hazels and birches clothing the bank stood blackly outlined. The sombre woods through which the avenue of the Dark Mile pierces its tunnel from the loch-foot to the Great Glen beyond, rose in funereal stillness, and the charred towers of Achnacarry Castle lifted their mutilated crests among the leaves in voiceless mourning. There was no sign of living being, nor fire nor smoke, amid the desolation. Alone the voice of the River Arkaig lamented in the wood, running strong and heavy from the loch to the muffled roar of its short falls.

Noiselessly two ghosts came gliding through the trees that draped the slopes of the North Bank at the issue from the Dark Mile. The man stepped forward out of the shadow into the hazy moonshine on the bank, and the woman checked him.

"Beware, Charles!" whispered Darthula, "will you be letting them take you on the very evening of deliverance?"

"The boat is late," answered the Prince anxiously, "it will be light before it comes. Oh! for the moment when it shall appear out of those mists, and I shall know that I am free!"

"What way," queried Darthula uneasily, "must you travel by the boat? It is conspicuous."

"Have no fears! The red-coats are departed this region, and we must spare Lochiel every foot of walking that we may. Should his wounded legs fail him before we come to Borrodale what will befall us all? For I will never sail, and leave him behind to the mercy of Cumberland's wolves!"

He had seated himself on a rock in the shadow close by the shore, and was gazing hungrily through the elusive mists as they swirled with pearly glimmers in their tantalising dance.

"It is you are the true Prince," she murmured, laying her hand on his arm, "that will not save yourself and leave your friends behind!"

"That," answered Charles, with a sudden passion in his voice, "is a small thing since I must sail and leave my love behind! Oh! Darthula, Darthula, they bow the knee to me, and call me Prince and Lord of all, and to me it seems sometimes that I am no more than a rag blown about by every gust of wind. Why, ah! G——! why did I desert you by Loch Cluanie that day, because of the reasonings of Glenaladale?"

"He reminded you," she replied in a peculiar tone of trembling firmness, "that you are indeed Prince and Lord of all, and cannot be free from your destiny. Our last days will have been together, over there so far away by Cluny's hut on Ben Alder, and I have sung my last songs to you, and the last drops of happiness are drunk."

"There was always Cluny, always Lochiel at the hut. For how many hours were we alone?"

"Think no more of me, my love. For it is you that must go forward along your path of grandeur . . . and of duty.

I was angered then, at Cluanie, but now I know the truth. It is that I will never be Queen or wife to you."

"But if I come again—"

"Darthula will be waiting for you, and she your servant while she has life. *Non obliviscor.*"

"What pledge of that will you give me?"

"And is it any pledge but my word you will be needing?"

"Words go up into the air and are borne away by the breeze! In three years . . . in five . . . in seven . . . will you remember the words you spoke by the shore of Loch Arkaig?"

"Must you have a token? Woe's me! The white heather is brown and withered!"

"Will you exchange locks as gage of fidelity?" he asked eagerly.

"They will be lovers' tokens. I will give token only of loyalty."

"Do not trifle with words. Give me your gage! Then I can still hope. See, here is my dirk for the shearing!"

She bent her neck obediently, while he severed a short, dark curl. Then, with a quavering smile, she took the dirk and gained for herself one of his brown-golden locks. "Now I rank with Mistress Flora Macdonald!" she said. "Ah! it is but a children's game!" she sobbed suddenly.

"It is no children's game!" he insisted. "I have your promise that, until I return this lock of your dear hair to you . . . that is to say never . . . you will wait for me to come again?"

"I promise . . . but I do not think there was any need for an outward pledge of Darthula's fealty! . . . Oh! Charles! Charles!" she cast herself weeping into his arms, "I know this is the end!"

He clasped her to him in an agony of remorse and frustration, while the salt brimmed over his own eyes. "Darthula!

Darthula! You are surely the noblest of all Scotland's royal treasures!"

They stood thus for a few minutes weeping in each other's arms; then they were aware of shadowy figures emerging cautiously upon the shore at the loch-head, and stepped down out of the wood to join them.

Lochiel walked first, limping on a crutch, with his kinsman Cameron of Clunes, in the ruins of whose house near the loch they had passed the night, giving him a hand now and then over the roughness of the ground. Lochgarry followed, Macpherson of Breakachie, and two or three servants.

"The boat is late, sir," said Lochiel to the Prince. "But Archie will not leave us in the lurch. In two days we will be safe aboard the French ship at Borrodale!"

"Lochiel, you shoulder a heavy burden gallantly! You leave your home here in ruins to seek exile! Methinks even the hut on Ben Alder were dearer to you than a mansion in Paris will be!"

"Our hut has sheltered our Prince these last weeks—and now I am ready to be gone. Indeed, sir, those left behind have perhaps more reason to complain. Poor Cluny—!"

"Do not judge me harshly, dear Lochiel! Someone had to stay, to hold our friends together, and to keep watch on . . . you well know what."

"Yes, sir, I understand necessities of state. None the less, Cluny has a hard post . . . and so too has my little cousin here!" He smiled with wan affection on Darthula.

"I besought Miss Maceachan to accompany us . . . she knows how earnestly . . . but she persists that her first duty now is by her brother . . . if perchance she may alleviate his lot."

"Darthula, you are of the antique mould!" Lochiel bowed with the awkwardness of a crippled man, but there was in his voice that which warmed Darthula's poor heart with gratitude. "Remember," added Lochiel, "there will be two of my men coming for you in an hour to bring you safe to my brother at Fassifern."

It was already ghostly daybreak, with the mist like a thick smoke veiling the softly-lapping water. The party stood in silence, ears pricked, till at last another sound mingled with the wavelets, the dip and splash of discreet oars.

A shadow fell athwart the mists; then a black shape came slowly through them, a boat with four oarsmen, and a man stood up in the stern.

"Is it yourself, Archie?" demanded Clunes in a low voice.

"It is. But for why in G——'s name are you all clustered here in the open? . . . Is His Highness there? . . . I crave pardon, sir, for my bluntness, but we have been sore frighted as we came along. There are strangers searching in the wood by Achnasaul."

"Ha!" exclaimed Charles, "so soon! Then let us waste no more time. Lochiel, let me give you my arm. Clunes, hold his crutch! . . . Are you comfortably seated, Lochiel? . . . That is well. . . . Come, now the rest! . . . Precede me, Mr. Cameron, it is my wish!"

They crowded into the boat, while Charles, left alone upon the shore, ran to Darthula, and drew her away from view into the mist.

He was crying like a baby, as he took her for the last time into his arms. "I cannot go!" he sobbed. "Oh! I cannot go!"

"Leave me, leave me, Charles!" she whispered with a choked throat. "Your life is everything! . . . I shall be waiting . . . Good-bye, my love . . . oh! my love, good-bye!"

Abruptly he tore himself from her, and pressing his bonnet down on his brows with both hands, ran down the shelving shore without looking back, and clambered into the boat.

Darthula ran after to get the last glimpse of him. She saw

the stir and rearrangement in the boat, as place was made for him. But he did not sit down; he stood up, peering towards the shore, seeking vainly with his hands to dissipate the vapours that hid her form from him. As he gave no word, Lochiel, alarmed at the delay, signalled silently to the rowers to start. They dipped noiseless oars into the loch; the little drops fell back into the ripples as they lifted the blades again; a rowlock squeaked softly, and the boat glided into the mist, its dark figures turning in an instant to grey, and then into shadows.

Darthula, standing on the shore, and continuously wiping the tears from her eyes lest she should lose the last sight of her Prince, saw a figure that was only a phantom stretch out arms towards the spot where she stood, and then melt away into the dancing torment. . . . There was nothing now save this shifting veil, but, piercing her heart with a sword of agony as if it spoke the irrevocableness of the parting, she heard behind the curtain the squeak of the rowlock once more, the soft dip of the oars, once . . . twice . . . and not again.

Darthula sank down blinded where she stood and lay upon her face. She was without the power any longer even to wipe her tears away. There seemed nothing left to struggle for. Why should she ever rise again?

Behind the Dark Mile at her back now, the sky was waking. A roseleaf blush overspread it till it clothed the whole pure and iridescent dome that curved over the Great Glen. And as the sun thus mounted, changing the heaven to a satin-blue faintly gauzed, the mists upon the loch began to sparkle and to thin. In time the warmth of the triumphing day stole over Darthula's chilled limbs; and after a while she stretched herself to take in this faint animal comfort. At last she sat up, still covering her wet eyes with her hands, and the wooing sun fell on her face, and made a brownish-pink transparency through her fingers. . . . She let them fall away, and turned her gaze to the lake.

The mists were drunk up and vanished. In the loop of its wooded shores the steel-blue water sparkled under the sun. A tiny green jewel of an islet gleamed near its foot; while, beyond, the shadowy promontories ran down on either hand to indent its shining ribbon, which lay unrolled for miles in softening mystery to where the huge mountain-shapes, still lightly veiled in vapour, stood sentry over the dream-worlds of the West. Birds were calling to one another; the sounds of falling water came more clearly to the ear, no longer muffled by the vapours; all seemed happy and tranquil in this virginal recess of Nature's playground . . . and task her eyes as long and as hard as she could, the girl could see no speck to indicate the boat on which the Commander of the Mists had vanished into his Kingdom.

Darthula sprang to her feet. An odd apprehension and urgency had come over her. An hour ago she had told herself that she did not care if she was taken, or left to starve among the ruins of Lochiel's castle. Now she felt a violent impulse of self-preservation.

She must not linger here in broad sunlight, to be observed by any who passed. But why had Lochiel's two gillies not come to find her as promised? Could some evil have befallen them on the way? She must hide herself until either they or darkness came.

Hurriedly she betook herself into the haunted wood of Achnasaul near by, so eerie despite its bright autumn foliage. The sun was striking through the branches, making a cobbled pattern of the hummocks of brown grass. Where the birch gave place to firs, the red trunks glistened like basaltic pillars. If she had come into this wood to escape fear she had failed of her purpose. It seemed to be all around her here, the more pervasive and baffling from the impossibility of locating its source amid these lucid vistas. She only knew that she dared not stay still, or creep into a thicket to hide as she had purposed to do. Always she had the feeling of ambush behind the trunks at her back, and she had to keep upon the move, struggling with herself not to turn her walk into a panic run.

She went on through the wood, panting slightly, and asking herself what madness was driving her, along the side of the loch towards the west. Then, as she came to a cluster of firs on the edge of a dip, she saw a sight that rooted her with terror.

Down in the dell below her, already lightly strewn with fallen leaves of autumn, three or four men were crouched together over a black hole that looked like a grave. They were absorbedly bending over it, stretching their arms down, and by degrees lowering a rope, as though seeking to fish up some object from the depths. Then one of them stood upright, straightening his back for relief, and, incredulous, she found herself staring at the face of . . . Alastair Ruadh!

A moment and his eyes fell on her, peering between the firs at him. He started forward, and Darthula, on an impulse she could not contend with, turned and ran as if for life back towards the loch-foot. She heard a pursuing foot rustle over the dead leaves; uttered a gasping cry of panic, and tripped over a root to fall headlong.

A rough hand gripped her neck, turned her on her back, and her great eyes, dilated, rested again upon the face, distorted with fury and fear, of young Glengarry. His dirk was naked in his other hand.

"Alastair!" she gasped. "Alastair! Let me go; you are hurting me!"

He recognised her voice and peered down into her altered face with amazement. "Darthula!" he gasped, letting go his hold. "Darthula Maceachan! Mother of God! Is it possible?"

"How come you to be here, Alastair, and you a prisoner in the Tower of London?" she whispered.

"My grief!" he smiled. "Is it yourself only that can effect an escape? For you to me, Darthula, have the air of flying someone."

"But how will you have contrived your escape?"

"By my own wits," he said dryly. "There was none would help me."

Remembering Charles Edward's parsimony where this faithful servitor was concerned, Darthula felt herself blushing.

"May I get up," she asked, "or will I still be dangerous?"

He laughed as he lent her his aid, but the laugh was a little shrill, and a magpie mocked it in reply from a branch.

"For what were you and your friends digging in this wood?" she asked curiously.

"And have you never seen a grave dug before in these troubled times?" he answered.

"A grave?"

"*Dieu me damne*, a grave, I am telling you!" He blazed into fury again. "Do you doubt my word?"

"For why should I doubt you, Mr. Macdonald?" she retorted coldly.

He wiped his forehead, and laughed with the same shrillness as before.

"I will be asking your pardon, Darthula," he said. "I am over-driven with anxiety and responsibility. We were burying a comrade, one of my own Glengarry men, whose corpse we were not willing to leave to the Sassenach vultures."

"Why," thought Darthula, "be burying a Glengarry Macdonnell down here in Cameron country?" But aloud she said only, "Are the red-coats then at hand?"

"Are they at hand! They have trussed up and hanged two Cameron men this morn by Clunes Bay. We passed

the bodies, and they not pretty! They will have been put
to the question before they were . . . set free." He began
to bite his nails; his jutting tooth crept over his wavy lip.
"I am wondering," he looked at her sharply, "what is the
question they will have been asked."

"My poor escorts!" thought Darthula, and was silent.

"I am wondering if you could give me the clue, Darthula?" said Glengarry suddenly.

"Is it I will be in the counsel of the English, Alastair
Ruadh?" she asked him.

"I did not say that!" he cried angrily. "None of us will
be in the counsel of the English, I trust! God's clear light!
Let us maintain Highland honour, if we have thrown away
all else!"

As his full, handsome face flushed in his indignation, she
became aware of a deep scar over his eyebrow that purpled
too. "You have a wound that is new, Alastair," she cried.
"How came you by it?"

"My grief! Fighting! Would I be getting it . . . at a
party of dice? But you, Darthula, how come you to be
wandering in the wood of Achnasaul alone . . . and ragged
. . . and the sorrow of all the world on your face that was
so fresh, my dear?"

She told him her plight in a few rapid sentences, but
nothing of having parted from the Prince at this spot a few
hours before.

"The men you saw tortured," she concluded, "Lochiel
had sent for me; the red-coats will have wanted to learn
their errand."

Glengarry made an impatient sound. They were sitting
side by side now on a bank, and he was driving his dirk into
the moss. "Do not ask me to believe," he said, "it was to
secure an unarmed girl like yourself they were at such heavy
pains! There was a more precious secret the red-coats were

so fierce to burn out of them. . . . I was thinking you might
have known. . . . But will Lochiel be still in Badenoch,
then?"

"I am not knowing where Lochiel will be at the hour that
is." She could not analyse the reason for her persistent pre-
varication to her old friend so strangely returned. But she
told herself now that the Prince's secret was not one she
would be at liberty to disclose without permission, even to
her own brother.

"Well," said Alastair, "I see you have no news to give me.
You are sure of that?" he added, glancing at her sidelong, as
if wishful to give her the opportunity to amend her story.
But she replied only, "I have told you all I can."

He sighed. "If I were knowing more I could be helping
you better." He began to dig his dirk into the moss again.
"What will you be doing with yourself now, Darthula?"

She paused with a perplexed look. That was not easy to
answer either. Lochiel's scheme for her had tragically miscarried, and she had in truth no desire to go to Cameron of
Fassifern, the dour man who had done his best to keep his
brother from joining the Prince's standard. Fassifern would
not help her to get to London to aid Hector. She groaned.

"It's I would be going to London, Alastair, to give what
help I may to Glenmarisdale. But woe's me, I have no
friends."

"No friends! My grief! Will you be saying that while
Alastair Ruadh lives?"

"You cannot, Alastair, find me the means to get to London."

"And what for no? Shall the purse of a Macdonnell, however slender, be locked, when Darthula Maceachan has
need?"

"I have guineas," Darthula confessed. The Prince had
pressed this provision on her from his funds the night before.

"But I have none to bear me company."

"Ah!" He looked extremely curious again. "Will you not be going to your uncle in Edinburgh to take his counsel?"

"Never! Alastair, never! James Maceachan is to me henceforth as a dead corpse!"

"Why, then, my dear, 'tis you are the lonely girl of the world! I see no other way but we must journey to London together, you and I!"

"You would go with me to London? How?"

"You as lady. I as servant." He smiled gaily. "You will be admiring my trick of disguises, Darthula. I was . . . scoutmaster, it will be called . . . in the *Royal Ecossais*. I will be taking another name as your lackey when we have crossed the border . . . Fergusson or Jeanson . . . aye, Jeanson. . . . Leave you all to me now, Darthula!"

"And will you do so much for me, Alastair?" she asked in a softened voice.

"Will I be the fair-weather lover only, my dear?"

She sighed. "Little there is left to love in my face, Alastair!"

"And much in your soul, true girl! 'Tis I am not unfaithful to my vows!"

He turned and whistled. In a few moments his gillie Mungo appeared out of the dell, regarding Darthula unastonished with his watchful lizard's eyes.

"Call the men away," Glengarry told him in Gaelic. "There is no more to be done yonder?"

"There is no more to be done, Son of Alastair."

Glengarry sighed. "Gather the men, then, to the *Mile Dorcha*." * And as the little attendant flitted away again among the tree trunks, "You shall see now, Darthula," said Glengarry, "with what good cheer we live by the ruins of Invergarry."

* Dark Mile.

"You will not be afraid of the red-coats, Alastair?" asked Darthula anxiously.

"Red-coats! Tach! I will be having my own way of dealing with the *saighear ruadh*. I will be Mr. Mackenzie from Kintail that sells them cattle."

"It is you are the sly one, Alastair!" she murmured admiringly.

"Will you go before me, lady?" he bowed.

"You are my preserver, Alastair Ruadh!"

"I am your faithful servant . . . Jeanson!"

BOOK THREE

THE RECKONING

1 7 4 6 - 1 7 4 7

Chapter I

FOR THE DEFENCE

THEY came into London by way of the Angel at Islington and Moorfields in the coppery dusk of an autumn evening, and Darthula felt stunned as she peeped from side to side of the hackney coach they had taken on leaving the stage coach at Holborn Hill. There had been nothing in Edinburgh's single busy street to prepare her for the bustle and clamour and rudeness of London under its dun smoke-pall. Exhausted in frame and spirit by her continuous ordeal, she felt as though everyone were shouting at her; and when their coach ran down an apple-woman's barrow in Fleet Street, and a crowd collected swearing at the driver, she sank back behind the worn leather window-curtains in panic.

An unshaven face peered in at the window and surveyed her with hostility. "Will you be leaving me alone?" she cried, rallying her spirit. "Take your head from my coach!"

"Whoo'oo! Another b—y Scotch rebel! Down with the Devil, the Pope and the Pretender!" shouted the man, detecting her accent, and her blood went cold. The next moment Glengarry had leapt down from the box where he was riding beside the coachman, and crashed his fist on to the fellow's jaw. He fell back with a grunt into the gutter, striking his head so that a rivulet of his blood mingled with

413

the garbage that clogged the kennel. Darthula was already at her prayers, expecting to be dragged forth to murder by the English mob; but to her utter bewilderment there was an immense roar of laughter, hats were waved, and a dozen voices shouted, "Well hit, Sandy man!" "Tapped his claret, by G——!" The coachman whipped up his horses, and they rolled off in a sort of triumph towards the Strand.

She reflected, as they rumbled along, that Alastair had indeed been wonderful. He had held to his character of Jeanson the lackey; had been alert, deferential and never presuming the whole of their toilsome journey from the north. Sometimes she had been unable to refrain from smiling at his solemn face, as he went about his business of waiting on her. But he had been clever enough at Stamford in the English Midlands when the landlord conceived a suspicion of them, and took them to the magistrates to be interrogated. Jeanson had had an answer to every question, explaining how he had been entrusted, gentlemen, with the safety of his young mistress on her journey to visit relatives in London by her father, the Reverend Alexander Murdoch, garrison-chaplain in the Castle of Inverness. She had bit her lip at this, for the Castle of Inverness was in ruin; but Master Shallow seemed to swallow it all, and they set out again the next day unmolested.

The coach jerked nearly to a stop, and peering through the front window, Darthula saw a great shadowy arch, adorned with statues, crossing the road in front of them, and slowing the traffic as it filtered through. She knit her brows for a moment—then suddenly the colour drained from her face. This was, this must be, Temple Bar, on the summit of which were set on spikes after treason trials, for a dreadful warning! . . . She dared not think further, but covered her eyes with her hands. She was still cowering in the corner of the coach when, after jolting a little way downhill toward the river, it stopped in Essex Street, and Glengarry, jumping down from the box again, obsequiously opened the door for her.

They were to lodge here at the house of a London attorney of Scots blood, named Campbell. It was an arrangement Glengarry had made by letter, and he had assured Darthula that Mr. Campbell, despite his name, was a good friend of his own, and was, further, employed about the defence of several of the Jacobite prisoners. Mrs. Campbell, a stout, middle-aged lady of a sandy complexion, well dressed and with gleaming shoe-buckles on her neat feet, was sitting in her parlour when they entered, and rose to welcome them. Her face in the firelight, for the candles were not yet lit, was slightly porcine, but shrewed and by no means unkindly. Behind her in the shadow the figure of a tall man rose from its chair at the same time.

"And is it you, at last, Miss Maceachan? Is it yourself, Glengarry?" she said cordially, putting out her hand. "Betty!" she called, "bring the cannles! There will be a dish of tay here in a trice to comfort you, Miss Maceachan. Are you tired out wi' your journey?"

Darthula had not spoken. She was looking beyond her hostess at the lank figure in the darkness behind her. And as the maid hustled in with the candles she uttered a cry. "Allan! . . . Allan Duncanson! It is never you!"

Glengarry pushed himself to the front with his tooth jutting in a furious face and his scar throbbing. "I will be asking an explanation of all this!" he declared truculently. "What is this person doing here, and *Dieu me damne*! Mrs. Campbell, what way have you thus betrayed my confidence?"

"Hoots, Mr. Macdonnell!" retorted the hostess, smiling but imperturbable, "there is nae betrayal here! I marvel, sir, that you should deem me capable of such. Duncanson of

Inveralsk is my clansman . . . and a very gude friend to all here!"

"It is that will remain to be proved!" said Glengarry sulkily. "At least, sir, I am hoping you will take it to be your part as a gentleman not to inquire the reasons why another Highland gentleman should be constrained in these ill days to travel disguised."

"I have no curiosity concerning your affairs, Mr. Macdonnell," replied Allan. "It is with Miss Maceachan my business lies—at her own good time."

"And what will be your business with Mistress Maceachan?" demanded Glengarry, puffing contemptuously. "Let me be telling you now, sir, this lady has constituted *me* her friend and protector!"

"That is for her to determine. My purpose in coming here is to confer with her upon her brother's affairs!"

"And for why would she be conferring with you on her brother's affairs, seeing that it is notour you are a partisan of the Government that is thirsting for his blood?"

"Simply for this. I am a lawyer, and I am prepared to be briefed to defend my friend."

"*Dieu me damne!*" said Glengarry again under his breath.

"He speaks truth, Mr. Macdonnell," declared Mrs. Campbell, "and I may tell you, my husband approves highly of the young man's purpose."

"He approves that Glenmarisdale be defended by an enemy—a political enemy, I am meaning, sir?" Glengarry bowed ironically.

Darthula found her voice. "Mr. Duncanson is no enemy, Alastair!" she cried. "It was he, and none other, saved Hector on Drummossie Muir!"

"Saved him to hand him over to the hangman?" inquired Glengarry.

"I am of opinion," interjected Duncanson quietly, "that

it would very little advantage Glenmarisdale to be defended
by some notour enemy of the established Government."

"And it will very little advantage a friend to Government
to appear as defender of a notour rebel," said Mrs. Campbell
shrewdly. "Hae you weighed that well, Mr. Duncanson?"

"In truth, madam, I did not weigh it at all—in the balance
of my friend's life," replied Allan.

"Give me your hand, sir!" cried Glengarry effusively.
"Soul of me! but it's you are the gallant gentleman! . . .
You will be forgiving me for mistaking you. . . . Come!
tell me your plans! On what line will you be making your
plea, now?"

"That is a matter for much thought, Mr. Macdonnell."

"Aye, and for a time when Miss Maceachan is less
fatigued!" added Mrs. Campbell. "Come, my dear! Here is
the tay must not grow cold! Afterwards you shall to your
bed, and we will speak of a' this the morn, when our heids are
clear!"

"I," said Glengarry, bowing, "will be asking leave to retire, and find habiliments more worthy of a gentleman before
we dine, Mrs. Campbell."

"Allan!" murmured Darthula, crossing over to him as soon
as Glengarry had left the room. "What way will you be
doing this for us? Must we be ruining *you*, too?"

"I am not so sure I will be ruined by this," answered Duncanson cautiously.

"Allan! Do not you be angered against Alastair Ruadh
either! It is he has been the true friend to me. You may
be trusting Alastair; it is no lie I am telling you!"

"Would you be carrying your milk in a sieve?" retorted
Duncanson chillily.

Over the dinner-table an hour later he was, however, a
trifle more communicative. He had secured admission to the

Tower of London to see Hector, he told Darthula; and when she cried out, dropping her knife, to know at once how her brother did, he answered, "Stronger in spirit than in body, if I must speak the truth."

"My sorrow! Will he be ailing then?" wailed Darthula.

"The Tower is a place of fevers," Duncanson reminded her, "and he, I surmise, will have been weak ever since his wound at Culloden. We must labour to secure his freedom without superfluous delay."

"No doubt a most desirable consummation!" cried Glengarry with a touch of sarcasm. "But, my good sir, the difficulty will be precisely in that kittle bit! . . . To release our dear friend . . . and see he is not released from the mortal coil! . . . It is not to be done by talking, whateffer!"

"I am nevertheless of opinion that talking may play a not unimportant part in his defence at law, as in any man's," retorted Allan drily.

"And what is it you will be saying on that day, Mr. Duncanson?"

Allan diverted the conversation; but, pressed by all three to disclose something of his mind, he confessed he was preparing a plea of youth and unpremeditation on Hector's behalf. Glengarry slapped his hand on the table. "By Gott!" he cried, "that will be a braw notion! Youth and unpremeditation! I am thinking that might well carry the day with a soft-hearted jury, and he a dear youth to be sending to the scaffold!"

"It is, I believe, the only plea we may employ with hope of success," answered Duncanson.

After dinner Glengarry excused himself on the ground that he had friends in London he desired to visit, and Darthula had a few more words with Allan Duncanson alone before he went. He assured her that it was hopeless for her to think of getting an order to visit her brother, at all events, for the present. Permits to visit prisoners arraigned for high treason were hard to gain, and she must not forget that she herself was liable to arrest. "With the Government," he told her, "though not with the world, your name is as notour as Mistress Flora Macdonald's, whom they have taken to bring to London for trial." No doubt, he added, the Government was not anxious for the odium of bringing more women to trial for loyalty to their families or their principles, but it would be reckless to walk straight into the lion's jaws.

"Allan!" she faltered, "where will Hector be finding the money to pay Mr. Campbell for his services . . . and . . . and . . . yourself?"

"Campbell can well wait," he answered drily. "A lawyer is always paid in the end—and I am acting as Hector's friend. But I may tell you I waited upon Lord Brounhill in Edinburgh before I came south to inquire his pleasure in these matters. It seemed to me that Glenmarisdale's Tutor had a duty to provide the funds necessar' to defend him."

"You will have had little satisfaction by that visit, Allan!"

"He drew me into his oratory, and, without word spoken, turned the pages of the Bible to the text: 'In the place where the tree falleth, there it shall be.' Yon is a hard man, Darthula!"

"I am thinking he has a stone where his heart should be. Is it a stone? It is many stones, all the stones of Glenmarisdale and its fields! And they are more to him than his flesh and blood. Let us not be speaking of that man ever!"

The next morning Darthula went out into the Strand to make some necessary purchases at a linen-draper's. She happened to look up through the window of the shop while waiting at the counter, and nearly dropped the stuff she was holding.

Past the door went her uncle and his daughter Jean. The

judge moved along with his face expressionless, and with his eyes on the pavement, as if he were studying the cracks in it. One or two persons who ran against him in the throng through his indifference to his steps, recoiled as if they had struck a rock; he appeared not to have noticed the collisions.

But Jean had her eyes brightly on the shop windows as she went by, and it was she caught sight of Darthula. Her eyes opened wide and she set one of her plump little fingers on her lips as she followed her father. In a moment she came running back and burst into the shop.

"Darthula!" she cried aloud as she hugged her cousin, without thought of the danger of proclaiming her name, "it can never be you! Oh! my dear, I have only a moment, you ken! I have told father I have a commission for my mother, and that he may walk on and I will rejoin him." She seized Darthula's wasted hands in her nicely-filled mittens, and gazed at her. "What terrible days have you been through?" she murmured. "Do not answer now, for I cannot stay, but tell me, where do you lodge? Campbell's in Essex Street? It is Campbell the attorney, is it not? Aye, I have heard of him. Keep your doors to-morrow morn, I will be with you. Do not fail me!" She flitted off as breathlessly as she had entered, and Darthula tried to re-examine her stuff through a mist of tears.

The next morning Jean arrived, as she had promised, in a sedan, and burst like a sunbeam with her golden bands into Mrs. Campbell's dark little drawing-room overhead, where Darthula awaited her.

"Now, tell me," she cried, flinging her wide hat down upon a sofa, "now tell me all you have been doing. . . . Or, stay," she checked herself, "tell me nothing in particular, neither names nor places; for if I am examined, I am so bad at the fibbing that I aye pull at some ribbon or button, and father says, 'Jean, you are pulling again!' and I know I am found out. How came you here?"

"There was a good friend conducted me," answered Darthula cautiously.

"I will not ask his name," Jean's eyes threatened to come out with curiosity. "But you were plundered of all, were you not? Are you provided, Darthula?" She felt for her placket.

"I will be provided, dear Jean, I thank you."

"Well, then," whispered Jean in an awestruck voice, "what has become of yonder . . . Young Gentleman?"

"You will not be needing to pull," said Darthula a little bitterly; "he is overseas beyond the reach of my uncle's malice."

"Not a word against father, or you and I will quarrel! You have never understood him, Darthula! He has been dour to you; but he is aye striving to do his duty by his family and the State, and what can man do more?"

"For why is he in London now?" demanded Darthula bluntly.

"For why? To do all he may to help poor Hector—what else, gudesakes?"

"You are believing that, Jean?"

"You believe otherwise, Darthula? Shame on you!"

"What is he doing? What steps is he taking? Answer me that, Jean!"

"Indeed, and how would I know? He is now with the Ministers, and now he is with the judges. We lodge with one of them, at his house in Queen Square. And last week, will you believe it, he had audience of His Majesty?"

"German George?"

"It makes no matter what you call him, so long as he may perchance grant a pardon to poor Hector. Now will not you come and be reconciled to Father?"

"Would he be welcoming me? . . . You need not pull! It is I know well he would not!"

"Darthula, there is no one but my Father can fee counsel to defend Hector!"

"I am thanking you, but all that will have been arranged."

"Arranged? How? . . . Who is his counsel?"

"Allan Duncanson."

"Allan Duncanson!" Jean's eyes rounded again. "It is he my Father would have had me wed, but," she smiled roguishly, "he was no willing."

"His affections are not fixed then!" cried Darthula, as if a little load had been taken off her.

"It is you should have pulled then, Darthula! You ken fine Allan's affections *are* fixed . . . and where. . . . But oh! it is ill, this jesting with our hearts so heavy! It is mine would break if I did not know my Father would save dear Hector. For oh! Darthula, why should I conceal it further from you? . . . I love him myself, I have ever loved him"; the tears suddenly flowed out of her eyes, "and if he is to die, or if he will not have me, I will go unwed the whole of my days!"

"You . . . are loving . . . Hector, Jean?" Darthula stared at her, for the moment unable to readjust her ideas of her cousin.

"And what for no, Darthula?"

"You were never giving sign of it to me—and I his sister!"

"Must I wear my heart upon my sleeve? And have you been always sisterly, or cousinly even, to me?"

"Jean!" Darthula stretched out her arms and embraced her cousin. "I have behaved very ill to you!"

"Whisht! Darthula. There is no need of apologies to be made to me!"

"Jean! Jean! We are both loving him! Try you to prevail upon your Father at least not to be cruel to the lad!"

"You will never be trying to do my Father justice, Darthula! If I thought he was the man you take him for, father or no, I would leave his doors for aye! But he is no the cruel man you think—just, but not cruel. And he will do for Hector all that can be done. . . . I am glad, though, that the poor lad has young Duncanson to be his counsel. They think much of Allan here in the Courts, I can be telling you." She jumped up. "Now I must be away, or I will be having to invent the names of a dozen places I was chaired to when mother asks me at dinner. . . . And I pulling the whole time!"

"Good-bye, dear Jean!" Darthula kissed her tenderly. "It's I am glad of you in this hour!"

Chapter II

SIMON FRASER

1

THE weeks that followed were weeks of heart-straining delay. The proceedings against Hector seemed to stand still; neither Allan Duncanson, his counsel, nor Campbell, his attorney, could penetrate the intentions of the Government or understand why he was not brought to trial. No friend was admitted to see him; difficulties were even made for his legal advisers, though mysterious Government agents from time to time visited him, trying to extract voluntary information of which he could not always comprehend the bearing. Allan advised Darthula that it was vain for her to hope to procure an order to visit her brother—and he cautioned her to be careful in her goings about the city, and to wear a hood.

Thus Christmas passed in sadness, and it was not till spring was advanced that Duncanson came one day to the attorney's house in Essex Street, obviously excited under his formal demeanour.

"I am of opinion, Miss Maceachan," he said as soon as she entered the parlour, "that the time has come when you may have a glimpse of your brother."

"Will I be speaking to him, Allan?"

He shook his head. "That, I fear, will be impossible. But it would cheer him so much to have even the sight of you. . . . There is not, I think, overmuch risk in what I am asking you to do. These last months I have not heard your name so much as mentioned in the places where such things are their concern, and I have kept my ears well pricked, I can tell you! I should say they are no longer interested in you. You should be safe if you go hooded, and take a mask. Mrs. Campbell will be your escort."

"Is it to the Tower?"

"No, to the precincts of Westminster. They have decided to summon Hector to the Bar of the House of Lords to take his testimony against Lord Lovat. I cannot see what need they have of him, and it is scarce humane when he has his own defence to ponder, and his health, I must not conceal it from you, Miss Maceachan, grows daily more precarious—"

"And I may not nurse him! Ah! the cruelty of them!"

"The Crown has hopes that by holding out some expectation of leniency towards himself they may induce him to add his mite to the burden of evidence against Simon Fraser."

"Sorrow's me for the name of Macshimi! He has shown himself little better than a traitor to both parties. But Hector —it's little they know him! He will not be for incriminating the old man."

"We shall see sad sights at this trial, Miss Maceachan. There will be no need of Hector's evidence to seal Lovat's doom. And yet, if he withholds it, I am bound in honesty to tell you this, they will harden in their determination to bring him to the scaffold himself. Poor fellow! He is so low in spirits, so greatly in need of support, that I am taking the risk of placing you somewhere near the entry to Westminster Hall, to give him a glance from your eyes as he goes by."

"My grief! It will be a small service I am called upon to

give, while you, Allan, are doing so much, imperilling your prospects too!"

"I am glad you do not shrink from it, none the less. For there is certes a modicum of danger."

Darthula felt her usual terror of the London mob when, a few days later, hooded and masked after the custom of the time, she made her way with Mrs. Campbell to the approaches of Westminster Hall. This crowd was so different in its boisterousness from anything she had experienced in Edinburgh at the most exciting crises. Mrs. Campbell, however, pertinacious and good-humoured, edged her way for them both through the seething of the throng until they had squeezed inside the great doors, close behind the line of mitred grenadiers that was keeping the august assemblage within free from the intrusion of the mob. Mrs. Campbell, glancing sharply round, discerned the foot of a staircase and skipped up it, beckoning Darthula to follow. It emerged upon a crowded gallery, the door of which was guarded by an usher, who at first looked sour, but yielding at last to Mrs. Campbell's plump, agreeable smile, stood back and let them edge their way inside.

They could look down now into the body of the hall. At its far end opposite them stood the empty throne, with the crimson Yeomen of the Guard resting on their halberds around it. Below the dais the law lords in their long wigs were seated in a semi-circle on the wool-pack, with the Lord High Steward presiding in a funereal black cocked hat, his white wand upon the table before him. Nearby glittered Garter King-of-Arms, with the Usher of the Black Rod and the Bearer of the great embossed Purse. Ranged around the Steward on three sides upon benches were the peers, looking like toy-figures in the uniformity of their robes and ermine, with small, three-cornered hats perched on their powdered perukes, and only the ballooning lawn sleeves of the bishops breaking the regularity.

Darthula craned about in vain to see the dock and the prisoner, but it was not until Mrs. Campbell had insinuated them into a corner right down at the front of the gallery that she was able to see almost immediately underneath the well-known corpulent figure, dressed now in black, and standing deferentially bowed as it leaned over the barrier to listen, one hand curved round its ear, for hearing was not easy in the high, vaulted hall. Bewigged barristers and attorneys with green bags were clustered below the dock, and halberd-points gleamed round Macshimi's great white wig; together with the axe-head held by the gentleman-gaoler, and still turned away from the yet uncondemned prisoner.

Darthula knew not why her eyes grew misty with tears at the sight of him patiently standing there. She knew how proudly he had been used to boast of his many hiding-holes, and the impossibility of his ever being taken. And here he was, the ancient spider, caught fast at last in the web of his enemies.

Down by the table in front of the High Steward an assistant of the Attorney-General's was reading through some long document in a droning voice that was caught up and lost among the carved angels supporting the beams of the roof. Her attention was beginning to wander, when she was tapped upon the shoulder from behind. She turned round. Mrs. Campbell had been separated from her by the pressing of the curious spectators, and she found herself staring at a man in the dress of an English country gentleman, with a hunting-crop in the crook of his arm. . . . She looked again, and it was Glengarry. She had not seen him for weeks, and she had attributed the cessation of his visits to the Campbells to pique at her acceptance of Allan Duncanson as her brother's counsel. Allan, it could not be denied, had continuously rebuffed Alastair's curiosity about his projects for defending Hector with an almost insulting sharpness, and Darthula knew the touchy character of Glengarry well enough to know that he would furiously resent such an apparent affront. But she could not on his account deprive herself of Allan Duncanson's services. It had pained her thus to seem ungrateful for his kindness—but she did not see what else she could have done. Now, however, he was smiling at her in the friendliest way, his full chin pressed upon his bucolic linen neckcloth.

"You know," he whispered, "they will be bringing Hector here to-day?"

"Have you come to greet him, too?" she whispered in reply.

"To greet him? That would scarce be prudent. . . . To have a sight of him—aye." He gnawed a finger with his jutting tooth as he squinted down to try to catch a glimpse of Lovat below in the dock.

The reading of the tedious document was at an end. The lawyer rolled up his parchment and knelt to the throne. Abruptly old Lovat lifted his hand as if demanding to be heard. He shouted something in a cracked voice across the floor to his judges. Darthula could not make out what he said. There was a remonstrant murmur among his counsel, however, and a loud laugh among the nearer spectators. At once the ushers bawled for silence, and a few persons were hustled out of the galleries. This produced so dead a stillness that Darthula clearly heard a voice cry, "Call James Murray of Broughton!"

She started, and turned to Glengarry in dismay. "Will they have Mr. Secretary, too, in their toils? Alas, poor man!"

To her surprise, Glengarry looked at the witness not with compassion, but with disgust, and spat upon the floor. Darthula listened bewildered while Murray was sworn, and after an exhortation from the managers of the prosecution for the Commons to "Give your answers distinctly and raise your voice as much as you can that my lords may hear you," began to unwind the spool of his carefully prepared evidence with his sharp, precise utterance, as though he were delivering a lecture.

After a few minutes Darthula began to think that her troubles had at last unseated her reason. She could not be hearing correctly. She clutched the wooden barrier of the gallery and looked around again with a wild query at Glengarry. He was standing, with his arms folded, still exhibiting the same savage sneer upon his face. It was true then! James Murray of Broughton, the Prince's friend, had become a King's evidence! He was betraying his ineffably sacred trust, and building up with relentless precision from the secret papers of which he had charge the case against the prisoner at the Bar. She looked now at his face, while his lips were moving. There was no possible doubting: he knew his infamy. His waxy cheeks, the shifting of his eyes, the way in which from time to time he wiped both his forehead and his mouth with a clean cambric handkerchief, revealed his inner distress. Still he held on grimly, in a voice that from time to time rose almost to a squeak, disclosing Lovat's share in the preliminaries of the invasion, his intrigues after the Prince's landing to gain the promise of a dukedom, his attendance at a secret conclave at Muirlaggan on the shore of Loch Arkaig after Culloden, where he had promised to raise men to carry on the struggle. The witness gave him money to pay his contingent.

"Whence came that money?" asked the prosecutor.

"From France."

"What was the sum of the money that came from France?"

"Thirty-five thousand louis-d'ors at that time."

An excited rumour rang round the court, and the ushers had difficulty in restoring order. Amid the buzz Darthula heard Glengarry crying in a shrill tone, "Pe tamned to them, pe tamned to them. Where did they hide it? . . ."

Darthula was nearly overcome by nausea. She had known exhaustion, hunger and thirst, bloodshed, the menace of torture, the outraging of her modesty, utter despair—but this was the worst moment in all her life. . . . She had never before seen the face of Judas.

Quiet had been restored, and now a Catholic peer, Lord Talbot, rising from his bench, was questioning the witness. He demanded to know, was he a voluntary evidence?

At once the prosecution were on their feet to protect their man, but Talbot persisted. He desired to be informed "Whether the witness is not an evidence in hopes of a pardon? And whether, if he himself were pardoned, he would be an evidence at all?" Again the Government advocates rallied round; there was objection and legal argument. At last Murray spoke in a low voice, very different from the hard confidence with which he had hitherto been giving his evidence. "I say that possibly, and very probably, had I been in another situation of life, I should not have appeared before your lordships as a witness against the noble lord at the Bar."

There was a complete silence at these words. It was as though the very nakedness of the pitiable admission had brought shame upon those who had engineered the man's downfall. The poor little figure seemed even to gain a certain dignity by the frankness with which he avowed his degradation.

A few more questions were put to him, and then suddenly the prisoner heaved his grotesque bulk nearly over the ledge of the dock, and shouted: "Ah, ye rascal! Ye would be saving your own heid by fause witness against my grey hairs!"

There was another throb of emotion in the assembly, and

the High Steward rose austerely to his feet. "My Lord Lovat," he said, "if there are no questions you have to ask this witness, you must be silent."

Murray of Broughton fixed his eyes for a moment upon Simon Fraser with a look curiously blent of abject terror and mortal hatred. "Had you not been false to us," they seemed to be saying, "I had not sold you now!" His warder touched him on the shoulder, and he slunk from the witness-box.

"And is not that the filth of the world?" whispered Glengarry to Darthula. "Is it not stranche that the sun should shine on one who sells his associates for his dirty life?"

"Poor man! poor man!" sobbed Darthula, "it is I have compassion for him!"

The next moment all these thoughts were struck from her head, for the Attorney-General cried, "Call Hector Maceachan of Glenmarisdale in the county of Inverness-shire."

There was a movement in the witness-box, and the next minute Darthula saw her brother.

At the first look he seemed to her in a better state than when she last saw him, which was while he was still prostrated by his wound from Culloden. Then she became conscious of his extreme fragility. His face was so thin, his form so slight, with his clothes hanging upon him, that he seemed already half a spirit, already half withdrawn from the material frame of the world. He looked cheerful enough, none the less; and she surmised that his mercurial spirits had risen by the mere relief of being brought by water from his prison to this place, and catching a glimpse of the living world as he went by. She longed to wave her kerchief or do anything to attract his notice, but knew it would be suicidal. Allan Duncanson had told them in a note sent to them before they left home that it was while Hector was being re-embarked that she would have the best opportunity of drawing near and giving him at least an unspoken message of cheer. Allan, wigged and gowned, had entered the court at the same time as Hector, to watch over his interests.

Meanwhile he had been sworn, and the Attorney-General upheaved himself to begin the examination.

Before he could answer the first question, the irrepressible prisoner cried from the dock, "Hector! Hector! do not you join them to swear away an old man's life! I was ever your good friend, Hector, bear that in mind!"

The High Steward banged upon the table as he rebuked Simon Fraser again, while Hector gave the old man a re-assuring smile and cock of his eyebrow.

"Be pleased to attend to my questions only, Mr. Maceachan!" the Attorney-General warned Hector, and began his examination. After some formal questions, "Were you with the prisoner at his Castle at Beauly by Inverness in the month of October of the year 1745?" he asked.

Hector agreed.

"Did you at that time ever see the prisoner in arms at the head of troops raised in the interest of the Pretender's party?"

"It would have given me much surprise to do so."

"Why would it have occasioned you surprise?"

"His lordship is too old and infirm," answered Hector delicately, "for feats of arms—on either side." There was a slight rustle in the Court at this barb.

"Did you hear the prisoner on several occasions profess his intention to take up arms for the Pretender?"

"I can never remember that he did so in my presence."

"Let me awaken your memory. In the month of October of 1745 were you not present with other chieftains in his Castle at Beauly when he gave command to attack Mr. Forbes, the Lord President, in his house at Culloden?"

"That attack will not have been carried out by Lord Lovat."

"But it was by his orders."

"I saw no orders."

"Did you take it on yourself to attack Culloden House without orders from anyone in higher authority?"

Allan Duncanson sprang up. "My lords, I must oppose that question being asked. This gentleman is shortly to stand his own trial, and he is not to be made to incriminate himself."

Mr. Attorney scowled. "He has sworn to deliver the whole truth."

"Concerning the cause between the King's Grace and the defendant. He is not an evidence in his own cause."

The Attorney-General flicked over the pages of his brief. "Now, Mr. Maceachan," he resumed, "did the prisoner at any time in your hearing give order to his son, the Master of Lovat, to raise his clan and take the field in the Pretender's cause?"

"Never!"

"Did he not, Mr. Maceachan, on a day of March in this year say to his son in your hearing, 'My dear child, raise my banner, as I have taught you to do, for King James'?"

"Not for King James, I am thinking."

"I am not asking you what you are thinking, but what you will swear to."

"Then I will not swear to King James—upon this occasion."

There was a titter at this audacity, and Darthula saw Allan Duncanson look grave.

The Attorney-General laid down his brief on the table, and looked severely at the witness. "I would put you in mind, Mr. Maceachan, that this is a very grave matter, and no subject for jesting—for you."

"Why, will I be upon my trial in this place, after all, Mr. Attorney?"

"You will be pleased to answer my questions and not to

question me!" Mr. Attorney's foot tapped the ground.

("Hector is fitting the noose to his own neck!" Glengarry murmured to Darthula.)

"Come now," the Attorney-General spoke more gently, "you are aware that I desire to treat you with every consideration, Mr. Maceachan." Hector bowed. "Did not the prisoner say 'for King James'?"

"As I recollect—we were at table—his lordship swallowed a small bone as he spoke those words, and I did not hear exactly what he uttered."

"In the circumstances of the conversation was it possible the prisoner could be directing his son to take the field for his lawful Majesty?"

"I would not be surprised at that either."

"Not when it would be contrary to the whole tenor of his action?"

"Lord Lovat is a very contrary man." There was another uncontrollable titter at this.

"Could he have said 'King George' and the Master immediately have betaken himself to the Pretender's Standard?"

"I know nothing of that. But I have observed that sons do not always obey their fathers."

"Did you, then, not see the Master of Lovat fighting on your side at the Battle of Culloden?"

Duncanson sprang up again. "I oppose that question, too, my lords. It directly incriminates the witness."

There was a murmur of assent among the peers, and Mr. Attorney sat down looking black as night.

"Hector has thrown away his only chance!" declared Glengarry.

Before she could answer, Mrs. Campbell had whispered to her over her shoulder from behind, and, without speaking to Glengarry, she hurried out after the attorney's wife.

Mrs. Campbell led the way past St. Stephen's Chapel to the

edge of the river-stairs. Several boats were in waiting with military guards. In a few moments came a file of soldiers, and a gaoler, with Hector walking slowly in their midst. He supported his steps on a stick, savouring the sunlight, and looking in its spring brightness an even more attenuated shadow of himself than he had done in the hall. A number of loafers by the river-bank collected in a small crowd to see him pass.

"Have a care, now!" whispered Mrs. Campbell. "Do not disclose yourself! Stand by me close, and drop your mask as he goes by!"

The rowers of the boat from the Tower stood up as Hector's guard approached. Darthula lowered her mask, and, taking a step in front of Mrs. Campbell, tried bravely to smile at her brother through her tears. Hector started, and gazed at her as if he had seen an angel. His walking-stick fell from his hold, and Darthula, swiftly stooping, handed it back to him. Their fingers met in a passionate pressure; then Mrs. Campbell dragged her back by her skirts, as a soldier interposed his musket, and another wrenched Hector's hand open to see if anything had been passed to him.

"You should be more careful! much more careful!" said Mrs. Campbell breathlessly to Darthula, as she hurried her away through the crowd round the steps. "What if they had stopped to interrogate you? Allan Duncanson will flite you for this, see if he doesna, Miss Maceachan!"

Allan certainly shook his head when Mrs. Campbell related the incident to him, on his rejoining them at the doors of Westminster Hall. He begged Darthula earnestly not to expose herself thus again to the public notice, but he did not scold. Indeed, as he accompanied them back along the Strand towards their house, he seemed in a hopeful mood.

He made light of Glengarry's predictions about the effect of Hector's evidence that morning. "He could not do otherwise, having regard to his honour," he said, "though it were to be wished he could abstain from unseasonable jocosities. They would, doubtless, have given him his life if he had followed Murray of Broughton to infamy, but I am not without hopes that I will secure his life by worthier means. The indictment against him, I am now to tell you, Miss Maceachan, will likely be presented a few days hence, at Southwark Court House, and this very morn, I have had a letter from Duncan Forbes on his subject."

"Why should the Lord President interest himself in Hector?" asked Darthula, surprised.

"You marked how I interposed when they were for questioning your brother anent the Frasers' attack on Culloden House? It is true that Hector was with Fraser of Foyers directing the attack. But it is also true his arm stayed the man that would by Lovat's orders be shooting the Lord President on the battlements of his home. Forbes kens well to whom he owes his life."

"Hector never told me that!" exclaimed Darthula, "but his memory was not good after his hurts at Drummossie. He would be talking of nothing but his childhood then."

"Forbes hath the better memory. He promises in this letter to use his good offices in the time and manner that shall seem most advantageous, at the trial or after as may appear fittest."

A faint warmth of hope crept into the chill that seemed to Darthula always to be bathing her heart in these days.

"Then, Allan," she said with a little sigh of relief, "I need not be troubling myself overmuch with Alastair Ruadh's forebodings!"

"I would counsel you not to trouble at all with that young man and his clack!" said Duncanson impatiently. "I think he is gone clean gyte these days, and I cannot rightly make out what his purposes are. I learn he was in the Cocoa Tree

Coffee-house on a night of this week, bragging to a crowd of broken gamesters and ruined Scots gentlemen of riches that he should soon be enjoying in his own right. Whence should he have expectations of riches, Miss Maceachan? Is his father dying, know you?"

"I have heard nothing of that, Allan."

"Nor I. Nor do I know why he, an escaped prisoner from the Tower by his own way of it, flaunts himself in all the places of pleasure in this metropolis, as though he had nought to fear from any man."

"That will ever have been his way, mad Alastair! He vows there is no path to safety but through the heart of peril."

"That is not the path that leads to old age," said Allan.

"Poor Alastair! I will not be forgetting it was he saved me from the red-coats by Loch Arkaig."

"And I think he has had enough thanks for that!" said Allan almost peevishly.

2

FOUR days later Darthula was again in the gallery of Westminster Hall with Mrs. Campbell to hear sentence given on Lord Lovat. She had not this time told Allan Duncanson of her intention, feeling sure he would oppose it; but she could not resist her impulse. Of Macshimi she knew much that was bad; she summed him up as a traitor to every cause but his own advancement . . . but he had been the greatest figure in the North in her childhood. Like almost every other woman she had found something not to be resisted in his wheedling ways, false though she knew them to be. Anyhow he was old and beaten now, ringed round by his enemies. Battered in honour, he yet stood in this mortal hour for the dignity of the tartan. . . . How her presence this day could aid him she could not see, but her heart in her melted at his defencelessness and distress.

Mrs. Campbell had been glad enough of the diversion of another visit to the chief spectacle of the day in London. Well enough known to the smaller law officials at Westminster, and always an agreeable figure to them with her ample bosom and pawky wit, she had again no difficulty in edging her masked companion and herself into the public gallery. The scene before their eyes was unchanged from what it had been four days before. Indeed, it was difficult to believe that the actors had not been in continuous session since then. There were the uniform rows of peers, robed and black-hatted, the judges on the wool-pack, the High Steward with the wand before him on the table, the glittering group of maces and heraldic tabards. The only difference was an unoccupied strip in the red benches, where the bishops had withdrawn from the ultimate business of butchery.

Below them, as the week before, the enormous head and white wig of the prisoner hung over the ledge of the dock between the halberd points, and the axe still rose beside him, with its edge turned away. Lovat was making, as Darthula and her companion entered, one of his long, rambling speeches, the best part of it inaudible, to show why judgment should not be passed upon him. At last the Lord High Steward interrupted his irrelevancies; he yielded with a rueful shrug of his great hunched shoulders; and following the laborious ceremonial of trial by the Lords, the peers filed out in procession to their own House for more formalities.

"Is it all over, indeed?" Darthula murmured to Mrs. Campbell, the tears running down her face. "Is there no hope for Macshimi?" She watched the Peers return.

The Lord High Steward spoke long before pronouncing sentence, with all an old lawyer's delight in the moralising and orotund phrase. But there was a deadly hush, as he paused at last, and then said solemnly:

"The sentence of the law is, and this High Court doth adjudge: 'That you, Simon Lord Lovat, return to the prison of the Tower from whence you came; from thence you must be drawn to the place of execution; when you come there, you must be hanged by the neck, but not till you are dead; for you must be cut down alive; then your bowels must be take out, and burnt before your face; then your head must be severed from your body, and your body divided into four quarters; and these must be at the King's disposal. And God Almighty be merciful to your soul.'"

There was a flash just underneath where Darthula was sitting; the gentleman-gaoler had turned the edge of the axe to the prisoner. . . .

The great Hall swam before Darthula's eyes. She had never before learnt the horrible terms of the sentence for High Treason, and for a moment it was Hector who filled her mind as she listened, and not the ancient sinner below. Then she saw Lovat's face turned towards her in the pale spring sunshine. He seemed to look about everywhere helplessly as if for some aid. His crumpled countenance was deadly white, the eyes starting out with terror. It was obvious he had hoped for some last minute intervention in his favour and was shattered by its absence. The Steward asked him a question, and with an astonishing effort he recovered his dignity. With his cracked tones uplifted more clearly than usual, "I have nothing more to offer," he said, "but to thank your lordships for your goodness to me. God bless you all, and I bid you an everlasting farewell." The Lord High Steward and the peers touched their hats. "We shall not meet all in the same place again; I am sure of that," added Simon Fraser with a chuckle, and turned to depart, with the Lieutenant of the Tower at his side, his face still creased as if he had made a good little joke in his parlour at Beauly.

There was a sharp crack in the Hall, as the Lord High Steward broke the white wand of his commission.

"Come," said Darthula to Mrs. Campbell, "come quick! I must see him depart; I must take farewell of him!"

Mrs. Campbell, demurring, sought to restrain her; but she hurried down the stairs and threaded her way, careless of remonstrances or the treading of heavy feet upon her toes, out into Palace Yard. Round the doors by which the prisoner would come out the crush was alarming, but she endured the buffeting and the risk to her ribs with a return of one of her old moods of exaltation. The mob surged and the wave of it bore her forward against the soldiers who were keeping the passage clear. She clung for support to the belt of a tall grenadier behind his back, and with the weight of his accoutrements he did not notice the frail addition to his burden.

Suddenly up went a storm of hooting and hissing, as Lovat appeared in the midst of his gaolers with the axe going before him. He had been cheered by this crowd every morning on his way to trial, so long as he seemed to have a sporting chance of acquittal. Beaten and condemned now, he evoked no feeling but moral indignation. Stones and handfuls of mud flew through the air, aimed at his old head. "Down with the Devil, the Pope and the Pretender!" roared a voice, and immediately the whole crowd took it up. "Down with the Devil, the Pope and the Pretender!"

Darthula could not bear it. She ducked under the elbow of her grenadier, and flung herself at Simon's feet. "God bless you, Macshimi!" she sobbed, "God sustain you in your hour!"

Lovat's eyes, changed to a childish candour, opened wide. "Is it Darthula?" he said, and a fatherly joy transfigured him. "May God and His Holy Mother protect you too, my dear child!"

"Hold that woman!" cried the Lieutenant of the Tower angrily; but before the soldiers could move, a strong arm had plucked Darthula away, and the grenadiers made only a faint-hearted attempt to break through the surging mob after her.

Instead their own line was for a moment broken. Gutter faces swirled round the ancient nobleman, fists menaced him.

"You'll get that nasty head of yours chopped off, you ugly old Scotch dog!" screeched a harridan from St. Giles's, puffing gin-fumes in his face.

"Why," said Lovat, as with unwonted agility he hoisted himself into the coach that was awaiting to take him, "why, I believe I shall—you ugly old English b——!"

3

IT WAS with a gaoler's rather than a deliverer's grip that Allan Duncanson guided Darthula, after rescuing her from the crowd, into a maze of slimy alleys and wharves between Whitehall and the river, where they were little likely to be pursued.

When at last he let go of her, she could see that his eyes were blazing palely with fury—a sight she had never seen before.

"I marvel at you, Miss Maceachan, I marvel at you! This is the second time you have committed a grave imprudence, and after warning!"

"I have a woman's feelings!" retorted Darthula sharply, for the exaltation was still on her and her spirit reared under the lash of his tone.

"Your feelings! Of what advantage are your feelings to yonder doomed old villain? What if you had been arrested, or we both had been trampled to death? Had you no care for your life . . . or mine?"

"If you are still shaking for your skin, Mr. Duncanson—"

"Had I not good reason?"

"Every man I suppose has that." She shrugged her shoulders. "Though the gentlemen I have frequented will not have been used to give so much thought to the matter."

"So you expect a man to throw away his life . . . idly . . . uselessly . . . to extricate you when you have endangered yours by some theatric whim?"

"My grief, Mr. Duncanson! I never did hear a gentleman make such clatter over helping a lady in a small distress!"

"Had I been killed by that mob—they were in the mood for it—what would have become of your brother's defence? Do you know they have found a true bill against him this very morning, and it is only five days to his arraignment? How could a new advocate gather the threads in that time?"

She hung her head. "I owe you an apology, Allan. I will never be forgiving myself for using you in the terms I have!"

"Then, I will beg you to observe more care after this! It is not for myself I am tender, however you may please to put it. Life is not so sweet in these times of ours that one should struggle to go on living—lacking the one thing that makes life desirable." He broke off, and a look of grievous concern came into his face. "Miss Maceachan," he stammered, "you are injured, you are bleeding!"

He fell on his knees at her feet, bringing to her attention what she had not observed first in her excitement and then in her anger, that her ankle had been lightly cut by a flying stone or perhaps by a kick in the mob, and that a drop or two of blood were oozing through her stocking.

"Let me bind it for you!" he stammered, pulling out his handkerchief. "Oh! let me try to staunch the flow!"

His hands shook so that he could not tie the kerchief round the tiny hurt.

"There is no flow at all!" she said, overcome by his immense tenderness. "Indeed, and you are troubling yourself for a trifle, Allan! It is a mere scratch!"

"Scratches must be looked to!" He rose and cast desperate glances around him. "If I could find a coach! There is none to be had in these foul little ways!"

"I need no coach," she said with a trembling smile. "I will be taking your arm instead, Allan—if I may?"

Chapter III

"HACKTOR MACKEICHEN"

1

THAT night in Mrs. Campbell's parlour Allan Duncanson disclosed to Darthula an anxiety that had arisen in his mind on studying the copy of the bill of indictment against Hector, with which he had to-day been furnished. After the customary preamble there was the expected charge that Hector had, "moved and seduced by the instigation of the Devil," joined himself to "a great multitude of traitors and rebels, against our said present sovereign lord the King" to "wage and levy a public and cruel war." To that accusation there could be no possible reply; the pleas of youth and unpremeditation would be all that could be advanced. But the indictment for armed rebellion had been preceded in the bill by a charge that the prisoner did "in the month of July 1745 with divers other traitors and rebels, compose, write and send a treasonable letter to the eldest son of the said Pretender, being then in France, whereby it should appear that His Majesty's dominions were to be invaded with the aid, assistance and encouragement of the said Hector Maceachan."

"I know nothing of any such letter," declared Allan.

444

"Hector is positive he subscribed no such document. What will this mean, and what evidence are they intending to produce?"

Darthula was as astounded as he was. "The poor lad," she declared, "was never meddling with politics before the Prince landed to claim his fealty! Cartes, golf, hunting the deer—such things were all his ploys!"

"As I would have testified from my knowledge of him. Is it possible, do you think, Miss Maceachan, they will have induced him in some moment of rashness to set his hand to one of their invitations to the Chevalier?"

Darthula paused a moment. "Without telling me?" she then said. "I am not believing it was possible in those days."

Allan set his lips grimly. "I begin to suspect foul doings here. If such a document can be proved, what becomes of our plea of unpremeditation? They ken that well. Maybe they harbour a deeper rancour against him than I supposed for his unwillingness to testify against Lovat. But they have had Lovat's head! What ails them that they must fabricate false evidence against a boy, broken in health, that can do them little more harm, howe'er it fall?"

Darthula could find no answer to this question either, and they both sat oppressed and anxious in the chilly twilight, gazing at the flicker of Mrs. Campbell's frugal fire.

Later that evening, long after Allan Duncanson had departed, came another, most unexpected visitor, asking to see Darthula. It was Alastair Ruadh, dressed this time in the top of fashion like a young buck of the town; but with his peruke slightly awry and a thickness in his tone, showing that he had been drinking deep before he came.

Darthula was no more surprised than any other woman of her time at finding a gentleman drunk after his dinner; but she was perplexed by Glengarry's excited and nervous manner.

After a few skilful excuses for his long absence as a visitor from her lodgings, he said abruptly, "Darthula, you will not be forgetting, will you, that it was I brought you in safety out of the hands of your enemies into England?"

"I will never be forgetting your goodness to me, Alastair. Sorrow's me, that I have so little in my power whereby to be showing my gratitude to you!"

"Then, girl of all the world, the opportunity offers tonight! A great thing I will be asking of you to do, but it is for your own deliverance as well as my happiness." He stood for a moment in his fine, figured crimson coat, his hand on his polished sword-hilt, looking down on her, with his single jutting tooth biting into his lip, attractive and debonair in his florid handsomeness, but swaying slightly on his feet as he gazed. "It is this," he said abruptly, "I am loving you better than all the treasures of the earth. Will you be accepting of me as your husband . . . and accompany me to France without any delay?"

She looked at him reproachfully. "Alastair, you should not use these wild words to me at such an hour, even though you be in wine."

"*Dieu me damne!* It is not the wine that speaks, but the red blood of me, Darthula! And pay you heed to my words! It is necessar' that you disappear from England without lingering, if you would not find yourself, too, in a cell of their Tower."

"Allan Duncanson tells me—"

"My curse on your whey-drinking Whig! *He* tells you you are safe and he lies! *He* tells you your brother will be acquitted and pardoned . . . and he lies again!"

"Take shame to yourself for those words, Alastair! And for why would you be quenching my poor hopes that Hector will be delivered from his foes?"

"It is because I *know*! It boots not, Darthula, to look unbelieving. I am the man that goes hither and thither upon the town," he flirted a lace handkerchief, "that is received into any house, that hath friends in all classes, all parties; Papist and Protestant, loyal and Hanoverian, I can worm their secrets from them."

"Alastair, my heart is heavy and my thoughts distracted. I am not having the time this night to listen to your boastings."

"Boasting!" He scowled, bringing his full chin over his cambric neckcloth. "Is it boasting I am? Darthula, have a care! There is an engine charged against Hector of which you know nothing, and Master Advocate from Edinburgh knows nothing, howeffer he may champ his lanky jaws!"

Darthula started to her feet. "If you know anything, Alastair, tell me in pity—"

"That you may carry it to Duncanson, is it not so, and that he may profit by your gratitude. May my soul be doomed if I will be the complaisant fool to be cheated—this time!" He drew himself up with an effort at dignity, leaning against the back of a chair as he did so. "Darthula, I am asking, will you have me? It is a soldier woos you with short words . . . but a long love and a true loyalty whateffer!"

She threw out her hands despairingly. "Alastair! It is you must be knowing I could not think of wooing and marriage at this hour! But if you will wrest an answer from me, and you ungallant to be doing so, the answer is no . . . and no. I am pledged elsewhere."

"Ha! To Duncanson, the Campbell traitor!" He looked very ugly in the feebly wavering firelight as he said this.

"It will be no concern of yours, I am thinking, Alastair Ruadh. You are answered!"

"Wait you!" He drew the dainty handkerchief over his forehead as he stood with his foot on the fender. She saw by the flame striking up from below that his face was pearled with tiny sweat-drops. "If it were in my power . . . mine alone . . . to save Hector from the gallows, would you be reconsidering of your answer, Darthula?"

"If . . . and if. . . . If you were our friend, you would not be haggling over a piece of knowledge of such moment to us. You would be running to Allan Duncanson, who alone can make use of anything you may have gleaned. And shall I trust you when you speak to me upon this tone? Either speak plain, tell me what you believe yourself to have discovered, or leave me to my grief, Alastair Ruadh."

He bowed to her with a look of sullen offence pinching his ordinarily expansive face. "If a shentleman is not to be trusted when he gives his word, there is the end of it! See now if it is Allan Duncanson will be your succour!" He stalked to the door, and then turned round with a tragic look in his eyes. "It is you are the foolish one of all the world!" he cried. "*Dieu me damne*, you will never be knowing what you have lost in rejecting the treasure of my heart! Farewell, Darthula, farewell! You will be remembering me still, though, I am thinking!"

As he turned about once more and passed with his swaggering step through the door, she was reminded again of that night long ago when he had walked through Lady Stair's door proudly bearing her small token of friendship.

She sighed, and let him fall from her melancholy thoughts.

Outside on the doorstep Glengarry stood swaying irresolutely and gazing about him.

Up from the direction of the Temple by the river, where he had been loitering, came, with a patter of steps, his little black-complexioned gillie.

"No, Mungo," said Alastair thickly, in answer to his enquiring eyebrows. "There will be no message to carry to my lords." He snapped his fingers in the air. "*Vive la baga-*

telle! Complete your packing of my bags, and come and fetch me from the Mitre Tavern . . . at daybreak."

2

THERE was none of the pomp of Lord Lovat's impeachment when Hector was brought to his trial five days later. A plea by his counsel for more time to prepare his defence against the unexpected particulars in his indictment had been refused on the ground that the long period which had passed since his arrest had allowed him and his advisers superabundant time to find witnesses (if they could) on his behalf and to prepare every detail of his defence. So within the time assigned he was brought into the dingy court-house at South-wark, evil-smelling, packed to suffocation with witnesses, counsel, curious observers from the great world, and ghoulish spectators from the mean streets of the neighbourhood. The red robes of the three judges under the faded Royal Arms of their canopy were the only splash of colour in the dull light that filtered through the grime of the windows. Darthula, who was with Mrs. Campbell, masked, in a gallery, was sad-dened by Hector's look of complete detachment from the proceedings, as he rested his head on his elbow upon the ledge of the dock, with abstracted eyes that focussed them-selves nowhere.

The prosecution were not long in unmasking their bat-teries. "Call Captain John Johnstone," said the Solicitor-General, who was leading for the Government, and into the witness-box stepped a straw-haired creature, so thin that it appeared he would, if he turned sideways, disappear alto-gether like a sheet of paper, at whom Hector in the dock, Darthula in the spectators' gallery, and Allan Duncanson in the well of the court stared with equal astonishment. None of them had ever set eyes on him before.

He deponed that he was a Scotsman holding a commission in the King of France's Scottish Brigade. He had formed part of a small detachment sent over in the autumn of the year 1745 to reinforce the Pretender's troops in Edinburgh. Their ship had been wrecked off the coast of Yorkshire, and he and the rest had been apprehended and brought to London to the Tower. As he had been a subject of his Britannic Majesty by birth, he had not been able to avail himself of the privileges of a foreign prisoner of war. While in confinement he had meditated on the unnatural sin of rebellion and assisting to levy war against his lawful King. Hence he had resolved, in no hope of pardon or other leniency, to do all that lay in his power to make reparation for his misdoings, and to aid His Majesty in uncovering the designs of his enemies. In particular he had communicated a treasonous document, subscribed in the hand of the prisoner at the Bar, which would be produced in the Court, and to the provenance of which he would swear.

"Your lordships and the jury shall presently hear the document read," said the Solicitor, "but I will first ask the witness to relate how he came by it."

Captain Johnstone swept his arm over his forehead with the air, thought Duncanson, of a man making a mighty effort of invention, and started off again. In the month of July, 1745, he had been on furlough in an inn near Nantes. There was a Scottish gentleman there the day before had been in a bruilzie with the landlord about his reckoning. They had come to quarrelling and blows, a drawer had been wounded by the angry Scotsman's sword, and the traveller had escaped, leaving his saddle-bags behind him.

"Did you learn the name of this traveller?" asked the solicitor. The witness shifted from one foot to the other. "He will have gone by the name of a Mr. Davidson."

"And did you and the landlord examine the baggage he left behind him?"

"We did, and found the letter you now hold, sir!"

"Let the letter be read," said the presiding judge.

The Clerk of the Court obeyed. The letter was an appeal to Prince Charles Edward to defer his coming into Scotland until the winter, when the signatories engaged themselves they would be found ready with their respective powers and friends to support him, and the weather would more severely hamper the movements of the English Government's troops. It was subscribed by nearly a dozen names, including Cameron of Lochiel, Lord Lovat, Lord Elcho, Murray of Broughton, and last of all "Hacktor Mackeichen."

Captain Johnstone explained that his intention had been to deliver the letter himself to Prince Charles, but on reaching Paris he had learned that the Prince had already set sail for Scotland.

"What did you do then with the letter?"

"I knew of no one remaining in France meet, in my opinion, to be entrusted with a document of such consequence, and I resolved if I could get to these islands and there join the Pretender's forces, to deliver it to him in person."

"How came it not to be found on your person or in your baggage when you were apprehended?"

"I had it sewn with other precious papers for safety into the sole of my boot. It escaped the notice of the searchers until I determined to disclose it—as an act of reparation."

Hector had scribbled a note to his counsel from the dock during this testimony, and Allan Duncanson, after a moment's intense study of the scrawl,

Hacktor Mackeichen

rose to cross-examine. He demanded to know whether Johnstone had given his evidence in expectation of a pardon; and though the Solicitor-General objected at first to the question, the witness glibly declared that no promise of any sort had been made to him; he had acted to satisfy his conscience solely.

Allan tried to elicit from him some more facts about the mysterious "Mr. Davidson" who was carrying the letter about France and had so culpably lost it; the Captain had not seen him and had nothing to tell about his rank, character or appearance.

"Were the words 'Hacktor Mackeichen' on the document when it came into your hands?"

"I did not tamper with it in any way! I am a man of honour!"

There was a faint titter in the court at this, and Captain Johnstone, swinging round to the public, cried, "You may laugh at me, but there are not many of you in my place would have acted otherwise than I am doing! I have a wife and three children in France who depend for their living on my pay!"

The presiding judge rebuked him sternly. "Answer learned counsel's questions, and do not make speeches to the people here."

"Were you ever acquainted with the prisoner?"

"I never set eyes on him before to-day."

"Did you conceive yourself to have any cause of quarrel or grudge against him?"

"Only for his being a rebel against his lawful King."

"Have you ever seen his signature subscribed to any other document?"

"To none."

"You are not aware that he signs always 'Maceachan of Glenmarisdale' and not in this style or with this spelling?"

"I am not."

"Would you be surprised if evidence were brought that the prisoner has never used this form of signature?"

"I am witness only to the finding of the document, which was as I have said, upon my oath."

Duncanson sat down, and the prosecution called "Alexander Macgliskin."

Into the box limped the one-legged landlord of the Hellfire Club in Edinburgh. He was dressed in black almost like a minister, his face shaved, his hair combed, an expression of profound gravity on his features.

"You are Alexander Macgliskin, a tavern-keeper in the street known as Canongate, in Edinburgh?" asked the Solicitor.

"I have been for fifteen year!"

"Cast your eye upon that letter. It is subscribed 'Hacktor Mackeichen,' as you see. In whose hand is that subscription?"

"In the hand of the prisoner yonder, the Laird of Glenmarisdale."

"You are well acquainted with his hand?"

"Very weel. I have mony times obleeged him wi' money on his note of hand."

"Is that his usual form of subscription?"

"It was not his most common style—he had several. It was a style I have known him use."

The Solicitor-General handed him a paper from his green bag.

"Do you know that document?"

"Aye. I delivered it to His Majesty's officers a while syne."

"What is it?"

"A promise to pay three hundred guineas, signed 'Hacktor Mackeichen.'"

"Let it be read," said the Judge. . . .

"We have heard," resumed the Solicitor-General, "that in this document the prisoner at the Bar promises to pay one Alexander Macdonnell, Younger of Glengarry, or bearer, three hundred guineas on the first day of February, 1746. How came it into your hands?"

"I discounted it for Mr. Macdonnell, for the sum of twa hundred and twenty guineas. He was leaving for France the morn, and needed money."

"You say the morn. Pray tell the Court what day that was."

Sandy rolled his tongue round his hollow cheeks, as though in deep reflection. "I canna mind the exact day to swear to," he said at last. "But I mind it would be the morn after the prisoner at the Bar had been fechting wi' Mr. Macdonnell in ma cellar over a wee bit o' tartan ribbon. I couldna mak' out the rights or wrongs of it, but Mr. Macdonnell was gey and ill mishandled, cut o'er his eye, to bleed like a pig!"

Hector suddenly smote his forehead with his hand, as though some startling recollection had dawned upon him. One of the assisting judges, who had been watching the prisoner closely, drew the jurymen's attention with his goose-quill to this agitation.

"You are satisfied, then, that the subscription, 'Hacktor Mackeichen,' was that of the prisoner?"

"I hae nae doot! Would I have advanced ma money if I had not been certain sure?"

"Pray compare the signatures to the two papers before the Court. Are they the same in every particular?"

Sandy pored over the two documents. "I can see nae difference. I wad accept baith as the prisoner's ain handwriting."

The Solicitor sat down, and Allan Duncanson rose.

"You are aware that the prisoner at the Bar was still an infant at law in the year 1745?"

"I kent it weel."

"You knew it at the time?"

"Aye. It was weel-known his Tutor was Lord Brounhill."

"Then you knew that he could sign no instrument having force in law?"

"I was no parteecular upon that point."

"You tell us you were not particular when you lent him money, several times, I think you deponed, whether his promissory note had force in law or not?"

"I hae been wont to trust the spoken or written word of a gentleman in these matters, and I canna mind when it has gane ill with me for sae doing."

"You were prepared to advance . . . another gentleman two hundred and twenty guineas on this valueless note of hand?"

"I had the security of Lord Elcho's backing. I wasna perturbed."

"Are you a careful man with money, Mr. Macgliskin?"

"I am nae fule."

"Did you ever try to present this note for payment?"

"What chance suld I have, a loyal man, o' being paid by a parcel o' pestilent Jacobites, as they hae syne been proved to be?"

"Nor did you attempt to recover from Mr. Macdonnell of Glengarry?"

"I havenae set eyes on him fra that morn to this hour," said the witness, smiting the ledge of the box for emphasis.

"I suggest you never advanced a penny on this note of hand to anybody!"

"It is fause!"

"I suggest you never saw that note of hand in your life till shortly before the beginning of this trial."

The Solicitor-General rose remonstrant, and the presiding Judge said testily, "What is the use, sir, of expecting the witness to aver the contrary of all he hath deposed? Are you asking him to admit to his own perjury?"

"With submission then, my lord, I beg for an adjournment of the case until Mr. Macdonnell of Glengarry can be served with a *subpoena*."

The Solicitor rose. "We would ourselves have called Mr. Macdonnell, but we learn he left this country four days ago by packet for France."

"Was any attempt made to apprehend him?" demanded Duncanson. "He was a prisoner evaded from the Tower of London!"

"He was released from the Tower of London under his Majesty's pardon," retorted the Solicitor, as though surprised at the allegation.

"Proceed with the hearing!" ordered the Judge ruthlessly.

Darthula saw Allan pass his hand slowly over the back of his wig, the only mark of worry he had so far shown.

"I desire to ask the witness," he said, "whether he has seen this form of signature, 'Hacktor Mackeichen' on any other document, known to be signed by the prisoner."

Sandy Macgliskin studied the cobwebby rafters of the Court. "I canna mind that I have," he said.

"This is the only time he signed 'Hacktor Mackeichen'?"

"Except, at any rate," put in the Judge with the licence of the period, "in the letter he wrote to the Adventurer."

An ex-secretary of Lord Elcho's was then produced, who identified the handwriting on the promissory note as his former master's, and even asserted that he remembered his lordship speaking of having signed the note. "He was doubting of his prudence," said the man. After these evidences and the failure of the defence to damage their testimonies, the trial became a rout for the prisoner's side. Two renegades from

clans not Hector's own, deposed to his presence at the raising of the Pretender's Standard at Glenfinnan; English officers and privates to his actions at the battles of Gladsmuir and
Culloden. Darthula in her numb despair felt a little touch
of pride in the fact that no member of his own clan had been
gained over to testify against him. She had been expecting
with a faint flicker of hope that some evidence would be
called to bear witness to Hector's having protected the Lord
President during the attack on Culloden House, but the topic
was not raised, she could not comprehend why. When the
Solicitor-General at length said: "There I rest it," the verdict seemed already as good as given.

Nor was it possible for Allan Duncanson to make much
play with his speech for the defence. The argument he had
hoped to found upon Hector's youth and lack of premedita-
tion in his conduct had been undermined by the production
of his apparent signature to a letter inviting Charles Edward
to make his attempt at the first convenient season. He was
made to appear a confederate with Lochiel, Murray and
others known to have been for years working towards the
end of an invasion. To protest the forgery of the signature
was a duty, but what weight could the protestation carry
when Sandy Macgliskin had sworn to a similar form of signature, and Elcho's servant had corroborated it? The production by the defence of two Edinburgh gentlemen of
Whig principles, frequenters of the Hellfire Club, who were
prepared to testify that to the best of their knowledge Hector had been a youth immersed totally in pleasure and sport
before the landing of the Adventurer, evidently made small
impression upon the judges or the jury.

The Judge's summing up was heavily against the prisoner.
He remarked on the uncontested evidence of Hector's actual
participation in the rebellion. To this the evidence of pre-
meditation in the form of the letter to the Pretender's son

was only accessory. If they credited the assertion of the defence that the signature was fabricated, it would not impair the weight of the evidence convicting the prisoner of actual treason and rebellion. But nothing had been advanced to invalidate the subscription, no motive had been shown why any person or persons should perpetrate so shocking a crime against God and their conscience as manufacture false evidence to overwhelm a young man already in sore peril of condemnation. The testimony of Captain Johnstone was not to be rejected merely because he had returned from evil paths and the monitions of the Devil to his true and natural allegiance. They had to consider whether the inn-keeper Macgliskin, a careful member of a careful nation, was likely to lend money without assurance of the genuineness of the note of hand promising repayment. The legal force of the document might be contested; but they might be assured that among gentlemen a pledge to discharge debts of honour, as gambling debts were unfortunately reckoned, was jealously observed. If they believed that, then they would necessarily believe that "Hacktor Mackeichen," written in the style of the subscription to the treasonous letter, was a form of signature actually in use by the prisoner at the Bar. If so, the last shadow of doubt as to the deliberate and premeditated character of the prisoner's most unnatural and cruel rebellion against his sacred Majesty and against the lives, liberty, property and religion of His Majesty's faithful subjects must be banished from their minds. He bade them consider their verdict without fear or favour as loyal Englishmen and faithful subjects.

The jury returned the verdict of "Guilty" without leaving the court and without recommendation to mercy. Mrs. Campbell was able to lead Darthula, half fainting, from the place before the ghastly pronouncement of the sentence for high treason. As she led the girl out her sharp glance caught

sight of Glengarry's little black servant in the well of the
court, regarding them with expressionless eyes.

3

IT WAS a terrible meeting between Darthula and Allan Duncanson later that evening when the advocate came hotfoot
from the Tower, where he had been interviewing Hector, to
Mrs. Campbell's house. The kindly lady, who had been doing her materialistic best to comfort Darthula in her affliction
with sal volatile, hartshorn and offers of brandy, slipped out
of the drawing-room and left them together. "It is Glengarry!" choked Darthula; and "It is Glengarry!" said Duncanson at the same moment in a voice that vibrated with
penned-up passion.

"I still cannot believe it of Alastair!" she sobbed.

"I can piece things together now," said Allan in a hopeless
tone. "They quarrelled that night of Lady Stair's reception
over the trifle of ribbon you were pleased to give Glengarry.
. . . Forgive me, I saw it pass."

"Sorrow's me. Oh! Sorrow's me! It is I am Hector's assassin!"

"You must not say or think that!" said Allan warmly.
"God save us all if we are to be held so far responsible for
what may flow from our unconsidered acts of carelessness or
caprice! Was it you made Alastair Macdonnell his crooked
soul?"

"If I had known it was Hector cut that scar above his eye,
I had been forewarned. He never forgives!"

"Hector tells me he was drugged by Macgliskin that night,
and remembered nothing of the quarrel but a vague chaos.
There is more than mere malice here, I fear. We have learned
to-day that Alastair was pardoned, and did not, as he told us,
escape from the Tower. . . . Do you think he was pardoned

for nothing? By what Hector tells me—for prisoners aye find means to communicate with one another—he was sent north to search for the treasure of French *louis d'ors* that Murray of Broughton buried by Loch Arkaig before he was taken himself. Ah, Glengarry hath taken service with new masters!"

"His old ones left him to rot in prison," confessed Darthula. "Yet there was thirty-five thousand pounds on the head of our Prince, and not one poor man in the Highlands to claim it!"

"I have learnt to-night that these past months . . . since he came to London in brief, he has been in and out of the Tower, drawing disclosures from some prisoners, doubtless, under his braw mask of friendship, corrupting others to bear false witness, and among them, I need scarce insist, this luckless Captain Johnstone. The man has a wife and children in Paris, as he said. . . . Now he will see them again; I cannot find it in my heart to curse him as he merits. For Macgliskin, 'tis a sewer-rat of the Canongate ready to cut any throat or swear any man's life away."

"Glengarry could not do this of his own influence, Allan. Who stands behind him?"

"Ah! There we enter the shadow. But there is this to be told you, Darthula. You were wondering, no doubt, that I did not make Hector's delivery of Forbes at Culloden House avail to weigh the scales in his favour. Well, I dared not! I had late last night an express from the Lord President. He confesses to me—a sore confession for one in his position to make to one in mine!—that after all he discovers his credit is so shaken with Government that for him to intervene as witness in a rebel's favour, or even to intercede for mercy for him, were to doom the object of his appeal as surely as it would further weaken his own standing. 'Let Lord Brounhill intercede for his nephew,' he writes me here, 'for I, it is as certain as the Divine Providence that watches all our steps, can do the lad little good, and muckle harm.'" Allan folded up the letter.

"It is because Duncan Forbes had a heart to pity us poor Highland folk that he is now persecuted!" sighed Darthula.

"Aye; it is Cumberland that would hound him down. He watches him like a beast in ambush to spring upon him. So much I have long suspected, and now it is confirmed. Duncan Forbes is a broken reed for us. . . . Darthula, there is but one hope . . . it is bitter for you, but will you go and plead with Lord Brounhill? He is Cumberland's fast friend."

"Allan, I will be on my knees to my uncle at daybreak to-morrow."

4

It was so early in the morning when Darthula reached the great house, owned by one of the English judges, where her uncle was lodging in Queen Square, that the footman who opened the door was wearing an apron, and there was a maid with a feather brush dusting the big china vases in the corners of the hall.

It was scarcely a moment, however, before Jean came running down the stairs in her dressing-gown, her eyes reddened, her face deadly pale, and took her cousin in her arms.

She had not been allowed by her father to be present at the trial, but had been told the verdict and the sentence by him the night before. She understood at once what Darthula had come for, and said, "We will go to him together. He is still in his bedroom, but I know he is up and working, for I have been hearing the papers rustling since daylight."

They went up to the first floor together, Jean supporting Darthula with her arm round her waist; and after a tap at Lord Brounhill's door, Jean led her cousin straight in without waiting for his permission.

It was a fine, large room, with window-curtains of red damask, and contained a stately four-post mahogany bedstead draped in tasselled silk, a dressing table bearing a gilt mirror, a marble washstand with a basin and curved ewer, and several comfortably upholstered chairs. Seated by a little round table near the hearth, the Scottish judge, wrapped in a dull brown morning-robe, with his nightcap still on his head, seemed rudely incongruous with the splendour of his surroundings. Darthula noticed, as she entered, that his bed had not been slept in.

He raised his head from his work with a crackle of parchment, and stared unresponsively at the two girls. Darthula tried to speak, but her throat filled, her eyes overflowed, and mutely she fell on her knees holding out imploring arms to her uncle. Jean threw her arm protectively round her shoulders.

Lord Brounhill dropped the deed with the dangling red seal that he had been reading. "I expected ye wad come to me," he said abruptly, "but what boots it to be coming now? I advised ye baith at Glenmarisdale, now laid in ruins by your wickedness; I entreated you, Darthula, at Fort Augustus, you will scarcely have forgotten it, to take the hope of clemency held out by His Royal Highness. Ma gude offices were flung insolently back in ma face each time—what mair is there I can do? What will ye be hoping for now?"

"You," Darthula found a few choked words, "you . . . can . . . save him, uncle!" Lord Brounhill struck the table impatiently with his fist. "It is what I canna do. Nor I, nor ony man that breathes!"

"Will you be saying that, father?" cried Jean indignantly. "I ken you are no speaking truly! They have sentenced the poor lad, but they would never carry it out, if you would intercede for him. What ails you, father, that you hang back? I cannot make it out. Your brother's son, your own near kin,

Darthula's brother, my dear, dear cousin and playmate! And you could gain his life for us!"

Lord Brounhill stood up with a jerky motion. "If it were my ain son I couldna . . . and I wouldna!"

Darthula uttered a despairing cry, and Jean an exclamation of furious bewilderment.

"Do I hear you rightly, father? My ears must be deceivers! *You* cannot save him? Is there a man in this kingdom that the Duke of Cumberland will harken to more readily than yourself? There is not, by my way of it! What was it the Secretary of State said to me at dinner in his house last week? 'Your papa, my dear, is the Government of Scotland to-day, not I! What he says will be done, what he forbids will be left undone. I have only to affix the seal.' I ken well he was not speaking all in jest. Get you to His Royal Highness, father! Tell him Hector *must* be pardoned for your sake, and the boon will not be denied!"

Lord Brounhill walked the length of the splendid room and back, his head sunk forward between his hunched shoulders, his hands holding the skirts of his mean, old dressing-gown behind him. Then he turned to his daughter, and said calmly, "I will not obsecrate the pardon of this traitor, Jean."

Darthula sank in a heap upon the gaily-wreathed flowers of the carpet; Jean stood, pale and staring, her pretty mouth open.

"Do you think," continued the judge, "that I too have not bowels of compassion, and yearnings to save ma ain flesh and blood fra the hangman's rope . . . forbye the shame to our fam'ly of sic a base felon's end to its chief? But I stand here the living battlefield of a conflict o' duties, in the whilk reason, law, and the word o' God itsel' bid us follow the greater one and cleave to it rather than the lesser. 'If thy hand offend thee cut it off!' Judge ye, which is my greater duty—to the State and the commonweal, and their lawfully appointed head, or to the claims o' kinship, so small a part of a' that we maun give account for in the Last Day? It is the King hath placed the sword of justice in my unworthy hands, not for the advantage of my fam'ly, but for the *salus reipublicae!*"

"Father," pleaded Jean. "For once forget the judge! The Saviour will forgive you for erring once upon the side of compassion!"

"Will you teach me divinity, girl? I will gie you a lesson, then. 'The soul that sinneth, it shall die!'"

"The sin of Hector was the sin of youth and thoughtlessness, father!"

"It appeared otherwise at his trial yesterday."

Darthula struggled to her knees. "The court was abused by a wicked forgery, uncle! Hector never signed that letter to the Prince!"

"Are ye so sure, Darthula? I am no so sure . . . and I will not perjure mysel' in the court of conscience by saying I am sure."

"Who will be knowing better than yourself, uncle, that Hector never in his life, but once, signed 'Hacktor Mackeichen'? And from that one signature there is a villain, who brings shame upon the name of Highland Chief, hath forged his subscription to the letter that ruined him!"

Lord Brounhill's eyes went glassy. "What avails this advocacy, Darthula? It was all said yesterday in the court. There was nane to credit it then . . . nor do I now."

"You believe Hector was a plotter, father?" exclaimed Jean. "Fie upon you!"

"He plotted weel eneuch to hae the arms ready for our clan to rise in war against His Majesty! There his secret designs stood revealed! Darthula, you were aider and abettor, there! Had you delivered them to me on my demand,

I had perchance been inclined to credit your disclaimers to-day!"

"Bury the past, father! Let Hector live! He will never do harm again. Let them banish him! What mischief can he wreak from exile?"

"A muckle mischief, ye daft lass! While he lives, he is Chief of Clan Maceachan. No law of the Sassenachs can abolish his right to that title. And while he is Chief there will never be ony peace for Glenmarisdale, never ony recovery for our stricken lands. It will be waiting and plotting, sharpening claymores, not growing corn, writing letters of conjury overseas, not tending cattle to enrich our native valleys. Must Glenmarisdale remain for aye a hotbed of sedition and ruin for Scotland?"

"They will take the lands from us, we know," sobbed Darthula. "My loss! let them go, if only my brother lives!"

"Let them go!" exclaimed Lord Brounhill in an exasperated tone. "So ye wad be for handing over Glenmarisdale to the English? For the life of ane brainless callant, fit only to waste our substance at the gaming-table, ye wad pull down the line of the Sons of Hector, take our kingship from the lake, and efface our crest from the keep o' Glenmarisdale! May my soul be doomed if it iss I will be accomplishing the great betrayal! Jean, in your veins runs the blood of the Maceachans; you shall rule, and your son and your son's son in the House of our Fathers!"

"Hear you me, Father!" cried Jean, her face a sheet. "I will be the wife of Hector Maceachan or I will be no man's wife! Let you save him to be Father to our next Chief, or I will expire and be buried in his grave; or, if I must live, live on a withered maid!"

Her Father confronted her for a moment with his fists clenched. "And you will be rebelling, too, is it e'en sae?

Weel; there will be time to tame you, hizzie!"

He walked to the washstand and took off his gown. "You keep me fra the duties o' the day," he said peevishly. "I hae nae mair to say to the twain o' ye. If you would aid Hector, get you to your prayers!" He lifted the ewer and splashed water into the basin. "Bid Hector repent and seek the comforts o' religion!"

With a gesture of utter hopelessness, Jean lifted Darthula from the floor and helped her from the room. At the door Darthula for a moment broke from her grasp and took a step again towards her Uncle.

His back was away from her, as he stood at the washstand in his patched shirt and black knee-breeches, rubbing and wringing his fingers in the basin with the energy of a little wooden figure worked by a handle. . . . A look of horror came over his niece's face. She ran and left him alone in the gorgeous bedroom.

Chapter IV

LEAVE-TAKINGS

1

"You have an hour," said the turn-key to Darthula, with the usual shame-faced harshness of his calling, and his keys jangled and echoed as if shutting her into an eternity of confinement, as he left her inside Hector's cell. She was in her brother's clasp in a second, and it seemed to her she was embracing an armful of thistledown, so wasted was he with his illnesses and imprisonment. His arms that held her seemed like brittle twigs; and it was borne in upon her that they might have spared their labour of butchery upon the frail body doomed soon in the course of nature to the grave. Her tears brimmed over, defying her efforts to show courage. They fell in a veil that made a crystal star of the tallow-dip on the table, and hid the grim walls and barred window, beyond which the River Thames flowed blackly through the night.

Then she found herself crouching at Hector's knee, her tears falling on his hand, as he sat in the wooden arm-chair that had been granted as a concession to his weakness, a wistful smile on his face, while he fondled her coppery curls with their silver streakings.

"I am sorry, darling," she sobbed, seeking vainly to master herself, "sorry I must waste our time together like this!"

He bent and kissed her hair. "For why will you be distressing yourself, little sister? Are you not showing me your love, so precious . . . so little merited!"

"Ah! Hector! Hector! It is I have led you to this cruel end . . . with my wanton recklessness! And now it is you will be paying and I will be living. God of all the graces! It is not just!"

"Never say so, Darthula! That you live is what keeps me from madness!"

"My darling, my darling, I was your evil counsellor! . . . Yet, sorrow's me! what could I do? . . . It was the Prince who summoned us!"

"It was the Prince!" He smiled with a dim shadow of his old irony. "We have all of us sacrificed ourselves for a dream . . . but it was a dream that had a right to our loyalty. You know it is not I have ever valued overmuch the scrambling hazard they call life. Yet, did I value it more, like that old villain Lovat . . . or poor Mr. Evidence Murray . . . or worthy cousin Lochiel, who has better reason to do so than any . . . even then I am thinking I should not regret to have thrown it away for the illusion that is called honour."

"It is the empty word honour seems in this hour! Oh! Hector, my little, little boy, I want you, I want your limbs and your dear face and your smile . . . no shadowy praises of your valour will give those back to me!"

"Ghostly laurels seem indeed unsatisfying!" He picked up and dropped again the Prayer Book lying at his elbow upon the bare wooden table. "Yet we must be bending our brows to them!"

"Oh! if only *He* were here!" exclaimed Darthula wildly. "He could answer, he could show us! He would be making us a reality of all that now seems so unsubstantial, so worthless! He would give you courage, me consolation to endure!"

"I am not thinking," answered Hector, with a light, little laugh, "that I will be lacking in courage to face the . . . ceremony . . . of to-morrow morning. It will be another phantasy, for all I know, the importance of bearing a stout heart . . . but I am not sorry it possesses me."

"Yet if our Prince were here in the flesh, Hector, it would be added assurance, faith—"

"My dear! He is never there in the flesh when man or woman would lean upon him! What will that line of the ancients be Dr. Hay was wont to quote:

" '*Ter frustra comprensa manus effugit imago*.'

"I am not blaming him. He is as he was appointed to be by the smiling gods. And we have put our trust in an airy spirit!"

"No more than that, Hector?"

"What more can I say? Well, I will be saying this. That were he to come again to-morrow, and I free to fight for him and die for him, I would do again as I have done . . . and come to this same end. . . . Maybe I will, for what do the wise say, but that all things are upon a perpetual wheel, and come again . . . and come again . . . and always without fruit or profit."

He was silent for a moment, and she touched him from his reverie. "Hector, you have some last commands to lay upon me?"

"Must I be doing so? Well, well, I know, it is a custom for the dying to enjoin . . . and for the living to neglect the injunction laid upon them. . . . Nay, do not shrink. . . . Will I be a changed man, think you, Darthula, because to-morrow I must be hewn in quarters? . . . I fear rather my last words will be an attempt to make the hangman smile! . . . But at least I am serious in this, and if you will be making it my dying injunction, be it even so. . . . Darthula, I beg you, grant Allan Duncanson his heart's desire!"

"My sorrow! Is this the time I should be thinking of marrying myself?"

"It is the time," he said gravely. "Darthula, if you will harken to me with patience, here is what I most wished to say to you to-night. We have come thither by a roundabout path, but it will serve as well as any. Do you know what is to be the fate of Glenmarisdale?"

"It is little I know. They say the English will forfeit all our land to the Crown. Jean thinks her father aims to receive it back from Government as the reward of his betrayal, and to establish himself as Chief in your place."

"Then all are wrong! I know more than they. Brounie will *not* receive his reward. Glenmarisdale is to be sequestrated, and an administrator appointed. And the administrator will be Allan Duncanson. He knows what he may not yet make public, and hath imparted it to me. Brounie has overreached himself; Cumberland begins to weary of his insistences and to doubt he may be setting up another Pretender in the Highlands, if he yields to all his demands. Poor Brounie! He reasoned close and he reasoned wrong. He could not save me, he reckoned, and the lands too. If I should live, they would be taken from the family. . . . He chose the lands, for the sake of the family. Now it is he will lose all . . . and Glengarry, too, who hoped for his slice of the cake! For, look you, there is Duncan Forbes, honest Duncan! who bears me a good will for preserving him into what seems like to be a sour old age. He is not yet so far fallen from grace that he cannot give a secret pull to the wires of the St. James's puppet-show. He will have been in counsel with Maccallum More, Allan's Chief and patron. They two are still a pair of pretty men in a combat political! There seems little doubt: Allan will be administrator of Glen-

marisdale. . . . Darthula! Allan's wife . . . *she* can bind
up the wounds and soften the lot of my people! I would be
departing with a free and happy mind if I thought I had left
them that much redress for all I have brought upon them."

"Oh! Hector, you do not know what you are asking—"

"My grief! Will you still be dreaming of being a Queen?"

She shook her head. "I am not mad. But if He should
come again—"

"That he will never."

"I am pledged to await him."

"In maidenhood? I am thinking that would be an odd vow
indeed! Come, Darthula, be frank! You had ever a *tendre*
for dear Allan to whom I am owing so much!"

She wavered. "If he took me, after all, he would have to
be understanding—"

"He would be understanding without any particular caution that if he took you, he would be taking a child of the
storm, be anchoring his barque to the floating isle of St.
Brendan, be making a snare to hold quicksilver. . . . In
brief, I believe it is Darthula Maceachan he loves, and not
some patron cut to the measure of the precepts!"

"Hector, dear, I can be making no promise—"

"I am not seeking a promise. Say only you will weigh well
my desire, and I will die content!"

She gave a cry. "Oh, Hector, you are to die; you are to
die! I can be thinking of nothing else . . . and there is
nothing else in the ways of the world that matters. . . .
Hector, my own, my darling, I cannot endure it. . . . Will
they not let me die by your side to-morrow?"

"Hush, little sister! We have but a small piece of our hour
left to us, do not you be squandering it! . . . Nay now, do
not scream . . . each second is worth more than gold!
Come you upon my knee now, your arms round my neck,
so! . . . Sing me, very low, one of your songs! It shall do

better than a priest's dirge to waft your brother into the Realm Unknown. Sing, Darthula, sing!"

Three times she vainly tried to gratify the longing in his voice. Then there came flowing from her the words of her last song, her lament for Neil the son of the Bard:

"Split is the sapling, by flame from the clouds,
   Amid the green-glancing boughs of the forest its brown leaves
      hang shrivelled.
They have smitten thy youth, while the gnarled oaks stand
      rooted in pride;
And all the Glen laments with the tears of eventide . . ."

Her voice gave way, and she lay sobbing on Hector's breast.

"That is a sad song for a dying man," he said gently. "Let us now be thinking of happier things. . . . We are in our little boat on the loch, drifting together while the day dies in the water, and peace falls from the hills into our hearts. . . . Be still now! We are on the peak of Fraoch Bheinn, with the world and its turmoils far below, and the clouds that turn their silvery edge to kiss us as they pass. . . . For we are only two children, you and I, a ragged boy and girl who will ever be tearing our clothes . . . and we do not dream what trouble we will one day be making for the great ones of the earth, we who intended so little evil to any! . . . We are knowing only that we are together, and having each other, have all in the world that is. . . . Darthula, my little mother, do you not think the time will come when we shall be that again, just children, happy in each other's love? . . . Sometimes I am wishing I had never read Davy Hume . . . but what is the matter for that? Naught can take the past days from us, my dear. . . . We have had our dream . . . and what will there be but dreams in this life or another?"

Darthula shook in his tight embrace as the key clashed in

the door. Raising her tear-bedewed face from his wet shoulder, she saw the turn-key standing with uninterested face regarding them. "Time for the young 'ooman to go," he said. "I have brought the gemman to the foot of the stairs to take her."

"Mr. Duncanson?" asked Hector, rising. "That does my heart good! Darthula, before we part, promise me this one thing . . . you will not be tempted, will you, to come . . . to . . . the place?"

She was making incoherent, sobbing sounds, which he hoped were her pledge not to be present at his execution. He knew of Jacobite wives and sisters who had faced even this ordeal, and he would protect her, if by any means he could, from its ghastliness.

He took her in his arms, and kissed her pale, drenched cheeks with the passion of all his life that was slipping from him now so fast; her eyes were closed. "Take her, jailer," he sobbed, breaking down at the last, "take her! . . . Gently, man, as you ever hoped for a kindly hand! . . . Give her to the gentleman below . . . it is he will be caring for her now!"

2

THE night wore on, and a deeper silence fell upon the ancient prison by the darkly running river. The jingle of keys grew rarer in the stone corridors, and at length only the cries and footfalls of the sentinels, in the courts, by the Jewel House and on the ramparts, broke the stillness. From the City nearby the clocks in Wren's new steeples made meditative answer to each other, as they spoke the small hours of the morning. Night trembled away in shadow; the river changed to a grey sheet; and the dim shapes of roofs appeared along its banks.

Then from the eastern marshes, in a glittering ball, the sun rose behind the pepper-pot turrets of the Tower, and woke the stagnant water in the moat. It lit the golden orb of the Monument, gleamed on the white classical spires, and bathed the swell of Paul's dome in purple light. Colour crept into the ancient houses on London Bridge, into the mediæval huddle of Southwark on the farther shore, into the crowded roofs of St. Stephen's and the fresh-looking Abbey towers below the curve at Westminster. Here and there a climbing-boy, like a negro imp, peeped out from a City chimney. Clamour swirled up from the markets at Smithfield and Billingsgate. In the still slumbering West End, maids in mob caps cleaned the door-steps of the Squares.

Immense, the dome of St. Paul's now overhung the stirring City in the blue of an unclouded April morning. The shutters clanged as the 'prentices took them down; wheels began to rumble on the cobbles; the painted shop-signs made a carnival of the streets. Over the crimson towers of St. James's Palace the Royal Standard flew, and a troop of periwigged Horse Guards moved with a glint of steel through the trees on the Mall. The blue Surrey Hills, the wooded heights round Hampstead, the leafy lanes of Knightsbridge and Kensington sent country messages up the ways of the small, red-brick capital.

Now the City roared with midday business. Crowds thronged the Exchanges, the coffee-houses, the taverns. The voices of street-singers and vendors, the bells of handcarts blended deafeningly with the smack of whips, the clangour of hoofs and wheels at the foot of the brooding Dome. In Hyde Park the horsemen bowed to the flutter of hats and ribbons on the paths; through St. James's the painted sedan-chairs swung sedately; in Mayfair the flunkeys lounged at the doors of the mansions, their eyes on the equipages rolling past in splendour of hammer-cloths and liveries. Underneath the pillared spire of St. Giles's-in-the-Fields a half-naked population of paupers, prostitutes and criminals quarrelled and blasphemed round the sculpture of the Last Judgment at the churchyard gates.

And as the afternoon drew on, with prattle lightly falling in Chinese drawing-rooms, and fiddlers beginning to scrape in rural pleasure-gardens, through all that network of squalid alleys, through the fetid rabbit-warren of the Seven Dials, through the fever-infected rags and worn boots hanging outside the Monmouth Street clothes-shops, there boomed hoarse voices that pierced the din of chaffering and disputation:

"Last dyin' speech and ballad of the dangerous Scotch rebel executed on Kennin'ton Common this mornin'! . . . Last dyin' speech and ballad! . . . Last speech of the Scotch rebel!"

3

Two evenings later, as the sun was setting in clouds prescient of coming rain, the butler at the house in Queen Square put his head out of the front doors and looked up the square towards its open northern end, where the spire of Hampstead rose over the fields. "Is that Scotch beggar still hanging around, 'Dolphus?" he asked the footman in the wicker-chair inside the hall.

"I haven't looked, Mr. Prentiss," answered Adolphus, coming lazily out of his chair. "Lawst time I see 'im he was leaning up against ahr railings."

"Why, o' God's name, must he choose *our* railings?" asked Mr. Prentiss testily. "Yes, there he is, sure enough, the ruffian! Still, we can't turn him off the public pavement, I persoom."

The two flunkeys were staring at what looked like a bundle of rags rather than a man, propped in a huddled heap against the area railings at the north corner of the house. "Wears the Scotch dress, too!" said the butler with a sniff. "As if that wasn't warrant enough for taking him to Bow Street. The impidence!"

"If that's a tawtan," sniggered Adolphus, "I'd say it was the clan of Macmud! I never did see sich a rig-out! Mr. Prentiss," he drew himself up to his six-foot, "shall I take my cane and drive the beggar away?"

"Best be careful, my lad," the butler checked him. "You never know what you're dealing with when it comes to the Scotch. Lord Brounhill might not be best pleased."

" 'Is lordship don't love the Scotch, that I *will* say."

"But he's a Scotchman, nevertheless, Adolphus!" The butler tapped his pocket.

"Here comes the kerridge!" said the footman, and hastened to throw open the doors.

From the coach which the English judge had courteously put at the disposal of his guests, Jean was descending in black with a mourning veil.

As she came slowly up the steps there was a sudden scuffle at their foot. The tattered Scotsman in the plaid of undistinguishable colours, so stained and faded was its pattern, had come running towards her, and been caught in the arms of six-foot Adolphus. The butler came down the steps waving an outraged hand.

"What is all this?" demanded Jean in a flat voice, raising her veil and showing a white face with reddened eyes. "Is the man a beggar?"

The starved-looking scarecrow thrust Adolphus against the railings with a sweep of one long arm, and eyed Jean inquiringly from deep-sunk grey orbs. "Will you pe Mishtress Jean Maceachan?" he demanded in a hoarse voice.

"I am. How comes it you know my name?" she answered coldly. "You are a Scot, are you not?"

"Aye, and she waas thinking a Hieland shentleman, efen if she waas not kin to you, might pe looking for a petter welcome at your hands, cousin!"

"Cousin!"

"The impidence!" said Mr. Prentiss.

"Be hoff with you!" menaced Adolphus, rubbing the back of his powdered head.

"She will pe Angus Maceachan of Maol."

"Maol! That is one of Glenmarisdale's farms, is it not?" asked Jean, restraining the servants.

"It is. She will pe ta tacksman, and foster-brother to Himself."

Jean curtsied. "A thousand pardons, Maol. I did not recognise you. Will you come in and take some refreshment?"

Angus smiled wanly. "Herself will pe glad of a dish of brose! It will pe two days syne she waas laast eating!"

"And how came you to London?" asked Jean.

"On ta shoes," he pointed at his raw toes wryly, "and then on ta feet. Ta stones will pe harder than ta heather on ta Hielant man's feet."

"Come inside, cousin, now, and rest yourself!"

The ragged creature stiffened his back, and darted a furious gleam from his sunken eyes at the butler. "Will you not pe first dishgraacing and punishing this rogue that waas for peating a shentleman, your kinsman?"

"These are not my servants, Maol. Take my apologies on their behalf."

Angus swept off his tattered wisp of a bonnet with dignity. Then he took her hand and kissed it.

She led the way into a little downstairs parlour and closed the door.

"Where," he asked her at once, "will she pe finding his sister, Mishtress Darthula?"

"Angus," said Jean, "some good friends took her away to Edinburgh it is now three nights gone. . . . In mercy they would not let her pass in London the dawn that was to see"—her voice shook—"that was to see. . . . Oh! cousin!" she sobbed, "your Chief—"

"Aye. What of Himself? She waas here to preak ta London tolbooth and release him, if you will show ta way to ta place!"

"Oh! Angus!" she sobbed, "it is too late. You come too late!"

He staggered back, his wearied knees sagging, at the look on her face. "What is t'at you will pe telling me?" he gasped.

"The son of Hector was hanged and beheaded by the English three mornings gone."

The Highlander gave a yelp like a hurt hound, then fell upon his knees on the carpet, clasping his head in his bony hands and rocking himself to and fro with hoarse, moaning noises.

The butler appeared in the doorway with a tray containing a decanter of sherry and biscuits. Jean took it from him and motioned him away, shutting the door firmly on his blatant curiosity.

As the door closed Angus, who had been wiping his eyes on a corner of his ragged and defaced plaid, sprang up like a stag. "She will pe raising the bones of Himself and bringing them home to Glenmarisdale," he thundered. "Where will his grave pe?"

Jean made a despairing gesture. "I know not where his body is buried," she answered. "But his head, ah! his dear head, cousin, they have set over their city gates for a sign of derision!"

Angus uttered a furious Gaelic oath; his hollow cheeks turned purple. He clapped his hands to the places where

his sword and dirk should have been. "And she unarmed!"
he said simply.

A sudden light burned in Jean's reddened eyes. "Will
you . . . Angus . . . will you take down his head with me
and give it burying? Oh, cousin, I have been unable to sleep
for dreaming of that dreadful thing. . . . I ken well I will
never sleep while that barbarity continues. Hector, my love,
oh! my love; let them take me and kill me too. But you shall
not stay there in the burning sun and bitter rain to be their
mock and triumph! Will you take him down, Angus, will
you? I will come with you and lend aid. Oh! I know I am
not brave like Cousin Darthula; I am not strong as she is, but
I will not leave my beloved there, if it costs my head. . . .
Angus, will you?"

"Will she?" The Highlander snorted contemptuously.
"Let us pe going at once, cousin." His face fell. "Woe's
me! Where shall she pe finding weapons to slay ta guards?"
He stretched out his long arms. "Her hands will pe all she
haas, and they enough!"

Jean shook her head and put her finger to her lips. "It is
not to be done by violence, Angus. It must be effected at
night and by craft. You must climb Temple Bar . . . can
you do it? You are a craigsman, and you can climb anything, can you not? It will be my part to keep watch that
you are not surprised . . . and to receive his dear remains
under my cloak." She took a step nearer to him, her eyes
still burning fiercely, a red spot on each haggard cheek. "It
will grow no easier with waiting and thinking, forbye that
my father, the judge, Angus, will be from home to-night.
Will you do it to-night?"

"Will she pe doing it to-night?" he nodded with a black
melancholy that had something fatalistic in it.

"Then drink now—but not too much, Angus! refresh

yourself, while we make our plans. Later you shall dine before we set out, for you will be needing all your strength. You must not wear those clothes either. I will find you a coat and breeches; there is one friendly footman here will lend them to me. Oh! Angus, I am sore, sore afraid. . . . But we will do it to-night, together!"

A swish of raindrops beat suddenly against the window.

"It will be a wild night!" exclaimed Jean exultantly. "The better for our design, thank God! The streets will be empty."

4

THE same rain, driven by soft breezes from the west, was hissing, as night deepened, upon the façade of Temple Bar, spotting in their niches the stone faces of the two Stewart Charleses who had sat upon the British throne, and drumming upon the window of the perruquier's shop niched like a bird's nest among the upper curves of the arch. There was displayed human hair on blocks, as it were in ribald parody of the ghastly relics that stood overhead, dispersing their revengeful infection into the neighbouring windows of the narrow street.

There, facing the Sunset Isles, waited Lord Lovat, his mouth twisted dolefully awry, his pendulous cheeks withering. There waited Hector Maceachan of Glenmarisdale, his eyes closed and the old half-ironical, half-melancholy smile upon his pale lips; while on the third spike hung a decaying tuft, relic of a Jacobite gentleman whose head had been blown away to roll in the kennel months ago. There they waited patiently in the shimmering rain-mist, amid the stench of the running gutters, the gleam of the infrequent yellow lamps on patches of wet, uneven paving below. Beaten upon by the same western rain that was at the moment shrouding their native valleys and veiling their native peaks in mist, they waited for their time to be accomplished.

Now the wooden giants on the clock of St. Dunstan's-in-the-West hammered two strokes. The last lamps in the street had long since been extinguished; the aged watchman on duty at the Gate, after a last glance up the deserted roadway to the city, swept still by the slanting lances of the rain, had retired an hour ago to join his comrade sleeping in the hutch beneath the arch, and was now snoring, too, with his head wrapped in a handkerchief. From a dark court in the Strand two shadows stole out, a woman cloaked and hooded, and a tall, lithe man wearing the clothes of a lower servant in an English household, who stood for a few moments staring up at the unwonted pinnacle he must scale. The downpour had yielded by now to intermittent showers, between which a watery moon gave pale glimmers between the clouds; and it was to take advantage of one of these intervals of light that Angus Maceachan had emerged at this moment to attempt his task.

Fortunately for him the sculptured stone Gate, with its tall, central archway across the road, flanked by lesser arches for pedestrians on the pavements, was closely built about by the adjoining houses, the garrets and roofs of which had, as it were, encrusted themselves upon it. The practised eye of the mountaineer soon detected in a gleam of the fitful moon a narrow crack btween the outer masonry of the left-hand arch and the wall of the house nearest it. Up this, as if it were a mountain chimney, he thought he could raise himself by back and knee bracing to the flat stone roof of the minor arch, the first stage of the ascent. Removing his coat, stockings, and shoes, he bade Jean keep her ear to the keyhole of the closed wooden gates, to listen for any stirring by the watchmen within, and at once began his climb.

Without interruption and without great difficulty he

gained the platform over the side arch. Thence a curved piece of ornamental scroll-work, like a gigantic stone snail, reached a great part of the way to the summit of the elaborate structure, faced with Corinthian pilasters and adorned with the royal statues, over the great central arch. Up this scroll Angus clambered as though it had been a spine of rock, and thence made a step to the capital of the nearest pilaster, the stone acanthus leaves of which, though slippery from the rain, gave his bare toes foothold, while his hands gripped the projecting lower line of the cornice over the statues. From here it was a simple pull-up to the cornice itself.

There he crouched a moment, listening and peering downwards. He planned next to work his way to the right along the ledge he had reached until he arrived at the carved wreaths and cornucopias embellishing the square moulding that rose from the centre of the cornice to its sloping roof. Abruptly, however, he was checked by the sight of Jean waving a warning arm from below before she ran noiselessly into the shadow of the right-hand arch. The next moment he heard the grating sound of the gates being unlocked from within, and writhing his way in among the floral sculpture lay there as still as if he were part of the hewn stone himself. In answer, he fully believed, to his fervid prayer, a cloud passed at that moment over the moon.

The decrepit guardian of the gate put his head out, to be greeted by a spatter of rain-drops. Angus heard him grumbling to himself, "D——n the rats! D——n the vermin! . . . Gr-r-r-cha!" he snarled loudly, to frighten the fancied disturbers of his slumbers; and then, after a minute more of listening, withdrew to shelter, locking the gate again.

Angus lost no more time. Over the top of the moulding he scrambled perilously, using his cat's eyes in the dark, and lay breathless from his late alarm upon the slope of the roof. As the moon again parted the clouds he glanced swiftly up

Fleet Street and down the Strand. There was no one in sight either way; he could discern only the tiny female figure just underneath him, now patiently at its watch again. On his hands and knees he crawled with caution along the curve of the roof, slimy as it was with the wet; saluted the head of Simon Fraser as he crept past it, and laid his hand upon the iron pole bearing Hector Maceachan. Rising to his feet, with his bald skull glistening in the moonrays, he lifted his chief's head with a gesture of ceremonial dignity by its dank, soot-begrimed locks from the spike; then, reaching down prostrate over the rim of the cornice, let it fall gently, as arranged between them, into the outspread cloak of the girl below.

Jean did not flinch as she received the bitter fruit dropping from the cruel tree. With a quiet reverence she undid the strings of the large velvet bag, hitherto dedicated to her own vanities, which she had prepared for the reception of her lover. Then, before laying the head inside, she wiped the streaming countenance and kissed the marbled lips. A few minutes later, taking Angus Maceachan's arm without a word as he rejoined her after descending the way he had come, she walked sedately away with him along the Strand.

Beyond St. Clement Danes another old watchman peeped out at them from the cover of his box. He gazed incuriously at the small hooded woman walking past on the arm of a tall fellow dressed like a servant, and carrying a large velvet bag on her arm. He wondered that they walked so slowly through the rain which had now set in once more with violence. They might, he thought, as he withdrew yawning into his hutch again, be mutes pacing at a funeral.

The two went on together thus in silence, dwindling figures that moved towards the West.

EPILOGUE

THE WRAITH—1753

1

THE raw March weather had turned clammy at midday, and at the fall of evening a slight haze had veiled the lower parts of Edinburgh. Counsellor Penicuik pulled up the windows of his sedan and drew his muffler round his throat. Susceptibility to rheums was a mark, he recognised, of advancing age; so was the unwelcome fact that he was often compelled out of fatigue to hire chairs to carry him about—as this evening to his favourite tavern at the foot of Leith Wynd by the little gate giving on to the sea-road; and so was the most unwelcome fact of all that he often found life dull in these days.

There seemed to him in truth to be very little life of any kind in Edinburgh now, and it was very hard to get material for his anecdotage. Indeed he was so often compelled to fall back now on ancient stories that once or twice he had seen people looking at him as if they knew what was coming. And often the story he wanted to tell he would forget when the moment came. Aye, these were dull days beyond doubt. Not that he wanted a return of such times as they had known in "forty-five"—things had then been too close to a bloody stramash for his taste. Wonderful how all that business had been forgotten! . . . He was not, he chuckled, the only person in Edinburgh who seemed to have a poor memory. . . . A bloody stramash in sooth, sirs, and nothing had come out of it but the black snuff to which he still remained addicted. . . . It had done the Young Person himself little good, if rumours were to be trusted. The bottle and the life of a conspirator hunted by all the spies of the Continent had made sair havoc of him this last six years—by all they told.

If Government had had longer memories, he reflected, while the chair lurched down the steep, rough lane outside the Netherbow, some people would not have the sufficiency to show their faces boldly in Scotland as they did to-day. There was an acquaintance of the Counsellor's lately returned from the north was ready to swear he had seen that Dr. Cameron in Inversnaid. If he was flisking about the Highlands it was no doubt with the intent of stirring trouble, if he could. What was quite certain was that this very morn Mr. Penicuik himself had been accosted in the Lawnmarket in broad daylight by Young Glengarry, smiling and swaggering in his gay clothes as if there were no Tolbooth a few yards away to engulf him. Well, that was Government's concern! Certainly the young man had been much improved by his years in France. He had lost the touch of the Hieland cateran in his speech and manner, and was quite the fine gentleman. Mr. Penicuik had been pleased with his manners.

The chair stopped outside a ramshackle house with a lantern glimmering through dimmed glass outside the door. There was a sea-tang in the haze that had crawled up from Leith. It was perhaps the eccentricity of age that made the Counsellor pass his evenings now in this rather mean resort known as Hugh Mackie's. But it had its merits in Mr. Penicuik's opinion. The appointments might be mean, but there was no place where they gave you fresher oysters, fried a collop to a neater turn, or could serve a better glass of brandy (Mr. Penicuik preferred not to think how this excellent French brandy came to their cellar). Moreover, the company was always entertaining in its variety. There would be, as everywhere, two or three of his own profession, Writers who attended the affairs of shippers and traders at Leith. There would be sea-captains often, with tales that needed a lot of snuff to help them down, Hieland drovers and cattlemen, a grave merchant or two who had walked up from Leith or down from the High Street, perhaps a party of fashionable young bucks priding themselves on their knowledge of Edinburgh by-ways and taste for good liquor, in brief, an odd and variegated company that helped to while away evenings intolerably lonely to the old man in his own chambers.

Mr. Penicuik climbed out of the sedan, and stood for a moment peering at the grizzled chairman while he fumbled for his change. His ancient face had shrunk away till it seemed all beak and eyes.

"There, Ned Burke," he said at last. "There are twa, three bawbees additional, to buy yourself a dram. But yin alane, mind ye! Dinna be drinking mair, and getting yoursel' into trouble, ye daft Hielander!"

"She will pe keeping hersel' fra trouble!" answered Ned with a grin, broadening his speech to amuse his venerable patron. "She waas not so young, now, Counsellor! A gude nicht to ye!"

He picked up the poles, with the youth he was training as his assistant following behind, and went back at leisured pace up the uneven wynd, absent-mindedly humming a stave.

> " 'But a' to no end,
> For the times will neffer mend,
> Till the King shall enjoy his own again!' "

He recollected himself, glanced round nervously, and went on his way with sobriety.

Mr. Penicuik entered the humble tavern and blinked round in the thick atmosphere of pipes and smoke from the fire where the cooking was going on. The long, low-browed room, stretching back from the wynd, was full as usual, since the place had become fashionable with the knowing ones; and Mr. Penicuik perceived, as he had done several times lately, the one feature he did *not* like about Hughie Mackie's. It was what he might have called, if the expression had then been common, an odour of *police*. They could not trick an old lawyer like himself. He knew the three fellows at the table behind the door who never even sipped their mugs of porter were spies. No doubt there was justification for the way they haunted Mackie's. Among the clamjamfrey there might well be smugglers as well as honest traders; the Hieland cattle-drovers might number also cattle-stealers. French secret service men occasionally slipped in and out of Edinburgh from Leith, dangers to the State even in peace-time, and possibly some of the poor crazed Jacobites might now and again be found flitting to and fro—hoping for God knew what! Still, Mr. Penicuik doubted if the landlord was any more pleased than he was by the presence of those fellows with their hard mouths and elaborately nondescript appearance occupying one of his snuggest corner-tables.

There was a fourth of the kidney, too, to-night, by the chimney corner—these rogues always seized the best seats—a tall fellow with a black wig and the longest nose the Counsellor had ever seen in his life, a bit conspicuous for a spy, Mr. Penicuik thought; and this creature had actually had the sufficiency to take the day's copy of the *Courant*, which the

Counsellor began every night by reading—an economy that added sensibly to the attraction of Hughie Mackie's—and looked like holding on to it, too!

Mr. Penicuik sighed, and finding a seat at a table, ordered half a dozen oysters in a rather peevish voice. The agents by the door kept looking at him, he thought, and that irritated him, also.

Suddenly the doors opened again, and in walked with an air of unfamiliarity, but with complete self-assurance, a most unexpected arrival. It was Mr. Allan Duncanson, Administrator of the Crown Estates of Glenmarisdale in Inverness-shire, an imposing-looking man now that he had added a little stoutness to his height. Mr. Penicuik, who had so far recognised no acquaintance in the tavern, rose with alacrity and signalled to Allan to take a place beside him.

"You are a stranger at Hughie Mackie's I'll uphaud you, Mr. Duncanson," he said, holding out his snuff-box with a glint of his old curiosity in his eyes. "Now, what, may I be bauld to ask, brings you amang us the nicht? Gin I may be your counsellor, I wad advise you order a glass o' their auld brandy for the gude o' the house."

Mr. Duncanson complied, and then said with his grave smile, "'Tis true I am a stranger to this house. But I am trysted with a cattleman who drives a big business 'twixt the Highlands and Edinburgh. I hope to persuade him to take some of my Glenmarisdale herds, the best stock, I make bold to think, in Inverness-shire to-day, if he will pay my price. He is rather a rough fellow to be introducing into my home, so I bade him name his own trysting-place."

"And how does your gude lady?"

"Why, very well, I thank you, Counsellor."

"And the bairn?"

"Stronger. My master makes flesh at last."

"That is a gude sign, too!"

"Aye. We were greatly fearing we would lose him in his first year. Now he has turned the corner." Allan looked around. "Is not that Herries the Writer from Leith yonder?" he asked. "I was wishful to speak a word with him when I found him. Will you excuse me, Counsellor?"

Mr. Penicuik nodded as he swallowed an oyster, and Allan Duncanson crossed the narrow room to accost the Writer.

Mr. Penicuik, while he dipped his beak into his mug of porter, reflected on the vicissitudes of the House of Glenmarisdale. The young Chief perished on the scaffold up to London—a sair tale that, sirs!—my lord Brounhill, who should have succeeded in the natural order, robbed of his heritage by his nephew's sedition, and dead so suddenly two years syne. Over his desk in Advocates' Close they had found him, with his heart stopped, mid-way in a memorial to the Secretary of State supporting a plea for pardon of a sorry wretch convicted of murder. The fact, Counsellor Penicuik remembered, had been pretty clear, but there had been a doubtful point of law to which Lord Brounhill when he died had been directing attention.

If you would have Mr. Penicuik's opinion, the learned judge's heart had stopped years before when he saw his hopes of succeeding to Glenmarisdale crumble, and when his daughter had refused to live with him longer, staying at Brounhill when he was in Edinburgh, with an aunt in Edinburgh when her father was at Brounhill. Always in mourning she went, and had gained the face of an old maid before she was five and twenty. Mr. Penicuik had puzzled a lot over the mystery of that family quarrel. For Lord Brounhill's political downfall, Mr. Penicuik believed that douce Duncan Forbes had worked it, together with Maccallum More, before he died.

There was only one member of that luckless family had come into safe harbourage, the daftest of them all, the girl

Darthula. Now if all the ins and outs of *her* story could be traced . . . Mr. Penicuik chuckled sardonically, and ordered a second mug of porter and six more oysters. Some said she had been mistress to the Pretender's son, but Mr. Penicuik ventured to doubt that, sirs! Allan Duncanson of Inveralsk would be no buyer of soiled linen. But there was no doubt that the young woman had gone clean gyte in "forty-five"—so had many another. She was fortunate in having suffered neither exile nor imprisonment, and in being married to one of the most rising men of the day.

Aye, she was very lucky and had best keep quiet now and busy herself with her husband and her baby. . . . It was odd, by Mr. Penicuik's way of it, that they should have chosen to make their home in Lord Brounhill's old chambers in Advocates' Close. But they were doubtless convenient, and Mr. Duncanson was not the man to believe in bogles. . . . Would that fellow with the long nose *never* have done with the *Courant*? He was a singularly ill-favoured rogue, with his thick eyebrows and swart chin, as he sat reading and sipping brandy.

As Mr. Penicuik disposed of the last oyster of the second batch, two friends of his entered, and after greetings proposed a game of cartes. All three retreated to a quiet corner to play. It was getting late hours for Edinburgh, and the tavern was emptying. The secret service men behind the door, however, did not stir.

2

ALLAN DUNCANSON got up from his place with a yawn, and strolled over to the fireplace, now deserted, for the landlord and his wife had gone into a back room to get their own suppers. The clock on the wall was pointing close to eleven, and the Highland cattleman had not kept his tryst. Allan wondered if he meant to break it as they so often did.

As he stood rocking on his heels, and gazing in boredom round the room, he heard a queer little slapping noise close to his elbow. He turned and saw that the dirty-looking rogue with the long nose who had been perched in the chimney-corner had moved to a small table nearby, where he was sitting alone with a half-empty decanter of brandy beside him, and playing with a pack of cards, which he took up, shuffled, spread in fans and threw down upon the table again.

Suddenly he looked up at Allan. "You were observing my cartes, sir? They are unusual in your country, are they not?"

Allan had in truth been idly noticing their brilliance and the queer figures painted upon them. "I am indeed unacquainted with that game," he said with brief courtesy.

"Let me explain it." The stranger pointed to the chair opposite himself, and Allan, he hardly knew why, found himself compliantly sitting down at the table in face of him. "This is *tarot*," said the stranger in a voice much more agreeable than his looks. "One wearies, sir, of the old game of king and knave. Here," he made another bright-coloured fan of the cards, "here are all the notabilities of this world and the next! Look!" He slapped down a carte before Allan's eyes. "There is the Devil!" He shuffled and produced another. "There is the Pope! And—" he dropped the pack, leant forward over the table on his elbows, and thrust his face right into the astonished lawyer's, so that he almost touched him with his long nose. "I think," he said in an almost soundless voice without appearing to move his lips, "*I think you know the Third!*"

Allan sat as if there were cobbler's wax in the seat of his chair. He did not know how the miracle had been worked; how the bleary-looking eyes turned to a deep, defiant blue, how under the black wig, the wax nose, the soot-smeared chin, there appeared in an instant a face he knew only too well—a face he had seen entering the gateway of Holyrood-house between saluting Highland sentries, riding at the head of an army through King's Park on the way to Gladsmuir, white and agonised in the last flurry of Culloden as the Argyll-men burst through the broken walls. He only sat stupidly staring, while cold drops came through his periwig and gleamed on his forehead.

"Do not glare so!" said Charles Edward in the same dead voice. "Those are secret service trusties over by the door. They are not hunting me but Archie Cameron; yet you may put a thought even into their thick heads."

Allan glanced over his shoulder. A ship's officer snored at one table. At another Mr. Penicuik and his companions played languid whist. He heard the Counsellor's voice. "'A pair of sorry rogues that have come from overseas to levy war upon oor Sovereign lord, King George,'" he tittered. The Administrator of Glenmarisdale gulped and then whispered hoarsely, "Why do you betray yourself to *me*?"

"Needs must," Charles tapped the horned card on the table, "when this gentleman drives. It is a fortunate chance meeting you, and you will have to help me, Mr. Duncanson."

"Help you, Monsieur?" whispered Duncanson savagely back. "Do you not comprehend that it is my duty to hand you over immediately to yon officers, if they be officers indeed."

"Oh, they are that!" answered Charles Edward lightly, spreading a hand of cards before him. "Make as if we were gaming together. . . . I do not think you will hand me over, Mr. Duncanson, because—here I play a Queen—you would be the unhappiest husband in Scotland for ever if you did!"

Allan groaned, and the Prince winked angrily at him to desist. It was curious to see the quenching of his former dignity in the arts and little tricks of the conspirator. As

Duncanson fell silent, miserably fingering the gay, mocking cards, he poured out a full glass of brandy from the decanter and drained it.

"What do you wish of me, Monsieur?" asked Allan at length.

"First, a place of refuge for the night. Then that you will be so good as walk to Leith to the *Ship* tavern, and look discreetly about for the Doctor. He was to have *rendez-voused* with me here and has perhaps mistaken the place of assignation. Unless, indeed," a troubled look came into his eyes, "some mischance has befallen him in Inversnaid on the way hither."

"I will *not* be your accomplice," said Allan furiously.

Charles gave a faint shrug of his shoulders. "I cannot compel you. But I would remind you, sir, that by declining this errand you may be knotting the rope for your own wife's cousin . . . as by declining to shelter me you will be guilty of high treason—in *her* sight."

He looked across the table with an almost spiteful glower in his darkened eyes. "I would not stand in your shoes when she gives you that look. And she shall know, depend upon it, Mr. Whig!"

Allan returned his glance with hate. The conspiratorial impudence in his glance stripped him of any vestige of royal glamour in Duncanson's eyes; he could trace the dissipation in the face below the mask. But the lawyer in Allan knew when the time had come to compromise.

"If I shelter you this night, will you pledge your word of hon—" he shuddered. "Will you give me a promise to leave Edinburgh the morn?"

"I am not used to be given orders." The Prince poured another glass. "In the morning we will have a conference . . . the three of us. . . ."

"No, by G——, Monsieur."

"You, I and your lady wife!" Charles looked at him with contemptuous malice dancing in his eyes, and drank another glass; his voice thickened a little. "We will decide the future then. . . . I may wish to return to France in the morning; more likely I will not. . . . There are great plans afoot . . . not for you to know, however, Mr. Whig!"

Allan Duncanson sat in hell. Unrolled in dreary panorama he saw the long cavalcade of "forty-five" passing again . . . this time with only one possible ending for Darthula and himself.

Charles pushed the glass over with an unsteady hand towards him. "Better take a dram," he said insolently. "They tell me you Whigs drink only whey. You will not get through your night's work, my fine fellow, on that tipple! . . . Cut the cards, d——n you! They are looking at us from the doorway.

Allan Duncanson rallied himself. He removed the decanter to his side of the table. "You will not leave here unbound, Monsieur, if you continue on *this* drink." He leaned across. "Now hear me, sir! I will give you the key to the private door of my lodging in Advocates' Close on one condition. You will pledge your word as Prince . . . you *are* a Prince still, remember . . . not to confer with my wife till I return, but wait in silence in my study."

"If she sees me!"

"Sustain your disguise! . . . But she need not. Pledge me your word to that . . . or I leave you now to your friends by the door . . . whatever the consequences."

Charles looked keenly at him. "*Touché!*" he said. "I, too, know when to yield. We will talk it out in the morning. You have my word," he put out his hand with dignity; Duncanson ignored it. He dropped it with an understanding nod, and fell to picking up and dropping the cards with a melancholy air. "You will go in search of Archie?" he asked at length.

"With more good will, Monsieur, than I assist you."

"And I comprehend that, too! Where is the key?"

"Take it, under the table."

He gave the Prince some more directions, and watched him while he rose and walked boldly towards the door. As he went up the room, the voice of Mr. Penicuik could be heard droning on " 'Ah! ye schauchling land-louper, to whom, then, will ye be leal?' "

Duncanson thought his heart would stop! Charles had halted deliberately opposite the secret service "trusties" and accosted them. Drawing a cutty pipe from his pocket, he leaned over and borrowed a light from the candle on their table. He spoke to them again, and Allan could see from the spies' evasive eyes that they wished him to be gone and not to draw attention to them. Charles laughed and swaggered out of the room, clacking the doors behind him.

Duncanson sat for a time with his head on his hands, utterly dejected. The future since he entered the shabby little tavern had blackened past recognition. What was to become of Darthula . . . of their child . . . indeed, of Scotland? *All that was beginning over again*, and on the desperate gamble of a man who was only the insolent shell of his former gallant if hare-brained self. Duncanson groaned and looked at the clock once more. No prospect now of the Highland cattleman arriving, even if Allan was in the state to drive a careful bargain with him when he came. He had better be about his errand—he had less reluctance, at any rate, about trying to deliver Dr. Cameron, if he was in Edinburgh, from the web. He went out in his turn into the haze, which had now turned into a heavy white sea mist.

Counsellor Penicuik's associates, too, had departed after a

last short game. He was alone in the tavern with the agents, knowing it was bedtime, but reluctant to face his cold and lonesome chambers up in Mylne Court. He suddenly realised that the long-nosed stranger had departed, leaving the *Courant* on the floor beside his seat. With an indignant grunt, the Counsellor hobbled over and picked it up. At last! He settled himself to read.

About twenty minutes had passed when the doors were clacked open from outside with violence, sending a cold draught through the room, in which the fire puffed smoke. The Counsellor glanced up in annoyance, and beheld with some surprise the face of Mr. Macdonnell of Glengarry, the Younger. He was scowling, and his eyes roved round the room and into every corner of it with a gleaming, hunter's look. Then—Mr. Penicuik saw it clearly—he made a little sign to the three trusties, and they rose and followed him out into the street.

Mr. Penicuik sat for a moment with his shrunken jaw fallen. So *that* was the corner where the wind sat! That was the secret of Mr. Macdonnell's immunity as he flaunted himself in the streets of Edinburgh. "Weel," thought the Counsellor, "I dinna love a Jacobite, but there is yin thing I love less—a traitorous rogue that sells his Prince for siller!"

Again he applied himself to the *Courant*, determined, in spite of all these interruptions, to read it through ere he went home to bed.

3

The big room at Advocates' Close that had once been Lord Brounhill's was cheerfully lit with wax candles, and a fire on the large stone hearth sent flickers over the lovely mouldings of the arched ceiling. At a small table drawn near the fire, Darthula Duncanson sat bending, with furrowed brow, over a bundle of papers. There was a quill in her hand, a tiny smudge of ink like a beauty-spot on her slightly worn but delicate cheek. With the silvery threads running through her dark curls, and her features refined by past sorrows, she had the look of a Muse just about to exchange the fire of youth for the authority of middle age. Before her on the writing-table was a large sheet on which a letter was begun to:

> "*Master James Macpherson,*
> *at the University and King's College,*
> *Aberdeen.*"

and after the opening compliments there were passages of poetry transcribed in her angular, elegant writing, its points and flourishes like so many dagger-thrusts. She had taken a fancy to this industrious youth, training at Ruthven, in the intervals of his schooling at Aberdeen, to fit himself for a dominie's work. Nobody had ever shown quite so much interest in her songs and recitations from Ossian and the ancient Bards, or pored with more enthusiasm over her attempted English versions, than this queer boy whom she had met during a visit to Aberdeen. One day, she thought, she would leave him all her papers to do as he liked with. Meanwhile she was transcribing him a few songs and epic passages from her notes taken down while Ewen the Bard was singing to her so many years ago.

Darthula poised her pen and raised her sharp ear. Surely she had heard the key grate lightly in the lock of the lodging. Allan would be returning then! Her face, for an instant, became that of a young girl again. But though she listened for a minute or two she heard no further sound in the passage outside, and concluded she had been mistaken. Then a troubled look clouded her grey-brown eyes. Had the child made some choking sound? She rose and darted with a rustle of skirts out across the dark passage, and into the bedroom, where a dip burned.

The little boy was sleeping quite peacefully, not even making any sucking noises. But, for she was a fidgety mother, she felt she could not leave him there. She caught up a plaid of Maceachan Clan Ranald tartan from the window-seat and carried him in her arms into the warmth of the great room. He murmured a little at the motion and change of temperature, but she merely cooed, "Hush! Son of Hector! Hush!" and laid him down, well-wrapped, on the sofa near her writing-table where she could keep her eye on him. The baby was soon slumbering tranquilly again. His mother applied herself once more with deep concentration to her poetic work.

Inside her husband's study meanwhile—the coffin-shaped little room where Lord Brounhill had been wont to sit over his law-papers and the *Pandects* that Darthula had once flung upon the floor—Prince Charles Edward was lighting a candle from the embers of the fire on the grate. Then he straightened himself, gave a swift, practised glance round, and dragged the rug up against the door, that the line of yellow light should not stream out underneath it into the passage and betray his presence.

Then, with a peculiar, bitter smile on his dissipated face, he set to work to remove his disguise. Heating his fingers in the candle-flame, he softened the wax that held in place his *nez à la Saxe*—the device he had learnt from Marshal Saxe's spies on the continent. His wig came off; he rubbed the black from his eyebrows. Now he was himself, brown-eyed, fair-haired, handsome as a haggard caricature of his former looks.

He had promised Duncanson not to hold conference with his wife. That was no reason, his eyes glittered maliciously, why he should not show himself to Darthula . . . why he should not ask her to give him something to drink. . . . They need not talk politics!

There! he was ready! He pushed the rug from the door, opened it with a hand practised in noiselessness and, crossing to the door of the big room, which was on the jar, looked through the narrow opening.

For some minutes he stood there, watching Darthula's back as she bent over her papers, scribbling, crossing out and writing in words, and never looking up except towards the baby wrapped in the Clan Ranald tartan on the couch. In the firelight Charles Edward, a long, thin shadow stretched himself and dwindled by fits upon the wall behind her, but she never looked up to see that either.

There was a wonderful peace about the beautiful old room, a homeliness about the furnishings, a tranquillity on the face of the sleeping infant. Charles felt he would give kingdoms to call out and have a glimpse of Darthula's face, but something withheld him; he could only remark the elegant prosperity of her dress, and the flash of a bracelet on her arm as it moved with the pen. . . . Last time he had seen her she was a half-starved creature in muddied rags, with the memory of death and torment stamped into her expression. . . . If he made a sound and she turned round now, would joy come into her face, or merely the strain and suffering of old memories?

He still stood silent, while the quill quietly scratched and the fire purred like some happy domestic animal. Slowly the cruel smile passed from his lips; the eyes glinting in the light that streamed through the door darkened and veiled themselves like little blue lakes. The conspirator's crouch with which he had been peering through the crack of the door gave way to a royal dignity as he stood upright and took a soundless step backwards. On his cheek, glazed with much drinking, a tear sparkled, then another which fell upon his rough disguise-coat. He gave one deep sigh as he felt in an inner pocket. Out of it he drew a small bag, untied it and drew forth a thick lock of brown hair, with a coppery tinge and a couple of silver threads in it. It was tied with a Royal Stewart tartan ribbon. For a moment he looked at it dolefully, as it lay in the palm of his hand; then he kissed it and crept back to the crack of the door again.

He saw Darthula sitting with her hand over her eyes, her slim fingers drumming on the table, seeking a rhyme or a rhythm. . . . She was not thinking of him at all . . . it was the bitterest stab of the moment. Then his hand went slowly through the door, his eyes watching her to see if she stirred . . . and dropped the token of release upon a stool just inside.

4

TEN minutes later a shabby figure with a long nose peeped cautiously out into the Close from the door under the inscription INTROIBIT REX GLORIAE. The steps towards the Nor' Loch ran down now into spangled mist, and the Close itself was hazy. Charles stood an instant listening. He heard hurried steps coming up the High Street outside. Blotting himself against the wall, he glided, like the shadow of a swiftly moving cloud on a hillside, down the steps towards the loch. He was buried in twirling vapour in a few seconds; then, out of the mist loomed suddenly a man, who made a clutch at him. His fist shot out; there was a click and a thud. The spy, as he fell with a crash on the stones, saw a shadow dance past him and dissolve into the white mists below. He raised himself on his elbow, but sank down again, half stunned.

Meanwhile two more men had crept into the Close from

the High Street. They went up a few steps of the stair and listened. "Will he be within yet?" whispered the first, "or is he awa' by the stairs?"

"Thomasson will be waiting to tak' him there," answered his companion. "He is a braw lad at the wrastling! Dinna tirl the pin. If he is within and we alarm him, I doot the leddy will be at some of her pliskies, and maybe find some passage for him to slip awa'. We will tak' him at the door as he comes down onthinking!"

They waited some minutes, then, "Yonder comes Thomasson hirpling!" said the first of them abruptly.

Out of the mist at the foot of the Close appeared the third spy, limping, with his hand to his head.

"What ails ye, mon?" demanded the leader hurriedly.

"He is awa'," growled Thomasson, "by the stairs to the loch. I couldna stay him, I tell ye! He knocked me o'er like a pushpin. Ma heid is still birling wi' the dunt of it!"

"Ye fushionless fule!" exclaimed the leader. "How lang syne was't ye let him gang by ye?"

"I dinna ken. Minutes! I hae been lying yonder onable to find ma feet."

"Rin! Mak' after him!" said the leader, starting to run down the Close into the mist.

"Whaur are ye awa' to?" asked a fourth man, who had come silently from the High Street into the Close, catching his sleeve. "Ye ken they have ta'en the Doctor in Inversnaid?"

"Muckle matters the Doctor!" growled the other, shaking off his hand, "when we hae lost the big fish o' the creel!"

He disappeared, running down the steps into the mist, with the companion of his watch panting behind him. Thomasson took a step or two after them, but lurched against the wall and stood leaning, nursing his head. "I canna rin," he said to the new-comer. "So they hae the Doctor, is that a fac'?"

"Aye, in a wood by Inversnaid. They hae ta'en the Doctor."

The echoes in the filthy porchway seemed to repeat in a whisper, "They hae ta'en the Doctor!"

Glossary

SCOTS ENGLISH TERMS

arisaid, woman's plaid
birling, whirling, spinning
bogle, spectre, goblin
brose, kind of porridge
bruilzie, broil
callant, lad
cateran, freebooter, brigand
chappit, pounded
clachan, a small village
daffing, jesting
fortalice, outwork of a fortification
gaberlunzie, beggar
glisk, glimpse
guiser, masquerade
gyte, crazy
havers, nonsense
hirpling, limping
ilka, each, every
jowk, duck
kelpie, water sprite

laigh-shop, oyster cellar
panel, prisoner
pibroch, pipe music
pliskie, prank
shielings, shepherd's mountain huts
sib, akin
thole, endure
tirl, twist
tuilzie, struggle

GAELIC TERMS

beanshith, banshee, female spectre
bocan, ghost
Cruachan, a mountain in the land of Clan Campbell
dorcha, dark
greas ort, make haste
Na Siosalaich, the Chisholms
Phrionssa Tearlach, Prince Charles
saighear ruadh, red soldiers
sithiche, Silent One, i.e. fairy

A NOTE ON THE TYPE IN WHICH THIS BOOK IS SET

The text of this book was set on the Linotype in Janson, a recutting made direct from the type cast from matrices (now in possession of the Stempel foundry, Frankfurt am Main) made by Anton Janson some time between 1660 and 1687.

Of Janson's origin nothing is known. He may have been a relative of Justus Janson, a printer of Danish birth who practised in Leipzig from 1614 to 1635. Some time between 1657 and 1668 Anton Janson, a punch-cutter and type-founder, bought from the Leipzig printer Johann Erich Hahn the type-foundry which had formerly been a part of the printing house of M. Friedrich Lankisch. Janson's types were first shown in a specimen sheet issued at Leipzig about 1675. Janson's successor, and perhaps his son-in-law, Johann Karl Edling, issued a specimen sheet of Janson types in 1689. His heirs sold the Janson matrices in Holland to Wolffgang Dietrich Erhardt, of Leipzig.

COMPOSED, PRINTED, AND BOUND BY H. WOLFF, NEW YORK. PAPER MADE BY S. D. WARREN CO., BOSTON.